PRAISE FOR

THE UNWEDDING

"Ally Condie's adult debut, *The Unwedding*, is a clever, witty, and fast-paced whodunit. I read it in one sitting and can't wait for the next."

—Harlan Coben, #1 *New York Times* bestselling author of *I Will Find You*

"Mesmerizing! Equal parts a clever whodunit and compelling character's journey, *The Unwedding* will speak to anyone who's been there, done that, and had the vacation from hell thrown on top of it all. This Big Sur luxury resort closed-room mystery will stay with you well past the final page."

—Lisa Gardner, #1 *New York Times* bestselling author

"Dead bodies, brutal secrets, and a fabulous view—*The Unwedding* is proof that Ally Condie knows exactly what we love and what we fear. Come take a wonderful roller coaster of a trip, but don't expect much sleep."

—Brad Meltzer, *New York Times* bestselling author of *The Lightning Rod*

"A knife's-edge whodunit that's as much a thriller as it is an exquisite meditation on grief and loss."

—Nicola Yoon, #1 *New York Times* bestselling author of *Everything, Everything*

"A classic mystery for a modern world—I couldn't put it down!"

—Ally Carter, *New York Times* bestselling author of *The Blonde Identity*

"An idyllic setting turns deadly in Ally Condie's smart and twisty debut adult thriller. With an isolated resort, a killer on the loose, and a cast of compelling characters, *The Unwedding* kept me on the edge of my seat from beginning to end. A clever and suspenseful mystery where everyone has something to hide."

—Megan Miranda, *New York Times* bestselling author of *The Only Survivors*

"Ally Condie's dazzling debut, *The Unwedding*, is a wild and mysterious suspense novel that will have you turning pages long into the night with the lights on! A lovely wedding is planned at a remote resort with a fresh, original, and shady cast of characters. In the author's brilliant hands, the happy occasion can only lead to murder. Buckle up!"

—Adriana Trigiani, bestselling author of *The Good Left Undone*

"A gorgeous murder mystery that explores what it means to be human—the pain and the love."

—*Kirkus Reviews* (starred review)

"This is an engrossing story with an interesting take on grief and forgiveness, with pieces of art found at the resort adding a fun element. Edgar Award–winning YA author Condie's adult debut is an unpredictable locked-room mystery for Agatha Christie fans and all readers looking for an intelligent read."

—*Booklist*

THE UNWEDDING

ALSO BY ALLY CONDIE

THE UNWEDDING

ALLY CONDIE

GRAND
CENTRAL

New York Boston

Grand Central Publishing
Hachette Book Group
1290 Avenue of the Americas, New York, NY 10104
grandcentralpublishing.com
@grandcentralpub

Originally published in hardcover and ebook in June 2024
First trade paperback edition: June 2025

Grand Central Publishing is a division of Hachette Book Group, Inc. The Grand Central Publishing name and logo is a registered trademark of Hachette Book Group, Inc.

The publisher is not responsible for websites (or their content) that are not owned by the publisher.

The Hachette Speakers Bureau provides a wide range of authors for speaking events. To find out more, go to hachettespeakersbureau.com or email HachetteSpeakers@hbgusa.com.

Grand Central Publishing books may be purchased in bulk for business, educational, or promotional use. For information, please contact your local bookseller or the Hachette Book Group Special Markets Department at special.markets@hbgusa.com.

Print book interior design by Marie Mundaca.

Library of Congress Control Number: 2023052688

ISBNs: 9781538757598 (trade paperback), 9781538757604 (ebook)

Printed in the United States of America

CCR

10 9 8 7 6 5 4 3 2 1

For Lindsey Leavitt Brown, Ann Dee Ellis, Josie Lauritsen Lee, and Brook Davis Andreoli.

I love you.

Thank you for coming to find me.

Let's go somewhere fun.

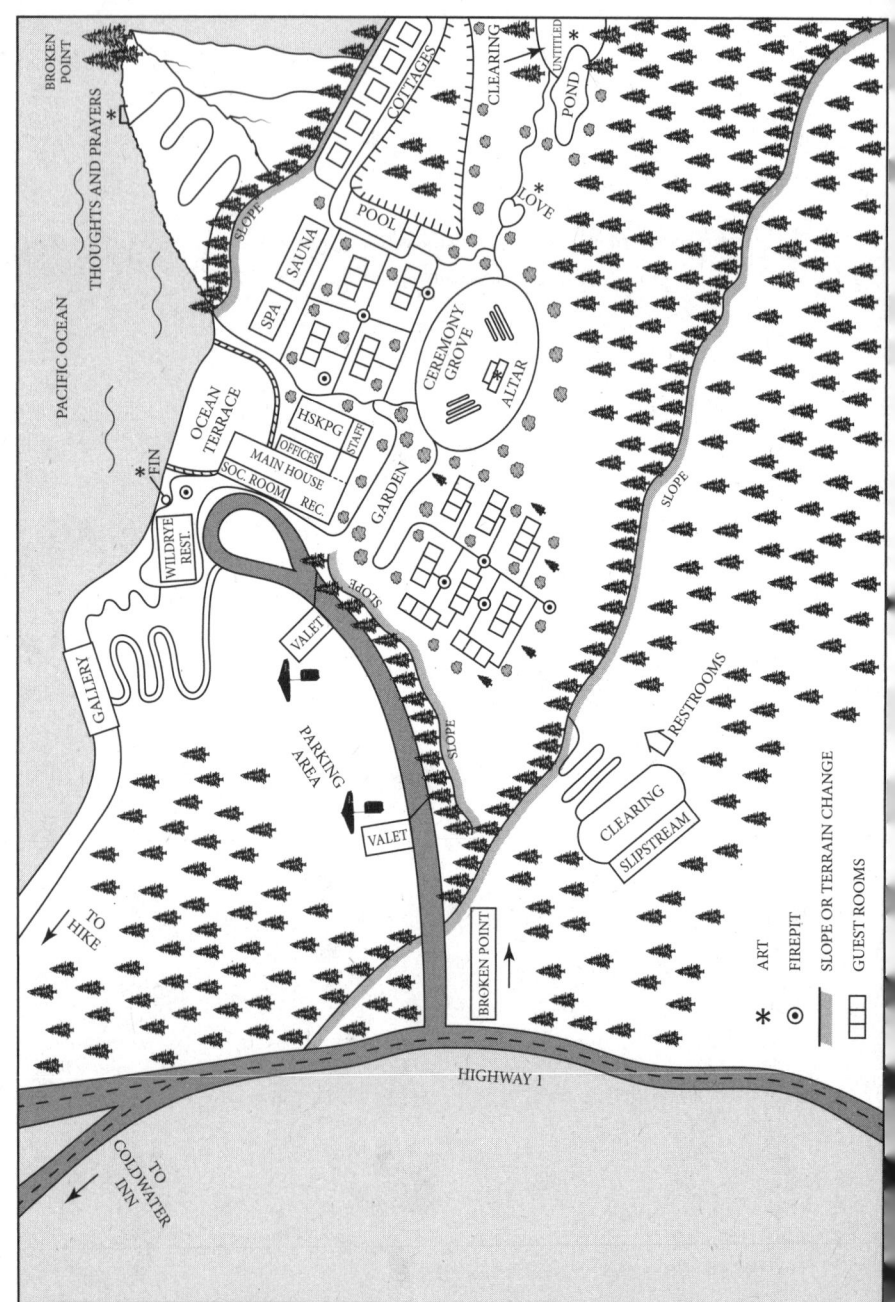

Something old, something new.
Something borrowed, something blue.
Someone lost, someone wed.
Someone broken, someone dead.

SUNDAY

*I*t wasn't yet sunrise when she left her room. Once the rain began it had never stopped, pounding and pouring down, turning into white noise, background.

She was drenched within two steps, but that didn't matter. She was wearing her swimsuit and heading for the heated infinity pool. She hadn't brought her phone or her towel or her flip-flops. The rain was too constant for a phone, made a towel pointless, and she trusted her bare feet more than any shoes when things were this wet.

She kept her head down. The light was gray, and she didn't want to fall.

It had been one of those nights that felt like she hadn't slept at all, but she knew she must have, because at some point she'd had a dream in which she was racing through a forest, darting among dark, wet trees, slipping, sliding, trying to find the people she loved, who were lost.

She just hadn't slept deep.

The soles of her feet found careful purchase on the flagstones. The water had pooled in any indentation it could find. It ran, stream-like, down the sides of the path, flooding some of the carefully tended plants.

If she went swimming when it was raining this hard, would it be like everything were water? As if there were no longer any separation between earth and sky?

Someone had stacked all the lounge chairs and shrouded them in plastic to protect them from the rain. Steam rose from the pool's surface, and for a moment, as she paused at the edge of the steps, she wondered if it were possible to drown with her head above water, gasping in the rain-thick air.

She had just started to go down the steps into the pool when she saw it.

Something dark and human shaped, in the water. Another guest, swimming? No. Floating.

A person, floating face down in the infinity pool, butting up against the glass-paneled edge that looked out over the trees.

Before she knew what she was doing, she was racing to the other side, feet slipping dangerously on the stone. She jumped into the pool as close to the figure as she could. It was a man; she could tell when she came up next to him. Her fingers slipped as she tried to turn him over. Something was wrong with his head, she noticed on some level; it was not shaped right at the back. There was something dark clotted in the back of his hair. She had to get him turned over, people died with their faces in the water, they couldn't breathe...

She heaved him over.

His face. Eyes open.

His clothes. Wet through.

He was still in his wedding finery, she realized, a suit, leather shoes, gold cuff links at his wrists, a bedraggled white flower pinned on his lapel. A camellia? Why was she noticing this? That didn't matter. Nothing mattered except getting him out of this pool, out of this water—

She reached under his arms. His clothes were sodden, and underneath, his flesh and bones—

Don't think about it, don't think don't feel.

She pulled him toward the steps at the end of the pool.

He's dead. He's not moving. This is a body. I'm touching a body.

"HELP!" she screamed.

Nothing.

She yelled again, as she hoisted him up the stairs and onto the flagstones next to the pool. She tried not to notice how his legs dragged across the pool's edge.

"HELP!"

No one.

She couldn't bring herself to look at his face again, but she felt like she could hear the rain on it.

She ran.

She raced toward the Main House, her bare feet slipping, shouting it over and over.

Help.

But she already knew. Even as her mouth formed one word, her brain said another.

Gone.

And she thought, Not again.

FRIDAY

TWO DAYS EARLIER

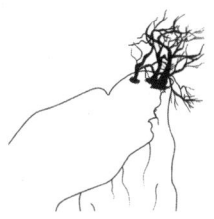

Today at The Resort at Broken Point

"If you know wilderness in the way you know love, you would be unwilling to let it go."

—*Terry Tempest Williams*

Weather: Sunny

SUNRISE: 7:12 A.M. .... HIGH: 66° F

SUNSET: 6:33 P.M. .... LOW: 55° F

ABOUT THE ART:
Intimation
by Clare Han
2013
oil

While much attention is often given to the dramatic vistas of Big Sur—its ragged cliffs, the ever-changing ocean—Han's piece focuses on one of the smaller but no less beautiful landscapes that exist if one looks closely enough. *Intimation* depicts a temporary pool created by rain in the forest. The colors of green, blue, and taupe provide a backdrop for small moments of red, which Han intended as a reference to Tennyson's lines about "nature, red in tooth and claw." The enormous scale of the painting also serves to draw attention to the smaller landscape and moment.

1.

No one could believe it when Luke and Ellery Wainwright got divorced the summer before their oldest child's senior year. Everyone was astonished by the speed with which it happened—they were still together, everything just fine at the neighborhood last-day-of-school party, their children running through the sprinklers or lounging bored on the grass along with all the other neighborhood kids. Ellery brought the strawberry rhubarb crumble she always did, warm and smelling of fruit and brown sugar. Luke hung out with the dads over by the barbecue and returned wayward basketballs to the teenagers playing in the Humphreys' driveway. They ate together on a blanket with their children. Later, Kat Coburn said she was sure she saw Luke put his hand on the small of Ellery's back when they were leaving.

No one had known they were putting on a good front. That Luke had already called the game, that Ellery was electric with grief and still hoping he would change his mind.

But by the Fourth of July, Luke had moved out. By the middle of September everything had been finalized, and in October Ellery was vacationing by herself on the trip they had planned for their twentieth anniversary.

"We'll seat you out on the patio," the hostess told her. "Please, follow me."

Ellery did.

She felt like she had been besieged by beauty since she had touched down at the airport in Monterey a few hours earlier. The drive to Broken Point was breathtaking, astonishing, Big Sur vistas around every turn, and the resort itself was also stunning. When she'd checked in at reception at the Main House, she'd been greeted by a staff member at a low midcentury desk flanked by a gorgeous gilded screen. Small fires snapped and flickered in stone pits throughout the property, a sculpture made of glass, steel, and granite looming near the largest one. Globe lights hung above on strings, swaying slightly in the breeze.

The restaurant, called Wildrye, was located adjacent to the Main House, and an enormous blown-glass chandelier graced its lobby. The tables on the patio were dressed with white linen cloths, ivory candles, and fresh flowers in tiny ceramic vases. A tree-scented breeze from the sea came up through the forest and the open windows. The full moon hung over the ocean in the distance, glimmering the waves. A glassed-in building clung to the edge of the cliff a few hundred yards up to Ellery's left, shimmering with light and shadowed with the shapes of people moving around.

"That's the art gallery," the host said. She was a doe-eyed young woman with a name tag that read *Brook*. "It's booked for a cocktail event for a wedding party tonight but will be open to all guests tomorrow."

Ellery knew all about the gallery and the other features at the resort. She was the one who had done the research, found the place, booked the trip.

She'd stumbled onto the website by accident the previous winter, via a "50 Places to Visit Before You Die" article. (Since she'd turned forty, two years prior to *that*, she'd been reading a lot of those kinds of articles online: "100 Novels You Need to Read," "The Best 100 Songs of All Time," etc.)

The Resort at Broken Point, the website read, in a font that managed to be both subdued and emphatic. The automatic photo gallery scrolled unbidden through pictures showing ocean vistas, sleek, low-slung modern buildings tucked discreetly among redwood trees, a woman enjoying a spa treatment with a row of smooth gray stones marching down her perfectly tanned back, delicious-looking meals arranged on creamy stoneware plates and decorated with flowers grown on-site in the organic kitchen garden. Guest rooms were arranged in groups of three per building, and there were five cottages. (Ellery's jaw had literally dropped at the price of booking one of those.) There was a sauna and a spa, Pendleton blankets thrown over lounge chairs on the terrace, heated pools, piles of fluffy white towels, mist threading through greenery. There was an art gallery, quiet trails winding through a cathedral-esque grove, a collection of fine art and sculptures scattered throughout the property, a full-sized Airstream trailer converted into a bar and nestled in the trees.

When Ellery had shown the website to Luke, he'd said "Let's go for it." He was standing behind her and kneading her shoulders precisely where they tended to tighten. She loved it when he did that. "Really?" she'd asked, because it was very, very expensive. "Of course," he'd said. "You only celebrate your twentieth anniversary once."

"You should still take the trip," Luke said later in mediation when they were dividing things up. His tone was gentle, as if he were committing an act of profound generosity. "The deposit's nonrefundable. And you really wanted to go there."

Didn't you? she'd wanted to ask. *Or were you pretending when we booked it? Had you already decided you were done?*

"Here we are." Brook pulled out Ellery's chair. "Your waiter will be with you shortly. Enjoy." She gave Ellery a menu—cream-colored paper, letterpress print. Moments later, a waiter in a cuffed white shirt stood at her table, listing the evening's specials.

Ellery couldn't concentrate. She felt an acute, sudden pain scything through her body. For a moment, she knew exactly where her heart was in her chest within a precise millimeter or two, thudding as it was against the muscle and bone that kept it contained.

But, as her therapist kept telling her, *the human body can't live at that high a level of pain for long.* Whatever systems made it so that you kept on going—even as your life was a shatter of sharp-edged glass around you—kicked in eventually to make it so you didn't actually die. And then you'd be back to the basic, chronic, ubiquitous pain, the one that never left, the one you were beginning to realize you might live with for the rest of your life.

Ellery glanced up. At the table to her left, what seemed to be a father and daughter were seated. There was something similar in their careful, heads-inclined attentiveness to what the restaurant host was saying. The father wore a button-up shirt with khaki pants. His daughter's long curly hair was twisted in a bun on top of her head, and she had a fresh-facedness about her, a cleanness to the line of her profile.

It seemed like everywhere Ellery looked, every life she saw, cut her to the quick. Everyone had a person. Everyone else's lives were going so well.

It wasn't that she wanted their lives.

She wanted her own life back.

She had known, of course, that there were problems in her marriage. Luke had definitely been in the throes of a midlife crisis for the past few years, but she was so sure it would pass. She thought they'd weather it together, the way they had everything else. Grad school, babies, toddlers, job changes, moves, illness, teenagers.

Sometimes, he was wonderful.

Other times, he said things that broke her heart.

I shouldn't have gotten married so young.

I was so busy doing what everyone expected of me that I didn't think about whether it was what I wanted to do.

I shouldn't have gone straight to grad school.

I should have tried to be a musician instead.

I never had time to find myself.

I didn't get to see what was out there.

They were laughable, the things he said. They were the things the crappy ex-husband says in the movie before the heroine goes home to her small town to heal and remeets her super-hot high school boyfriend, who is now a veterinarian raising his deceased sister's precocious daughter.

But she'd always thought that she and Luke would make it. They were both good people. They had had great times, so many of them, small and big. They had raised each other up, cheered one another on, held each other when they cried. They knew what the other looked like when they were sleeping, kissing, sobbing, brushing their teeth, seeing their children for the first time.

The kids.

Ellery stood. Her napkin fell from her lap to the ground and she didn't bother to retrieve it. She turned, almost blindly, and began walking back the way she'd come. A waiter moved to the side to let her pass. Her sandaled heels made snick-snack, clip-clop sounds on the stone of the patio as she made her way between the tables. Did the others glancing up at her know it, too? How nothing and no one was ever as it seemed? Not even this beautiful place, not even their beautiful lives.

Luke had told her he was done in May, two weeks before school ended. They were sitting at the kitchen table after the kids were in bed. Kate, their oldest, had a cello recital coming up. Ethan, their son, was just finishing his freshman year in high school. Maddie, the youngest, had a new best friend who they both found hilarious. Those were the things she'd thought they would talk about.

"I'm not happy," Luke said instead. "I don't like anything about my life."

He was holding her hand. He had said things like this before. At first, it didn't register that this time he was serious. That he wasn't blowing off steam.

She'd looked back at the counter where she'd packed the kids' lunches for the next day, still scattered with paper bags and jammy knives and apple cores; at the shoes on the floor, the dollops of socks they hadn't picked up when they'd peeled them off after school; the dishes in the sink. Earlier that evening she'd thought, *How is it possible to work literally every minute of this day and have nothing to show for it?*

Ha. How little she had known.

She'd had *everything* to show for it.

And now it was all being taken away.

2.

In the restaurant's bathroom, she pulled out her phone and dialed her best friend, Abby.

"How are you?" Abby asked without preamble.

"It's going great," Ellery told her. "I'm having a grief attack in the bathroom."

"Perfect," Abby said. "Get it out of the way. Do you need to cry into the phone?"

"Probably." Ellery took a shuddery breath. The bathroom had a small alcove with a sofa. Maybe she could just lie down on it. Maybe that wouldn't be weird. "There's a wedding here this weekend."

"We knew this might happen," Abby said. "It's going to be okay."

"Remind me again why we thought that?"

"You've never actually been to Big Sur or Broken Point with Luke," Abby said, reciting the reasons. "So it's new geography. You didn't want to waste the money because the deposit was nonrefundable. And—"

"I didn't want him to bring Imogen on the trip instead of me," Ellery finished.

Imogen was Luke's new girlfriend, whom he had obtained within a month of the divorce. She was tiny (Ellery was tall), had beautiful red hair (Ellery had basic brown), was five years younger than Ellery and Luke, and was Irish—like actually *from Ireland*. Which meant she had an accent.

There was no competing with an accent.

These were thoughts Ellery had expressed to Abby before, so she held off on expressing them again now. Instead she said, "I wish you were here, Ab." She had invited Abby to come with her since the trip was over fall break, but Abby had already made plans with her family.

According to their freshly signed divorce decree, this was Luke's year to have the kids for fall break. He was taking them camping. Ellery had never loved camping and now they were probably going to do lots of it without her. Ellery was great at hiking. And she used to be great at rock climbing. She could run, she could ski, she could kayak and paddleboard. But she had sucked at camping ever since she was a kid. She could never seem to sleep when she was out in the wild.

She would camp with Luke now, if he'd give her the chance. Do all the things she hadn't done. He was also doing the things that she'd hoped *he* would do. Now he listened to Brené Brown and talked about emotional vulnerability, and he had started exercising again. It was all very exciting for Imogen, Ellery was sure.

"I wish I were there, too." Abby's voice had softened. "This is hard," she said. "It was hard enough for me when I'd been married for seven years. You guys were married for twenty. You can do this."

"I don't think I can," Ellery said. Not dramatically. Truthfully. Even checking in to the room she'd been supposed to share with Luke had felt impossible. Honey-colored wooden walls, crisp and cozy white bed linens, a gray-and-red Pendleton throw draped across the foot of the king-sized bed. Simple leather chairs, black-and-white art prints, a plate with two chocolate covered strawberries and a handwritten note on a thick card letterpressed with the resort's logo (a spare line drawing of three trees clinging to a cliff's edge). *Enjoy your stay*, it said. When Ellery walked into the bathroom and she saw the vast, sleek glass shower with two showerheads and two fluffy white robes hanging on Eames-inspired hooks, she'd slid down to the cool tile floor and put her head in her hands.

Was she going to spend this whole trip crying in various bathrooms?

"You can live through anything for three days," Abby said.

"I don't think that's right," Ellery said. "Like, you think you could live through *labor* for three days? Could you grade *ninth-grade research papers* for three days?"

"Okay." Abby laughed. "You've made your point."

Ellery and Abby both taught social studies at Dutch Fields High School. Ellery had been a teacher her entire marriage, first to put Luke through grad school, then to help pay off his student debts, and now to help save for the kids' college. Plus, when she wasn't mired in grief, she loved her job and was good at it. Six years ago, Abby had started teaching across the hall right after *her* divorce, and they coached the girls' track team together. Abby was feisty and smart and gorgeous and funny and loyal. She made Ellery laugh harder than anyone else. She threw parties every time she felt like there was something worth celebrating—a new album by her favorite artist, friends' promotions, her kids' half birthdays. She had a habit of patting people's backs when she hugged them that Ellery teased her about, telling Abby that it was like she thought the world was made up of her babies and she was going to burp them all. Ellery had always felt lucky to know Abby, but over the past few years, they had been each other's lifeline.

"I know this is ridiculous," Ellery said.

"It's not ridiculous," Abby said. "You're grieving. The life you thought you had exploded in your face."

Ellery stood up and walked over to the long marble countertop with the sunken-in copper sinks. She squirted some of the fancy lotion in its amber bottle into her hands, rubbing it into her skin. Her face in the mirror looked dim and half-formed. "It really did."

"And now everything feels super shitty. Luke let you put him through the hard part of life. Now he's walking away in the middle of his midlife crisis. Some other woman you don't even know is hanging out with your kids. He's started putting gel in his hair and shaving his arms and wearing V-necks and posting wrongly attributed inspirational quotes on social media. Do you need me to keep going on about why it's okay for you to feel bad?"

"Please don't," Ellery said, trying not to cry-laugh. She sat back down on the sofa. The lotion smelled like an upscale, herbal version of the Creamsicles she used to eat in the summer during her childhood.

"It's going to get better," Abby said. "I swear to you. It is."

Abby's ex had cheated on her with their next-door neighbor. Abby had two little boys who hadn't even been old enough to be in school yet when her husband had left for good. She was now happily remarried and had made it through, as she said, to the next part of her life.

Ellery felt tears well over. "Everything feels wrong, Abby. On a cellular level."

"I know," Abby said gently. "I really do."

"Maybe I should leave," Ellery said. "This place, I mean. It's supposed to rain later this weekend anyway."

"You're not going to waste the money," Abby said firmly. "Tonight, dinner. Tomorrow, you're going to go on a hike because you loved hiking before Luke and you will love it again. You'll sit by that heated infinity pool in your bikini and breathe in the air of a place you have never, ever been with him. You will feel horrible some of the time but you'll try to put together a few minutes or hours or whatever when you feel a little better. Distract yourself. Pretend to be someone else if you have to give yourself a break. Fix your eyeliner before you go back out there. Call me anytime. You're going to be okay."

"Okay."

"I need to hear you say the whole thing."

Ellery drew a deep breath. "I'm going to be okay."

"We've been through worse," Abby said, gently.

Abby didn't say the words *two years ago* or mention *the accident* but Ellery knew what she meant. And, even in the depths of her agony, even feeling that losing her marriage and her family was the worst possible thing, she knew empirically that it wasn't.

Because she had been there when the worst thing *had* happened.

And she would never be able to leave it behind.

3.

Ellery was almost back to her table when someone stopped her.

"Excuse me." An extremely handsome man stood in front of her. He wore a chambray shirt with the sleeves rolled up and his warm brown eyes were kind. "Are you dining alone?"

"I am."

"Would you like to join us?"

The man, whose name was Ravi, handled everything with perfect grace. He signaled to the waiter and swooped a chair over to where he and his dining companion were sitting a few feet away. "This is Nina," he said, indicating the woman across the table from where he placed Ellery's seat.

"Ellery," Ellery said, slipping into her chair. "It's kind of you to let me sit with you."

"It's no problem at all." Nina's voice was warm and pleasant. She wore a fantastic pantsuit and her dark hair was in the kind of messy, perfect chignon that Ellery could never quite get right. Nina's eyes were shrewd, intelligent, and evaluating. But not unkind. Just...clear. Unhoodwinkable.

The waiter arrived with another menu. Ellery had planned on ordering the farfalle pasta, because it was the cheapest item on the menu, but she found herself eyeing Nina's filet mignon and ordering that instead. Why not?

"Nina and I are friends," Ravi said in an explanatory tone after the waiter left. "We've been traveling together for years."

"That's fantastic," Ellery said. "Plus, it's so much cheaper when you can split a room."

"Um, no," Ravi said. "We *never* share a room."

"We'd kill each other," Nina agreed.

"Oh." Ellery could feel herself flush slightly with embarrassment. Of course. Most of the people who came here wouldn't be worried about the price of the rooms. She had a stab of misgiving about the filet mignon.

"We've been on enough trips together to make a few ground rules," Ravi said. "Never share a room is one of them. Eat dessert every night is another. Also, we steal something on every trip."

"Ravi," Nina said. "Don't give away all our secrets." She rolled her eyes in mock-exasperation. "We just met her."

Do they really steal *something?* Ellery wondered with a thrill of misgiving. Neither of them seemed the type. Nina caught Ellery's eye and gave a wry shake of her head, as if to contradict Ravi's statement.

"And we always invite someone else to eat with us the first night," Ravi said. "The only criteria is that they have to look interesting."

"I'm not interesting," Ellery said automatically, and she immediately heard Abby in her ear. *Why do you always deflect? Stop selling yourself short!*

"Yes, you are." Ravi leaned back, studying her, smiling. He was so friendly, so disarming, that she grinned in return. "A beautiful woman, sitting alone, a certain sadness in her eyes..."

Ellery's smile faltered. Was she that transparent? Could *strangers* see how sad she was? How nothing felt right, ever? She straightened her spine. She was not going to give these elegant people her sob story. For one thing, that wasn't the point of this trip, and for another, they'd have to earn it. She had some pride.

"Actually, I think you're being taken in by the eyeliner," she told Ravi. To her delight, this made him laugh. "I'm a high school teacher." Because she was curious and because this conversation was centering entirely too much around her, she asked, "What do you both do?"

"I'm a landscape architect," Nina said.

"World class," Ravi confirmed. "Look up *Nina Ruiz* online and you'll see her work everywhere."

"Wow," Ellery said. "What a cool job."

"I love it," Nina said simply.

"She does sustainable landscape design for extremely rich people and companies," Ravi said. "It's a whole thing."

Ellery was intrigued. But before she could ask Ravi what he did for a living, he'd moved on. "So, what do you think of the resort?"

"It's beautiful," Ellery said. No need to mention how she found the place daunting. Or how it was becoming clear to her—despite the resort's supposed eco-friendliness and its attempts to blend in with its environment—that a place like this did not belong here. This was a land of cliff edges and living beaches and wild waves. Not heated pools and retaining walls and expensive buildings. She wondered why she'd been so taken with Broken Point when she'd stumbled across it online. She wondered if the other guests felt the strangeness, or if she'd brought it with her.

"It's exactly what I need," Ravi said.

"Ravi just broke up with his boyfriend," Nina said.

"I'm sorry," Ellery said.

"It's all right," Ravi said. "Or, if not, it will be. Eventually." He lifted his glass in a toast and Ellery and Nina raised theirs to clink with him.

"We got here this morning," Nina said. "Flew in from New York. What about you?" Her sleeve slid up as she took another roll from the basket, revealing a small tattoo on the inside of her wrist. Ellery wished she could see what it was.

"This afternoon. From Colorado."

"Apparently there's a wedding on the property this weekend." Ravi gestured with his wineglass to the gallery on the hillside above. "I'm hoping for scandal."

"Ravi's always hoping for scandal," Nina told Ellery.

"I do better when I have a problem to solve," Ravi said. "Even on vacation."

The breeze shifted, fluttering along Ellery's neck, the backs of her hands. "I get that." She would love her brain to have a problem to work on that might actually *be* solvable, instead of the ones it kept pacing around, circling.

"Hey." Ravi had lowered his voice. "Speaking of problems to solve.

Mysteries to unravel. Did you know there's a shadow celebrity staying here? We've got to figure out who it is."

Ellery wasn't sure what he was talking about. "A what?" She darted a glance at Nina.

"Someone who's sneaky famous," Ravi said. "Who can go unrecognized among the masses, but who wields tremendous power. Like the head of a movie studio who prefers not to be known. Or the founder of LikeMe. Or the person who invented a cryptocurrency that funds an entire nation."

"Oh," Ellery said, a small thrill running through her. "How can you tell that someone like that is here?"

"Don't listen to him," Nina said. "He's always making things up. And the worst part is, he believes them."

"People are not always what they seem." Ravi's eyes searched Ellery's. "Don't you agree?"

"I do," she said. "Everyone has a shadow." Even the waiters with their bright eyes and cheerful voices, even the people across from her, even her best friend, her own husband, herself.

Before Ravi could respond, the waiter arrived with Ellery's entrée. A few twists of black pepper, a murmured *Can I get you anything else? No? Please enjoy* and it was only the three of them again.

Ellery took a bite of the filet mignon. It melted in her mouth. This was nice. Eating with other people was helpful.

"I like the way you said that." Ravi held his knife loosely in his hand, his eyes thoughtful and direct as he looked at her. "There's that saying that everyone has a secret. But I think that *everyone has a shadow* is much more accurate."

Ellery glanced away, accidentally catching the eye of a very cute guy standing at the bar. He wore a flannel shirt and khakis, his brown hair curling around his ears. He appeared to be in his twenties. How could someone so young afford to be here? Probably a trust fund baby. Although he didn't look like a trust fund baby. In fact, he looked... uncomfortable. (But didn't good-looking people fit in everywhere?) His shirt wasn't hipster-flannel but seemed legitimately worn. And the way he moved—when he took a to-go box from the barman, nodded his thanks, and walked away—spoke more of actual outdoorsiness than studied casualness. He was the kind of guy she'd see up in the canyon rock climbing back when she was in college.

Well. The light was dim. Ellery was probably making things up. Creating a story that didn't exist. She did that often. She'd done it with her own life, for crying out loud.

"He's the best-looking guy here," Ravi said, catching her eye when she looked back.

"That's contestable," Ellery said honestly. "I mean, you're very handsome."

"Thank you," Ravi said. "You're quite attractive yourself."

"What about me?" Nina asked.

"Oh, please," Ravi said. "You know you're stunning."

Nina yawned. "I'm also weirdly tired. What is it, eight p.m.?"

"If that." Ravi shook his head. "You're losing your edge. It's painful to watch."

"You did fly in from New York," Ellery said.

"Still, I don't usually get tired this early," Nina said. "I must be getting old."

With their good hair and their excellent outfits, Ravi and Nina had initially appeared to Ellery to be in their late twenties. But upon closer inspection, she saw that they were likely only a few years younger than she was, maybe thirty-six, thirty-seven.

"Will you get the check?" Nina asked Ravi. "I'll cover tomorrow night."

"Sure," Ravi said. "See you at breakfast."

Nina lifted her purse from the back of her chair and smiled at Ellery. "Nice to meet you."

"You too." Ellery watched Nina wind her way through the candlelit tables, wishing the waiter had brought the bill so she could leave, too. Was it going to be awkward sitting alone with Ravi?

But the waiter came by within moments. And after they'd signed their receipts, Ravi turned to Ellery with a wicked twinkle in his eye.

"So," he said. "I know we just met. But do you want to crash a wedding with me?"

4.

Technically, they weren't crashing a wedding. Just a cocktail party.

Ellery didn't know what had gotten into her. She hadn't had any of the wine. But she felt lightheaded and boozy-eyed with adventure and newness and not-wanting-to-be-aloneness. And Ravi was so funny and charming.

"Why are we doing this again?" she asked him. They were following the path up from the restaurant to the gallery through the trees. The trail moved in gentle switchbacks undulating up the cliffside to the top where the glass-and-steel building perched. It came and went through the trees as they climbed, and an ocean breeze sifted the leaves. Some came free and floated to the ground, drifting past the lights set into the path. Their feet made gentle sounds on the wood-chipped path.

"It's one of the rules of travel, remember?" Ravi said. "We're stealing something."

"So we're doing an art heist?" she asked, and he laughed out loud, which made her grin the slightest bit.

"I don't think you say *doing* an art heist," he said.

"What do you say, then?"

"Hmmm." He ran a hand through his hair, picking up the pace slightly. "I don't know."

"Conducting an art heist?" she said. "*Committing* an art heist?"

Ravi laughed. "Don't worry, we're not stealing art. Just a drink or an hors d'oeuvre. With any luck, we won't even have to go into the main room of the gallery. We can sneak in a side door and find the serving area and snag something."

"Does it count if Nina's not here, though?" she asked.

"Full disclosure," Ravi said. "Nina never actually steals anything."

"It's always you?"

"Every time," he confirmed.

"That you know of, anyway," she countered, and he turned to look at her full-on, grinning.

"Good point."

The sound of the ocean was growing subtly stronger as they closed in on the top of the cliff, and Ellery thought she could feel the salt on the air. Somewhere near here, not quite visible in the dark, was the outcropping that gave the area and the resort its name—a jagged, broken-away promontory with three ragged trees clinging to the cliff. She'd seen it driving in but had lost track of it now.

"So," Ravi said. "Why were you eating by yourself? Are you here with anyone?"

"No," she said. "I came alone." And then, because he'd been so forthright with her about his recent breakup, she said, "It was supposed to be a trip with my husband for our twentieth wedding anniversary."

"But…" Ravi prompted.

"We ended up getting divorced, and I didn't want him to bring his girlfriend here instead of me." Ellery glanced over her shoulder, thinking she'd heard someone coming along the path behind them, but there was no one.

"Good for you," Ravi said. "Don't let him get away with that. What's he like? The ex? Paint me a picture."

"He was nice and cute and smart and great and he decided he wanted to see who else was out there," she said.

"So, not that nice and smart and great after all."

"I mean, he *was*," she said. "Now I feel like I don't even know him anymore. He said he should have been a rock star. As soon as we got divorced, he started wearing all new clothes and got a girlfriend and bought a motorcycle. *Two* motorcycles, actually."

Ravi snorted. "That all seems a little on the nose."

They came out of the trees, and there was the gallery, light spilling from the windows in rectangles onto the dark ground. She could hear the ocean crashing louder in the distance. Its edge was gray and faintly discernible in the night. A line of cliffs fell sharply below the building. Ellery's heartbeat picked up, right on the edge of panic. *What was she doing here?*

The well-lit walkway, the proximity of other people did nothing to slow her racing heart. Ravi seemed kind, but what did she really know about him? What did she really know about anyone or anything at all?

Ravi didn't seem to notice. "So, what's the ex named?"

"Luke," she said, and she was surprised when Ravi snorted in laughter.

"What?" she said. "Lots of people are named Luke."

"It's also just a little on the nose," Ravi said. "It's a very good name for someone who is white and having a midlife crisis."

"So? And Luke Skywalker was *hot.*"

Ravi groaned. "No," he said. "No. *Please* tell me you did not have a crush on Luke Skywalker over Han Solo."

"Um."

"Yikes," Ravi said. "It's so good we met."

They were at the gallery. She followed Ravi around the part of the building that faced away from the ocean, and there was indeed a side door. It was slightly ajar. *Perfect.* Before Ellery could say, *Are you sure about this?* Ravi pushed the door all the way open.

5.

The key," Ravi said, "is acting like you belong. If anyone catches us, we smile and say hello. Then turn your back on them and find a piece of art to stare at. We'll pretend we're deep in conversation and *very* knowledgeable."

"Got it." Ellery glanced down at her dress. She was 100 percent sure it wasn't even close to as fancy as it should be for something like *this*. Through the door into the main room of the gallery, where everyone was gathered, she caught glimpses of shoes and dresses so gorgeous she wanted to reach out and touch them.

Standing in front of the glass windows was a young woman in a white slip dress who had to be the bride. Her brown hair was twisted up in a beautiful and complicated braid, and she glowed with youth and happiness. Next to her, a handsome, dark-haired young man slid his arm around her waist and they smiled at each other so fully that their eyes crinkled. Ellery's heart did a painful flop in her chest. They were lovely.

"Okay," Ravi said. "We're out of luck in this part of the gallery. All that's here are the bathrooms."

Ellery tore her eyes away from the couple and took in her immediate surroundings. Ravi was right. They were in a part of the building with black walls and two discreetly marked bathroom doors. The floor was the same shiny, gorgeous wood that led into the main room of the gallery. An enormous painting hung on the wall of the gallery opposite the bank of windows, the colors and lines striking even from this distance. Ellery wished she could move in for a closer look.

"No drinks," Ravi said. "They're either in that main room or somewhere along the other side. Shall we?"

Something in her expression made his face change, from adventurous and wry to gentle and understanding. "Never mind," he said. "You wait here. Or right outside. I'll bring you something. Okay?"

"Okay." She was certain her relief was audible. "That sounds good."

Ravi slipped away into the main room. Slender, dark haired, and graceful, he blended in even though he was slightly underdressed. She, on the other hand, had barely made it across the threshold before the wrongness of it all had stopped her in her tracks. She should be home with her family. How was that no longer an option?

I shouldn't be here alone. I shouldn't be here. I shouldn't be.

Ellery took a step for the door. She'd feel better outside. The resort, the people, the things that felt out of place, she herself—the ocean and the trees were what she needed. They didn't care that her life was falling apart. They didn't care about anything at all.

"Hey." Ellery flinched at the sound of an unfamiliar voice behind her. *Oh no.* She turned to see a young woman—*the* young woman.

The bride.

"Hi," the woman said. "Are you waiting for the restroom?"

She had a gentle voice. She was likely closer to Kate's age than to Ellery's—midtwenties.

"Um, no. I was just leaving."

The bride's engagement ring glittered even in the dim light where they were standing. Ellery glanced down at her own wedding band. After twenty years, she felt naked without it. She'd switched to wearing the band on her right hand a few weeks ago. Abby said it was time to stop wearing it altogether.

Ellery hadn't managed that yet.

"I'm sorry," she blurted out, looking directly into the bride's eyes. "I know this is a private event. I'm leaving right now."

"Oh, no worries at all," the young woman said easily. "I'm sorry you're staying at the resort while we're overrunning the place. I'm the bride, by the way. Olivia."

"Ellery. It's nice to meet you." Ellery glanced at the door. Olivia had been beyond gracious, but it was time to leave. Ravi would find her outside. "Congratulations. It's a beautiful location for a wedding."

But Olivia kept talking, chatting away easily as though Ellery were a wedding guest and not an absolute interloper. "Thanks. My mom picked it." She sighed. "This whole thing is so much bigger than Ben—my fiancé—and I had in mind. We wanted to get married at city hall with a couple of witnesses." She looked down at her white silk dress, which was alternating liquid gold and shimmery silver under the muted lights. "This was what I was going to wear." Olivia shrugged. "But in the end, it's not only about us."

"That was generous of you," Ellery said. "Families are important. And friends." She thought of Abby and all they had been through together.

"They are," Olivia agreed. "Friends, especially, for Ben." Her voice softened. "His parents died in a car accident when he was a teenager."

"I'm so sorry." Ellery's voice caught. *There are far too many hard things in this world,* she thought. Even beautiful people who married other beautiful people in startlingly beautiful places couldn't escape them. Her heart went out to Ben. "Does he have siblings? Other family?"

"No," Olivia said. "He's an only child." She smiled, shifting the tension. "But once we decided we were going to do the wedding this way, he didn't want to leave any of his friends out. So now he has seven groomsmen. And two best men."

Ellery smiled, too. "Do you have as many bridesmaids?"

"Just one," Olivia said. "My cousin, Rachel." She reached up to brush a tendril of hair away from her face.

Ellery found herself wondering if Olivia could be the shadow celebrity. But Ravi had made it sound like someone who was here on vacation, trying *not* to be noticed. And a bride always drew attention.

"Olivia?" someone called out from the other room. *"Olivia?"* It was a woman's voice, clear and commanding.

"That didn't take long," Olivia said ruefully. She glanced behind her. "My mom. She's kind of stressed out about the whole wedding. She's paying for everything. Because, you know. Ben's parents can't help out."

"Oh." Ellery took another step toward the door. *Time to go.* She doubted the mother of the bride would be as generous about Ellery's trespassing as Olivia had been. "It was nice to talk to you." *Thank you for being so kind about my being here, intruding in my on-sale Anthropologie dress and drugstore eyeliner.* "I hope tomorrow is perfect."

"Thank you." Olivia had turned toward her mother, so Ellery slipped out the door into the night.

6.

"You," Ravi said admiringly, "have guts."

"No, I don't," Ellery said. She did not have any guts. She also did not have any bones or muscles. She was a heart longing for a family she no longer had and a brain thinking about things it shouldn't and nerve endings reaching out in every direction.

"Yes, you do. Talking to the bride like that? Guts. Guts for days."

They were walking back down the trail. Ravi was carrying a champagne glass and she held a tiny lemon lavender tart that he'd brought her in the palm of her hand.

"Here," he'd said, when he'd given it to her moments ago outside the gallery door. "I noticed that you don't drink."

"Thank you." She'd been touched by this. By his seeing her. She'd also been touched by his asking to exchange phone numbers. He'd given her Nina's as well. "In case you want company," he said. "We'll be around, driving each other crazy."

Now, Ellery popped the entire tart into her mouth. She didn't know what else to do. Somewhere in the recesses of her brain, the word *delicious* rose, disappeared.

The path from the gallery back down to the main area of the resort was barely wide enough for them to walk side by side. The lighting along the edges was so discreet and tasteful that it was as if the plants along the path had simply chosen to glow here and there, exactly where one would next need to see. Ellery brushed the crumbs from her hands. "We're like Hansel and Gretel being led ever so gently into the woods."

"Exactly," Ravi said.

WHEN EVERYONE ELSE WAS occupied—*drinking, eating, dancing, sleeping, hiding, kissing, crying, laughing*—*that was the best time to explore the paths, the forests, the views. Late at night, or early at the edge of morning. She loved both times, the way you saw what few others did. The midnight-blue moments, the in-betweens. Anything could happen then.*

The ocean was breaking itself against the shore. She could hear it and, after her eyes had adjusted, she could see it, the silvered sprays and curls dashing against the rocks, the cliffs. It was a lonely sound, as inevitable as it was inviting.

The sea, the sky, the smell, the ground, the trees.

She stepped a bit too close to the edge.

It was easy to forget yourself out here.

It was easy to forget what you had done.

What you still

might do.

SATURDAY

Today at The Resort at Broken Point

*"May your trails be crooked, winding, lonesome, dangerous,
leading to the most amazing view."*

—*Edward Abbey*

Weather: Sunny/Partly Cloudy/Rain

SUNRISE: 7:13 A.M. ....HIGH: 65° F

SUNSET: 6:32 P.M. ....LOW: 54° F

ABOUT THE ART:
Untitled
by Jamie Klein
2015
steel

This sculpture consists of two pieces, an adult whooping crane with its beak to the sky, and a nest of the same species, the latter of which may occasionally be submerged under water depending on the time of year.

7.

Ellery had vowed to herself that she would take advantage of all the healthy, healing things that were included with her stay. Like *sunrise yoga* or the *early nature walk* or the *morning meditation followed by green juice pressed from plants grown on the property's garden.*

What she did was sleep straight through all of them until 7:37 a.m. She woke up, startled, when she heard a door slam and slightly raised voices passing her window, the sound incongruous in such a peaceful place.

She'd better get moving if she still wanted to catch the group going on the day hike. According to the description on the website, the hike was stunning, ascending over the crest of the coastal hills and then down along the shoreline, passing several small waterfalls along the way.

Ellery hurried into her shorts and tank top and the pair of old running shoes she used for hiking, before grabbing her water bottle and backpack and heading out the door. Today would have been her twentieth wedding anniversary. Instead, it marked nothing at all. *Keep moving,* she told herself. Otherwise the sadness monster could get you. It was always waiting for any sign of weakness. Teeth bared, claws out. Sometimes she wondered if she were grateful for the lessons learned after the accident had happened just over two years ago—were they what had made it possible to survive Luke's leaving? Other times she felt that that was not the case at all—that the accident, followed by the divorce, was such cruel timing, so many things piling on top of the other, that there was no way she could possibly bear it.

We've been through worse, Abby had said. And she was right. Death *was* the worst thing, wasn't it?

Even asking the question was a luxury only afforded to the living.

Ellery slowed her steps as she came to the spot marked on the resort map as *Ceremony Grove.* A tasteful sign had been staked in the ground to the side of the path. THE HARING-TAYLOR WEDDING, it read, printed in the resort's signature font. Staff were setting up chairs and drilling more stakes into the ground so they could hang lanterns along the path.

"I'm sorry!" Ellery said. "Should I take another trail?"

"Oh no," said one of the young women holding the lanterns. "It's no problem at all. The grove is open until an hour before the wedding. We're hoping the rain holds off."

"When's the ceremony?" Ellery asked.

"Right before sunset," the girl said. "Golden hour."

"Oh." Ellery actually sighed. She couldn't help herself. It was too perfect. Olivia and Ben would be stunning, standing here in the forest together.

The staff was tying dark green ribbons around the stakes and the trees, and Ellery found herself feeling judgy about that. Ribbons? Really? *Leave it alone,* she thought. *Let there be trees and leaves and golden light filtering through the branches. You don't need anything else.*

Either it will rain, or it won't.

Either they will keep loving each other, or they won't.

Ellery slowed as she passed the altar in the grove.

It resembled an oversized version of the cairns you often saw on trails—long flat stones stacked on one another, tapering slightly as it came to the top. Some parts were rough-hewn, others smooth. An artist's mark was etched into one of the stones. For a moment, Ellery was confused. Then she remembered the sculptures scattered throughout the resort. This must be one of them.

Ellery wasn't sure how she felt about the altar, what the piece implied. Was it offering guidance along a path? Or asking for an offering?

She'd have to look more closely later. Ellery nodded to the last of the staff and hurried out of the grove.

8.

One of the three other guests who showed up for the hike was the cute guy that Ellery and Ravi had noticed the night before.

And it turned out that the staff member guiding the hike was also extremely handsome. Blond hair, wide green eyes, broad shoulders.

This was starting off as well as could be hoped. Abby would be pleased.

"Okay," the staff member said. "My name's Canyon, and I'll be leading you guys on the hike today."

Canyon? Could that be real? First Brook, now this. Maybe people who worked at Broken Point had to have special nature-y names, like River or Poppy or Sage.

"Everybody wearing sunscreen?" Canyon asked. "Everyone have plenty of water?"

Murmurs and nods from the group.

"I need to get a verbal confirmation that everyone is aware that this hike has been classified as moderate, and that it's almost eight miles long over challenging terrain," Canyon said. As everyone murmured their yeses, his gaze lingered on two of the guests in particular. It was the father-daughter pairing Ellery had noticed at dinner the night before. This morning, they were both wearing San Francisco Giants baseball caps.

"Don't worry," the older man said dryly. "You won't have to carry me." He gestured to the young woman. "I've got my daughter. Grace. She'll look out for me."

"*And* he has Stabby," Grace said cheerfully, pointing at the hiking pole her father was holding. Her smile made you want to smile, too. Even Canyon, who must have seen his fair share of charming young female guests, couldn't help but grin back.

"Grace is a certified wilderness first responder," her father said, pride evident in his voice. "And she runs ultramarathons."

Ellery swore she could see the handsome guy next to her perk up. "Andy," he said, holding out his hand to shake Grace's.

"Gary," the father said, shaking hands next. Then it was Ellery's turn. She introduced herself and shifted her backpack higher on her shoulders, feeling the heft of the water bottle inside it. She didn't want to shake hands. She didn't want to touch anyone. She never knew what small contact or kindness might undo her.

"Okay," Canyon said. "I've got extra water in my pack if you need it. I've got a map for each of you. You can all hike at your own pace. I'll go last and bring up the rear. The main trail is well-marked and you will eventually loop back here to the trailhead, but if you're *ever* not sure, stop and wait for me. It's not worth getting lost. It's easy to forget because of the resort, but we're in the wilderness. Stick to the path."

"Sounds good." Grace took her map. Ellery accepted hers, opening it so she could see where the hike had been outlined. It matched what she'd seen on the website.

"I'm happy to answer any questions you have as we hike," Canyon said. "And I'm here to make sure we all get back in one piece and on time." He pointed at Andy. "Especially you."

"You don't have to worry about me." Andy pulled a worn ballcap out of his back pocket and clamped it down over his curly brown hair. "I'll run if I have to. I'm not going to be late."

Late for what? Ellery wondered. She didn't have a chance to ask Andy before he started off. His walk was so natural and smooth that she felt envious. How would it feel to be that at home in your body, in the world?

She'd known that feeling before. Not anymore.

9.

Ellery hadn't brought enough water.

If her GPS watch was right, she was almost halfway through the hike, but she was well over halfway through the contents of her Nalgene bottle. The day had gone from cool blue to bright hot and was becoming unseasonably warm. She could feel the skin on the bridge of her nose starting to burn, and she wished the way she always did that she'd gotten her dad's olive skin instead of her mom's pale, easy-to freckle complexion. The first few miles had turned out to be uphill without any shade. She kept thinking each rise was the last one before they'd start coming down by the coastline but so far, no good. Ellery had been hiking since she was a kid, and she was in decent shape, but she'd made a mistake.

Lately she was thirsty all the time. It was probably because of all the crying.

She could turn back or wait for Canyon. He had extra water. But she didn't want to do either of those things.

What if I die out here, she thought, *and no one cares? What if I dry up into a shriveled pile of skin and bones and teeth?*

Back when they were young newlyweds, she and Luke had splurged on a trip to London. They'd gotten student rates on airfares and found a hotel with a teeny tiny room with a large casement window that opened up to the sounds of the city below. One of the places they'd visited was the British Museum, where a mummy had been on display in a glass case. Like, the *body* of the mummy itself. Not a gorgeous golden sarcophagus or other ornate container you saw in pamphlets.

Besides the obvious issues with the artifacts even being in the United Kingdom in the first place, Ellery had found it disturbing on a personal level. The card attached to the display case said that the mummy was a woman who'd likely had children. The woman's arms and legs were drawn up as if to protect herself, and her body looked like strips of dried leather affixed to bones. But she was undeniably, irrevocably human, and Ellery hated—*hated*—that the woman had been placed there for everyone to gawk at without her permission. She had turned away with tears in her eyes. Luke had given her a hug, wrapped his arms around her right there in the museum. *I'm going to die someday,* Ellery had thought, *but at least I have this. I have him.*

She was almost to the top of the hill. This time, though, the rise beyond had trees on it. *Get that far,* she told herself, *and you can have another drink.* The dirt path under her feet was still muddy from the recent rains, and small yellow wildflowers dotted the ruts and crevices in the road.

The second she came under the trees at the crest and could feel the shade soaking into her skin, she dropped her pack somewhat dramatically and exhaled loudly. *Ahhhh.* She couldn't see the full vista yet because of the trees, but the glimpses of ocean in the distance hinted that the views might, indeed, be worth it.

She pulled out her phone and texted Ravi. *You're going to be sorry you didn't come on this hike,* she wrote. *I'm getting SO MUCH exercise. And there are two cute guys.*

"You've got to be kidding me," someone said behind her. "You're getting *cell service* up here?"

Ellery spun around, her heart pounding. As if she'd summoned him with her text to Ravi, Andy was coming up the trail behind her. His baseball cap was still pulled down low and she couldn't quite see his eyes.

Had he meant to scare her? She would have sworn he'd been far ahead. She tried to smile, but she was aware of how alone they were,

slightest bit tempted to say yes. She could use the mind clearing climbing had always given her.

"Okay," Andy said. She kept expecting him to say goodbye and head off down the trail, but he continued to keep pace with her.

"So, is the groom a nice guy?" Ellery asked. "I talked to the bride last night and she seemed lovely."

"Oh yeah," Andy said. "Ben and I grew up together. Like, from kindergarten on. I'd do anything for that guy." His tone had gone serious. "He's the best. People always say that about their friends, but with Ben it's true."

"It's good to have friends like that."

"He'd do anything to help someone out," Andy said. "He's helped people get back on their feet, takes on clients for free if they can't pay him and he sees a need."

Ben did sound wonderful. But, like they'd discussed at dinner last night, everyone had a shadow. A secret. Something that they'd done, or could do, or that had happened to them that was so dark it followed them everywhere.

Everyone was hiding.

She was no different.

Ben was no different.

Andy was no different.

The uneasiness that had found its way in before was back.

Somewhere above, a gull screeched and wheeled. The sound sent Ellery instantly back in time to a dark highway road, screaming teenagers, her own heart in her throat, the wrenching and scraping of metal, the sound of bodies hitting the roof, the ground, one another. *The accident.* She and Abby always referred to it as simply that, those two words, though the news sites and television anchors gave it other names.

The one that had really caught hold was "Track Team Tragedy," after *People* magazine had run a cover story on the whole thing using those three words as the headline. Ellery and Abby had been hailed as the "hero teachers" who had "saved the day," their photos included in all the articles along with those of the students. Both she and Abby knew the truth, though. They weren't heroes. They hadn't been able to save anyone. They'd done their best, and it had not been nearly good enough. Later, one of the parents had accused them of moving kids who were injured and causing greater harm. Ellery had been surprised then how pain could compound on pain, how you could hurt, and hurt, and hurt.

She was still surprised at the way that worked. How much you could feel, over and over again.

"Hey," Andy said. "Are you all right?" He had glanced over at her and must have seen an expression on her face that caught him off guard.

"Yes," she said. She was not. She never would be again. But she was also here with the wind on her face and the sun on her back. "Just… remembering something. *Oh.*"

They'd come down another small rise, and as the view cleared in front of them, they both stopped short.

Aqua-blue ocean as far as the eye could see. The cliffs crumbled to the sea, streams of waterfalls shining down in several places. The hills leading to the water were green-and-gold-grassed, rippling in the breeze. Off to their right, up the coastline, the jagged cliff of Broken Point and its three trees was visible in the distance.

"Holy shit," Andy said. He glanced at her. "Sorry."

"No worries," she said.

"It's not a great phrase to describe how stunning that is," he said.

"There probably aren't *any* good words to describe how stunning that is," Ellery said. She and Andy stared out at the water, the sky, the heartbreakingly beautiful blue of it all, in silence. Ellery wanted to close her eyes. She wanted to disappear right now, while someone was standing witness in a gorgeous place at the edge of the world. She could wink out, like a candle, and Andy could testify that she hadn't meant for it to happen. *One second she was here,* he'd say, *and the next she was gone.*

She took her phone out of her pocket to take a picture, though no picture could ever capture this. But it would be something for her to look at later, in another harder moment—proof that she really had been here, that she really had done this.

Andy glanced at his watch again. "Well," he said. "I'd better get going. I was actually planning on running the whole way back. Got to get showered and help out with at least some of the wedding stuff."

"Good luck," she said. "Be the best of the second-best."

That made him laugh. "Hey," he said, gesturing to the phone she still held in her hand. "Can I give you my number for tomorrow? In case you change your mind?"

"Um, sure." Why not? The only way he'd hear from her was if she reached out to him. Which was unlikely.

After she'd added his contact information into her phone, Andy lifted his hand in a wave. "See you later at the resort. Assuming I survive this wedding." With that, he was off down the trail, running as easily as he'd been walking earlier, his backpack bouncing lightly against his shoulder blades.

As Ellery watched him disappear over the rise, she wished she'd asked him if he had any extra water. Her lips were parched. Her eyes prickled.

Her throat was as dry as a bone.

10.

Ellery was guzzling water straight from the tap in her room when her phone buzzed with an incoming text. She reached for where she'd set it on the bathroom countertop.

Luke Wainwright.

Her heart leaped in her chest.

This is Maddie, the message said. *Can I FaceTime you?*

Of course, Ellery wrote back. She filled her bottle with water and headed for the desk chair so she could sit down. Did she have time to find her AirPods?

She did not. The phone started to buzz almost immediately and she hit accept.

"Hey, there!" she said, holding up the phone, and she saw Maddie's dear little face. Then it disappeared momentarily as Maddie said, "Mom? Hi." The way the kids FaceTimed made her seasick. They were always moving the phone around to try out different camera angles. Right now, for example, Maddie was angling the camera so Ellery could see directly up her nose.

"How's it going, honey?" Ellery asked.

"Good," Maddie said, moving the phone from side to side so she could admire the way she was stretching her face into crazy contortions. She was eight, and Ellery's baby, and Ellery missed her so profoundly she had to swallow, hard, in order to speak.

"Are you home from camping already?"

"Yes," Maddie said matter-of-factly. "We had to come back early because it started to rain."

"Oh, shoot," Ellery said, though she felt a little surge of glee that the outdoor adventure without her wasn't going perfectly. "It's supposed to rain here tonight, too."

"Where *are* you?" Maddie asked, though she'd been told.

"California."

"Can I see your room?"

"Sure." Ellery did a sweep of her room with her phone. She loved this about Maddie, that she always wanted to be able to picture where someone was. Ellery was the same way. She tried not to look past Maddie to catch glimpses of Luke's new home, the one he'd bought and furnished using their (now closed) joint account. He hadn't wanted to take a single chair or plate or bowl from their home together.

It killed Ellery to know that there would be rooms in her children's lives that she would never see; ones they would walk into and visit and inhabit, that they would know intimately, with the kind of minute geographical detail—*there's a crack in the baseboard here, a particularly cozy spot in the corner there*—particular to childhood and to where you grew up. She'd known, of course, that they would live places without her. But she'd thought she'd have until they were eighteen at least.

"The rooms here have names," Ellery said.

"Like what? Like Caitlin?" Maddie asked. She had had a favorite teenage babysitter once named Caitlin and had decided it was the best possible name ever since.

"No, like nature names," Ellery said. "Of the plants and flowers that grow around here."

"What's yours named?"

"Milkweed."

"Ew." Maddie hated milk. "But it *looks* nice."

"It is," Ellery said. "So how *was* camping?" She kept her voice steady.

"Good," Maddie said.

"What did you guys do?" Ellery ached to know what their days were like. It felt foreign to have them pass so much time without her.

"Stuff," Maddie said.

This was the kind of answer Maddie had always given, even before the divorce. She was feisty and spunky and funny. But lately Ellery heard a new edge in Maddie's voice, a kind of brittleness, like someone keeping a fragile thing safe that she had been handed against her will.

"What did you have for lunch?" Ellery tried again.

"Food," Maddie said, pulling her cheeks down so that she looked like the *Scream* painting. Then Ethan came in and said something off camera.

"Hey, Ethan," Ellery said, and he said, "Hi, Mom," back, his face with its shaggy mop of hair and big brown eyes appearing for a split second.

Ellery loved them all so much, and these glimpses and conversations when they were apart weren't nearly enough. She wanted to truly *see* them all, to try to reach through the screen and touch them, pull them through the ether to California, to her.

"Where's Kate?" she asked.

Right then, she heard Luke's voice in the background. Her heart thudded, leaped, sank. "All right, guys," he said. "Time to go. You can call Mom again tomorrow if you want."

Was Imogen there? Ellery wondered. What would they have for dinner? How late would they stay up? What would they do after the kids were in bed?

Don't think about it, she told herself. *Throw the loop.* This was something her therapist, Macy, had told her. Instead of staying on the same circling feelings, spiraling down into *what ifs* and *what nows*, Ellery was supposed to imagine drawing a circle and then not completing it. During a session, Macy had had Ellery draw a bunch of unfinished circles over and over on a piece of paper. It had been at least slightly therapeutic, because it took concentration not to close the circles. There had also been an added hilarious benefit when they looked at the paper a few moments later and realized that the incomplete circles looked like a line of neat little sperm marching across the page. "I wanted you *not* to think about Luke," Macy had said, and that had cracked Ellery up the slightest bit, even in the midst of all the hell.

She set her phone down on the desk. A leather tray in front of her held a notepad and pen. It also held the room service menu, the daily card with information about the resort and its art and weather, and a slender, journal-sized booklet with WELCOME TO BROKEN POINT printed across the cover. Each item was emblazoned with the resort's logo.

The manager, a tall, wiry silver-haired woman named Nat, had given the booklet to Ellery at check-in. Ellery flipped through it, her mind half on other things. It had a map of the resort and listed information about Broken Point, from the titles of the artwork placed throughout the property to the kinds of cocktails they served down at the trailer bar during happy hour.

What were her kids doing right now? Without her?

Ellery stood up. She needed food. And something to drink.

And not to be alone.

11.

I did not expect the cocktail hour to be this hopping," Ravi said.

"Don't say *this hopping*," Nina told him. She was wearing a deep purple dress that echoed the shades of the plum-colored flowers in the vases on the tables. Ravi wore a soft navy button-up and black jeans. Ellery was wearing dark jeans and her favorite green sweater. For years, her goal at events (Luke's work parties, the random dinner she got invited to) had simply been to not wear the *wrong* thing. She didn't want to stand out. She wanted to be part of the background, the crowd. Not ignored or alone, but not the center of attention, ever.

She noticed Grace and Gary talking to a couple she hadn't yet met, two handsome men she guessed were in their fifties. Gary wore a blue Oxford shirt with the sleeves rolled back, and Grace had on the kind of skimmy, floaty floral dress that looked wonderful on the young and long-legged.

"There *are* a lot of people here," Ellery said to Ravi. She'd thought the cocktail hour would be kind of chill—the resort guests getting their drinks, mingling for a moment, diffusing out like fireflies into the night. But with the ocean terrace off-limits thanks to the post-wedding dinner, which was due to begin shortly, everyone else seemed to be lingering in the Main House.

"There's some kind of situation going on with the wedding," Ravi said.

"How do you know?" Ellery turned to Nina, preparing to be amused, to hear Nina tease Ravi about always looking for a scandal.

But Nina was in full agreement with Ravi. "We ran into the bridesmaid and the bride's mother earlier today coming out of the spa," she said. "They were whispering. They looked worried."

"Well, weddings can be stressful." For all the poignant and painful memories Ellery's wedding was occasioning in her right now, given today was her actual anniversary, she could remember moments of tension. Nothing major, nothing she'd thought about in years. But Luke's parents had invited his old girlfriend—not only to the reception but to the ceremony itself—without telling Ellery. And no one had thought to make sure the flower girl had brought the shoes that went with her dress. Things like that.

"It was more than normal wedding stress," said Nina. "Trust me. I've been a bridesmaid for all four of my sisters. Something's going on."

"Every time I see the mother of the bride, the Cruella de Vil song starts going through my mind." Ravi began to sing. *"Da doop de do da doopty, da doop de do da doopty…"*

"That's 'The Addams Family' song," Nina said fondly.

"You catch my meaning, though," Ravi said to Ellery.

"I do." She was legitimately cracking up. Ravi and Nina were smart and fantastic and elegant and did not take themselves too seriously. They were *goofy*, almost, in certain moments. It surprised her, and it also surprised her that she could laugh at all this weekend.

"There's more." Ravi lowered his voice. "I heard a member of the staff telling Nat that one of the art pieces was missing."

"Art piece?" Nina wanted to know.

"*Oh* my word," Ravi said. "We've *discussed* this. There's art all over the property. It's part of why we picked this resort! They tell you about it on those cards they give us every day!"

"I *know*," Nina said. "I meant, which art piece is missing?"

"Ravi." Ellery was thinking of last night, what he'd said about the rules for vacations, when they'd snuck up to the gallery to steal something. "Did you do it? Did you do an art heist?" She was half joking, half serious. She wouldn't put anything past him.

"No," Ravi said, momentarily diverted—and delighted. "Do you really think I could pull off something like that?"

Ellery tilted her head. "I don't know," she said. "Maybe being an art thief is your secret. Your shadow."

"No," he said. "Mine's much more serious than that." He shook his head. "And I don't know which piece is missing. I was lucky to hear anything at all. I went to the reception desk to ask for another welcome booklet because I'd lost mine, and Nat and Brook were there. When they saw me, they stopped talking."

"How would you even steal a painting?" Nina asked. "It's not like you can exactly tuck it under your arm and walk off. And where would you hide it?"

"Maybe it was a sculpture," Ravi said. "Some of those are small."

"What exactly were they saying?" Nina asked.

But before Ravi could answer, one of the bartenders—a redheaded thirtysomething whose name tag read *Owen*, ruining Ellery's hot nature names theory—offered them drinks on a tray. "We have beer, white wine, or red," he said. Nina took a beer, Ravi a white wine. Owen looked at Ellery.

"Do you have any mocktails?" she asked, slightly embarrassed.

"We do," Owen said. "We have a virgin sangria that people love."

"Would it be too much of a hassle to have that instead?"

"Not at all," Owen said. "I'll be back with it in a few moments."

"Ooh, can I get one too?" a woman asked behind them.

They all turned to see who had spoken. A young couple stood a few feet away, the woman blond and beautiful and wearing an orange sherbet-colored maxi dress. Her hair was braided up in an elaborate crown with a flower tucked behind her ear. The man with her had a hipster-husband look to him—he wore a short-sleeved button-up shirt, his face was perfectly stubbled, and his hair was combed in that way that always made Ellery think of a rooster.

"Of course," Owen promised.

"I'm *so* glad I heard you order that," the woman said, beaming at Ellery. "I can't drink because, you know." She cradled her hands around a tiny, perfect baby bump.

"How exciting for you guys!" Ellery looked at the husband, who smiled and said, "Thanks."

"Congratulations," Ravi said, looking vaguely appalled.

"I just *barely* started showing," the young woman said. "And it's *perfect* timing. We've been waiting for the right time to tell our followers. Now we can do that while we're here."

"Your followers?" Nina asked.

"On LikeMe," the woman said. "We're Morgan and Maddox. Or Morg and Madd. If you want to look us up. Two *d*'s in Madd, and one of those *and* signs between our names."

"That's called an ampersand," Ellery said helpfully.

The woman looked confused.

"Never mind," Ravi said. "So you're influencers?" He raised an eyebrow significantly at Ellery and she remembered their conversation at dinner the night before. How he'd said there was someone sneaky famous staying at the resort. But these two seemed the opposite of sneaky. And not the kind of famous Ravi had been talking about.

"Yeah," the woman said. "Have you heard of us?"

"I'm sorry, no," Nina said dryly.

"We're not your target demographic, though," Ravi said. "Which one are you? Morg or Madd?"

The woman thought that was hilarious. "I'm Morgan!" She shook her head playfully at Ravi. "And we have half a million followers who are going to totally freak out when they find out about *this*." She patted her baby bump. "Broken Point is supposed to be a no-children resort, but we have a *stowaway!*"

"She's definitely posting that as a caption on LikeMe," Nina said under her breath. Ellery smothered a laugh.

But in spite of the artifice of it all—the discussion about timing the announcement, the archness of what Morgan was saying, the cradling of the oh-so-perfect baby bump—it was real. There was a baby on the way who Morgan and Maddox would raise and love and they were people with actual feelings and lives.

Unintentionally, Ellery's gaze caught on Maddox. His shoulders, she noticed, were powerful, moving under his dress shirt every time he shifted position. They seemed like real muscles, not the souped-up gym kind you usually saw on guys like this. Briefly, her eyes met his. There was a baffled look in them. For a moment, she thought they were both thinking the same thing: *How did I end up here?*

No. There was danger in that, she remembered. You never, ever knew what someone else was thinking.

Just then she felt a shift in the atmosphere, rippling through the groups gathered in clusters throughout the room. Heads turned in the same direction, like flowers to the sun. Owen was walking toward them with their drinks but he stopped halfway, his head turning, too.

The mother of the bride stood incongruously in front of the bar, Nat and Canyon on either side. The mother of the bride's dark green silk sheath dress stood out among the more casually dressed cocktail crowd, as did her updo, her glittering necklace, her sharp eyes cutting through the gathering.

Da doop de do da doopty ran through Ellery's head.

"What presence," Nina said appreciatively. "Look at her posture."

"What's she doing here?" Ravi asked. "Shouldn't she be at the dinner?"

"Excuse me," said the mother of the bride to the crowd.

They could hear her, but guests a bit farther away were still talking. "Shhh," Ravi said, and the hush spread over the little knots of people holding their drinks.

"Excuse me." The mother of the bride spoke again into the growing silence. "I'm Catherine Haring."

"Um, okay..." Morgan said, under her breath.

"Why do I know that name?" Ravi murmured to himself.

"As some of you may have heard," Catherine continued, "the wedding today did not take place."

The crowd rippled again, this time with electricity, surprise.

"Oooh," Ravi said.

Olivia. Ellery's heart flopped in her chest like a fish as she thought about the bride. *Was Olivia okay? Was her heart broken? Or was she the one who had called it off? And why was her mother making such a public announcement about the whole thing?*

"We'd invited additional guests who were staying off-site to the dinner reception after the wedding," Catherine said. "We were able to tell them to turn back, but much of the food had already been prepared." Her tone was clipped, matter-of-fact. Now that people were quiet, her voice, low but clear, was easy enough to hear. "I've asked the staff to open the reception on the terrace to all the resort guests. Please feel free to help yourselves. There is no point in it going to waste." With that, she turned and walked away, Nat and Canyon following behind. Somehow, even in heels, Catherine didn't wobble or miss a step.

"What do you think?" Nina asked. No one was moving toward the terrace. "Do you still want to eat at the restaurant?"

"No, we're definitely partaking of the unwedding feast," Ravi said. "But I don't want to lead the charge."

It turned out that Morgan and Maddox were the first to head out to the terrace. "Of course," Ravi said under his breath, but Ellery was grateful to them for breaking the ice. It didn't seem greedy, somehow. It seemed gracious. Plus, she remembered how it felt to be pregnant and sometimes food sounded amazing and sometimes it sounded terrible, and you had to go with whatever your body was saying. Maybe Morgan was starving.

Ellery herself was ravenous.

12.

If you weren't involved with the wedding, it was turning out to be a pretty great night.

The food had been set up buffet style in silver dishes on long, ivory linen–draped tables. Floral arrangements of white and cream flowers and greenery had been placed in the center of smaller tables for dining. Candles flickered, and the food was excellent—gourmet sliders, tiny shrimp cocktails, fresh green salads garnished with wildflowers, ravioli, honey-mustard-glazed chicken, with chocolate pots de crème and lavender shortbread for dessert. There was a small bar nestled in an alcove in the terrace serving house cocktails and specialty drinks.

And apparently the band had arrived before receiving word that the wedding was canceled, so Catherine Haring had told them to play on.

It became clear almost immediately that Morgan and Maddox were fantastic dancers, exactly the right amount of fluid and dirty to be fun. They were young and beautiful and the way they laughed and moved made everyone around them smile. Morgan danced over to Ravi and Ellery and beckoned to them. Ellery begged off, laughing, but Ravi made his way into the center of a quickly forming dance circle.

"This is getting kind of hot," Nina said. "Or am I just super drunk?"

"It's hot," Ellery said.

A few of the off-duty staff were joining in. Some pushed the round tables slightly out of the way to enlarge the dance floor. The band started to kick back a bit, riffing on some of their songs, freestyling others. A few drops of rain came down, causing moments of exclamation and looking up, but the storm was holding off. A round moon kept peeking through the clouds and then sneaking back behind.

Ellery noticed a striking young woman she'd seen up at the gallery slip into the party. She wore a deep green silk dress and sandals and her cheekbones were high, her movements purposeful, the kind of woman you didn't forget. She didn't dance, didn't engage, didn't look at a single person. Instead, she made her way to the food table and took a plate, filling it. On her way past the bar, she leaned over it and said something to the bartender, who nodded. He handed her a bottle of wine and she set down the plate for a moment, deftly tucked the bottle under her arm, picked up the plate again, and disappeared into the night.

Was that the bridesmaid Nina had mentioned? Ellery was willing to bet on it. Her clothes looked like the outfit of someone who hadn't had time to fully change, who had gone straight from bridesmaid to consoling best friend. The food and wine had to be for Olivia, didn't they?

Ellery turned back to the party.

Ravi and Morgan were breaking it down, the crowd egging them on, when several twentysomething men in tuxedos walked out onto the terrace and toward the bar.

"Oh, hell," Nina said to Ellery. "They have to be groomsmen. Of course. They can't miss out on the drinks."

At first, Ellery tried to differentiate among the groomsmen but they were too much of a type, especially in the dusk. To Ellery they seemed profoundly entitled, from the unbuttoned collars of their shirts to their rumpled hair to their ruddy faces, visible as they stood under the hanging strings of lights. "Hey," one called out to everyone on the dance floor. "This was supposed to be *our* party. You're welcome!" The others laughed raucously.

"Lovely," Nina said.

Another groomsman had made his way up to the bandstand, and he reached for a microphone. The band halted as he hoisted a drink into the air. "To Ben," he shouted. "To his freedom!" The others cheered.

Ellery could feel the party turning. She caught Ravi's eye, and she could tell he felt it, too. He hugged Morgan, shook Maddox's hand, and headed over to where Nina and Ellery were standing. "Okay," he said, "time to call it a night."

A lone figure had detached himself from the groomsmen and was headed in their direction. *Ugh,* Ellery thought, but then, as he came closer, she realized it was Andy. "Hey," he said, looking grim. "Sorry about all of this."

She should have realized that one of the group was not quite like the others. Andy's shirt was ironed but not starched, his shoes weren't polished, his hair was in its usual state of unruly, not drunk-tousled. And, of course, his expression was entirely different. There was no trace of *oh well, let's have a good time anyway.* He appeared shaken.

"Are you okay?" Ellery asked. "You look like you'd rather be anywhere than here."

"I'm only here to make sure they don't make asses out of themselves," Andy said tightly.

"How'd you end up with that job?" Ellery asked, as Ravi said, "So these guys are your friends?"

"I'm Nina," Nina said, sticking out her hand.

"Whoops," Ellery said, embarrassed. "I should have introduced everyone before I started interrogating you."

"No worries," Andy said, though he did actually look very, very worried. He shook Nina's hand. "Andy."

"Ravi," Ravi said, and he and Andy shook as well.

"I don't really know these guys," Andy said. "They're Ben's friends from his college fraternity. And work."

They all looked over at the group. The groomsman who'd given the sardonic toast was now in deep discussion with one of the band members. Probably giving his opinions on the set list and making requests.

Andy's jaw tightened. "I'd better go get that guy off the bandstand.

For Ben's sake. I don't want him to have to deal with anything else tonight."

"Wait," Ravi said. "Can you tell us what happened? Who called it off? Was it the bride?"

"It was Ben." Andy shook his head. "I don't get it. We were all gathering in the grove for the wedding. I thought Ben was with the best man, Matt, who thought he was with me. Olivia thought he was with one of us. No one knew anything was wrong until we all got to the grove and Ben wasn't with anyone. About five minutes after the ceremony was supposed to start, a couple of us heard from him."

"Did he say why he didn't come?" Ellery asked.

"He didn't *say* anything." Andy's eyes flickered to the groomsman on the bandstand, who was getting more and more wound up. "He texted."

"Really?" Ravi asked.

Andy nodded. "He sent the same text to all of us. Olivia, me, Matt, Rachel, Olivia's parents."

What did it say? Ellery could see the words forming in Ravi's mind, but he managed to forbear.

"I don't get it," Andy said again. He glanced over at Ellery. She wondered how it had been for him the last couple of hours. Getting the text. Looking for his friend. Trying to find out what had gone wrong. Had he heard from Ben since?

There was a crash from the bandstand. Someone had dropped a wineglass and another groomsman had grabbed the microphone. "I'm Matt," he said. "I'm the best man, and I've got a speech that shouldn't go to waste—"

"Crap," Andy said. "I'd better go help." He walked away, his shoulders somehow both set and slumped.

"Poor guy," Ellery said.

"Let's get out of here," Nina said, Ravi already nodding. The dance floor was emptying quickly. Andy had reached the bandstand and was talking to Matt, who looked mutinous and drunk.

"I think I'm going to stay," Ellery said.

They both looked at her in surprise. Then Ravi grinned. "Good idea. Give Andy some moral support."

"Exactly." Ellery winked at them both, a gesture so foreign to her these days that they all started laughing at the stiffness of it.

"Breakfast tomorrow?" Ravi asked.

"Sounds good."

But as soon as they were gone, Ellery didn't walk over to Andy. Instead, she headed to a quiet part of the terrace, where the strings of lights didn't reach and the bushes clustered up against a low stone wall.

There. She hadn't imagined it. Someone was sitting there, half-concealed.

Alone, and watching.

13.

I don't have a glass," Catherine Haring said. She held a bottle of wine in her hand. Her voice was quiet and controlled, but Ellery could tell she was drunk. "But help yourself." She held out the bottle.

"No, thank you." Ellery already regretted her decision to approach the mother of the bride. She didn't seem to need any help or company. Plus, Ellery was a stranger. This wasn't her job. She'd just felt sorry for the woman. Catherine sitting alone had tugged at Ellery's heartstrings. She understood alone when you didn't want to be. When you hadn't expected to be. Catherine should have been celebrating here, too, and she wasn't.

Where was her husband? And where was her daughter?

"Olivia's locked her door," Catherine said, as if she knew exactly what Ellery was thinking. "She told her father and me to go away."

That alarmed Ellery.

Catherine might be drunk, but she was still sharp. She inferred from Ellery's silence what she might be thinking. "Rachel's with her," she said. "The bridesmaid. That's who Olivia wanted. Not me. So I came back out here to make sure this didn't all go to hell, too."

"I think Andy is on it," Ellery said. *So that* had *been the bridesmaid, with the food.*

"Who?" Catherine furrowed her brow. "Oh, of course. The one with the hair. The one who's not quite right."

It was such an odd way to define Andy that Ellery blinked.

Catherine laughed, bitterly. "Oh well. I always knew Ben wasn't good enough for Olivia. She may have dodged a bullet."

Olivia and Andy had both spoken highly of Ben, but that meant nothing. People could hide things. *Everyone has their shadow.*

Ellery studied Catherine's profile—the flicker of her tastefully done false eyelashes, the set of her chin, the rings on her fingers and the wine in the glass flashing in the light. There was an exhaustion to her, something almost dangerous, in the way she was watching the group and drinking her wine. She drank neatly, not spilling a single drop on her dress, and she set the bottle down so quietly on the stone next to her that it didn't make a sound. And no matter what she had said about Olivia dodging a bullet, Ellery sensed a deep sadness in Catherine. For her daughter? For herself?

"Well," Ellery said after a moment. "Good night. I just wanted to see if there was anything I could do."

This time, Catherine's laugh had a note of derision in it. "You *do* know you're not part of the wedding party, don't you? Sneaking into the gallery last night and hanging around here now doesn't mean you're one of us."

Ellery stepped back, stunned. Catherine had seen her last night? Embarrassment flooded her, and her eyes prickled with tears.

"I'm sorry," Ellery said. "I shouldn't have—"

Catherine waved a hand, dismissing her. "It's understandable," she said. "Some people are butterflies. Like Olivia. And others"—she turned, looked at Ellery, her eyes assessing—"are moths. Drawn to the flame."

A moth. That was exactly how Ellery felt. Small, gray, fluttering around, still searching for the right light.

"I'm sorry," she repeated. Her hands were shaking. She shouldn't have intruded. Not last night, and not now.

Without looking at Ellery, Catherine lifted the bottle again. "Good night."

14.

Ellery walked back alone. Near Ceremony Grove, the lighting along the path revealed that the chairs were gone, the lanterns removed. But there were still traces of the setup for the wedding ceremony. The wind was picking up, and it stirred the remaining flower petals scattered along the ground and across the altar. There was a definite smell of rain in the air, a heaviness to the night.

When Ethan was smaller, seven or so, they had taken a trip to the Wizarding World of Harry Potter at Universal Studios in Los Angeles. It was part of a family vacation that also included Disneyland (Ethan's favorite place in all the world and the one where he was the most affectionate—holding family members' hands, which he hardly ever did, giving them big bear hugs of his own volition, which was even more rare). Ellery had booked the extra day at Universal on a whim, wondering if it might be another place Ethan could love.

But he hadn't loved it. He'd tolerated the day and the rides but wasn't taken with them the way he was at the other park. Too computerized, she thought, the world hadn't actually been built up around him in intricate, tactile detail. However, the part of the visit he'd most liked (to her surprise) was a visit to the wand shop they'd done mostly for the other kids. Ethan had been attentive during the whole presentation and had asked afterward if he could have a wand, which (despite the exorbitant prices) she'd purchased for him. He'd carried it carefully onto the plane, refusing to let her put it in his bag or a backpack, and had treated it with similar reverence at home (this, from a child who sometimes went through the world like what she and Luke called a "teddy bear in a china shop," the misquote intentional, expressing Ethan's careless, clueless, adorable—and sometimes dangerous—lack of awareness of the world around him).

After they'd returned from the trip, Ethan asked her repeatedly to take him to a lake up in the mountains that they sometimes visited. It was a beautiful spot—blue water, perfect green pines, a sandier beach than you usually found in Colorado, a long wooden dock stretching out into the water from which you could launch kayaks or paddleboards. The day she'd finally gotten around to taking Ethan had been months after their trip to California, later in the year, when the air and water were cool bordering on cold. There hadn't been many people at the lake.

Ethan had climbed out of the car with a sense of purpose. "Wait for me, buddy," she said, trying to make sure she had her keys and phone, but he was off, stalking intently out onto the dock. Since he had a penchant for jumping into bodies of water fully clothed, she hurried after him, worried he'd gotten it into his mind to go for a swim.

But Ethan stopped at the end of the dock and turned to look at her. It was then that she saw he was holding his wand. She hadn't noticed that he'd brought it in the car. His blue eyes and the blue T-shirt he was wearing and the blue water behind him all brightened and deepened one another, and she thought, *This is impossibly beautiful.* He *is impossibly beautiful.*

"Mom," Ethan said, urgency in his tone. "Mom." To her surprise, he handed her the precious wand. "*Mom.* Turn me into a fish."

"Oh, Ethan," she said, her heart breaking. "I can't. I'm so sorry."

"No, Mom," he said. "You *can.*"

It built and built, the urgency in his voice, then the distress, the break in her heart, until she thought they would both shatter. Inward or outward, she didn't know, but neither of them could bear this much pain, this much *want*, this much failure. "Mom," Ethan kept saying, tears in his eyes. "Mom, *please. Please.* Turn me into a fish."

When he finally realized that she couldn't (oh, how she hoped he didn't think it was that she *wouldn't*) they got back into the car and drove home. They wound down the forest roads in silence, both of their faces tearstained.

She hadn't seen the wand since. He had never asked to go to the lake again.

She had thought, that day, that it was the worst she could possibly fail someone.

She'd been so absolutely wrong.

Catherine was right. Ellery was a moth. She couldn't turn Ethan or herself into anything other than what they already were. And right now, the light she could not stop fluttering around was her family. Her beautiful little family, that she'd spent her entire adult life creating and working toward.

A month ago, she and Ethan had been driving at night. Ethan had done well at school that day—no running away, no sweet but disruptive outbursts of singing his favorite songs at the top of his lungs—and so she was taking him to get a drink from the gas station, which was one of his favorite things to do. She wasn't certain what it was that he loved so much—the treat, obviously—but was it also the inherent choice of the whole experience? Getting to decide something when so much of his life was decided by the people around him? Whatever it was, she was glad to share it with him.

Ethan had selected music, which he also loved to do, and she was in that exhausted end-of-day state that came from single parenting without family help. It was past nine, dark, and her heart was heavy but her son was beside her, there would be stars, she had made it another day. It was always easier when she had the kids with her—it was the profound emptiness of a home she'd once lived in with her family that truly buckled her knees.

And then, out of nowhere, so fast she barely saw it before she'd hit it, a deer ran across the road. They hit it head-on, the airbags deploying.

"Oh!" Ethan yelled. "Ow! Ow!" She looked over at him. He didn't appear to be hurt, but who knew? And it was clear the experience had rattled him, as it had rattled her. It had been so sudden and sharp—that wasn't the word. It had felt like blunt force trauma. She'd gotten Ethan out and to the side of the road, and then she'd had to keep him from running back into traffic to get something he wanted out of their car. She'd needed help while she waited for the police, and she hadn't been able to get ahold of Abby. She'd stood there, staring at her phone.

Luke had made it clear that he did not want her to call him after the divorce. He preferred "written communication." So she texted him.

Ethan and I were in a crash, she wrote. *We're both okay, but the car is totaled. Could you come take him for a little bit? I've tried Abby but she isn't answering, and E keeps trying to run out into traffic.*

Luke responded hours later, well after they finally made it home. Some kind strangers who had seen the wreck pulled over and stayed with her and Ethan until the police had come, the car had been towed, and she'd gotten an Uber to take them home.

I'm sorry to hear about the crash, Luke wrote. *That must have been frightening. I am glad you are both okay.*

That was all.

Ellery veered from the main path onto a smaller, barely visible off-shoot. She didn't want to walk through the grove yet, through those ghostly remnants of a wedding that never happened. Her throat was tight with unshed tears. The thin thread of the other trail wasn't lit, so Ellery turned on her phone's flashlight as she wound deeper into the trees. But before she had gone far, the path dead-ended. She sighed. Wrong turn. She'd have to walk through the grove after all. As she was turning, her light glinted on something near the ground.

She shifted her light higher, and there it was.

A sculpture that said *Love.*

Oh.

When she'd glanced through the list of the resort's art and come to this one, she'd thought it might be a replica of the famous red *LOVE* sculpture, the pop-art one you saw in different cities.

But this wasn't shiny and slick and made of metal, with two letters on top and two on the bottom. It was carved out of wood and stood vertically, the letters soft-edged, wrapping around and into each other in a kind of lowercase cursive. Moss limned it, and her flashlight beam playing across the sculpture made it seem as if something there were moving, growing. Ellery shivered. That was when she saw something else—what was that huddled shape, a few feet back in the trees?

For a moment, Ellery thought it was Catherine again. *How did she get here so quickly?* But then she realized that the slender figure sitting against one of the trees was Olivia, her form much like her mother's.

Olivia's head was tilted forward, resting on her knees, which were drawn up to her chest. Ellery couldn't see Olivia's face, only the delicate bend of her neck and the tendrils of her hair, coming loose from the chignon she'd likely had done for the ceremony.

Ellery's heart caught in her throat. What should she do? What was Olivia doing out here alone? Hadn't Catherine said that Olivia was with Rachel, the bridesmaid? Had the plate of food, the bottle of wine, *not* been for Olivia? How long had Olivia been by herself?

Ellery knew that she shouldn't do anything. Had her experience with Catherine moments ago taught her nothing?

Olivia hadn't seemed to hear Ellery, or to notice the light from her phone. Maybe Olivia was wearing headphones and listening to music. Maybe she was so deep in hurt that nothing else mattered.

No one but Olivia knew her exact pain. When Ellery was in the thick of hers, there had been times when she wanted someone with her to bear witness, someone to say *I see you, you still exist.* Other times she'd wanted to dissolve without anyone noticing. To have never been anywhere, ever, at all.

Ellery would do things differently from here on out. She would not assume anyone wanted or needed her in the slightest. She slipped back into the trees, leaving Olivia alone.

THE RAIN CAME IN the middle of the night while she was sleeping.

It splattered on the plastic-covered golf carts lined up in front of the Main House.

It drenched the terrace, the firepits, the chairs stripped of their blankets. It ran in rivulets along the paths, threaded steadily down the trunks of trees.

It streamed from the altar, washed over Love.

And it fell, unrelenting, on a body.

SUNDAY

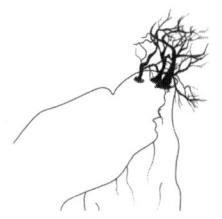

Today at The Resort at Broken Point

"Nature never did betray the heart that loved her."

—*William Wordsworth*

Weather: Rain

SUNRISE: 7:14 A.M. ....HIGH: 53° F

SUNSET: 6:31 P.M. ....LOW: 42° F

ABOUT THE ART:
Sketch
by Andy Warhol
1967

Known among staff as "the roving Warhol," this sketch by the famous artist is moved from room to room so that it can be viewed and enjoyed by a variety of guests. We decline to describe the work further so that the viewer might use a discerning eye and delight in their discovery.

15.

Ellery couldn't stop shaking. Someone had wrapped one of the ubiquitous Pendleton blankets around her shoulders. Her bathing suit felt clammy on her skin, water still dripped down her back, and she wanted to wash her hands. The fire in the fireplace seemed very far away. Everything felt dimmed and uncertain.

She was sitting in the Main House. She wasn't sure how much time had passed since she'd made it to the building. Nothing felt real. Where was she? Where was her family? She knew the answers to the last two, at least, but they felt wrong. No one was where they were supposed to be. They weren't all *home* together.

They never would be again.

And. *What had happened to Ben?*

Because it was Ben she had found in the water. Ben who she had tried—and failed—to save.

Ben. The groom.

Who'd called off his wedding at the last second and left the groomsmen to get drunk without him, his second-best man stunned and shocked, his bride-to-be curled up alone in the trees.

In the first initial rush after she'd arrived at the Main House, breathless and drenched and calling for help, Ellery had waited alone while Canyon went into the main office to try to contact the police. It had taken him a moment to understand her breathless alarm—"Someone's dead. At the pool. *Ben*"—but when he had, he'd moved quickly. "Stay here," he said firmly, and she'd sat right down on the couch, her shoulders shaking.

He'd also summoned Nat, who had gone to the pool immediately along with the resort doctor and the head security officer. Moments ago, Ellery had heard Nat telling another staff member that several security officers remained posted at the pool. "Keep the guests away," she'd said, grimly. "They'll be awake soon."

Ben. In the water. Dead.

The on-site doctor had inspected the body with Nat and the head security officer. Now they all wanted to talk to Ellery again. They sat on another couch across from her, expressions slightly expectant, as if *she* could elucidate anything here, give them information that would help this make sense.

"You've probably gathered by now that cell phones and landlines are out, thanks to the storm." Nat was calm, resolute. "We won't let up on trying to contact the police. Canyon's on the radio right now trying to get through. But we need to tell Olivia and the others soon. And it would be helpful to know a bit more about how you found Mr. Taylor."

"Is he really dead?" Ellery asked, hating both the stupidity of the question and the shakiness of her voice as she asked it. But she wanted more than anything to fix the unfixable. She wanted to go back in time, find the moment Ben died, and undo it. Barring that, she wanted to go back and stay in bed and never go to the pool, never find the body. Take herself out of this equation entirely.

"Yes," Dr. Anand said. It was the first time he'd spoken directly to her. He was a gentle-looking, older man with a shock of thick, gray-white hair that stood out in contrast to his brown skin. "And he had been for some time before you found him." He reached out to pat her hand. His was warm. "There was nothing you could have done."

"What were you doing at the pool?" the security officer, Craig, wanted to know. He was straight out of a movie—bulky, ex-Marine-looking build, gray crew-cut hair.

"Swimming," she said.

"In the rain?" Craig asked. "At five a.m.?"

"Yeah." She didn't know how to explain herself. "I couldn't sleep. Swimming seemed…" Ellery swallowed. "Peaceful? And I was wondering if all the rain would have turned the edge of the infinity pool into a real waterfall." How did you describe flights of fancy to people who didn't really understand them? ("What were you doing?" her parents, Luke, friends, would ask her when she'd had some random idea, an interesting impulse that had to be followed. "I was just—" she'd say, but then she hadn't known how to explain, or she'd tried and the explanations hadn't made sense to them.)

"Guests often swim early. Or in the rain." Nat's tone said *Leave it.*

"Okay," Craig said. "So you were going to go swimming. And then…"

"And then I saw him floating." Ellery gripped the fringe of the blanket tightly. Her fingers still felt cold. Anything could slip through them.

"Before or after you got into the pool?"

"Before."

"So why did you get in the pool if you saw there was a body in it?" Craig asked.

"I wanted to save him." Ellery's throat felt raw. "But it was hard to get him out of the water."

"Did you think he was dead when you ran for help?" Craig asked.

"Yes," she said. "But I had to try."

"Did you think about calling 9-1-1 or the Main House for help instead of running?" Nat asked.

"I'd left my phone in the room," Ellery said. "Because of the rain." She paused. "And anyway, you said the phones are out."

"Is there someone at the property that we can ask to come be with you?" Dr. Anand wanted to know. The consideration in his tone, his kindness, threatened to undo her.

"Ravi," she said. "I don't know his last name." Realizing again how alone she was—that the closest person to her here was someone whose last name she didn't even know—made it hard to breathe.

"We'll contact him." Nat stepped aside and gave directions to one of the staff. Ellery closed her eyes. Would Ravi come? Would they still let her leave for her flight? They *had* to let her go home. She was due to pick up her kids this evening. She could not stand one extra minute without them. And now, with the storm, she couldn't even contact them. Her throat throbbed and her eyes stung.

"I'm sorry," Dr. Anand said. "We'll let you go in a minute." Craig did not look pleased, but the doctor didn't seem to care.

"Okay," Ellery said.

"Did you notice anything unusual about the body?" Dr. Anand spoke gently. "I apologize, but I have to ask."

"I mean, *everything* about it seemed unusual," Ellery said. "He's so *young*." Her eyes filled with tears.

Dr. Anand reached out to pat her arm again. "Would you like me to give you something to help you rest?" he asked. Ellery must have looked alarmed because he held up his hands. "Nothing addictive, of course. We have a few over-the-counter medications on hand in the resort clinic. And melatonin."

"That's okay," Ellery said. "Thank you, though." She lifted a hand to push her hair away from her face. She could feel it drying slightly in the heat of the room, though the rest of her body still felt soaked through.

The lights flickered, and they all glanced up.

"Wonderful," Craig said. "That's exactly what we need right now, the generator going out."

"We're on our own generator?" Ellery asked. That would explain the dimness she'd been noticing in the Main House. She'd thought it was her own fogginess and shock.

"The storm knocked out everything." Nat had returned. "Not only the phones. We've been on auxiliary power since three a.m. Don't worry. It's happened before."

"Did you notice anything else?" Dr. Anand asked.

"He was dressed for his wedding," Ellery said. "The suit, the shoes, the accessories, everything." She thought of the cuff links, glinting at his wrists. The flower pinned to his lapel, crooked in the water.

And.

"His head," Ellery said. "Something was wrong." She tried not to think about the caved-in shape of it, the thickness at the back of his hair. "I think he hit it before he fell into the pool."

The rain, everywhere. The flagstones, slick with water. Ben could have slipped, cracked his head open, fallen in. She might have been swimming in his blood.

"You shouldn't have touched him," Craig said sternly. "You understand that now, right?"

Ellery's throat tightened. *Not again.* "I didn't know what else to do—"

"Whatever," Ravi said from the doorway. Ellery turned at the sound of his voice. He was wearing printed paisley pajamas and a deep blue robe.

She was so glad to see him.

"It's ridiculous that she's still here," Ravi said. Even in his night-clothes, his hair dripping with rain, his voice carried total authority. "She found a body and she's wearing a bathing suit and all you've done is give her a blanket."

Canyon had come up behind Dr. Anand and the others. He cleared his throat.

"Any luck?" Nat asked.

"Yes," Canyon said. "I finally got through on the radio for a minute." There was something odd about his tone.

"Great," Nat said.

"There's a problem, though." Canyon's glance flickered to the others. "Could I speak to you in the office, Nat?"

"Oh no," Ravi said. "I don't think so. We're right here in this."

"Go ahead," Nat said, apparently deciding that Ravi was not going to be easily deterred.

"The police can't come," Canyon said.

"What do you mean, they can't come?"

"Our road is out," Canyon said. "And Highway 1 is impassable in a lot of places. Boulders coming down, things like that. There's been a major landslide."

Nat closed her eyes briefly. For a minute, Ellery could imagine what it would be like to be in charge of this situation. A failed wedding, a storm. The highway cut off. Dozens of guests trapped at the resort. A body on her hands.

"Where is the slide?" Nat said. "Someplace easy to fix, I hope?"

"It's the bridge," Canyon said. "The whole thing is gone."

Ellery looked at Canyon and the others: Nat, Craig, Dr. Anand, Ravi. Every one of them, even Ravi, was a stranger. But she could tell from the expressions on their faces that they were all thinking a variation of the same thing.

Ravi was the one to put voice to it. "So now what?"

"It's likely that no one is leaving Broken Point for a few days." Nat spoke carefully. "If the bridge is out, it will take a significant amount of time to fix it, and the rain is still coming down."

Ellery's heart dropped. "No," she said. "*No.* I have to get home. My kids."

Nat attempted a look of conciliatory sympathy, but it was clear her thoughts were elsewhere, on other, bigger problems. "I'm sorry," she said. "I'm going to need to ask you not to tell the other guests about the landslide and the roads until we have a chance to do so. And I also need to ask you not to discuss Mr. Taylor's death with anyone else."

Someone dead. Roads out, bridges gone. *This can't be happening.*

"Would you like to give us an emergency contact?" Dr. Anand asked. "We can call the police to reach out and let your contact know you're all right."

Ravi slid a piece of paper and a pen toward her. With shaking hands, Ellery wrote down Abby's name and number instead of Luke's. After the car wreck with Ethan, she knew contacting Luke was pointless. He hadn't cared when she and Ethan had been in a dangerous situation together. He certainly wouldn't care when she was in one alone.

Abby would care. She would also be absolutely clutch, as she was in every circumstance. Luke would take Abby's call politely, express the right words of removed concern when he heard what had happened, assure Abby that things were fine there, that he had it covered. Then he'd have to tell the kids—*the kids*—

Dr. Anand took the paper from Ellery's trembling hand.

"Well," Ravi said. "While you're all figuring out what this means and what to do about it, I think you can let your guest change into some dry clothes." He took Ellery gently by the elbow and helped her to her feet. "Let's go." Together they walked over to the row of golf carts that staff had been lining up in a little fleet in front of the Main House. Preparing to go and tell everyone else, she guessed. The almost-bride. The second-best man.

"Excuse me," Nat said. "I don't think—"

Ravi ignored her. He pushed aside the plastic curtain on one of the carts, took a seat, and turned the key in the ignition.

"Andy," Ellery said, as she climbed into the passenger seat. "Someone should go be with him." Olivia had her mother. But Andy had seemed on the outside of the wedding party. Who did he have, besides Ben?

"They'll handle it," Ravi said. They pulled away from the Main House and out into the rain.

16.

The light in Ellery's room flickered when she turned it on. "Seriously," Ravi said. "If the power *does* go out..." He was gentle with Ellery, guiding her with a hand in the middle of her back. Her teeth had begun to chatter from shock and fear and sitting in her bathing suit for the last hour.

"Hot shower?" he asked. "Bath?"

"No." She didn't want to get in any water. But she did want to get warm.

"Of course," he said. "Here. Get dressed in your warmest stuff, then. Put this on, too." He grabbed the folded hotel robe from the foot of her bed as she gathered up items from her suitcase. Bra, underwear, sweatpants, shirt, hoodie. Ravi plopped the robe on top of the pile in her arms and she went into the bathroom to change.

Her hands were still shaking, but she found it comforting that someone was there on the other side of the door, alive. She pulled off her sodden swimsuit and dropped it on the bathroom floor the way her kids always did. She did not care. Her mind was skittering from this tragedy to the last one, though they were vastly different. *She wished Abby were here. She was glad Abby was far away.* What headlines would the news sites come up with for this heartbreak?

"The landslide," Ellery said through the door. "The highway. It's bad, right?" She remembered reading an article about something like this happening in Big Sur before. The road had been out for a full year. Could that be right?

"They'll figure it out," Ravi said.

It was reassuring having him there, but it also felt weirdly intimate talking to him while she was changing clothes.

When she finished dressing, she took a deep breath and opened the door. "I'm okay now." She wasn't, but was it possible to be so not okay that your body rounded the bend into a kind of numbness so you'd survive the hour? That's what she felt like might be happening.

"Are you sure?" Ravi asked.

He was so kind. But he was not the right person.

Something terrible had happened. Again. And she no longer had *her* person to tell about it.

"Hey," Ravi said. "I have an idea."

17.

Ellery rested her head against the wall of the sauna. Nina poured a ladle of water over the heated stones and steam hit the air. "Yes," Ravi said. "That's perfect."

Ellery sat on the highest bench, sweat soaking through her bra and underwear, her other clothes in a pile by the door. All three of them were stripped down to their skivvies. Usually Ellery would be self-conscious wearing so little in close quarters with people she barely knew, but right now it didn't matter. It was profoundly unimportant. Who cared if they could see that her underwear was sensibly cut boy briefs, and that they didn't match her bra?

It felt like some of the morning was finally coming out of her pores, slick on her skin where she could maybe wash it away later. She often overheated quickly in places like this. Right now she felt like she wanted to curl up and sleep forever.

"We have to take advantage of this before they shut it down," Ravi said. His eyes were closed. "I'm actually surprised they haven't already. It can't be essential. How much power do saunas use?"

"No clue." Nina exhaled.

"How long do you think we'll be stuck at the resort?" Ellery asked.

"Canyon told me that the last time there was a major mudslide, back in 2017, guests were trapped at Broken Point for a week before they could get them all out," Nina said. "He didn't think it would take that long, but he wanted us to be prepared."

"When did he tell you that?" Ellery asked.

"This morning," Nina said. "He was going room to room, I think. You and Ravi must have missed him."

"A week," Ellery said. Her voice wavered. *My kids.* The constant, aching drum of those two words, those three people.

"Because Broken Point has auxiliary power and extra food, we won't be the highest on the evacuation priority list," Nina said. "But Canyon thinks we'll be higher up than we would be because of our, you know. Tragedy."

"Poor Ben," Ellery said. And then she let it happen. Warm and safe—*ish*—in the sauna, she said out loud what she'd finally allowed herself to think. To remember.

She recalled her hand brushing Ben's head as she tried to save him, the way his skull sank in at the back. "Ben had been hurt. There was something on the back of his head. Thick. Stuck to his hair."

"Blood?" Ravi asked.

"I don't know." Ellery paused. "Yes. I think so."

"Was it more of a puncture wound?" Ravi asked. "Or, like, a bullet wound? Or blunt force trauma?"

"I'm not sure," she said. "His head was kind of...bashed in." She winced. "I was trying not to look too closely."

Other injuries, other faces, the screaming of students. She and Abby, seeing it happen, helpless. Racing to the sides of those who had been hurt, knowing they were too late, hoping, hoping, hoping, that they weren't.

Do not think about the accident right now. This is enough. Get through it and get home.

"Things like that *do* happen, though," Nina said, practically. "It was slippery last night because of the rain. He absolutely could have hit his head on the edge of the pool and then fallen in and drowned."

"But why was he still wearing his suit for the wedding?" Ellery asked. "And he couldn't have been at the pool last night when everyone was awake, right? Someone would have noticed him. So he must have come there later, after everyone had gone to bed. Why hadn't he changed by then?"

"Maybe he died earlier," Ravi said. "And someone brought him to the pool."

"Oh, come on, you guys." Nina stretched out on the lower sauna bench and covered her eyes with her forearm.

"The doctor didn't say anything about a possible time of death in front of you, did he?" Ravi asked Ellery.

"Not really," Ellery said. "All he said was that Ben had been dead for a while before I found him. He wanted me to know that there was nothing I could have done to save him."

"So when was the last time anyone heard from Ben?" Ravi asked. "Do we know that?"

"Andy said that Ben texted right before the wedding was supposed to happen," Ellery said. "So, right around sunset."

"What time was sunset?" Ravi asked.

"Um." Ellery tried to think. Sweat formed a rivulet down her back. She glanced at Nina. Perspiration was streaming down her face, and her arm was still over her eyes. Didn't she care that someone had died and it seemed at least possible that it had been foul play? Wasn't she worried about being trapped at the resort? Ellery wished she were as unflappable as Nina. "I'd guess around six or seven? Is that right?"

"I know!" Ravi sat up straight and grabbed one of the resort robes from a nearby shelf. "Those cards they hang on our doors every morning? The ones with the nature quotes? They have the sunrise and sunset times." He slid his feet into his sandals. "I'll be right back."

Ellery was left alone with Nina for the first time in their brief friendship. Which had begun only a day and a half ago. How could that be? So much had happened.

"Are you okay?" Nina asked her after a few moments had passed in silence. "Have you ever seen a dead person before? Besides at a funeral, I mean?" She didn't move her arm away from her face when she asked the questions, which, somehow, made it easier for Ellery to respond, though she gave only a partial answer.

"I don't think I am," she said, honestly.

"What was it like?" Nina asked. She sat up then, her dark eyes fixed on Ellery's. Her gaze was so intense, so direct, that Ellery felt additional heat rise to her cheeks. She didn't want to get this wrong.

"It was heavy," Ellery said. She swallowed. "I mean, he was heavy." There was a lump in her throat. *It was so sad,* she wanted to say. *Sad beyond belief, except it's not really beyond belief, because we will all die someday. Dried up in a museum, afloat in a pool of water, lying at the side of a road.*

We will all be a body in the end.

"It's okay," Nina said, gently. "I shouldn't have asked. I didn't mean to interrogate you." She reached for one of the small towels stacked on a shelf and used it to blot her face.

Before Ellery could say anything else, the door to the sauna swung open. Ravi entered carrying a card, the welcome booklet, and a pen.

"That was fast," Nina said.

"It would have been faster if they used numbers for the rooms instead of names," Ravi said. "I had trouble finding my own room. And they're all so tucked away, and everything looks alike." He removed his robe and sandals and sat back down on the lower bench of the sauna. "Which reminds me. We should know where we're all staying so that we can find each other. I'm in Willow, Nina's in Larkspur." They both looked at Ellery expectantly.

"Milkweed."

"So." Ravi held up the card. "This says that sunset last night was at 6:32 p.m. Which means Ben would have sent that text right around then. If—" Ravi looked at Ellery significantly, as if he wanted her to finish his sentence. As if she knew what he was thinking.

Which she did, because she'd been wondering the same thing.

"If Ben sent that text at all."

"Wait." Now Nina sounded interested. "You think Andy lied about that?"

"No," Ellery said. "I think they got the text. But who knows if Ben is the one who sent it?"

"Right," Ravi said. "What if someone had taken his phone?"

"Oh, for crying out loud." Nina lay back down and covered her face again, this time with the towel.

"Let's go with what we know," Ravi said. "We came back from the wedding dinner around ten thirty, I think. Right, Nina?"

"Yes," Nina said, her voice muffled.

"I wasn't long after you," Ellery said. "Maybe twenty minutes?" She'd had that awkward conversation with Catherine. But it had been short, and she hadn't stayed long on the path in the trees where she'd stumbled across Olivia.

"And none of us noticed anyone in the pool then," Ravi said.

"Well, but did we really look?" Ellery asked. "I feel like we would have noticed someone, but maybe we wouldn't have?"

"Good point." Ravi sighed. "That's a pretty wide window. From whenever someone last laid eyes on Ben—and we don't actually know when that was—until the time when Ellery found him." He opened up his welcome booklet and clicked his pen. "We're going to have to keep track of all this. Ellery, you've got to try and see if you can get a more exact time of death from the doctor." He scribbled something down.

"Okay." She might as well ask. Maybe she could make up some excuse, think of a reason why she'd be entitled to that information.

"Did you notice any signs of a struggle?" Ravi asked. "Like any blood under his fingernails?"

Ellery bit her lip. "No, but I didn't notice much." She was a terrible witness for these kinds of things. She remembered the way the rain felt on her hair, how it sounded on his face, the gray steps of the pool as she dragged him up them, the drumbeat in her head saying, *no no no please no no no*, the white camellia that had been pinned to the front of his suit, but these were not the kind of things that were useful.

"You noticed everything you should have," Nina said gently. "You noticed he was in trouble, and you tried to help him."

Ellery's eyes flooded with tears. She hadn't known Ben. She shouldn't be this gutted. She knew it wasn't only the loss of Ben, a human being who had his whole life in front of him, that was tormenting her.

It was other losses, too.

"And we're going to have to make friends with the other guests," Ravi said. "It's a good thing we're all cooped up here together."

"Is it?" Nina asked.

"For murder solving purposes, yes," Ravi said. "I admit it's less than ideal for staying alive purposes."

"No one else is going to die," Nina said. "This was a freak accident."

Ellery had thought of something. "Why would Ben even be at the resort? After he texted everyone that he wasn't going to be at the wedding, wouldn't he leave right away?"

"*If* he sent that text," Ravi said.

"Right."

"We should talk to Carlos," Ravi said, furiously scribbling down notes. "The head valet. He's the most likely person to notice someone leaving." He stopped writing for a moment and asked, "How many ways are there out of the resort? We flew into Monterey and then drove down on Highway 1."

"Same." Ellery held her hand out for the welcome booklet. "Let me look at the map."

Ravi handed it to her. "So according to this," she said, studying it, "the only marked way into the resort is Highway 1. The resort drive comes straight off it. There aren't really any back roads because we're on the ocean. Maybe you could cross Highway 1 and get to the Coldwater Inn? They're our only marked neighbors. But they're a few miles away." She handed the booklet back to Ravi. "Do we know where the big landslide is? All I remember them saying is that the bridge was out."

"I'll find out," Ravi said. "And I'll get a better map of the area." He looked at the one in the welcome booklet. "Maybe you *could* walk through the woods to the highway," he said. "Without a path or a road. Make your way through the trees?"

"That wouldn't be safe at all," Nina said. "And even if you got to the highway, it's damaged both to the north and the south."

"And either way, Ben *didn't* leave yesterday." Ravi tapped the pen against his mouth. "Or if he did, he came back. And it's very unlikely someone could leave or get in *now*." He looked at Ellery, his eyes shrewd. "What does your gut tell you? Do you think something's wrong?"

The question made her pause. She hadn't trusted her gut in so long. After the divorce, when she'd expressed concerns about the children and how they were handling things, Luke had said dismissively, "Kids are resilient. And I don't have to manage your anxiety anymore, Ellery." The words had hit her in the face like a slap. She hadn't even thought she was being unusually angsty. She'd thought she was parenting. It was your job to pay attention. Wasn't it?

Ellery took a deep breath. "I mean, everything's wrong. We're trapped here. The roads are out. I can't get home to my kids."

"You know what I mean," Ravi said. "Is anything wrong, like *murder?*"

Ellery tried to remember what Ben's head had looked like, what she'd thought in the moment. What came back to her most strongly, though, was the way it had felt. His head, when she'd touched the back of it. His body, in her arms. The water, on her face and his. She remembered other faces, those of her students, eyes staring up. *No.*

"Yes." The word sounded cold and distilled, like a raindrop falling into the heat of the sauna.

"Okay," Ravi said. "Okay."

They both looked at Nina. She must have felt their gaze because she lifted the towel from her face and glared at them.

"Oh no," she said. "You're not roping me into this. Playing detective won't help us get home any faster."

"Nina," Ravi said. "It's possible that we have a *murderer* in our *midst.* If we don't find out what happened, we might not get home at all."

Nina sat up and swung her long legs off the bench. "That's melodramatic," she said. "If someone actually did want Ben dead, it's done. Over."

"Don't you read *anything?*" Ravi asked. "Have you ever watched a murder mystery? There's never *one* body. Maybe Ben wasn't the intended victim. Maybe someone else saw something and now *they* have to die. Maybe there's a serial killer here and they've only gotten started—"

"Stop," Nina said. "I will not go down this path with you."

"Fine," Ravi said. "But one death isn't how it works." He clicked his pen shut. "It's never just *over.*"

18.

The staff was doing their best. Lunch had been set up buffet style in Wildrye, the restaurant, and it looked delicious. Ellery hadn't thought she'd be hungry, but after missing breakfast, her stomach was empty and she thought she might be able to eat after all.

The long tables were set with soup and salad and bread, labeled with cards delineating which were vegan or gluten free. It was all lovely food—rich salad greens in a variety of shades, garnished with ruby-red tomatoes and studded with nuts and cheese, creamy risotto, a seafood bisque, hearth breads with house-made chive butter. Salted dark chocolate brownies had been cut up into precise squares for dessert. Ellery filled her plate and straightened her shoulders, glancing around the room. She didn't see Nina or Ravi, though she imagined they'd arrive soon. And as they'd left the sauna, Ravi had pointed out that they'd have to make friends with the other guests if they were going to learn anything new.

The tables were filling up quickly. The staff had left cards by their doors notifying them that meals would be at certain times. The restaurant was full of people gathered around the tables, shocked expressions on their faces, voices low. A man Ellery didn't recognize was talking to Nat belligerently, brandishing his (presumably unusable) cell phone.

Ellery couldn't quite bring herself to ask if she could join an already-established group, so she made her way to an empty table and sat down. Right after she'd unfolded a napkin on her lap and given her drink order to a waiter, someone walked over to her table.

It was Andy. "Hi," he said, his voice exhausted. He held a plate with a single roll on it.

"Hey," Ellery said. She wanted to hug him, put a hand on his arm. Comfort him like she would one of her children, or her students. "Are you—" She stopped. *Are you okay?* The question Nina had asked her, that everyone asked, seemed pointless here. Of course Andy was not okay.

He swallowed. It sounded hard. Andy's face was pale, the shadows under his eyes deep. When he spoke, his voice sounded like he'd been crying. "Nat told me you're the one who found Ben."

"Yes," Ellery said.

"I've been looking for you everywhere."

She felt awful that he'd found her hanging out in the restaurant, her plate piled high with food. It probably looked like she was relaxing. Like she didn't even care what had happened.

"Can I— Can we—" He stopped. "Can we talk?" He looked around at the busy restaurant.

"Of course." She stood up, but he waved her back down.

"No, no," he said. "After you eat."

"Are you sure?" she asked.

"Yeah," he said. "I guess I should eat, too." He sat down with his roll. A waiter appeared to take his drink order, and Andy asked for coffee.

Before he or Ellery could say anything, Nat stood up and gave a little speech about the sadness and shock of Ben's "accident," the situation with the landslide and roads, and how the resort was committed to keeping them all safe and comfortable. "We have been through this before," she said. "It may take some time to evacuate you all, but this area experiences natural events somewhat frequently. It's part of the geography."

"Hey." The best man—Matt, Ellery remembered—dropped into the seat next to Andy, heavy and unorganized, like a bag full of stones.

Matt scooted his chair closer. It looked as if he hadn't slept at all.

His blond hair was rumpled, his blue eyes bloodshot. "Man. Man. This is some shit." His hands shook as he unfolded a napkin. "I can't believe this. When did you see him last? Where did we lose him, man?"

"I hadn't seen him all day," Andy said. "I went on that hike. Got back just in time to shower and head over to the grove."

"I didn't see him either," Matt said. "I mean, not since the brunch. We were texting, though." Then Matt collapsed even more, both in on himself and onto Andy's shoulder. "Why weren't we with him? Ben is *freaking dead*. What are we going to do now?"

Andy glanced over at Ellery. His eyes were weary.

"You're going to be all right," she said to Matt, but also to Andy. "Not right now, though. Not yet. But it will be okay." It wouldn't. It would never quite be okay again. But they already knew that. There was no need to say it out loud. Now was the time for lying.

"Who are you?" But the best man didn't ask it mean. "Are you one of Olivia's friends?" Then he laughed, and a cruel edge did creep in. "Wait. Does Olivia even *have* any friends?"

"Hey," Andy said. There was a warning note in his voice. "No reason to talk like that."

"No, seriously," Matt said, sitting up straight. He was either still hungover or maybe he was newly drunk, Ellery couldn't quite tell. "Do you think she had something to do with this? Olivia can be a stone-cold b—"

"That's enough." Andy put his hand on Matt's arm. It wasn't to steady him.

Matt didn't even seem to notice. He was growing animated. "When a girl dies, they always blame the husband or the boyfriend. They should do the same with this. Take a closer look at Ben's wife. His *almost* wife. Maybe she killed him because he bailed on her."

"Whoa." Andy's voice dropped a notch in warning. "Matt. Olivia had nothing to do with what happened to Ben."

"Were you with her every single second?" Matt asked Andy. He didn't wait for an answer. "Then you don't know." He appealed to Ellery. "You think a guy like Ben falls into a pool and drowns? You think that happens?"

"I don't know what happened," she said quietly. She was in the middle of this and still outside, in a strange gray area that seemed to shift with the moment, the conversations, the people surrounding her. Certainly not one of the wedding party, but not just one of the other resort guests either, not exactly. A moth, slightly closer to the light.

"Shit," Matt said, studying her face. The anger had disappeared. "I know who you are. You're the one who found him, aren't you?"

"Yes."

"Thanks for being there," Matt said earnestly to Ellery, tears welling up in his eyes. "They said you tried really hard to save him."

Ellery was suddenly finished. Yes. She'd found Ben. She wished she hadn't. But she *didn't* belong to the wedding party. She didn't belong to anyone anymore except her kids, and they were three states away and she didn't know when she'd see them next and she couldn't even text or call. She glanced up and saw that Andy had noticed, that he was already lifting his coffee cup and standing, gesturing for her to come with him.

"Okay," Andy said. "Let's go."

19.

She was surprised when Andy took her to his room. *Lupine*, it was called.

She was even more surprised to see Olivia in it.

"Oh," Ellery said.

Olivia was sitting curled on the sofa, her feet tucked underneath. Her eyes were red. The pain on her face was naked, raw. Ellery knew that feeling. When you were not a person anymore. You were a nerve ending. You were loss. You had become nothing and yet you felt everything.

"I'm so sorry." This time, Ellery couldn't help herself. She went over to Olivia and knelt down and hugged her, held Olivia as tightly as she'd hold any of her children if something like this had happened to them.

Olivia shuddered. Ellery held on for two, three seconds more. Then she sat back on her heels.

"Can you tell me?" Olivia asked. "What happened?"

Ellery remembered this feeling too, from both the accident and the divorce. You had to find out everything you could so you could fix it or say *No, see, there you are wrong. That can't be. That's not actually how it is. We should stay together. He's not actually dead.*

"I saw him in the pool," Ellery said. "I pulled him out. But it was too late."

Was that enough? Too much?

Olivia's eyes welled over with tears. Ellery couldn't bear it. She looked past Olivia, at the painting on the wall, the unmade bed, the lamp on the table giving off a dim, generator-subdued light.

"Can you tell me anything more?" Olivia asked. "Please."

"He was wearing his suit," Ellery said. "And the boutonniere."

Olivia made a strangled sound. Andy shifted. Even that was too much to say. Ellery had thought Olivia might want to know that Ben was still in his wedding clothes, that he likely hadn't left Broken Point. Maybe he'd meant to come to the wedding all along, or, at the very least, he'd had a good explanation as to why he hadn't shown up.

"I'm so sorry," Ellery said, looking back into Olivia's eyes. Holding them. "That's all I know. All I remember."

But it wasn't.

That dark patch, the shape of the back of his head…

Had Ben missed his wedding because he was already dead?

There was a sharp knock on the door.

"Whoever it is can come back later," Olivia said.

Another knock. And then, right on its heels, the sound of a key being inserted. Ellery stood, and Andy took a step forward. The door opened.

It was Nat. Craig, the head of security, was with her. So, oddly, was Maddox, the LikeMe husband. His sandy hair stood straight on end and he wore jeans and a puffy North Face jacket. "Hey," he said, looking profoundly uncomfortable. Ellery was confused. Why was he here?

"We didn't think anyone was in the room," Nat said. "We knocked."

"You didn't wait long," Andy said, an edge to his voice. He stood protectively between them and Olivia. "What do you need?"

"We're double-checking that all the rooms have working power," Nat said. "We have the generator going, but we want to make sure everything is satisfactory."

"I'm an electrician," Maddox blurted, glancing at Olivia. "I mean, I used to be. They came around asking if anyone knew anything about generators and stuff and could help them out. So that's what I'm doing.

Why I'm here. Sorry." Ellery felt a flash of sympathy for him. At this point, he seemed to be apologizing for his very existence.

"Our electrician was off-site when the slide happened," Nat explained crisply. "She's been unable to get back."

"So, um, seems fine in here." Maddox reached for the door handle. "Lights are on, looks good."

"We're also letting everyone know that the dinner time has been adjusted slightly." Nat's eyes had already caught on Ellery and registered surprise, disapproval—But why? The *please don't discuss Mr. Taylor's death* request couldn't possibly apply to Ben's fiancée—and moved on to Olivia. "We're serving a modified menu in the restaurant from seven to eight. Ms. Haring, we will, of course, bring anything you like to your room, if that's preferable."

Olivia stood up. Her tears had stopped. "Thanks," she said to Andy and Ellery. "I think I'll be going to my room." Her glance flickered to Nat. "If you could have someone bring me a soup or a salad or something when it's dinnertime, that would be great. Thank you."

She pushed past them all and went out the door.

"Well," Nat said, after a moment. "We'll see you two in the restaurant later. Excuse us." Within seconds she, Craig, and Maddox were gone, and Ellery and Andy were alone.

"All right," Ellery said. "I guess—"

"Olivia's not—" Andy said at the same time. "I don't want you to think—"

Ellery stopped talking.

So did Andy. Then he tried again. "She's not rude, she's…" He trailed off.

"However Olivia acts is absolutely fine," Ellery said, gently. "No explanation required. Her fiancé died. And I think I told her too much a minute ago."

"No, she wanted to know," Andy said. "She asked me to find you." He opened the door for Ellery. "She and I had to go identify the body."

"But I—" Ellery stopped herself from finishing. *But I already told them who it was. Nat knew who Ben was, too.* None of that would matter, she realized. Someone who really knew Ben would have to say it was him. And the police weren't even there yet. So did the identification formally count? Would Olivia and Andy have to do it all over again when the officers arrived?

"The doctor told us you were the one who found Ben. And then after we got back Olivia asked me to get you so she could talk to you about it, and then Nat comes barging in with extra people…" He exhaled. "It's a lot."

"I understand," Ellery said gently. "I mean, I don't, but I do."

One of the parents at Maddie's back-to-school night had come up to talk to Ellery while their daughters were chatting. Ostensibly, it was to make sure Ellery was doing okay post-divorce, but there was that peculiar, particular light in the woman's eyes, the one some people get when they are in the presence of another's misfortune.

"How *are* you?" the woman had asked, and Ellery, for the first time in her adult life, had simply stared straight forward and walked past someone she knew was trying to speak to her.

You don't even know me, she'd thought. *I owe you nothing.*

20.

Later, after dinner and before she went to bed, Ellery reached for her phone to text Abby. She wanted to tell her what was happening. She'd powered her phone all the way on before realizing—again—that it didn't work. How many times was she going to do this? And how many times was she going to try to contact her kids, even knowing she couldn't? She felt sick.

I'll write it all down, Ellery decided. *Everything I want to say.* She could send nine million texts the second they got cell service again. Ellery opened the notes app in her phone but then hesitated.

What if the generator failed at some point? Should she be saving her phone's battery? The darkness and rain outside seemed to be pressing down. They were in the middle of nowhere, cut off. She didn't know anyone here, not *really*.

Breathe.

Ellery remembered Ravi writing in the sauna. She went over to her desk and picked up her welcome booklet, flipping through the pages. Sure enough, there was a section of empty pages at the back for note-taking. She took out a fine-point Sharpie from her purse. She hated the ballpoint ink of hotel pens.

Ellery labeled a page ABBY. Underneath, she wrote everything she wished she could text to her friend:

I found a body.

It was the groom.

He might have been murdered.

Seeing the words written out both helped and hurt. It acknowledged what had happened, and it also made things real.

I wish you were here. I don't know what to do.

Before, she at least had Abby.

"Get on the bus," she'd told Colby Howard, who was notorious for dawdling or wandering off in search of fast food right before they were about to depart. "We'll leave you behind this time, I swear."

"Right, Coach," Colby said. He knew she would never do it.

Annabel Walsh was getting a head count for the girls' team. She was a senior and the team captain, and one of Ellery's and Abby's favorites. "Can we follow her to college?" Abby had asked. "Would that be weird?" Ellery had understood. It was hard to see some of the kids leave after coaching them for years.

It was getting dark. Her phone had lit up with a call. Luke.

"Answer that so he doesn't get pissed," Abby said. "I'll make sure we've got everyone."

Luke hadn't understood when Ellery had wanted to start coaching track. She had wanted to do something that was hers. *Yes, it was about the athletes, yes, it was kind of an extension of her job, but it was also about her, Ellery. She'd been a runner in high school and had kept it up since. "It doesn't pay well," Luke had said. "It's only a few months a year," she'd countered.*

"Are you close?" Luke asked.

"We haven't left yet," she said, turning her back on the team and climbing down off the bus for a minute for some privacy. Hayley Verlander and a few other girls were trickling toward the bus, Hayley filming something on her phone. She was always *filming something on her phone. Ellery gestured for them to hurry up. They climbed aboard, chattering, and she was alone.*

Luke was silent. That meant displeasure. "Okay," he said at last, in a tone of great forbearance. "The kids are missing you. They thought you'd be home by now."

She doubted that Kate was missing her very much—the girl's social life was boundless—but her heart tugged at the thought of Ethan and Maddie waiting on her. "I'm sorry," she said. "It's the Lakewood meet, remember? So we've got a bit of a drive home. And they had a couple of false starts, and then they couldn't find one of the timers, so we're running a little late. Did Michaela already leave?" She always made sure to get a sitter for the days she had track meets so that Luke wouldn't have to come home from work early.

"Yes, she left at six thirty," Luke said.

"There's some enchiladas to heat up for dinner," Ellery said.

"I found them."

"Okay." She saw the students through the bus window above her, finding seats, laughing, one of them handing Abby something. "I'm sorry again about being late. You good?"

"I'm fine," Luke said. "But the kids miss you when you're gone this much. Track season is hard on them."

There it was. The guilt. Luke articulated it for her, but she always felt it. Why was she choosing to be with other kids when she had hers at home? Once, she'd said to Luke, "Do you think I'm a good mom? A good wife?" and he'd said, "I think you're a good friend," and it had cut her to the core.

"Okay," she'd said. "I'll be home soon."

She exhaled roughly. *Keep going.* She wrote down the texts she wanted to send to each of her kids. What she wouldn't give for a disorganized, disjointed FaceTime with them now.

Ellery turned to another page in the booklet and labeled it QUESTIONS. There, she wrote down some of the things she and Ravi had wondered in the sauna.

Who was the last person to see Ben?

What time did he die?

Why was he still wearing his wedding suit?

Did he ever leave Broken Point?

And one more that came to mind:

What exactly did Ben's text say?

She wondered if she could ask Andy about the text. She tapped her Sharpie against her notebook, thinking, her mind racing faster and faster.

It was all too much. Poor Ben—his body—

She took a deep breath and wrote down two more questions. The most pressing ones.

How did Ben die?
How do I get home?

————

Someone hammered on her door. Ellery jumped, her head snapping up from where she'd fallen asleep on the desk. She took a deep breath, waiting for a moment before she walked quietly to the door. She wasn't sure she wanted to answer a knock like that. Who was it? What had happened now?

Ellery looked through the peephole and saw—*Nina?* In the strange, rainy early-morning light, Nina's face was the color of ash.

Ellery opened the door.

"You and Ravi were right," Nina said. "Someone else is dead."

*R*AIN THUDDED DOWN ON *her hood, on her jacket, on her shoulders. Mud sucked at her boots; the trees screened her. They wept on her, too, sometimes steadily, sometimes in torrential, wind-driven sobs. She could hear the ocean between the drops. She could feel the cliffs beneath her feet, waiting for time and water and wind to carve them in new ways, reveal what was below the topsoil, the plants hanging on for dear life.*

Everything is something else underneath.

MONDAY

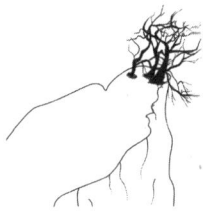

Today at The Resort at Broken Point

"Nature provides exceptions to every rule."

—*Margaret Fuller*

Weather: Rain

SUNRISE: 7:15 A.M. .... HIGH: 66° F

SUNSET: 6:29 P.M. .... LOW: 55° F

ABOUT THE ART:
Parts
by Anonymous
2016
bronze

When coming upon *Parts* in the forest, one might at first mistake the exquisitely sculptured faces and hands winding around the tree for enormous fungi. Indeed, that was the intention and inspiration of the artist, who wanted the viewer to be drawn into the beauty of the human parts by the natural world. The installation of this work in one of our redwood trees was undertaken carefully, using a tree that had already died. No living creature was harmed with the installation.

21.

S tay *back*," Nat said. For the first time, she seemed ruffled.

People had swarmed along the path to the viewpoint that gave the resort its name—the broken cliff with the three trees clinging on and the best vista of the ocean. They were in various states of early-morning attire—some fully dressed, others wearing coats and boots thrown on with pajamas, all come to see what was happening. Ellery noted the groomsmen gathered in the group nearest the railing, one that included Nat and Carlos, who both looked grim. Ellery glanced over the crowd—no sign of Olivia, Andy, Catherine, or Catherine's husband (What *was* his name? He'd been largely invisible all weekend). Grace was there, gripping her father's arm and trying to make their way upstream, through the gathering and back toward the resort. Gary held his walking stick—Stabby—tightly in his hand. "Excuse us," Grace said. "Please, can you move?" The path was paved, but it had been washed over with mud and narrowed by the rain. The railing was completely gone in several places, clinging to the earth in others.

It took the frat boys a moment to understand what Grace and Gary were trying to do, but once they did, they made room by squashing together along one side of the path. "*Walk*," Grace said to them, her voice sharp. "Go *back*. The last thing we need is another accident."

"Listen," said the frat boy with the reddest nose, "that's our *friend* out there, we have every right—"

"Awesome," Grace said. "You can rubberneck all you want once we get past you."

Ellery, Ravi, and Nina hadn't made it very far along the path. They were closer to the main resort area, so there was more space. As the father and daughter passed them, Ellery's eyes met Grace's in a flicker of connection. Before Ellery could offer to help, Grace spoke. "We're good," she said, and Ellery swore she could hear the wilderness first-responder credentials right there in Grace's voice. A moment later, and they were both gone.

"They're the ones who found him," Nina said. "They were walking along the path toward the viewpoint and saw that Matt had fallen."

"What the hell were they doing out there in this weather?" Ravi asked.

"I don't know," Nina said. "But they saw the body, and they came back to get Nat and Carlos, and then they took them out to the path to show them where they'd found Matt, and while all that was happening word spread like wildfire, of course."

"How do you even know it's Matt?" Ravi asked. "They all look the same."

"*Ravi,*" Nina said.

Nat had finally succeeded somewhat in shepherding the group back toward the resort. Several of the staff surrounded her. Canyon's face was white. Carlos looked tired but laser-focused on the matter at hand. "It's going to be difficult to get to him," he was saying to Nat.

"They're picking off white men," the red-nosed frat guy called out. "Any of the rest of us could be next. We're the ones in the most danger. We've been under fire for *years.* People don't pay attention. They don't listen."

"Jason," said another frat guy, one with giant bags under his eyes and a wedding ring on his left hand, "shut the hell up."

Jason did not shut up. "This is exactly why the Second Amendment matters," he said. "If the resort allowed guns, none of this would have happened."

"I cannot," Ravi said. "Can we lock them in their rooms?"

"How about the sauna?" Nina asked. "And turn it to high?" When

Ravi and Ellery stared at her in surprise, Nina flushed. "Look at me," she said. "This is getting to be *Lord of the Flies*. And it's only been a couple of days."

"Canyon," Carlos was saying, gesturing to the frat guys, "get these people out of here." His gaze caught on Maddox. "You," he said. "The electrician. Can you help us?" Before Maddox could respond, Carlos pointed at someone behind Ellery. She turned around to see that Andy had joined the group. "And you. Everyone else, go back to the Main House or to your rooms. In case it wasn't obvious before, you should not be hiking around on any of the trails. The last thing we need is another one of you going over the edge."

22.

"Nat would be so pissed at us right now," Ravi said, as he, Ellery, and Nina stepped carefully along the path out to Broken Point half an hour later.

"For good reason," Nina said. "This is stupid." The three of them had changed into hiking boots and parkas and they were moving slowly. Every step took full concentration. Some of the paving material that had constituted the path remained, but much had given way to mud or pools of water. Ellery went first, having been deemed the most athletic of the group, and she was trying to follow—without actually stepping in and ruining—the prints from what she believed were Carlos's boots. The others were doing the same.

"We have to look before the crime scene is compromised." Ravi spoke behind her.

"What makes you think it isn't already?" Nina asked.

"Oh, it is for sure," Ravi agreed. "But it's going to get more compromised by the minute. The rain's not finished yet. And they'll definitely rope off this whole trail. I'm surprised they haven't already."

"Here we are," Ellery said. She squared her feet and looked up from the path for the first time since they'd embarked on the precarious, unsanctioned journey.

They were at the spot in the fence where Nat and Carlos had been standing, partway to Broken Point. The three trees rose up in the distance, farther along the trail. A wooden guardrail lined the more sheer of the two sides of the path, but the once-tidy barrier was compromised. Ragged pieces had broken away with the force of the weather, remaining posts sticking up from the ground like snaggly teeth, newly broken wood an almost-white against the sodden ground. In the spot where they stood, the guardrail had also come away, but more cleanly, the wood disengaging from the post like a fence swung open and right off its hinges. The missing piece had fallen a few feet and was now embedded in the mud below. And beyond that, all the way at the bottom of the cliff...

"We'll have to take their word for it that that *is* Matt," Ravi said quietly.

Ellery had a sense of unreality as she looked down at the figure. Yes, it did look like Matt, but it also felt entirely impersonal, like when she was sitting in an airplane looking at a city with cars and roads and schools and blue pools pressed into the landscape like thumbtacks below and thought, *Either that's not real or I'm not; something about this whole situation does not compute.*

Maybe if you got closer it made more sense.

Although she'd been right up close to death before and that hadn't made sense, either.

It was dark, and they were thirty miles from home, almost back to Colorado Springs. The track teams were giddy because they'd performed well at the meet— training at their high altitude always came in handy when they went lower in elevation, and plenty of the kids had scored personal bests. They were engaged in the usual post-meet, late-drive-home activity—some sleeping, some playing cards, some sharing music, a rowdy game of truth or dare going on in the back.

Ellery was tired and happy. Up front, she and Abby were sitting near Henry Solomon, the head boys' coach. And Pete, a bus driver they all knew and liked, was at the wheel.

It was like dozens of other bus rides over the past few years. She and Abby and Henry were talking about their kids, or their spouses, or plans for the next meet. It could have been any of those things. She couldn't remember.

What she did remember: turning around to holler at the kids playing truth or dare to keep it down, because it was getting a bit loud, and then turning back to see the lights bearing down on them, hearing Abby say, "Shit," and Pete, his face terrified and bleached white in the light, hitting the horn, slamming the brakes, turning the wheel...

"I'm trying to look through the footprints out here," Ravi said. He aimed his phone at the ground. "But it's all muck."

"I'm pretty sure we've been following Carlos's footprints," Ellery said. "That was my goal, anyway. I think his are the work boot ones."

"Interesting how Nat is relying on him instead of Craig right now," Ravi said.

"He's much more competent," Ellery said. "Maybe he'll get a promotion after this."

"He'd better," Ravi said. "Promotions for everyone who does a good job during this mess. And if we solve the murder, medals for us."

"I don't think we're going to get any medals," Ellery said. "We're actively compromising what might be another murder scene right now."

"Here are some sneaker prints," Nina said. "Closer to the edge. Maybe they're Matt's?" Ravi zoomed in on his phone and took a picture.

"These could be Nat's," Ellery said, pointing to another pair of smaller boot prints. "Or Grace's. And maybe these are Gary's?" A larger set of prints, not as deep as the ones she thought might be Carlos's. "Or I'm all messed up and we've been following Gary's footprints this whole time."

"Do you see any other prints?" Ravi asked. They scrutinized the path, the waterlogged areas near it. "There?" Ellery said, pointing. "And maybe there?" It was hard to tell. Ravi snapped a couple of pictures on his phone and then turned it off to save the battery, sliding the device into the left pocket of his parka and zipping it shut.

"We can try and get print matches on Grace, Gary, Nat, and

Carlos," Nina said. "Follow them around or something? This is all so bizarre."

"It really is." Ravi had begun the return trip and was concentrating on each step, his stylish leather hiking boots now slathered in mud. "Two people falling to their deaths, in different ways. We're dropping like flies."

Ellery stood for a moment more, her eyes not on the body below, but on the gap in the guardrail. It had come away so neatly here. So unlike the other places in the railing.

"Yeah," Nina said, very quietly. "I see it, too."

23.

They were rounding the corner by the Main House when they came upon Rachel, the bridesmaid. Her long blond hair was piled up on her head in that effortless-seeming way that young women often managed, and Ellery realized that the two of them were the same height, around five ten. Rachel's eyes met hers and held them.

"Find anything good?" Rachel asked.

"I'm sorry?" Nina asked.

"I saw you guys out on the path looking around," Rachel said. "Don't worry, I won't tell Nat that you broke the rules. See something useful?"

"Not really," Ellery said truthfully. That clean break in the fence was strange, but did it mean anything?

"This whole thing is a mess," Rachel said. "Matt was an ass, but he didn't deserve to die. Jason, on the other hand…I wouldn't mind if someone took him out." She shook her head. "His mom died last year, and so Ben felt bad for him and kept him around even when he shouldn't have."

"And Ben?" Ravi asked. "Was he an ass who didn't deserve to die? Or would you not care too much if someone took *him* out?"

"Ben was the best," Rachel said simply.

"That's what we keep hearing," Ravi said. "Although he did leave his bride at the altar."

"I'm sorry, are you involved with the wedding in some way?" Rachel's tone wasn't as hostile as Catherine's had been the night before, but it carried a cool weight. Rachel tipped her head inquisitively, her expression focused. "Because in spite of what you were just doing out there hunting around, you're definitely not detectives. So I'm not sure why you're all so interested in this."

"We're trapped at a resort where two people died," Ravi said. "Of course we're interested in this."

"I found the body," Ellery said. She met Rachel's gaze. "I'm worried."

Rachel nodded. "Olivia told me. She said you were nice." Rachel said the word *nice* in a way that sounded flat, without depth.

Ellery was so sick of being described as nice. She'd lost her person and would never have him back. She missed her kids. She had seen death up close. Where was *nice* in all of that mess and loss and complexity and humanness?

"I am," she said. Without thinking, she mirrored Rachel's tone exactly. "I'm super nice."

Something flickered across Rachel's expression. "I'll leave you all to it," she said. "Let me know if I'm a suspect." She headed off in the direction of the restaurant, pulling her deep green parka around her as she walked under the breezeway.

Ravi and Nina were looking at Ellery approvingly for some reason. "Well, well, well," Ravi said. "I knew you had it in you."

"You knew I had what in me?"

"A spicy streak," Ravi said. "I had a feeling it was there. You'll let people get away with a lot, but when you hit your limit—"

Nina smiled. "It was nice to see."

"It's good you found the body," Ravi said. "It means people give you a little extra leeway when you're asking around about Ben."

His tone was gentle, though, and from the look he gave Ellery, she could tell that he hadn't forgotten how stunned and shocked she'd been yesterday morning.

"Okay," Ravi said, after a moment. "Rachel thinks something's off, too. She's not stupid. Everyone with any common sense has figured out that two deaths within twenty-four hours can't mean anything good."

"How many guests are staying here, anyway?" Nina asked.

"I don't know, but there are thirty-six guest rooms," Ellery said. "And they're arranged in little groupings of three rooms per building. Plus five cottages, but those all have a king-sized bed." Ravi and Nina stared at her. "It's in the welcome book," she told them. "But I don't know how many people are *actually* staying here right now. We'd probably have to ask the staff for an accurate number."

"And make sure they've subtracted two," Nina said dryly.

"I still don't know where all the guest accommodations are," Ravi said. "I've got all the big stuff down. The gallery, the Main House, the restaurant, the spa, the pool."

"It's very well designed," Nina said. "They've managed to make it feel like each of the guest buildings is tucked away in its own area without being highly visible to the others."

"We need to get the lay of the land," Ravi said. "Literally. We need to look at some maps. And go over what we know."

"Where?" Nina asked.

"Let's meet in the sauna in fifteen," Ravi said. "Bring those stupid welcome books and anything else you can find in your rooms that might be useful."

24.

The sauna was cold and dark. A few small safety lights placed along the bottom of the room gave off a faint residual light, but the boards were no longer soaked in heat and the stove had clearly been shut down. When Nina ladled water over the rocks, there was no sizzle, no steam.

"Damn," Ravi said, depositing his bag on the floor and zipping up his coat. "They've turned it off."

"Maybe that's good," Ellery said. "Now we can be sure of having it to ourselves."

The wood of the walls was caramel colored, organic. It gave off enough of an illusion of warmth that she still felt drawn to the space.

"I wonder how soundproof it is," Ellery said.

"Go outside and listen," Ravi said. "We'll scream."

Ellery stepped outside. The sky and air were soggy and heavy. The mulch in the plantings near the sauna had been washed away by water cascading down the rain gutter next to it, some kind of thin-fronded plant clinging on despite the deluge. Nina would likely know what it was, since she was a landscape architect. Ellery should ask her. It was interesting how every single person in the world had some kind of specialized knowledge, whether it was from the work they did or the passions they had or the way their lives had turned out. You came to know certain things specifically and deeply, sometimes by choice and sometimes by circumstance, occasionally by both. Ellery had remembered this fact anew when she'd gone to the movie theater where Kate had gotten a job over the summer. She realized that Kate knew how to run projectors and fix soda machines and make popcorn, that she knew terminologies and had little expertises that were entirely foreign to Ellery. It was like how your spouse had a full work life that you couldn't truly begin to conceive of, even if you tried.

And you could never live through what the other had lived through, in the moments when you were apart.

That truck isn't stopping, Ellery thought. Not stopping not stopping not stopping. She looked at Pete, who was turning the wheel of the bus as hard as he could. In the seat next to her Abby was screaming "SEAT BELTS!" to all the students, and then Ellery saw the white lights coming closer, bearing down on them, and then

the impact
Pete's blood on the windshield
her body thrown forward
the end
of everything.

Ellery shivered. She couldn't hear anything from inside the sauna, so she pushed open the door. "Nothing," she said. "Were you actually screaming?"

"Oh, we were," Ravi said. "But let's make sure. I'll go out. You two scream."

Ellery settled down on the bench below Nina. "Okay," Nina said. "On the count of three. One, two, three…"

Nina let out a scream, throaty and piercing and long. The hairs on the back of Ellery's neck stood up at the rawness of it. Her own scream was coming out reedy and short, higher-pitched than she would have expected.

Weak.

It turned out she did not, actually, know how to scream.

Nina's face was a mixture of empathy and concern. "You're going to have to get better at that," she said. "Especially with a murderer around. Let's try it again."

But then Ravi opened the door. "I didn't hear a thing," he said. "You were screaming, right?"

"Oh yeah," Nina said. "We really got after it."

"This is excellent," Ravi said. "We've basically got a soundproof murder room here."

Nina cleared her throat.

"I didn't mean it *that* way," Ravi said. "I meant a place where we could talk about murder. Not *do* murder." He pulled a map out of his bag and unfolded it on the bench in front of them. "I grabbed this from the front desk," he said. "We really are on our own. There aren't any other resorts for miles, and Highway 1 is the only main road we connect to."

"Ugh," said Nina.

Ravi unfolded another map. "This one shows the trails in the area. The ones in Broken Point itself, and a couple that link to the resort from elsewhere. You would have gone on one of those for your hike, right?"

"Yeah." Ellery tapped the map. "I think it's this one."

"Do you think anyone could hike out on one of them?" Ravi asked.

"Not really," Ellery said. "The ones on this side of the highway lead to the ocean. I guess you could try to hook up to the highway from one of the trails, but it would be really risky. And even then, the highway isn't in good shape."

"It would be a fool's errand," Nina agreed. "Plus, it's still raining."

"Here's the layout of the resort again." Ellery opened up her booklet to the two-page spread. "But of course this doesn't have everything on here. Like the little service roads the staff use for the golf carts in addition to the paths we know, and where the staff who reside on-site actually live. I mean, I saw some of those buildings when I was driving up to the resort the first day, but I don't know anything more than that."

"Who all lives on-site?" Ravi asked.

"I think Nat, Carlos, Brook, and Canyon all do," Nina said. "And the doctor. And the chef and the kitchen staff. And the security guy. What was his name again?"

"Craig," Ravi said with distaste. "So there are a lot of staff who are still here."

"Do you think they're suspects?" Ellery asked.

"I mean, they have to be, don't they?" Ravi said.

"You remembered right, Ellery," Nina said. She was looking at the page Ellery had looked at earlier, the one entitled ACCOMMODATIONS. "It says here that there are thirty-six guest rooms and five cottages. And they're each double occupancy only."

"Even the cottages?" Ravi asked.

"Yeah," Nina said. "It says the cottages are larger in case people have come with a group and want to gather during the day, but even those only accommodate six to eight people at the dining table, things like that. And each cottage still only has a king-sized bed."

"Are the wedding party staying in the cottages?" Ravi asked.

"I'm not sure," Ellery said. "Olivia mentioned that she was staying in a room when I was talking to her with Andy. But maybe she meant a cottage."

"Was Ben staying with her?"

"I don't know."

"The cottages are insanely priced," Nina said. "I looked into them. You're talking $10K per night."

"I know." Ellery truly couldn't imagine having that kind of money. That was half of a beginning teacher's salary, back when she'd started.

"So we need to figure out who is staying where," Nina said.

"We can knock on their doors kind of early, before they've had time to go anywhere else for the day," Ravi said.

"Upon what pretext?" Nina asked.

"Goods and services?" Ellery said. "If we have something that people want or need, they'll forgive us for intruding."

"Like what?" Ravi asked. "Do we bake them cookies?"

"I mean, maybe?" Ellery said. "The staff is overworked. They're having to fill in with tasks they don't usually do, and I don't think they're getting much rest. So maybe we talk to Brook. See what we can do to help."

"Oh no," Ravi said. "Are you saying we're housekeeping now?"

"It's a thought," Nina said. "And not a bad one."

"If you say so." Ravi turned the page from the map and Ellery and Nina did the same. It was another two-page spread.

The Collection at Broken Point

The Collection at Broken Point is one of the premier private art collections in the state of California, and its location at a luxury resort is truly singular. Originally encompassing nine pieces when the resort opened in 1996, the collection now numbers thirteen works in total, including paintings, textiles, sculptures, screens, and sketches. While the Gallery hosts different shows throughout the year, the thirteen pieces of the Collection remain at Broken Point permanently and are located throughout the property. A curator is on retainer to ensure that the art is cared for properly and to keep an eye out for other pieces whose addition might facilitate the purpose of the Collection. It is our belief that art is meant not only to be curated, protected, and admired, but also experienced, shared, and appreciated within the context of its surroundings, including the natural world.

The Collection at Broken Point is also unique in that we invite our guests to embark upon a journey of discovery through art. Information about the works is included here, but we do not provide photographs of or locations for the pieces, inviting you instead to locate the art during your time at Broken Point. You may find the works in the Gallery, in common areas, tucked away in the landscape, at the end of hidden paths—and even, if you are fortunate, in a guest room.

Below were thirteen listings, one for each work. The listings contained the kind of information you often saw on cards next to pieces in museums or galleries.

"That's right," Nina said. "We've been forgetting all about the stolen art. Do you think that could be connected? Cause and effect, somehow?"

"Do the rest of the guests know that anything's missing?" Ellery asked.

"Who knows," Ravi said. "But our showing an interest in the art won't set people's teeth on edge as much as our sniffing around the deaths will. It would make sense that we'd be interested in finding all the pieces, since there's not much else to do now that we're locked in."

"They've been putting those art descriptions on the cards we get every day, but I admit I haven't been giving them the attention I should," Nina said. "Check this one out." She held out her book, her finger marking one of the descriptions:

> *Altar*
> by Kristin Sands
> 1996
> granite
>
> Commissioned especially for the Resort at Broken Point, *Altar* was installed immediately prior to our opening and remains an iconic artmark of the area. Sands, known for her outsize sculptures made of stone, envisioned the cairn shape for the altar knowing that it, unlike many other works, would be in active use.

"An artmark?" Ellery asked. "Is that a word?"

"Who wrote these descriptions?" Ravi asked. "Werner Herzog? But I do like the altar itself."

"I do too," Nina said. "It makes me uncomfortable as hell. And I kind of love the idea of people getting married in front of something like that."

"Here's another one I've seen," Ravi told them. "This was in the gallery, in a display case."

Driftwood Crown
by Camille Gray
2013
driftwood, stones, beach glass

Gray uses only found objects in her sculptures and is willing to wait for exactly the right piece of wood or stone, a process that can take years. In a reversal of the way crowns are often presented, with stones or jewels as the focal points on a base of gold or other metal, this crown is covered in glass and stone but left unadorned in the places where gems would usually be arranged, revealing the driftwood below as the ornamentation.

"Thirteen pieces in the collection," Nina mused. "What do you think they were trying to do? Tempt fate? Show that they didn't care about the numbers?"

"Be provoking?" Ellery guessed.

"Ravi?" Nina asked. She waved her hand in front of his face. "Hello? Where are you?"

Ravi looked up wide-eyed from the welcome booklet. "You guys," he said. "Look at this."

It took Ellery a moment to make sense of the words.

The collection is selected and its installment overseen by Catherine Haring, a renowned curator and art dealer based in San Francisco.

"*Interesting,*" Nina said.

"No wonder Olivia's mom didn't want her to have her wedding at city hall," Ellery said. "Catherine already had the perfect place in mind."

Ravi and Nina looked at her, surprised.

"I talked to Olivia the night before the wedding," Ellery explained. "Briefly. It was up in the gallery. Remember, Ravi? You saw us. She said that she and Ben had wanted to get married at city hall, but that they hadn't because of her family. *It's not only about us.* That's what Olivia said."

Ravi and Nina were still staring at her. "It feels like you've talked to everyone in the wedding party, one way or another," Ravi said.

"Not really," Ellery said. "And I think people have been talking to me because I'm alone. You know. Everyone else is with someone or part of a group."

"Still, we should keep you on the suspect list," Ravi said, grinning. "Are you *sure* you didn't know Ben?"

"I didn't," Ellery said. The image of him in the water, his eyes open to the rain, came back and she took a shaky breath.

"Hey," Ravi said, reaching out for her arm. "That was a crappy thing to say. I know how hard it was for you to find him. I'm sorry."

"It's all right," Ellery said. "It's much worse for everyone else. For the people who loved him and knew him." *Don't go there,* she told herself. *Don't think about any other tragedies, any other deaths, any other eyes open wide and seeing nothing.*

"Nina and I saw something strange," Ellery said, changing the subject. "Out at the viewpoint. The gap in the guardrail where Matt probably went through. Did you notice it too, Ravi?"

He nodded. "It was a clean break. Not jagged like the other places where the railing had been torn away. Like someone had unscrewed the rivets or bolts to make it easier for the guardrail to come apart right there."

"Exactly."

"Okay," Nina said, after a moment. "I think we need to divide and conquer. We've got to find out more. I can ask the staff about the art. I could say I'm using some large pieces in a landscape project I'm working on and that I find what they've done here inspiring. Something like that."

"Ellery, you're already partially in with the wedding party," Ravi said. "Olivia might be willing to talk to you again. You have a connection with Andy. And maybe you can also talk to Brook or Canyon? Figure out some way to learn more about the guests and how many people are staying, things like that?"

"We've got the hardest jobs," Nina said dryly. "What exactly are you planning to do?"

"I'll try and talk to Nat," Ravi said. "See if I can get any more info. She's not crazy about me but I don't think she's crazy about anyone. Maybe Carlos will be easier, but that guy is handling everything so he might be impossible to find. I also might give Rachel a try. I feel like we'd get along."

"Okay," Ellery said. She did not want to do any of this. But she *had* to get home.

25.

Ellery wasn't certain where Brook would be, so she went to the Main House first. She found the young woman hurriedly cleaning up after some sort of gathering in the social room, the large common space next to the reception area. Crumpled napkins and smudged glasses and mugs littered the tables and floor, and a fire crackled in the enormous stone fireplace that opened onto both reception and the social room. The storm had taken a breath earlier that morning but it was coming down again now. Though it was drawing close to noon, the light outside the windows was watery, green and gray from trees and rain. Ellery again had the sense that they were underwater or suspended in a cloud.

"Let me help you." She reached for a napkin that had fallen to the floor.

"No, no, you're a guest." Brook straightened up, holding a glass that showed the traces of what looked like a Bloody Mary. "What can I help you with? Is everything all right with your room?"

"My room is fine," Ellery said. "I was coming to see if there was any news, which I know is unlikely." She was deliberately vague about what kind of "news" she hoped to hear, letting Brook tell her whatever came to mind first.

"We're still in contact with the police," Brook said. "They'll be here as soon as they can." She hesitated, as if she wasn't sure what more she should say. It was obvious they were dealing with something other than two separate "accidents," and it was also clear that Nat had not yet fully decided how to address that with the guests. Brook settled for saying, "They said there have been emergencies everywhere. But we're a high priority now."

"I'm sure they'll be here soon," Ellery said. "I'm glad you're still in touch with them. Are they giving you any updates on the weather?"

"Yes," Brook said. "It's supposed to keep raining for at least two more days."

So that's not great, Ellery thought. "Was there an event here that I missed?" she asked, reaching for one of the unused napkins to wipe up a sticky spot on a side table.

"It was only a few guests," Brook said. "The groomsmen wanted to have a toast to their friend, the one who was found today."

"That was kind of you to arrange."

"They want to have a memorial tonight for both Matt and Ben," Brook said. "So I'm afraid that if you'd like to be here in the social room past eight, we'll be closing it off for them. Reception will still be open, of course."

"I understand," Ellery said. In her mind, she could hear Ravi saying, *"Memorial? It's not like they were army veterans."* But they were people who were loved, and her heart hurt for Olivia, for Ben's friends, for Matt's friends and family. Had they been told yet? She thought of Matt yesterday, his ruddy face, his bloodshot eyes. His concern and grief for Ben. "And I'm sure Olivia and her family, and Andy, will be glad there's some kind of service as well."

"I'm not exactly sure who all is attending." Brook had stopped cleaning for a moment and was contemplating a wine stain on the rich red-and-brown rug that stretched over the perfectly weathered hardwood floor. "It's a bit difficult keeping up with all of the different requests and what we're arranging for whom." She sighed. "We're understaffed. Some of the people who work here live off-site, and they haven't been able to get back. Of course, the safety and comfort of our guests are our top priorities."

"I'm sure you have your hands full," Ellery said.

"These kinds of things do happen up here," Brook said, "but not like *this*. I mean, the road washes out. We have mudslides. It's part of living in such a wild place. But the guests—" She stopped short. *The guests dying,* Ellery imagined Brook was going to say. *That's new.*

"You're doing a wonderful job," Ellery said. "This is an impossible situation."

The front door of the Main House opened, and Ravi, Nat, and Canyon walked in. Ravi waved at Ellery. She waved back. Nonchalant, casual, as if they both didn't know exactly what the other was doing.

"Hey!" Ravi said. "There you are! I've been asking Nat what we can do to help. There must be something. We can't sit around while the staff bears the brunt of everything. It's unconscionable."

Ellery raised her eyebrows at Ravi. *You're overselling it,* she tried to convey. *Be cool.*

I can't, his eyebrows said back. *This will work, though. Watch me.*

A golf cart pulled up in front of the building, almost skidding out in the rain. A staff member Ellery had seen around but whose name she didn't know climbed out and held the plastic covering open for a tall, well-dressed man in a cashmere sweater with graying hair and a slight potbelly. "Right through here, Mr. Haring," the staff member said. "Nat will be with us shortly." Nat nodded to him, and the two men disappeared through a door behind the reception area.

A long-suffering look flickered across Nat's face. She had a weary energy about her, the kind you get at the end of a very, very long party you agreed to host and now profoundly regret.

"I'm sure Brook can think of something for both of you to do to help," Nat said to Ravi and Ellery. She went through the door and into the back offices.

Brook furrowed her brow. "Let me think for a second."

"Give us something mindless and annoying so that you don't have to do it," Ravi said. "But not cleaning toilets. I'm not *that* bored."

Brook laughed. She gestured for them to follow her toward another door at the back of the Main House that Ellery hadn't really noticed before. "I know. You can write out the cards that we hang on the doors every morning. You might have noticed that the weather is filled in by hand each day."

"Do we know the forecast?" Ravi asked.

"We got one this morning from the police." Brook led them out of the building and under a short, covered walkway to a low, gray-shingled building that Ellery had assumed contained more guest rooms. Brook opened the door with a key and ushered them through what appeared to be a staff lounge (microwave, a few round tables, several squashy chairs, and a kitchenette) and into what was clearly the housekeeping headquarters. Unlike the rest of the resort that Ellery had seen, this was utilitarian and industrial. A long, stainless-steel counter for folding laundry and organizing supplies ran down the center of the room. A bank of industrial-sized washers and dryers churned away, and one of the walls was lined with large standing baskets that could be loaded onto golf carts or rolled to different locations. There was another door on the opposite side of the one where they'd come in. "I wrote down what they told us and I'll give you a copy to work from. The weather could change, of course, but it's the most up-to-date information we have." Brook unlocked several cabinets and opened them, revealing cards, cleaning supplies, towels, washcloths, and charming little rows of in-room toiletries.

"We also need someone to stock the housekeeping baskets," Brook said. "Our head housekeeper lives on-site, but not all of her staff does, and she's a bit overwhelmed at the moment. They've been cleaning up the restaurant and kitchen after breakfast so that everything will be ready for lunch."

"Good idea," Ravi said. "After food, housekeeping is the first thing people start to lose their minds over."

"There's a list on the inside of this cabinet with what needs to go in each basket," Brook said. "Housekeeping will be back around to pick them up. They'll be delighted to see they don't have to do it and they can load up the golf carts right away."

"This all sounds excellent," Ravi said. "Shall I start stocking the baskets? Or doing the cards?"

Brook gave him an evaluative look. "Nat's picky about the cards looking perfect. How good is your handwriting?"

"Gorgeous," Ravi said. "An actual dream."

"Let's see you both write something." Brook handed them each an inky black pen and a piece of paper.

It turned out that Ravi's handwriting was atrocious. He looked up at them with puppy-dog eyes.

"Um," Brook said, a slight grin crossing her face. Ellery was glad to see the smile, a moment of levity in the heavy situation. "It looks like you're going to be stocking the baskets."

Ravi feigned utter dejection. Ellery patted his back.

"Don't feel bad," she said. "It's part of being a teacher. We have to have good penmanship so our students know what we're writing on the board."

"False," Ravi said. "You don't even write on boards anymore. You all have smart tablets or screens or whatever. And I had teachers whose handwriting was absolutely illegible."

"That can happen," Ellery concurred. "But we're not known for our bad handwriting the way doctors and lawyers are." *Wait a minute,* she wanted to ask Ravi. *What do you do?* She still wasn't sure. There had been that whole conversation about her work and Nina's, but Ravi had changed the subject before they'd talked about his job. They'd moved on to the resort, the wedding. The shadow celebrity.

Maybe that whole conversation was a trick, she thought. *Maybe Ravi himself is the shadow celebrity.*

"The cards are preprinted." Brook removed a stack from a shelf in one of the cabinets and set them down on the counter. She reached back into the cabinet and took out a cup full of black felt-tipped pens. "We rotate through the cards in a specific order so that you don't ever overlap with the same quotes and art information unless a guest stays longer than thirteen days. Housekeeping writes in the weather by hand for a personal touch. There's a schedule taped to the inside of the cupboard that tells you which card to do on which days. They're all organized according to the daily quote. The Stegner quote is day one, and so on. You keep moving through the rotation. For tomorrow, we'll be on the Emily Dickinson quote."

Ellery looked at the stack of thick, letterpressed, cream-colored cards. The ink that had been used to print them was a deep, russet-y orange, an unusual color. She liked it. It reminded her of how her grandmother always used to write her letters and cards in brown ink, saying it was more unusual than black or blue. "It's nice to have a hallmark," her grandmother had said. "A calling card, if you will. Handwriting is one, of course, but I always like to have a few."

Murderers would have calling cards, too. That's what all the shows and books said, anyway.

"How many cards should I fill out?" Ellery asked, holding her breath.

But Brook didn't hesitate in giving the information. "Twenty-seven," she said over her shoulder, as she headed down to the other end of the room with Ravi, who turned and gave Ellery a thumbs-up from behind Brook's back.

They'd learned something. Twenty-seven of the rooms and cottages were occupied.

It was oddly satisfying to write on the creamy, high-quality paper. Ellery could hear Ravi chattering away with Brook as they worked together on the baskets, filling them with towels and toiletries and folded sheets. "So I have to admit," he was saying now, "that I overheard something earlier about the art. One of the pieces was stolen?"

Ellery heard a clatter of bottles being dropped. She drew in her breath. "Oops," Ravi said. "Let me get those."

"Where did you hear that?" Brook asked.

"Well, from you," Ravi said apologetically. "I swear I wasn't eavesdropping. It was the day of the wedding. I stopped by the front desk that morning and you and Nat were talking for a second with the office door open before you saw me."

"Oh, right," Brook said. "Everything's fine. Nothing to worry about. I think you must have misheard, but I'm sorry if that caused you any distress."

The door swung open and Maddox stepped inside. He was dirty and wearing work gloves, and his waxed jacket bore a sheen of rain. His boots were so muddy that some of it had leached onto his jeans.

"Where's Nat?" he asked Brook. "I need to talk to her about the generator." His voice was rougher than Ellery remembered, as if he'd been yelling or screaming. He looked exhausted.

"Of course. I'll be right back." Brook hurried after Maddox, who shot them a slightly confused look over his shoulder.

"Well, well, well," Ravi said, making his way closer to Ellery. "Did you hear any of that over the washers and dryers?"

"I think all of it."

"Interesting, right?" Ravi said. "She literally dropped the Aesop hand soap bottles on the floor when I brought up the missing art. That stuff is *expensive*. So I don't buy that line about it all being *fine* and *nothing to worry about*."

"I don't, either."

"Do you think we can get away with pretending we're housekeeping and deliver all these supplies ourselves?" Ravi put his hands on his hips, surveying the stocked baskets and the pile of cards Ellery had finished.

"I think that would be pushing it."

"You're right, of course," Ravi said. "It's for the best. Still, though. Brook trusts us. We're in here without supervision. Anything else we should take a look at?"

The door opened. A staff member with dark hair in a neat bun entered the room, carrying herself in a perfect-postured, no-nonsense kind of way. "Brook told me you were in here. I'm Isabel, head of housekeeping." Isabel didn't sound pleased, and she looked around as if she were surprised to see that the room hadn't been trashed entirely. Her glance lingered on Maddox's muddy boot prints. *We didn't do that,* Ellery wanted to tell her. "Thank you for your help," Isabel said. Was it Ellery's imagination, or had Isabel infused the last word with a touch of sarcasm? "I'll take over from here."

"Nice to meet you, Isabel." Ravi held out his hand. "I'm Ravi."

Isabel nodded at him, but she was already opening the door to one of the dryers and two of the other staff had begun loading baskets onto a golf cart parked near the exterior door. "Lunch is being served in the restaurant now."

"I think we've been dismissed," Ravi said quietly, and Ellery nodded. They sidled out the door and started past the plastic-sheeted golf carts that the housekeeping staff were using. Rain drummed down on slick green leaves and puddled along the flagstones, which another staff member was squeegeeing off. Immediately, Ellery felt the damp seeping into her bones, smelled the lush and near-decay scent of land and vegetation that were absorbing too much water.

"To lunch?" Ravi asked, holding his coat over his head.

"To lunch." Ellery flipped up her hood, which, as always, gave her the feeling of a horse wearing blinders, which she hated. "I'll catch up with you. I need to go back to my room and grab something."

The familiar feeling had started up again—grief and fear coming for her as ponderous and inevitable as a bus and also as quick as electricity, ready to lightning through every nerve in her body on its way to re-shatter her heart. *Alone.* She needed to let herself fall apart so that she could go on keeping it together.

26.

Ellery barely made it back to her room.

She sat on the edge of her bed and bent in half. After a few moments of breathing in, out, in, out, she kicked off her shoes and let herself assume the fetal position, curling up around the pain.

This was the other version of what had happened the first night at the resort, when she'd had to leave her table at the restaurant and go to the restroom to cry. She would be pushing through, functioning at least somewhat normally from the outside, getting things done, teaching a lesson, driving a car, making the kids dinner, but she would feel it coming for her. The pain of grief and loss and *everything*. Sometimes she had to get away and cry. Other times she had to fold up and ache.

Her eyes were shut tight but she could still hear the rain on the roof.

Ellery had that suffocating feeling again, where she was suspended in heavy air, and she was either going to drown there or fall to earth and break. She was alone, cut off physically as well as emotionally from the people she loved and the life she knew, and the uncertainty of when she'd get back to them in any way felt untenable. It was bringing back that other time, just over two years ago, when the world was upended.

It happened so quickly that they were all in the middle of it before they knew what had begun, and yet there were so many moments that stood out, discrete and imprinted, their own small universes in which a world began and ended.

The semitruck careening toward them

Ellery staring into the white-hot headlights, blinded, willing the driver of the truck to wake up, to look up, to see them in time

the force of the turn as Pete cut the wheel even more sharply, trying to pull the bus out of the way

her body, slamming painfully forward into the seat belt, Abby's body doing the same in the next seat

her eyes, catching Pete's in the rearview mirror, the fear in them

how quiet it all became.

And then

the screams

the brute force of the impact, a cataclysm of scraping metal and screeching tires

the turning over and over and

over.

She had to go to lunch. She had to keep moving. Get to the kids. It was all narrowing down to that one clear point. *The kids.*

"Okay," she said, out loud. "On the count of three. One, two, three..."

She sat up in the bed and met her own eyes in a mirror hanging over the desk.

She hadn't made a mental catalog of the art in her room. But wait. Had that mirror always been there? Hadn't it been a painting or a photograph earlier?

She remembered other things about the desk. The vintage telephone, made of black metal, with a rotary dial that called only four numbers (Reception, Concierge, Room Service, Housekeeping). The flowers—sunset and ivory colored, interspersed with green and gray-blue foliage—arranged in a small gray vase. The leather tray that had held the welcome booklet. Her eyes stared back at her in the dim light of the room, the power seeming to ebb and surge—according to the generator, perhaps. It gave her a flickering, ghostly look.

Breathe. The mirror has probably been here all along.

What if it hadn't, though? What if it had been the roving Warhol and she'd been too stupid and sad to notice, and now someone had taken it and replaced it with a mirror and was going to frame her for the art theft and then the murder?

Now she was actually losing her mind.

Ellery went to the door and reached for her muddy boots. A movement along the pathway caught her eye. It was Maddox, coming out from one of the other walkways that led to the guest buildings. He was barely visible through the screen of trees. Had he been checking on one of the rooms? Did he have an update on the backup generator?

She was about to call out to him when he stumbled, putting out a hand to grasp one of the trees and right himself. Ellery caught a glimpse of his face, cold and grim, set in lines that made him look like a much older, harder man. He looked up suddenly, almost furtively, in her general direction, but his eyes didn't alight on her, as if she couldn't be seen.

Maddox let go of the tree and, with a slight sound that could have been a curse or a moan or nothing at all, something in her imagination, walked away down the path. He was gone. He might never have been there at all.

She needed to keep moving, too.

27.

Ellery picked up one of the boxed lunches set out on the table and looked around the restaurant. Her heart was still thudding, but Maddox was nowhere to be seen.

Ravi was already seated at a table near the front with Rachel, deep in animated conversation. Even though getting to know other people had been part of the plan, Ellery felt her heart sink. In a very brief time, she'd become accustomed to being with Ravi and Nina. Now she was on her own again, albeit temporarily, and it felt worse than before. Now there was death in their midst.

Someone waved at her from a table near the front. Grace. Relief washed over Ellery as she made her way over to where Grace sat with her father. She liked Grace and Gary, their clear affection for one another, the way they appreciated the outdoors and not only the luxury surrounding them. She was sure Ravi would be delighted that she'd managed to sit with them, and she knew he'd want her to ask them about finding Matt's body. But she wasn't completely certain that she could bring herself to do that. She knew what it was like, how it felt to want to avoid discussing something terrible.

But it turned out Grace and Gary *did* want to talk about it.

"Not with everyone," Grace said, after they'd exchanged *hellos* and *I'm so sorrys* and *I know you probably don't want to talk about its*. Grace lifted the bag and wallet from the chair that she'd been using to make it look like the place was saved. Ellery felt flattered, wondering if they'd been saving it for her. "We don't mind talking about it with you. You've been through the same thing."

"The body finders," Gary said. He wore a bright blue Patagonia jacket that brought out the tan in his skin. "It's a grim little club."

"Oh, Dad." Grace's hair was in two braids today, a few tendrils escaping. She wore a bright green hoodie and a Gore-Tex parka was draped over the back of her chair. Both she and Gary also had the boxed lunches sitting in front of them. It looked like Gary had already made his way through the sandwich and the chips. A soft drink with a lime perched on the rim sat next to his meal.

"It is," Ellery said.

"We were luckier than you were," Grace said. "We were at a distance. And it was pretty clear there was nothing we could do."

Ellery wondered how much they'd heard about Ben and how she'd found him. It seemed like they knew at least some of the details.

"We didn't have to identify him," Grace said. "Did you?"

"No," Ellery said. "The bride and his best friend had to do that."

"Young people dying is a tragedy," Gary said. "There's no excuse for it." His voice was tight. "So much waste."

I agree, thought Ellery, but she couldn't quite form the words around the sudden lump in her throat.

"Dad's been around a lot of hard things in his line of work," Grace said softly. "He used to be a district court judge."

Even though Gary was still wearing his Giants ballcap at the moment, Ellery could picture him presiding on the bench. There was a dignity about him, a confidence. Not arrogance, though. More like... seasoning. "I imagine you've seen everything."

"Quite a bit," Gary said. "Some truly terrible things. Photographs of them, anyway, and testimony that I'll remember for the rest of my life. Of course, it's always worse for the family members and the first responders. Of everything I did, though, child custody decisions were some of the ones that haunt me the most."

Ellery flinched.

"I'm sorry." Gary was quick on the uptake. "You've been through that yourself, perhaps. I didn't realize."

"You had no way of knowing." Ellery opened her lunch. The staff had again set out stoneware plates, cloth napkins, and full silverware, and someone had also made small floral arrangements for each table. Ellery felt her mouth twist wryly. Why not play violins while the *Titanic* was sinking? Why not create lovely little bright spots when cliffs were sliding down? It was like the daily cards she'd filled out in house-keeping this morning. "This weekend was supposed to be our twentieth anniversary," she told Grace and Gary. "I came because I didn't want him to bring his girlfriend instead. Which was a mistake. Clearly. I was already missing my kids, and now who knows when I'll get back to them." She couldn't quite keep her voice from wavering.

Gary patted her hand sympathetically. "You're not the only one who's made a mistake in coming here," he said. "This is my fiftieth wedding anniversary weekend." His eyes were sad. "My wife passed away five months ago."

"I'm so sorry."

"Big Sur was her favorite place," Gary said. "We used to come camping here decades ago. Now of course, it's very different with all the resorts. And it's not that we came to this exact spot every time we visited. We stayed up and down the coast. Sheila loved to try new places." Gary wiped his eyes with a napkin, looking embarrassed by the emotion.

"I think it's lovely and brave of you to come and honor your wife," Ellery said.

"That's what we were doing when we found Matt," Grace said. "We knew the weather was awful and that we shouldn't really be out. But we'd both brought good gear, and we didn't know if we'd get another break in the rain. We weren't trying to go on the whole hike. Only far enough out to the point that we could do what we needed to do."

Which was what? Ellery wanted to ask.

"We were honoring my wife, but we were also engaged in illegal activity." Gary tried to laugh, but his eyes were still swimming.

"We have my mom's ashes." Grace kept her voice low, so they wouldn't be overheard by the surrounding tables. "We were going to scatter them at Broken Point. That's where Dad proposed to her years ago. We were realizing that it was too dangerous with the path washed out."

"*You* were realizing," Gary said. "I was hell-bent on getting all the way to the point. Which was ridiculous, I see that now."

"You're grieving, Dad," Grace said. "It's okay. Anyway. We'd stopped and I was trying to talk him into scattering the ashes where we were when we looked down. And saw Matt. It was pretty clear from the way he was lying that he had broken his neck." She swallowed. "I've helped people on trails before, just first-responder stuff. It's not like I'm an EMT or anything, but I've seen that once before. When someone fell and you could...tell. Right away."

"It was far too dangerous to be hiking. I shouldn't have insisted we go out there," Gary said. "Even if it was Sheila's favorite place." He passed a hand across his face. "And besides," he said, "what if home was her favorite place? Or her garden? How can I be absolutely sure?"

"I don't think you can," Ellery said. "But I also think there's more than one right answer in a life that long. In a marriage that long." *That's rich, Ellery,* she thought. *Positing theories on marriage and life when you've so clearly failed at both.*

But Gary and Grace were both looking at her gratefully.

"Anyway." Gary cleared his throat. "This whole situation is a mess. We need to get out of here as quickly as possible. Take my advice, young woman. Don't go anywhere alone. If you think I'm letting Grace out of my sight..."

Ellery noticed that his walking stick, Stabby, was propped up next to his chair.

Well, I'm staying here alone, she thought about saying, but Gary was speaking again. And, she realized, everyone else *had* come with someone or as part of a group. And people were still dying. *Together* didn't necessarily equal *safe*. In fact, it could be the most unsafe thing of all, depending on who you were with.

———

The staff had announced last call for the food when Andy walked through the door, wearing a blue plaid shirt and a ballcap. Even from her seat, Ellery could see the stubble growing back on his face and the shadows under his eyes. He was looking around as if searching for something or someone, and she was surprised when his eyes landed on her. He waved, slightly, dropping his hand almost immediately as if he didn't expect her to acknowledge him. She waved back.

"That's the groom's best friend, isn't it," Gary said. "Poor guy." Andy made his way awkwardly to the buffet table, stopping in front of the rows of boxes as if bewildered.

"We talked to him a bit before the hike on Saturday," Grace said. "He seemed nice."

"Even though he *is* wearing a Dodgers cap." Gary winked.

"Do you mind if I invite him to sit with us?" Ellery asked. There was something forlorn about the lonely set of Andy's shoulders, the brown hair curling out from under his hat, the wave he'd given her earlier. More than anyone else, she felt that he was also here alone, though technically he was part of a group.

She had that sense from Olivia, too, she realized. Now that Ben was gone, both Andy and Olivia seemed to have lost their linchpin, their anchor. Which didn't make sense, did it? Olivia's parents and friends were here. And Andy should be with other young people. Charming, outdoorsy, beautiful, smart, kind ones. Like Grace?

"I don't mind at all," Gary said, and the glimmer in his eye made her wonder if his thoughts were running along the same track.

Heads turned as Nat, Carlos, and Craig entered the restaurant. They were wearing raincoats and boots that were particularly muddy. Ellery shivered, wondering what they'd been doing the last few hours. Had they been able to retrieve Matt's body? Who would formally identify *him*? Where were they keeping both of the bodies? And Maddox— what had he been doing? What was the situation with the generator?

"If I could have your attention, please," Nat called out, and more heads turned in her direction, the restaurant quieting. "There are a few things we need to let you know. I have some good news and some bad news and, well, just some news. I'm going to need you all to wait until I'm finished before you ask any questions, please."

Gary folded his arms across his chest. Ellery found herself leaning forward. What was the bad news?

"The first and most important update is regarding the police," Nat said. "They're obviously very concerned about your safety and want to get you all evacuated and home to your families as soon as possible."

"I don't know about *obviously*," someone at a table behind Ellery muttered.

"A natural disaster of this magnitude requires attention and manpower that is almost beyond belief," Nat said. "They've been working around the clock to get people out of campsites and other areas that were more compromised and much less safe than we have been. And until today, we didn't think that what had happened to Mr. Taylor was anything other than an unfortunate, onetime accident."

But Dr. Anand, Ellery thought. She could have sworn that he felt the way she did when she was sitting, dripping, on the sofa in the Main House. She realized she hadn't seen him since then. Where was he?

Nat was still speaking. "I need to point out that we still have no reason to believe otherwise. What happened to Mr. Colton"—*so that was Matt's last name,* Ellery thought—"could also have been an accident."

A small eruption from the groomsmen's table, and from a few other groupings as well.

"Carlos and a few other staff members were able to retrieve Mr. Colton's body and take it to a secure location," Nat said. "We're grateful to his friends for identifying him."

Ellery glanced over at the table with Jason and the other groomsmen. They looked mutinous, simmering. And sad. Two of their number were gone. They'd been spared the task of identifying Ben, but which of them had had to identify Matt? What had he looked like, up close? Somewhere out there in the world were Matt's parents, his family. Did they even know yet that he was gone?

Ellery's throat ached. *Don't cry,* she told herself. *This isn't your tragedy. Not yet. And, with any luck, it won't be. Not this time.*

"However, even that much of a recovery effort was extremely

dangerous, and it also gave us an inkling of what the police and other emergency responders might be dealing with right now," Nat said. "The resort road is largely impassable, and the police have said the highway is out in multiple areas."

"They should send in some choppers," one of the groomsmen called out.

"They will, when the weather is clear enough," Nat said. "But right now, the conditions are too dangerous for that as well. We don't want to add more fatalities to the situation." Her tone was blunt. "The police have asked us to shelter in place. I know it doesn't feel like it, but we are luckier than most."

Ellery knew this to be true. She also knew that her body didn't care, that every instinct screamed *Get out. Get back to your family. Whatever you have to do, do it.*

"The situation could become even worse if people continue to disregard our warnings about leaving the main area of the resort," Nat said. Ellery turned back to see Nat's gaze fixed on their table. Did she know about the excursion that Ellery, Nina, and Ravi had made out along the trail? Or was she looking at Grace and Gary? Ellery willed herself not to glance in Ravi's or Nina's direction again during the meal.

Nat gestured to two of the staff, who began opening several enormous cartons at the front of the room. "We'll be distributing a list of rules and safety measures for you to follow. We're also handing out emergency backpacks with flashlights, first aid kits, and other items that you should keep with you." One staff member began moving around the room, handing out thick white folders printed with the resort's logo, name, and the words EMERGENCY PROCEDURES. The second staff member began pulling out black, logo-emblazoned backpacks.

Jason had had enough. "So we're supposed to wait around for someone to drown us? Or shove us off a cliff?"

Nat's voice cut through the noise rising anew from the tables. "I will reiterate again that these could both be simple accidents, one due to the weather and another due to disregard for the natural disaster at hand."

"Or we have a serial killer on our hands," Jason said, standing up. "What about that?" Craig took a step forward, jaw clenched.

"Son," Gary said from their table, "this isn't helping." His voice held the kind of authority that some people were born with and some were not. And Gary's might be innate, but it had also been honed, Ellery thought. It was all the more effective because it wasn't always on display. She was reminded of earlier in the day when Grace had put the groomsmen in their place on the trail.

"I'm not your son," Jason muttered, but he sat back down. Craig folded his arms. Carlos looked at his watch. Ellery knew there must be other situations unfolding and problems to be solved of which the guests weren't even aware.

"We do recommend that you stay with a friend at all times," Nat said. "Both so that they can help you if something goes wrong—if you slip or fall, for example, since the rain is compromising even the parts of the resort that are open—and so you can feel safe knowing someone you trust is with you."

"So that's the emergency plan?" a guest Ellery didn't know called out. "The buddy system?"

Nat fixed the room with an icy glare, waiting until the chatter had died down and then for a few moments afterward, until the atmosphere became attentive, almost uncomfortable.

"We are closing the resort except for the guest rooms, this restaurant, and the Main House," Nat said. "That has largely been in effect since the storm began, but now it's official. This will also help us conserve power. Please read through the material in your folders, keep your backpacks with you, stay with your friends or family, and be safe." Each word held weight, as if she were putting some of the responsibility for what was happening back on everyone else in the room. *Do as you're told. Stop being children. This is an emergency.*

"It's very likely that we'll lose power at some point," Nat went on. "That's the nature of disasters and generators, even first-class ones like what we have here. The important thing is not to panic if it happens. Stay where you are, if it's dry and safe, until power is restored or someone comes to find you. That's all in the folder. Dinner will be served tonight in the restaurant at five o' clock so that we can take advantage of what natural light there might be at that time." Her glance flickered out across the room and came to rest on Ravi, who was standing up. To Ellery's surprise, Nat gestured for Ravi to join her at the front of the room.

"Thank you, Nat!" Ravi said brightly. "I asked if I could speak to you all. I've had an idea, and I'm hoping you might be convinced to join in."

Ellery saw that a few people who had not yet had the chance to be charmed by Ravi were looking slightly put off. The rest were brightening at the sight of him. Rachel was actually smiling. Had he gotten her to like him within the space of a single meal?

"As Nat mentioned, we'll likely be trapped here for a bit," Ravi said. Ignoring the mutters and groans going on around him, he continued. "And unfortunately, there's not really any way to go out. And we have limited access to the facilities. And the staff has plenty to do without trying to babysit us. As we know. So I thought it might be fun—"

"*Fun,*" someone muttered to someone else.

"—if we helped keep one another entertained," Ravi went on. "This is an interesting collection of people. In any other circumstance, we'd interact very little and go on being interesting to the groups we came with. But now that we're without Wi-Fi, we may as well be interesting to each other as well. For example, I have on good intelligence that we've got experts on art and landscaping and history and criminal justice and finance and rock climbing gathered here, to name a few."

Everyone began looking around to try to pinpoint who each person was.

"I'm a microbrewer," one of the groomsmen shouted. "Like, craft beer."

"I'm a licensed masseuse," Morgan called out. Ellery looked over and saw that she and Maddox were seated at a nearby table. *When did he come in?* she wondered.

"Oh, hell yeah," Jason said to one of the other groomsmen.

"Hell no," Maddox said. Ellery saw a slight narrowing of his eyes, a set to his jaw. He looked better than he had earlier, though. Calmer, more like himself.

Morgan's lips tightened, but then she called out, "I reserve the right to refuse service to anyone," in a cheery tone, and people laughed.

"Great," Ravi said. "So I have a sign-up sheet, and anyone who wants to can write down what they're willing to do. Nat said we can use the social room for any gatherings." He beamed at the room. "I'll post lists of the activities in the Main House when we have them scheduled. As Nat mentioned, staying together is a good idea right now, and this will help us accomplish that."

"Brilliant," said Gary. "That is a smart man." He was watching Ravi shrewdly.

From his table, Maddox caught Nat's eye and motioned that he'd like to speak to her. She nodded and withdrew, following Maddox into the restaurant's kitchen and past the staff, who were now clearing up.

Maddox is already so trusted, Ellery thought. There was something profoundly competent about him.

Where is *Olivia?* Ellery wondered. Oh, there were so many people to worry about. She felt her hands shaking under the table, her heart pounding. *Calm down. Remember. Staying calm is how you get home.*

28.

Ravi had hooked them up. When he'd gone around with his sign-up sheet, he'd signed Nina, Ellery, and himself up for the first three massage spots that Morgan had open. And, in spite of what Nat had said about closing down different areas, they'd agreed to keep electricity running to the spa for another day once Nat had realized Morgan was serious about her offer.

"It's probably hard to say no to either of them when Maddox is being so helpful," said Ravi. "Or maybe Nat realized that she might not have a guest insurrection if people were relaxed."

The spa was next door to the sauna and near the pool. Ellery was struck again by how tucked into the foliage all the buildings were, and realized she still didn't have a complete grasp on where everything was. She vowed to consult her map again. It was the way the buildings were low-slung and weathered, their glass reflecting back the verdant trees and greenery that grew among the entire resort. You were never completely sure where you were, especially not now with the fog.

Warmth engulfed them when they came out of the rain and through the door into the spa's reception area. Ellery's eyes took a moment to adjust to the dimness of the lights. Someone had lit a fire in the fireplace. Candles were set in large glass bowls and surrounded by smooth river rocks or floated in other bowls full of water and a few gently drifting blossoms. *Camellias,* Ellery thought, with a small shiver.

"Hey, there." Morgan was standing behind a wooden desk with a sculptural live edge. Rows of tastefully colored bottles and other spa products—baskets full of blankets, hand lotion and soap, essential oils—lined the shelves along the wall to her right. "It's good to see you." She came out from behind the desk. Her long blond hair was pulled up in a ponytail, and she wore a tidy black uniform that looked like slightly tailored scrubs. Even pregnant, she was so small that the stomach fit loosely. "The staff's letting me wear the spa uniform," she said, giving a little twirl. "What do you think?"

"You look fantastic," Ravi said sincerely. "Super professional. Thank you for doing this, especially since you're expecting."

"It's not like I'm *that* big yet," Morgan said. "And I haven't had any morning sickness." She consulted a piece of paper in front of her. "Nina, it looks like you're first. The women's dressing room is right through there, first door on your left. I've got robes and everything ready to go."

"Thank you," Nina said. "This is really lovely of you." She went through the open door behind Morgan and down the hall. Ellery felt a stab of misgiving. Would Nina be all right? Should she offer to follow her? They weren't supposed to be alone.

"It's nice that Nat is letting us use the spa," Morgan said. "I guess they figured that moving the massage table through the rain to the Main House or somewhere would be too much of a hassle. Of course, we're only using this foyer, the dressing rooms, and one massage room. Which is a shame, because the steam room is to *die* for." She grinned, apparently unaware of any irony. "Did you guys get to try it?"

"No," Ravi said, "but we did use the sauna before they cut off the power."

"Ooh, nice," Morgan said. "I didn't go in there because. You know." She patted her baby bump. "I actually didn't use the steam room either, but Madd did, and he said it was next level. And I took a peek."

"At Madd or at the steam room?" Ravi asked, and Morgan cracked up.

"This really is so nice of you," Ellery said.

"It's no problem," Morgan said. "I loved being a massage therapist. Seriously. But being a LikeMe influencer pays a lot better."

"How did you and Maddox meet?" Ravi asked. "Wait, let me guess. High school sweethearts? Where did you two grow up?"

"Just a small Midwestern town!" Morgan said brightly. Ellery was caught off guard by the forced sound of Morgan's voice, the way her expression seemed to shutter. She'd always been so open about everything. Ellery saw from Ravi's raised eyebrows that it had surprised him, too.

Before any of them could say anything else, Nina came back into the room wearing one of the sumptuous white resort robes and rubbery black spa sandals. "I'm ready."

"Perfect." Morgan gestured for Nina to follow her. Their footsteps padded down the hall. "You get all comfortable on the table," Morgan was saying. "I'll knock and make sure you're ready before I come inside. Speak up a little so that I can hear you." A door opened, closed. A pause. A murmur, a door opening and closing again.

"That was weird, right?" Ravi asked, sitting down on one of the curved-edge sofas near the candle-strewn coffee table. "What I wouldn't give to be able to do a deep dive on the backstory of Morg and Madd right now."

"It *was* odd," Ellery agreed. She was thirsty, so she stood up and walked over to where there were small glasses and a giant clear dispenser with a pillar of what looked to be amethyst inside. It was probably supposed to be infusing the water with certain properties. *How about peace and calm and instant rescue helicopters*, she thought. Ellery filled a cup for herself and one for Ravi, handing it to him as she sat down. "It was almost like she was reading a script."

"If she's the murderer, I didn't see that coming," Ravi said.

"Me either." Ellery took a sip of her drink. Was she easily suggestible, or did it actually taste like rocks? And should she mention that she'd seen Maddox earlier in the day, looking—what? Tired? Upset? They were *all* tired and upset.

"Maybe Morgan's a mastermind," Ravi mused, "and she'll use the massages to get everyone to talk. And then she'll solve the murders."

"People don't normally talk during massages, do they?"

"No," Ravi said.

"That's what I thought," Ellery said. "But it's been a minute." The last time she'd had a massage was…four years ago? Yes. It had been their sixteenth anniversary, and she and Luke had gotten a couples massage at a spa downtown. They'd never had one before and at first they'd looked across at each other, grinning and giggling, but then they'd both gone into relaxation mode (and in Luke's case, she suspected, to sleep). Afterward, rested and loose-muscled, they'd gone to get hamburgers and shakes and slid into the same side of the booth together, holding hands. Her chest clenched. It was before everything had really gotten tough, before Luke had started threatening to get an apartment and before the accident. But, according to Luke now, he hadn't been happy even then.

"So," Ravi said. "What did you accomplish in our time apart?"

"Not nearly as much as you did," Ellery said. "You canvassed the whole restaurant and got people to sign up to give lectures and massages and who knows what else, and you *also* made friends with Rachel."

"I don't know if we're friends," Ravi said. "But I sat with her, and we are officially acquaintances now."

"Did she say where Olivia was?"

"She did not," Ravi said. "And I did hint around trying to find out. But I learned something interesting. Olivia's father isn't her father."

"What?"

"I mean, he is," Ravi said. "He adopted her when he married Catherine. Olivia was five. But her biological father was never in the picture."

"Rachel told you all that?"

"Yes," Ravi said. "She's not a fan. Of this dad, I mean. I mentioned that he didn't seem to be all that involved in the wedding and she said yes, that was typical. That he has always been, and I quote, a placeholder."

"Ouch," Ellery said.

"Let's go get into our robes." Ravi stood. "I don't want to waste any time. These are only thirty-minute massages."

"Still generous," Ellery said.

"Oh, for sure," Ravi agreed.

Ellery walked into the women's dressing room. The tiles were cold against her bare feet when she stepped out of her boots and socks. She imagined that wasn't always the case. The floors probably had radiant heating that was usually turned on. The wood-paneled walls were a beautiful warm color that reminded her of the sauna. She folded up her shirt and jeans, took off her bra and folded that too, and put them all in a locker. On a whim, she powered up her phone to see if by some miracle there was service in this part of the resort. The screen lit up and she hoped, prayed, there would be something. Just one little bar. *"Please-pleaseplease,"* she said, but there was nothing. No cell service, no Wi-Fi. She'd have to trust that the resort's plan of having the police call out to update the guests' loved ones on the situation was working. Ellery powered down her phone and put it in the locker on top of her shirt, closing the door. The lockers were made of the same golden wood as the walls, only their locks and seams giving them away.

Should she even bother locking up her things? She sat down for a moment, overwhelmed by a small decision as she sometimes had been the past few years. In the dim light, she leaned her head against the smooth wooden paneling.

No one was screaming anymore. The students were keening or whimpering, animal sounds that went to Ellery's heart, to the marrow in every one of her bones. But better this, she thought, than if they were all silent. She reached to unbuckle her seat belt, to get out and get them out. Her fingers were stiff and strange (later, she would learn that four of them were broken, snapped when she had pressed them against the seat in front of her at some point during the fall, trying to brace against the further impacts as the bus rolled) and it took her a moment to figure out the latch. Once she had, she gripped the seat (she was still not feeling pain) and anchored herself, looking both ways as she moved for the aisle, as if she were about to cross the street. The bus was upright again. Later, she would learn it had rolled twice.

Oh, God.

Abby was okay, she saw. Her friend was standing in the aisle, talking on the phone to emergency responders, her forehead streaming blood. Coach Solomon had been thrown to the front of the bus. He hadn't been strapped in. She couldn't look.

Pete was still in his seat. The front windshield was shattered, and his body was limp and twisted to the side, his head at a terrible angle. Blood everywhere. Glass all around, like shards of ice. Some were in his arms—she could see from the blood—

And then she turned around.

Ellery sat upright.

She *should* be careful, what with a possible murderer on the loose, so she locked up her things and put the tiny brass key in the pocket of her robe. As she headed for the exit, she caught sight of herself in the floor-to-ceiling mirror near the door and both her reflected surroundings and she herself looked strange. *Where the hell was she? Was this actually her life?* She was reminded again of the mirror in her room. It had to have been there before. If it had been a painting, she'd remember that, wouldn't she?

Her mind had been so overwhelmed the past few years. And especially these last few months.

She and Ravi had been back in the reception area for only a few minutes before Nina came out, looking blissful.

"She says to give her five minutes, and then head on back," Nina told Ellery.

"How was it?" Ravi asked Nina.

"I'm never joking about Morgan again," Nina said, in a low and heartfelt voice. "And if she's the murderer, I feel like she probably had a very sound reason and I'd never testify against her."

"She's that good?" Ravi asked.

Nina nodded, rolling her shoulders. "I swear she got rid of that knot I've had for five years."

"I know that knot," Ravi said. "You talk about that thing nonstop."

"We need to protect Morgan at all costs," Nina said. "I don't like the idea of her being alone in that massage room with the groomsmen or whoever. Or anyone but one of the three of us. Or Maddox, of course."

"Ellery and I have been wondering if *Morgan's* the murderer," Ravi said. "Maybe we're the ones in danger."

"I highly, highly doubt that," said Nina. "My money is not on the cheerful pregnant blond with the super-capable husband."

"Goodness," said Ravi. "Next thing we know, you'll be following Morg&Madd on LikeMe. That massage really converted you."

"He's not my type," Nina said. "But you can't deny the attractiveness of absolute competency." She smiled. "And if I'm totally honest, I think I was converted back when they were dancing."

"If Maddox is so capable, *he* might be the murderer," Ravi said. "A capable murderer would be the *worst*."

Morgan appeared in the doorway and Ellery flushed. Had she overheard what they were saying?

"Come on back," she said.

"Thank you again," Nina said. "That was transcendent."

Morgan laughed and led Ellery down the hall to the massage room. Once she was alone, Ellery took off her robe and climbed onto the table, settling herself face down into the pillow and pulling the crisp sheet and soft blanket over her. The lighting was low and restful, and the white-noise machine sent soothing ocean sounds throughout the room. Ellery felt as if she'd climbed inside a gentle cocoon, or as if she were a long-ago insect that had landed in a pool of tree sap and had decided, *Oh well, this isn't so bad, I'll just let myself be preserved in amber.*

"All set?" Morgan asked, from outside the door.

"Yes."

Morgan entered quietly. She walked over to the white-noise machine and adjusted it slightly. *How much electricity does that thing use?* Ellery wondered. *What about these lights? They seem pretty dim, but every watt has to count. Were* electrical units actually measured in watts?

"The essential oils they have here are *great*," Morgan said. "Super-high quality. Which one do you want?"

Ellery turned her head so that she could see the little wooden box full of amber vials that Morgan was holding. "Um," she said. "I don't know. Lavender?"

"Here," Morgan said. "Close your eyes. I'll put a few of them under your nose to smell, and you tell me which one you respond to the most."

Ellery breathed in. *Too spicy. Too sweet. Too powerful.* "That one," she said at last. Something had zinged inside her at the scent. It was citrusy, not too sweet, reminding her of being outside and being okay. "That one for sure."

"Bergamot," Morgan said. "Okay. Hold on one sec." She took the oil and settled on a stool at the head of the table. She dropped a few drops onto the face pillow. "Go ahead and lie face down again," she told Ellery. She obliged, turning her head back into the pillow.

Morgan's hands were warm and strong. The ocean waves from the white-noise machine crested and fell. The bergamot smelled like home and far away at the same time. "Breathe in deep," Morgan said.

Ellery did. Her chest felt tight and knotted. She could hear how shallow her breath sounded.

"Again," Morgan said. Her voice was kind. "Deeper, if you can. Try doing it three times." Her hands were still moving along Ellery's back and shoulders, and Ellery felt like her muscles were drinking in the touch, trying to send it to every nerve ending in her body.

It had been so long since anyone had touched her. It felt absolutely wonderful. She took a deep breath, another.

And then she began to cry.

It was quiet crying, but unmistakable. Her shoulders moved up and down in the shuddering, deep motion of silent sobs. Her tears were streaming into the pillow. Her throat ached.

"I'm sorry," she told Morgan, her voice muffled by the face pillow. "I'm really sorry."

"It's all right." Morgan's voice was almost impossibly gentle. "This happens a lot." She moved her hands up to Ellery's shoulders, smoothing away the tension, the pressure exactly right. "I'll keep going," she said. "You keep breathing. You keep crying. Does that sound okay?"

"Yes," Ellery said. "Thank you."

Ellery apologized again at the end of the massage.

"Seriously, it's no big deal," Morgan said. "That was one of the parts I loved most about the job. Not that people cried or felt sad, I mean. Just that what I was doing really helped them." She smiled. "Of course, sometimes, people were pervs."

"I hope no one's like that here," Ellery said.

"They'd never," Morgan said. "Not with Maddox around."

Right then the ocean sounds flickered, stopped. The light disappeared. Out in the waiting area, Ellery heard exclamations, then quiet.

"Shit," Morgan said. "The power's out."

29.

Ellery and Morgan made their way down the dark hall and back to the waiting room. "Don't worry," Morgan was saying. "I'm sure Maddox will get things running again in no time."

In the candlelit waiting room, Ravi and Nina were sitting together on one of the sofas. As soon as Ravi saw them, he called out, "No power! Can you believe this?"

"I cannot," another voice said dryly from within the waiting room.

Two other people were sitting on the second sofa. It took Ellery a few more steps into the room to recognize Olivia—*so Olivia was safe and accounted for, thank goodness*—and Catherine. Both women had their hair pulled back and they were wearing leggings and pullovers, Catherine's a light-colored cashmere turtleneck, Olivia's a sweatshirt emblazoned with STANFORD UNIVERSITY. Their boots and coats had been left in the foyer, and two additional umbrellas dripped onto the tray surrounding the bucket where they'd been placed.

The low, flickering light of the candles played across the two women's faces. Seeing mother and daughter together, Ellery could better note the differences. When she'd mistaken Olivia for Catherine on the side path near the *Love* sculpture, they hadn't been side by side. While the Haring women *did* look alike, and their frames were similar—slight and graceful—their faces were not a younger version and an older version of each other. Olivia's eyes were larger, her mouth more full. Catherine's cheekbones were higher, her eyebrows shaped differently.

"Don't worry," Morgan said cheerfully. "We can keep doing massages for now. I don't need a ton of light for them. I'll take a couple of these candles into the other room. Ravi's next, but you two are right after. We should be able to get you in before it gets too cold."

"You ladies go ahead," Ravi said. "I certainly don't need a massage more than you do, given the circumstances." He moved for the coat pegs near the door without waiting for Catherine and Olivia to respond. "I'll go back with Ellery. Nina?"

"I'll stay," Nina said. "So you have someone with you, Morgan. You know, the buddy system and all that."

"Oh!" Morgan said, sounding surprised. "Right. That would be great. Thank you." She looked over at Catherine and Olivia. "Who wants to go first?"

Catherine looked at her daughter. "I will," Olivia said, reaching for one of the candles. "Should I bring this back with me for more light?"

"Sure," Morgan said. "I think they've got a couple of others around here. Let me look."

"I'll help." Nina got to her feet. "And we have those flashlights in our emergency packs that we can use." Catherine followed suit.

Ellery and Ravi slung their packs over their shoulders, pulled up their hoods, and opened the door.

The incessant sound of rain engulfed them immediately. Even though the waterlogged, late afternoon light wasn't bright by any means, Ellery still found herself squinting into the day after the darkness of the spa.

"I feel like a college kid," Ravi said, shrugging his on. "It's been years since I've worn one of these."

"I actually wear one a lot," Ellery said. "You give up on style when you're a teacher. It's all about ergonomics and practicality. What do you usually carry? Some kind of Italian leather shoulder bag?"

"Yes," Ravi said. "Which would get ruined instantly in this rain, so." He paused. "Interesting that Olivia and Catherine are getting massages and walking around the resort when two of their party are dead."

"Maybe they figure the worst has already happened."

"The worst has never already happened." Ravi nodded to another backpacked, be-slickered, and booted figure walking past them, and Ellery said hello. The man nodded back, and Ellery recognized him as someone she'd seen in the restaurant but never spoken to.

"Do you know him?" she asked Ravi as they went on.

"Nope," he said. "Just one of the guests I've seen around."

"How many massages does Morgan have scheduled, anyway?" Ellery asked. "Is she going to spend all of her time in the spa working for free?"

"Oh, we figured that out already," Ravi said. "We're going to say there were limited spots available. And now, with the power going out"—he shrugged—"she can cancel them all."

"That's good," Ellery said. "No way should she have to give the groomsmen massages."

"Except for Andy," Ravi said. "He's a decent human being. He's also the odd man out for sure."

"Poor Andy," Ellery said.

"You know how you meet someone and trust them instantly?" Ravi asked. "Even if you realize later that you probably shouldn't trust anyone, like if you're trapped at a resort and people keep dying?"

"Yes."

"That's Morgan for me," he said. "Even though she acted weird when I asked about her background. I still trust her. And it's Andy for you, isn't it."

"I think so," she said. "Or maybe Olivia."

"*Two* people?" Ravi said. "Okay, I also trust Grace."

"I get that," Ellery said. "She's great."

"Yeah," Ravi said. "But it's possible that you and I are too trusting. We should be more like Nina. Although, wait. She's all about Morgan and Maddox. See? Even she's not immune."

"I mean, the massage *was* amazing," Ellery said. "I'm sorry you didn't get one."

"That's all right," Ravi said, swinging his flashlight. "Hey. Do you think Nat realized she was giving us potential murder weapons when she handed these out? I'm no outdoorsman or whatever, but I can tell these things are state of the art. Maybe if you used enough force?"

Ellery flinched. She hadn't thought of that.

"They could also be weapons of defense," she said, trying to keep her tone light. "If someone came at us with *their* flashlight, maybe we could, like, swordfight them off."

"I'll have to practice my parrying skills," Ravi said. He held the flashlight out in front of him, feinting a move at one of the resigned, soaked-through trees that lined the path. Then he lifted it toward Ellery, as if daring her to fend him off. She laughed, but her heart panged, thinking of Ethan and Kate doing this when they were small with whatever they could find. Sticks from the yard, pool noodles, the skewers they were supposed to be roasting marshmallows with. Almost anything could be turned into a weapon.

"Oops," Ravi said, pulling up short. "This is me." They'd arrived at the guest suite with the name *Willow* on its discreet wooden sign.

"Okay," Ellery said. "See you at dinner?"

"Wait," Ravi said. "Chivalry demands that I walk you back to your door. Also, Nat demands it. Buddy system. Can't leave you out there alone, possibly getting flashlight-murdered."

"But then you'd be alone and I'd have to walk *you* back, according to Nat," Ellery said. "This could go on for hours."

"Or we could shack up together," Ravi suggested. "I'm a cuddler, though. You'd hate sleeping with me."

Ellery laughed. "Seriously, I'm fine," she said. "My room is super close. As you know."

"Oh, good," Ravi said. "Because I actually *don't* know. Even though I've been there before. I mean, logically, I'm aware that your room is near. Experientially, too, since I've walked there before. But I get turned around *alllll* the time here. Is your room that way?" He pointed.

"That way," she said, pointing in the other direction.

"Ugh," Ravi said. "Okay, got it. You're to the left of me when I come out my door. For some reason I always turn right when I come out of any room at any resort or hotel. I always think everything will be to my right. Even though I *know* that's impossible."

Ellery was laughing. "I'm the same way," she said. "I get it."

"I'll come and pick you up for dinner," Ravi said. "Now that I remember where you are."

"Perfect."

The lights above them flickered. Windows bloomed golden in the oncoming dusk.

"Oh, look," Ravi said. "Perfect timing."

30.

There was a note on her door.

Who would have left it there?

Ellery hesitated, glancing over her shoulder. No one. The paper was folded in half and stuck on with Scotch tape. She plucked it from the door and went inside her room, waiting until she'd heard the click of the latch behind her before she opened the note.

Memorial tonight after dinner, it said, in neat handwriting. *Please join us at 8.* There was no signature, but the penmanship was neat, almost blocky.

Who was the note from, and why hadn't they signed their names? Ellery didn't think it would be any of the groomsmen. She'd only talked to Matt, and he was gone. Andy? Olivia? She'd never seen their handwriting, so it could be either of them. Had Olivia left it on her way to the spa for her massage? Catherine certainly wouldn't have invited Ellery to anything.

Several hours later, she slipped from the restaurant into the breezeway, which remained slick and puddled, despite the staff's best efforts. Dinner had been a more formal affair than lunch, the food served in silver dishes rather than brown boxes, the whole setup slightly reminiscent of Saturday night's wedding feast (though there was, of course, no question of it being served on the terrace in this weather). Ellery, Ravi, and Nina had sat together near the back, with

Ravi whispering that they should split up and get to know other people after dinner but that they'd earned the right to eat a meal together. Ellery hadn't told him or Nina about the note on her door. She wasn't entirely certain why.

After dinner, Grace and Gary were hosting a discussion on who was the most likely team to win the World Series this year and, judging by the amount of people who seemed to be sticking around after the meal, it was going to be well attended. Ravi and Nina both lingered behind, talking to the other guests gathering where the staff were serving tea and dessert. For a moment, everything seemed civilized and under control. But only if you didn't look too closely at the shadows under the staff's eyes, the nervous gestures of the guests, the way the rain came down outside, still relentless.

Ellery was headed for the Main House, which was lit up for the memorial the groomsmen had arranged for Ben and Matt. The light was yellow orange through the windows, shades drawn. As she came closer, she noticed the groomsmen's silhouettes and heard one starting what sounded like a college fight song, the others joining in. Ellery wasn't familiar with it.

She pushed open the door. Canyon was sitting at the front desk in the reception area, looking grim.

"Hi," she said. "How are you doing?"

"I'm babysitting," he said, though that wasn't quite what she'd asked.

"I'm sorry," she said, but he was the obvious choice for the assignment. He was physically strong enough to overpower any of the groomsmen if they got drunk, which wasn't the case with Nat or Brook, who were both slight. "The memorial's in there, right? For Ben and Matt?" Ellery glanced over at the doorway that went through to the social room.

"Yeah." Canyon looked surprised. "Do you need to go in?"

She held out the note. "I'm not sure? I found this on my door, and I don't know about any other service or anything." Canyon took the paper from her and read it. His brow furrowed, then cleared.

"That's probably from the bride or the groom's buddy, the hiker guy," Canyon said. He snapped his fingers. "Andy. They're doing their own thing."

"Oh." What, exactly, did that mean?

"They're in the staff lounge." Canyon swiveled his chair and gestured in the direction of the gray-shingled building she and Ravi had been in earlier when they'd helped with housekeeping. "We're heating that building anyway. They brought their own drinks. All I really had to do was unlock the door and leave them to it." He tipped his head toward the social room. "Unlike this crew."

"You're all handling this very well," she said sincerely. "The staff, I mean."

"It's going to get worse." Canyon's warm brown eyes were tired but alert, attuned to what was going on around him. "I know two people have died and there's been a mudslide and that's pretty bad already. But everything hasn't fully hit us yet. You know? Tomorrow we're going to have to move guests into different rooms to conserve energy, which is going to make people mad. The food's not going to be as fancy. At some point the power will probably go out for good. Everything's going to hit the fan for real."

"Have you been at Broken Point during a disaster before?" Ellery asked. He seemed young to have been there for the last major mudslide, but it wasn't impossible.

"No," he said. "But my oldest brother worked here during the 2017 slide. He told me what it was like. And that was without any random or, you know, not-random deaths." The handheld radio on his desk crackled unintelligibly, then fell silent.

"Sorry." Canyon looked up at Ellery, his lips pressed together ruefully. "Shouldn't have told you all that about moving rooms and the power going out eventually. Nat and Brook would be pissed." The veneer was coming off Canyon, the carefully overlaid luxury-resort-employee facade eroding and his direct, plain-speaking personality coming through. Ellery liked him more for it. She appreciated it when people knew when to drop the pretense.

"Don't worry about it," she said. "I'll go to the staff lounge for the memorial, if that's okay?"

Canyon nodded. She walked behind the reception desk and out the back way, a nagging feeling that something was off catching at the periphery of her mind.

The door to the staff and housekeeping area was closed, but the windows at the front of the building glowed with light. She lifted her hand and, after a moment's hesitation, knocked.

She heard murmuring behind the door. Footsteps. The door swung open.

She'd thought Olivia's family might be there as well, but it was only Andy and Olivia, plus Rachel, who'd opened the door. They were all wearing oversized white sweatshirts with a photo printed on the front. Ellery couldn't quite make out what it was, but it was the same photo on each shirt, showing what looked like a toddler in a Halloween costume. They'd pulled three armchairs around a coffee table, and several six-packs of some kind of pale ale were sitting in the middle of the table. Their raincoats dripped from pegs near the door, and their boots had been muddily but neatly lined up in the boot tray. Both Andy and Olivia appeared red-eyed and exhausted, as if they'd been crying. They also looked surprised to see Ellery.

Rachel ushered Ellery through the door, letting it swing shut firmly behind them. "Hey," she said. "I'm glad you figured it out. I realized later I forgot to sign the note."

"What note?" Olivia asked.

"I left a note on her door inviting her to come," Rachel said, dragging over a fourth armchair to add to the grouping. She reached for another bottle from the six-packs. The packaging showed a leaping fish in bright colors.

"Ben's favorite," Andy said, indicating the beer. "Feel free to have one. We're not here to get plastered. We're here to honor him. Share memories."

"Oh," Ellery said, feeling staggeringly out of place. She didn't sit down. "I really—I only came because—"

"We're wearing these sweatshirts because this is the cutest picture ever," Olivia said. She sat back and straightened out the front of her shirt so Ellery could better see the photo. It was a baby Ben,

Ellery realized, a chubby-cheeked toddler looking extremely serious and wearing a penguin costume, sitting on a lawn covered in autumn leaves.

"It is," Ellery agreed. Her heart panged. There was nothing she loved more than a baby or a small child in a Halloween costume. Either they were nonplussed and hilarious, unaware that they were dressed as a penguin, a pea in a pod, a bear, a pumpkin, or they *believed* they were whatever they were costumed as, that there was a chance webs would come shooting out of their wrists while they were wearing their Spider-Man suit, that the magic wand they were carrying *would* work, that people *did* see an adorable flightless bird right in front of them, before their very eyes.

If only wanting could make things happen.

"I had them made as a joke for everyone in the wedding party to wear when they saw us off on our honeymoon," Olivia said. "So now I have a box of Ben's face staring back at me. I'm making Andy and Rachel take a couple. Do you want one?" She made a sound that was half laugh, half sob. "Of course you don't." Olivia covered her face with her hands, folding a bit in half, a move reminiscent of the way she'd been curled up under that tree the night of the wedding. "You didn't even know him."

"I'm so sorry," Ellery said. She looked from Andy to Rachel, and then moved toward the door. "I wasn't sure who'd invited me, and I didn't want to seem rude. But I don't really—"

"We're also here to figure out how he died," Rachel said. "That's why I invited you."

"Rachel." Olivia lifted her face, the grief so raw Ellery wanted to turn away. "She already told us everything she knew."

Ellery gripped the door handle. She hadn't, though. When she'd spoken with Andy and Olivia earlier, she'd never mentioned the back of Ben's head. But surely that didn't matter? Wouldn't Andy and Olivia have noticed the injury when they went to identify the body?

"Stay." Rachel was more than a couple of beers in, Ellery could tell, but the bridesmaid's eyes were clear and her voice authoritative.

But Ellery rebelled against the almost-command. "Thank you, but

I'll be going," she said, turning the door handle, opening the small, sorrow-soaked room to the rain and the smell of vegetation under siege, earth that could not possibly absorb one more drop. She would not be one of those people, the ghouls who hung around tragedy, trying to smell it out, hoping to roll in the scent so they could have some of it on them to signal that they were important, too. Trying to make any tiny thing they knew about the event or the people involved into something essential, themselves bigger and more attached than they actually were. *The grief humpers*, Abby called them. *They get off emotionally on the trauma of other people. They want to be around it.* There had been plenty of them after the accident.

"No, please," Olivia said. Ellery turned to see Olivia getting out of her chair, a bottle of water in hand, shoulders straight. "Actually, it would be great if you stayed. I was surprised, that's all. And I feel bad that we keep asking you about finding him. That had to have been awful."

Andy stood, too, again offering Ellery a drink.

"No, thanks," she said, uncertain—not about the beer, but about what she should do. Stay here with them, or go back alone?

And were *they* being entirely honest with her? Ellery wondered, briefly, if someone in here—one alone, or all three of them together—already knew what had happened to Ben, and who had done it. Maybe they were trying to find out what she knew so they could decide if they were safe. In that case, it would be better for her not to say anything about Ben's body beyond what she'd already told them.

Ellery remembered what Matt had said at lunch on Sunday morning. She wasn't suspicious of Olivia. But should she be?

Ellery walked over to the armchair without removing her boots or coat. She dropped her backpack to the floor and sat down. She'd noticed that no one else in the room seemed to have brought their packs with them, at least not that she could see. Her chair faced Olivia.

"There are two people dead now," Rachel said bluntly. "And we're trapped. We need to figure this out."

"I really don't know anything more than I told you," Ellery said, looking at Olivia and Andy.

"That's not true," Rachel said.

Ellery blinked.

"You and your friends have been trying to solve the mystery," Rachel said. "And between the three of you, you're bound to unearth something. I like Ravi. He's great. But I don't trust that guy any farther than I can throw him. *You* have that PTA mom look about you."

"Thanks," Ellery said flatly.

"It's a compliment," Rachel said. "A face like that can get you anywhere. And I bet it has. People talk to you, don't they?"

"Rachel," Olivia said wearily.

"It's fine," Ellery said. "They do. Even when I wish they wouldn't."

Andy looked surprised at the retort, but Rachel laughed. "Fair."

"We *are* trying to figure out what happened," Ellery said. "Obviously, we're not as directly affected by everything as you are, but we're still stuck here and we're still sorry that Ben died."

"I get it one hundred percent," Rachel said. "I'd be doing the same."

Someone pounded on the door. Ellery jumped, startled, but the others didn't flinch nearly as much as she did. "I was wondering when he'd show up," Rachel said, getting to her feet. She had just begun to open the door when whoever it was started knocking again. Rachel pulled the door the rest of the way open, so the person on the outside practically fell into the room with his first raised high.

"Whoops!" One of the groomsmen caught himself up short. "Sorry about that. I thought you didn't hear me knock the first time."

"Patience," Rachel said, "is a virtue. But thanks for coming, Trevor."

"Rachel." Trevor inclined his head in the sort of faux-southern gentleman style that Ellery hated very, very much. He had swoopy gold-brown hair and a deep tan. "Olivia. Andy." He bowed to each of them in turn. When his gaze landed on Ellery, he looked puzzled for a moment. Then he said, *"Oh.* The body finder. Nice to see you."

31.

In spite of the falling through the door and the tasteless way he'd addressed her, Trevor did not seem drunk to Ellery. Instead, he almost seemed to be acting the part because he wasn't sure how else to be.

"How are things going over there at the bro memorial?" Rachel asked.

"Pretty shitty." Trevor took off his coat and sat on the arm of Rachel's chair. She drew away slightly, but he didn't seem to notice. "Everyone keeps asking where you are." Trevor pointed at Andy. "You should come back with me."

"Thanks, but I'm good here."

"I know some of the guys were being jerks before the wedding, acting like you were the outsider or whatever, man, but we both know you weren't." Trevor's voice was fervent, reminding Ellery of the way Matt had spoken in the restaurant the day before he died. Trevor appealed to the rest of the small group—Ellery, Rachel, Olivia. "This guy knows Ben better than the rest of us did. That goes for you, too," he said, now pointing at Olivia. "If any of us think we knew Ben better than this man right here, that's ego talking. Don't you think?"

"Yes," Olivia said, after an infinitesimal pause that bespoke thought, rather than hesitation or a lie.

Rachel and Andy exchanged a look between them, something loaded but not romantic, it seemed to Ellery.

"We're trying to figure out who would want to kill Ben," Rachel said.

"Could have been you," Trevor said. "Because he was stealing your best friend or whatever."

"Olivia's my *cousin*," Rachel said impatiently. "She's family. She can't ever be stolen from me."

"Right, right," Trevor said, nodding. "Blood is thicker than wine."

"Water," Rachel said.

"Whatever," Trevor said. "That just gives you another motive. Would you *kill* for your family?"

"We're not in a shit mafia movie, Trevor," Olivia said. "Ben's dead, and we didn't kill him, and we're trying to figure it out. Would you like to help us, or should we also accuse you of wanting to kill him so that everything's nice and fair, and then we can give up on having a conversation that might actually be useful?"

The quick change in Trevor's face surprised Ellery. "You're right," he said. "We can all think whatever we want to think. But we should try to figure this out. And we can't forget Matt. Matt died, too." His face crumpled.

"Let's start with Ben because he was the first, and because three of us actually saw his body." Rachel's tone was softer than it had been before. "Olivia and Andy had to identify him, and Trevor, this is Ellery. Like you said, she's the one who found him."

"Sorry I didn't get your name earlier," Trevor told Ellery.

"Don't worry about it."

"Trevor, do you know if there was anything going on with Ben's work?" Rachel asked. "We can't think of anyone who would have a personal reason to hurt Ben. He was too…Ben."

"I know what you mean," Trevor said. "That's why I think it's a serial killer. Targeting young guys or something."

"It's not impossible," Rachel said. "But again. What about work?"

"I wouldn't know," Trevor said. "Ben and I both ended up in San Francisco, but it's not like we're at the same firm. I mean, it always seemed like he was doing well. Not that he bragged about it or anything." He sighed. "Most people get into investment banking because they want to make a lot of money. Ben got into it for that, sure. He liked nice stuff. And he really wanted to be able to take care of himself. But also because he was smart. It fascinated him in ways I don't think the rest of us really understood. And he took on smaller clients on the side, people who didn't have a lot of money and weren't sure how to manage what they did have. Immigrants, people he thought were interesting and wanted to help. He told his company that they had to let him freelance, too, and they wanted him bad enough that they agreed." He glanced at Olivia. "But I'm sure you know all that."

She nodded. "Yeah."

"Maybe one of these clients on the side had a problem with him or something?" Rachel asked.

"I don't think so." Trevor shifted, considering. "Ben stayed far away from anything shady. He's always been like that. Hasn't he?" Trevor appealed to Andy, who nodded.

"So no drugs or anything, probably," Rachel said.

"I keep *telling* you," Olivia said, her voice exhausted and exasperated. "Ben never would have gotten involved with anything like that. Because that's not who he was, and because of what happened to his parents." She glanced at Ellery. "Ben's parents were killed by a guy who was driving on the wrong side of the road. He was high."

"Maybe there is some kind of connection between the deaths, even if it's not a serial killer," Ellery said. "Do you know who the last person was to see either of them alive?"

"The guys and I have been talking about that," Trevor said. "We were all staying in our own rooms, which was insane, because this place is expensive as hell. But none of us really wanted to share because there's only one bed in each room." He glanced over at Olivia. "Your mom got us that discount for it being off-season, which was cool. But still, you know."

"I know," Olivia said. "That's part of why we had the wedding now. October's a slower time of year in Big Sur, so you can get off-season rates. And the weather is usually still good." She sighed. "That didn't prove true, obviously. And my mom loved the show they have up in the gallery right now. She thought it would be a perfect backdrop for the cocktail hour, plus if the weather wasn't good enough to hold the wedding ceremony outdoors, we could move it to the gallery."

"She really thought through every detail," Ellery said.

"And how," Rachel said dryly. "Too bad the weather didn't comply."

"Ben said it was easier to go along with whatever she wanted than to have an opinion," Trevor said.

So was there one small chink in Ben's armor of perfection? Ellery wondered. Was he not a fan of his mother-in-law, or, at the very least, of her taking over the wedding?

But Olivia didn't seem bothered. "She never really got to have a full wedding of her own. She and my dad weren't married, and when she and Rick got married, it was very practical."

"Ben said this whole thing was more for her than for either of you," Trevor said. Rachel and Andy exchanged another glance. Again, that interesting in syncness that Ellery had noticed earlier in the evening. *Should I tell him to shut up, or should you?* it seemed to say. But Olivia remained calm.

"Maybe," Olivia said. "You know how parents want to give their kids the things they didn't have? She was always doing that for me. By doing this wedding the way she wanted, I felt like I had a chance to give *her* the thing she didn't have." She sighed. "So I decided I didn't mind letting her plan the whole thing. But Ben did."

"Did you guys argue about it?" Ellery asked.

"Not really," Olivia said. "I could tell it was hard for Ben because I know him so well. But I shouldn't have pushed."

"You didn't push," Andy said. "He never once said that." He glared at Trevor, daring him to contradict, but Trevor was peeling the label off a bottle of beer and didn't catch the look.

"I know, but that makes it even worse," Olivia said. "I should have known better than to ask it of him. So Ben did what he usually did. He packed down his own feelings and went along with what was best for everyone else." As Olivia spoke the last sentence, she sounded furious, catching Ellery off guard. "He was always too selfless for his own good. He needed to stand up for himself now and then." Her voice broke. Anger, love, frustration, grief—they were all there, right at the edge.

"He *was* so damn selfless," Trevor said, looking up again. "You know how Jason's mom died and he hasn't been doing that well financially?"

Olivia nodded, her lips pressed tightly together.

"Ben covered the price of his room." Trevor shook his head. "Jason told us that tonight at the memorial. He was crying. Ben was such a good person. It doesn't make sense."

"Nothing about this makes any sense," Olivia said. "Not for Ben, not for Matt."

"So who was the last person to see each of them?" Rachel asked.

"We think it was me who saw Matt last," Trevor said. "Unless it was someone who wasn't in our group. He was in Huckleberry, I'm in Fir. They're next door to each other. We had a couple of drinks together last night after the other guys had gone back to their rooms. We were talking about Ben. How crazy it was. Matt was positive that Ben had been murdered. At that point, I was still thinking it had to be an accident."

"Did Matt say why he thought Ben might have been killed?" Rachel asked.

"Not really," Trevor said, scratching his head. "Not that I can remember."

"When did Matt leave your room?"

"I think it was around one."

"And he seemed..." Rachel prompted.

"He seemed not great," Trevor said. "He felt horrible about what had happened to Ben. Said he should have been able to keep him safe, since he was the best man and everything. He went on and on about the text that people got that said Ben wasn't coming." Trevor glanced at Olivia. "He thought someone hacked Ben's phone. He said no way would Ben have ever left you at the altar. And that even if he *had*, he would never have told you in a group text. No way."

"I agree," Rachel said.

"What did the text say?" Ellery couldn't help herself. They all turned to look at her. "If you don't mind my asking."

"I didn't get it," Trevor said. "He only sent it to Olivia and Matt, and Rachel, and Olivia's parents."

And Andy, Ellery thought. Rachel and Olivia both glanced at Andy, too, who shrugged, not bothering to correct Trevor.

"Ben's text said, *I can't do it. I'm sorry.*" Olivia closed her eyes. Everyone was quiet.

That's all? Ellery thought. Even though everyone (except Catherine) seemed to think that Ben was a really nice guy, she felt like calling off your wedding required more than six short words. Ben should have had so much more to say.

"I know," Olivia said, glancing at Ellery.

Are you angry? Ellery wondered. Olivia hadn't seemed angry the night of the almost-wedding, when she'd been curled up near the *Love* sculpture. She had seemed brokenhearted.

"Well, Matt didn't seem *depressed* or anything," Trevor said. "Not like he was going to jump off a cliff. If anything, he was pissed. Not literally. Yeah, he was a little drunk. But he was also motivated." Trevor shifted in his chair, reaching toward another pale ale. Across the table, Andy nudged the case closer to Trevor. "Like he had something on his mind." He twisted the top from the bottle with his bare hands, making Ellery wince. Wasn't it cutting into his skin? "I could be wrong. What is it they say? Hindsight is fifty-fifty, or whatever."

Twenty-twenty, Ellery thought.

"You didn't walk Matt back to his room?"

"No," Trevor said. "It's only a few steps away. And I think he did make it back to his room that night. Because he was wearing totally different clothes when they found him. He'd been wearing another shirt and pants when we were hanging out the night before."

"Who told you that?"

"*I* told me that," Trevor said, flatly. "When I saw him."

"Wait," Rachel said. "You saw Matt? *You* identified the body?"

"Not in person," Trevor said. "But Carlos and a couple of his guys went and moved Matt from where he was lying into a maintenance shed down there and locked it up. They said it was too risky to move him much farther because of the police eventually coming and needing to see the scene of the crime or whatever, but they felt like it was awful to leave him out there for who knows how long." He furrowed his brow. "They'd better not get in trouble for that. It was the right thing to do."

"I'm sure the police will understand." Ellery was sure of no such thing, but she agreed with Trevor. It seemed terrible to leave Matt out there in the rain, the elements and animals free to have at him.

"Nat showed me and the other guys some pictures they'd taken of Matt before they moved the body." Trevor swallowed, his Adam's apple moving up and down. "It was definitely him. The coat and boots were the same as what he'd had on the night before, but that made sense. We're all wearing that shit everywhere since the rain started. But his shirt and pants were different from last night."

"How did he...look?" Rachel asked.

"Dead." Trevor glanced over at Ellery, and a kind of sympathetic understanding flashed between them. "We have *got* to figure this out." He squinted, looking at Rachel, then Andy, then Olivia. "Wait. What the hell are you all wearing?"

32.

It's Ben when he was a baby," Rachel said briskly. "Olivia had them made for everyone to wear as a joke for when they left on their honeymoon." She jerked her head toward the boxes on the floor. "Help yourself. Take some back over to the memorial for the guys."

"Um, okay," Trevor said, but he made no move to do so. He seemed to settle, almost compress, deeper into the armchair, now that he knew what he was seeing. Baby Ben, before any of them (except maybe Andy?) had known him. Baby Ben, who was going to die when he was far too young.

"Okay," Ellery said. "If you're all thinking Ben might not have sent the text, then the question of who saw him last matters even more."

"Are you, like, an undercover detective or something?" Trevor asked Ellery.

"No."

He didn't look convinced. "You *did* find Ben's body. Maybe you had a tip? Someone told you where to look? Or that something was about to go down?" Their moment of understanding was gone. "Why else would you be staying at a resort like this by yourself? Are you holding out on us?" He leaned forward, glancing around wildly. "Are we in the middle of something that's bigger than we can even imagine?"

"Yes, in the sense that people are dying," Ellery said. "But I'm not a detective. I'm a high school teacher. I'm here alone because my husband and I just got divorced and we'd already paid for the trip."

"Well, hell." Trevor leaned back. "At least he isn't dead."

"There is that," Ellery agreed. "Can you walk me through the wedding schedule? You all know it, but I don't."

Rachel reached into her bag and handed Ellery a gold-edged card with a gilded drawing of a flower printed at the top. Ellery felt herself flush a bit as she read the first formal gathering on the list, for Friday night. *Cocktails and Hors d'Oeuvres at the Gallery at Broken Point.* The event she and Ravi had crashed, thinking it was daring and funny, with no idea of what lay ahead.

The next item on the schedule was *Rehearsal Brunch at the Slipstream Bar.* Ellery had seen pictures of the bar online. It was the repurposed Airstream trailer that had been restored to mint condition and tucked into the trees down on the other side of the hill from the ocean. In the photos, globe lights on strings looped from redwood to redwood, blooming against the soft greens and rusts and silvers of the trees, the foliage, the ground, the trailer. Groupings of redwood picnic tables—their planks smooth and soft in the filtered light—and Adirondack chairs, gathered around lower, circular tables, filled the clearing around the bar.

"And Ben was at the brunch," Ellery said, confirming.

"Yup," Trevor said. "We all did toasts and everything." He glanced over at Andy, who had missed the brunch. Ben had been a very understanding friend, she thought. To let one of his groomsmen do whatever he wanted on the day of the wedding until the ceremony seemed unusual. But then, Ben and Andy seemed unusual. The kind of deep understanding and acceptance that you often didn't see between men. Or brothers. Or anyone.

"I wasn't at the brunch." Andy glanced at Ellery. "I was on that hike. Ben told me all I had to do that day was show up in Ceremony Grove at the right time." His face clouded over. "I shouldn't have left. I should have been a better best man."

"Second-best man," Trevor said. "Matt was the best man."

"Sure," Andy said. "Right." His hands, Ellery noticed, had balled up into fists. It was the first time she'd noticed anything angry about him.

"But Ben wasn't pissed at you." Trevor seemed to realize how what he'd said could be taken. "He was glad you were out having fun. He was cool."

"I *know*," Andy said. The expression on his face wasn't one Ellery had seen before. It was stern, anger hovering right at the edge. "Because I'd already—" He stopped abruptly, his voice lowering. "Because I'd already been there for him."

"Yes," Rachel said. "You had."

"It *was* fine with Ben," Olivia said. She was looking at Ellery, as if she'd guessed Ellery's earlier thoughts. "He knows Andy. Toasts and big crowds and all of that—Andy hates that stuff." Her eyes flicked to Andy, then back to Ellery. "Ben's never loved it either, and he had to do so much of it for work. So he really did understand."

Ellery wished she'd had even one conversation with Ben. Learning about him from everyone else meant that she had to take other people at their word. She wondered what kind of descriptions her closest friends would give of her if they were asked. Would they know if she truly were fine with something? Was there anyone in her life who could see inside her anymore?

Abby, for sure. She wished Abby were here. Last time, that had made all the difference.

Ellery put her finger on the next item on the schedule and read it out loud.

"Wedding Ceremony, Ceremony Grove, Golden Hour."

Everyone was silent for a moment. The rain was still sheeting down outside in the pools of light cast by the exterior lights and from windows.

"I wish we'd never put 'golden hour' on the schedule," Olivia said at last. "My mom warned me about that. Everyone had to keep texting me about the time. I just thought it sounded so much prettier."

Ellery remembered Olivia telling her about the wedding being at golden hour when they'd spoken briefly on Friday night, and how Ellery herself had sighed. The words did have a lovely sound to them.

It was interesting that Catherine had let Olivia have her way in the phrasing rather than overriding her. "But Ben knew the actual time," Ellery said, making certain.

Olivia laughed, a sound without mirth. "Yes, Ben knew the time of the wedding."

Ellery bit her lip, embarrassed. "I didn't mean—"

"Even *Andy* knew the time of the wedding," Olivia said.

Andy flinched. Rachel and Trevor both looked at Olivia with surprise.

"Sorry." Olivia shook her head and met Ellery's gaze. "Everything is coming out wrong. I know you don't know Ben at all. So you couldn't know if he really was punctual, or what I'd told him, or anything. You only saw him dead. Gone, gone, gone." There was a bitter poetry in the repetition of *gone.* Ellery remembered how that was the word that had come to her mind, too, when she'd found Ben in the pool.

Olivia reached over and took Andy's hand, squeezing it briefly. "I'm sorry. You don't care about the little stuff. That's part of what Ben loved about you. And you always show up when you know it's important. *Always.*" Andy met her gaze. "Like you said. You'd already been there for him." She glanced over at Rachel. "You too."

A moment passed, and Ellery wanted again to leave. She'd been here long enough as an interloper. There were only a few more questions to ask. "So did anyone see Ben between the brunch and when the ceremony was supposed to take place?"

"I didn't," Olivia said. "We agreed to wait to see each other again until we were at the altar. It seemed romantic to do it that way, and besides, I had to get my hair done and all of that."

"I saw him after that," Trevor said. "Ben got us all matching cuff links to wear and he came over to our rooms to give them to us."

"Do you remember when that was?" Ellery asked.

"It was soon after we got back from the brunch," Trevor said. "I'll ask the other guys to make sure."

"How did he seem?"

"Good," Trevor said. "I mean, a little nervous or distracted or whatever. He was getting married, so of course he was."

"Did you see Ben then, too?" Ellery asked Andy.

"No," Andy said. "I wasn't with the other groomsmen until we walked over to the grove together."

"Ben didn't give you cuff links?" She felt pushy asking, digging down on such a small thing, but it seemed strange that Ben wouldn't have given Andy some as well.

"He'd already given me my gift," Andy said.

"Oh," Ellery said. "Because he knew you might be getting back late from the hike?"

"Right."

"Did you see him at all before the wedding, after the brunch?"

"I don't think so," Andy said. "Sorry."

Was he being deliberately obtuse? Ellery wondered. She remembered him coming out of the trees on that hike, startling her.

"Which room was Ben staying in?"

"He was in Yarrow," Olivia said. "It's next to me. I'm in Goldenrod. Rachel's on the other side of me, in Iris."

"None of you are staying in the cottages?"

"Only my parents," Olivia said. "I was using their cottage to get dressed and ready for the wedding, because it's larger. It's called Wildrose. My mom gets to stay there for free sometimes as payment for being the art curator on retainer. It's where they were delivering everything for the wedding, too. The flowers, things like that. *The bridal staging area.* That's what everyone kept calling it."

"So we don't know who saw Ben last," Ellery said. "Did anyone ever find his phone?"

"No," Olivia said. "It's not in his room. Nat looked. And she and Dr. Anand said it hadn't been with him when he was found. You didn't see it, did you?"

"No." Ellery frowned, trying to remember if she'd noticed anything on the deck next to the pool, or on any of the chairs. But it was no use. She'd only seen the body, the water.

"Before we all lost cell coverage, I tried to call it." Olivia swallowed. "It went straight to voice mail, every time."

"And they didn't find *anything* interesting in his room?"

"Just what you'd expect," Olivia said. "Clothes, stuff like that. His wallet was gone, and they haven't found it, either. The keys to our rental car were missing, too."

Rachel glanced at the others—Andy, Olivia, Trevor. It did sound like Ben had planned to leave the wedding, and the resort. But he hadn't.

And the suit. He was still wearing his suit. And the flower. Why hadn't he changed?

Was it simply that he was in a rush?

And why was he found here, at the resort, so many hours past golden?

Why hadn't he left?

Who hadn't let him leave?

Ellery read out the last item on the schedule. *"Dinner and Dancing on the Main House Terrace."*

Rachel snorted. "We all know how *that* turned out." She glared at Trevor. "You guys were total assholes. Especially Jason."

"And then, the rain," Ellery said.

"The weather was perfect," Rachel said. "Until it wasn't."

"You could actually say that about the whole day," Trevor said, struck by his own profundity.

Ellery quietly switched on her phone. She still carried it with her, out of habit and just in case. She was saving the charge and religiously topping it off whenever she was in her room (and the generator was functioning properly).

"Can I take a picture of the schedule?" Ellery asked. "To keep things straight in my mind?" She glanced down at her phone. Nothing from anyone. Zero bars, no Wi-Fi signal. They were still isolated.

"You can keep it," Rachel said. "I know the whole thing by heart."

"Are you the one who put the schedule together?" Ellery tucked the card into the front pocket of her backpack. Perhaps that had been one of Rachel's bridesmaid duties.

Rachel snorted. "You think Catherine would let me be in charge of something as important as the schedule?" she said. "Plus, I'd already—" She stopped short, at a glance from Olivia. Rachel's face flushed slightly, the most discomfited Ellery had ever seen her look. "Already made my peace with that," Rachel said. "I get it. Weddings are a big deal for people. Especially when it's your daughter."

Ellery wondered why Rachel had seemed slightly flustered, what the glance between her and the bride meant. Olivia was quite open about the fact that she would have preferred something smaller and that Catherine was running the show. She'd told Ellery, a stranger, as much on the first night when they'd encountered each other at the gallery. Olivia, at least, had been resigned to doing things the way her mother had wanted.

But had Ben?

There was true exhaustion in the slope of Olivia's shoulders again. She was rallying and then flagging, a pattern Ellery knew well.

"Who would hurt Ben?" Olivia asked. "It doesn't make sense."

"It does feel like it has to be a case of wrong place, wrong time." Rachel's voice was gentle.

Involuntarily, Ellery winced at the phrase. How many times had she heard those exact words, after? *If we'd only left a little earlier, or a little later, or if the truck driver hadn't been so tired, or if we could have seen farther down the road…*

"Well," Trevor said, "I'd better get back." He stood, reaching for one of the sweatshirts. "I'll take this, if the offer's still open."

"Of course," Olivia said. "Take a couple more for the other guys, if you want."

Trevor reached into the box and took out several more shirts, tucking them under his arm.

Andy stood too. "I'll walk you over to the Main House."

Trevor guffawed. "You think I need you to hold my hand?" He realized he hadn't put on his coat and set the shirts down on the table while he shrugged back into his heavy jacket. Ellery noticed a flash in the light.

"Wait," she said. "Is that the gift Ben gave you?"

"Yeah," Trevor said. "We all wore them tonight in honor of Ben and Matt." He held out his arms so Ellery could see the cuff links better. They were gold, engraved with *HYB*.

But those weren't Trevor's initials. She glanced up at him.

Trevor answered the unasked question. "It stands for Have Your Back," he said. "That's what our group of friends have said to each other since we were in college. It started with Ben, actually. And Olivia. He was going to ask her out and he was terrified. He had the biggest crush on her. We all told him to go for it. We told him, we'll have your back. It worked out, and he told us we were good luck. So we'd use that phrase when we needed something. We called it a have your back. When we were older we'd text just the letters to our group chat. Like, when I was applying for a promotion, I texted the guys, *Hey, I need a HYB*. And they'd all text *HYB* in response. Then you knew everyone was rooting for you or whatever. Eventually someone changed the group chat name to The HYB Boys." Trevor passed a hand through his unruly hair. "Damn. Ben was the sweetest guy. You couldn't help but love the dude because he genuinely wanted the best for everyone."

Ben had *been so sweet*, Ellery thought. He'd wanted to mark moments, which was something she understood. Ben, having suffered an enormous loss at an early age, seemed to want to say the things and give the gifts while people were still there to receive them.

"I'm gonna go," Trevor said. "You guys don't need me anymore, right?"

"You're good," Olivia said, gently.

"Can you tell me the name of everyone in the wedding party?" Ellery asked, after Trevor had left.

"Sure," Rachel said.

"Where did you teach?" Olivia's head was tipped, her brow slightly furrowed as she looked at Ellery. "I keep thinking that you seem familiar to me."

"Colorado," Ellery said. "You grew up in California, right? So I wouldn't have taught you." She reached into her backpack and removed the schedule card, returning it to Rachel. "You can write it all down on here."

Rachel scribbled the names on the back of the card, then handed it to Olivia. Olivia read over the list, her lips moving. "That looks right to me," she said, passing the card back to Ellery.

"That's all?" Ellery asked. It was not a large number. The groomsmen, the bridesmaid, Olivia's parents, the bride, and the groom.

"That's everyone who was here for the actual wedding ceremony," Rachel said. "There were people coming in for the dinner, remember. Catherine had called them off when Ben didn't show up. And there was going to be a larger reception back in San Francisco later, at a museum Catherine likes."

Ellery thought about how there were circles of people you knew. The work group, the friends group, the people you went to high school with, the family where you grew up, the family you created as you became older. Sometimes there was overlap, or circles within circles. And then there was the circle of people who knew you best. It could be tiny, including only you and a single other person.

Ellery's hands felt cold, remembering. The bus, the ice, the quiet and the crying...

There was Annabel Walsh, her long dark hair covered in blood. Ellery put her fingers to the back of Annabel's head and they came away wet. She wiped her hand on her jeans. God, please. Please please. She did not know what to do. Should she move Annabel? Should she leave her alone? Something about the way she was twisted told Ellery that this was impossibly bad, that Annabel was broken.

"I wasn't wearing my seat belt," Annabel said. She sounded so small and frightened.

"That's okay," Ellery said. "It's okay." She put her non-bloodied hand on Annabel's cheek. Was that the right thing to do? Annabel closed her eyes. Her skin was very cold. It was only the two of them there in that moment, the smallest circle.

Ben's parents were dead. But the person he'd loved most was still here: Olivia.

IT WAS NO LONGER raining, but the faces were streaming with tears, the water catching in cupped hands or spilling over trailing fingers.

The brochure had described this piece of art as exquisitely sculptured faces and hands *that might be mistaken for* enormous fungi. Perhaps, in different weather, in different lights, they might appear that way. But to her, they looked like people weeping, trying to catch, letting go.

The faces had been captured in a variety of expressions, the hands in a myriad of gestures. The faces showed laughter, surprise, ecstasy, peace, terror, other things she couldn't quite name but felt she recognized. The hands were clasped, flexing, curled up into fists, outstretched, reaching.

The sculpture started about three feet up the trunk of the dead redwood tree and wound its way up another ten or twelve feet. She could see where they'd drilled through to install each piece of the work, and the tree was reinforced in places by steel bars.

The booklet had also said that no living creature was harmed with the installation. *That was never true, she knew. Living things were always harmed, and harming.*

She kept moving.

TUESDAY

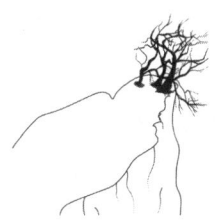

TODAY AT THE RESORT AT BROKEN POINT

"Nature is a Haunted House—but Art—a House that tries to be haunted."

—*Emily Dickinson*

Weather: Intermittent Rain

SUNRISE: 7:15 A.M. ....HIGH: 67° F
SUNSET: 6:28 P.M...LOW: 54° F

ABOUT THE ART:
Fin
by Page Horowitz
2018
glass, steel, granite

In naming *Fin*, Horowitz referenced a quote by painter Ala Bashir ("Darkness is where we begin and where we end"). *Fin* refers not only to the shape of the piece, but also to the French word for "end." The glass and steel formation mounted on raw granite calls to mind several different shapes—a dorsal fin, a liquid bonfire, or a spray of water.

33.

Ellery woke to a woman screaming.

Was it the middle of the night or the very early morning? She glanced over at the clock, but there was no light in the display or, she realized, anywhere else in the room. The power had gone out again.

Ellery reached under her pillow, her cold fingers closing around her flashlight. She liked the heft of it, the solid feel, but she remembered that everyone else at the resort was similarly armed. Should she stay put? Should she make her way to Ravi's or Nina's? She caught her expression in the mirror that she wasn't sure had always been there. With the flashlight on her upturned face, she looked scary. It reminded her of the sleepovers she'd had when she was a kid and they'd made their faces ghastly to terrify one another as they told ghost stories.

Out of habit, Ellery reached for the light switch at the bed beside her. Nothing. Of course. It was strange, the way the body kept trying to do what the brain had already registered wouldn't work. Based on the temperature of her room, the power had likely been out for some time. There was a chill in the air. There was a breath, a pause in the noise and chaos.

And then it began again.

The screaming.

It was coming from the room next to Ellery.

With renewed vigor, Ellery climbed out of bed and into her boots, pulled her coat around her, and opened the door. The morning was misty and gray, fog making it hard to see very far in front of her. But, as she stood outside listening, three things became clear within moments.

It was no longer raining.

It was Catherine who was screaming.

Olivia was missing.

34.

All this time, Ellery had assumed that no one was staying in the room next door. She'd never seen anyone enter or leave, or heard any sounds through the walls until this morning. It now seemed like an egregious error that she hadn't found out who was actually next to her in a situation like this, even if they didn't have connecting doors. Had they heard her talking to her kids? Had they heard her crying?

Now that Ellery was standing outside, she could hear Catherine's words clearly. "*Olivia. Olivia. Where is she?*"

It was primal, the sound of a mother missing her child. Ellery closed her eyes. She could not do this again.

She should walk away. She should take herself to the Main House and find out what was going on with the power or go to Ravi's room and ask if she could stay there for an hour or two.

But she did neither of those things.

Rachel opened the door of the room, stepping outside. Before she closed it behind her, Ellery caught a glimpse of Catherine sitting on the bed, her head in her hands, of Catherine's husband and of Brook and Canyon, standing next to her, their faces stricken. *How had they all come to be in that room? Had they been there all along? But no, Olivia had said her parents were in one of the cottages. And this wasn't Rachel's room. Hers had been next to Olivia's, which was Goldenrod. So whose room was it?*

Ellery's mind was doing that thing where you focused on minutiae, on the inconsequential things you didn't understand surrounding the thing that was too large to look at.

"My room's next door," Ellery said to Rachel. "I heard the screaming. Olivia's gone?"

"We can't find her anywhere," Rachel said. "Catherine is losing her mind."

"What can I do?" Ellery's eyes darted over Rachel's face, the ashen, shocked look of it.

"I don't know," Rachel said. "Nat and Carlos are gone, too."

"Wait," Ellery said. "They left with Olivia?" She was trying to wrap her brain around what was happening. For some reason, the absence of the rain was making everything strange. She had become used to the white-noise constancy of it. It had become a kind of companion—a dangerous one, eroding the landscape around them, keeping the police away, making the terrain slippery and changeable—but a steady one, nonetheless.

"No," Rachel said. "When we went to tell Nat and Carlos that Olivia was missing, only Brook and Canyon were there. Brook told me that Nat and Carlos left when the rain broke, right at first light."

"Why did they leave?" Ellery asked.

"I guess they were going to try to find the police." Rachel shook her head. "I honestly don't know. All I know is that they're gone, and Brook and Canyon are in charge now."

"What time is it?"

"About nine," Rachel said. "We noticed Olivia was missing about twenty minutes ago. She and I have adjoining rooms, and she gave me her extra key. When I woke up this morning, I walked over to see if she was awake and how she was doing."

"You walked over?" Wasn't Rachel's room next to Olivia's?

"I got moved here in the middle of the night," Rachel said. "My ceiling started to leak. I didn't want to wake Olivia up by asking if I could come in with her. So I went to the front desk and Nat gave me a key to this room so I'd have someplace to sleep tonight. It was probably close to one in the morning when that happened, I'd guess."

Ellery had not slept this late in quite a while. Was that why she felt an underlying layer of grogginess under the fear, the adrenaline?

"When I couldn't find Olivia this morning, I went over to Andy's room. But he hasn't seen her either." Rachel put her hands to her head, an unconscious gesture that mirrored her aunt's. "So then I went to tell Nat and Carlos. But only Brook and Canyon were there. And they went and told Catherine. She came here to find me."

Why hadn't Rachel gone to Catherine first? Ellery thought she knew the answer. When you were acting in an emergency, you went on instinct. To the most likely person to know what had happened or how to help, and then to the next most likely person, and the next. Rachel had not thought Catherine would know where Olivia was, or be able to help find her.

The door opened behind them and Canyon came out. "This is bad," he said, looking discomfited. "We've got to find her."

"Where did Nat and Carlos go?" Ellery still couldn't fathom why they'd chosen to leave when the rain stopped. It seemed unlike both of them—they had been steady at the helm throughout the entire disaster.

"They took one of the all-terrain vehicles and went to try and reach the police, since they didn't show last night," Canyon said. "Maybe they'll have some luck."

"But don't the police have better vehicles and equipment than the resort?"

"Nat and Carlos didn't explain their decision to us," Canyon said dryly. "They left me and Brook in charge and said they hoped to be back by late afternoon. The power went out last night and Maddox came to take a look. He said we're unlikely to get it up and running again. That might have been the final straw for Nat. Plus, if we *brought* a vehicle down to the police, they could use ours to come back up and check things out if all of theirs were already being used. I think Nat wanted to get officers on-site as soon as possible." He exhaled. "All that reasoning was *before* a third person went missing."

"Well, we know where the other two people are now," Ellery said. "I mean, in theory. I don't actually know where you're keeping Ben.

Or, for that matter, Matt." She paused, but Canyon didn't seem like he wanted to share that information. "Where's Andy?" she asked.

"He and some of the staff are out looking," Rachel said. "Olivia's boots and coat are gone. When I was walking around, I found some prints that might be hers. They look like they were made right after the rain stopped."

"So she's only been gone a couple of hours." Ellery tried to sound soothing "She could turn up any minute."

She hadn't noticed the door open behind her. "Anything can happen in a couple of hours," Catherine said, her voice wild.

Catherine was right, of course. Ben had died in a matter of minutes, or seconds. So had Matt.

There had been many times in the past few years when Ellery had looked around, thinking, *Where is the expert, the person in charge? Who can help me?* only to realize that there *was* no one else. She was the person, older and wiser, at least in theory. You couldn't ask kids to fix the thing that was unbearable. If you were the adult, then, by default, it was your job to assume the role of the leader. To take on everything you could so that they didn't have to.

This time, though, there might be someone else.

———

Gary opened the door of his cottage. "Shhhh," he said. "Grace is still asleep." Through the door into the living room, Ellery caught a glimpse of a tangle of blankets on the cottage's couch. Grace's curly hair spilled across the pillow. The interior was light-filled and spacious, with a jaw-dropping view of the ocean. Ellery found herself wondering how a judge could afford to vacation in a place like this, even for an important anniversary.

Gary stepped outside, leaving the cottage door slightly ajar behind him. He fixed Ellery with his direct, blue-eyed gaze. "How can I help you?"

"I take it you know what's going on," Ellery said. "Olivia is missing."

"I came out for a moment when I heard screaming," Gary said.

"The bride's parents are in the cottage next to mine. Wildrose." He gestured across at the modern slant of another roof barely visible among the vegetation.

"They're all gathered in the room next to mine," Ellery said. "The mother's distraught."

Gary knew what she was hinting at. "It's best to let the staff and the other professionals handle it."

"Carlos and Nat are gone," Ellery said. "They left when the rain stopped."

Gary looked surprised but shook his head. "Still, there's likely nothing I can do that would be helpful."

"Probably not." Ellery looked pointedly over his shoulder, at where his daughter lay sleeping. *Someone else's child is missing.* "But should we try?"

35.

I need you to understand that I'm not a detective," Gary told Catherine. When Ellery had returned to Rachel's temporary room with Gary, she learned that the entire group had moved over to the social room at the Main House. Rachel had escorted them to where Catherine and her husband, Rick, were holding cups of coffee. "Or a police officer. I used to be a judge. A local one, nothing fancy. That's all."

"We do understand," Rick said. "Right?" He looked at Catherine, who was perched on the arm of the leather sofa, poised to fly away to search for Olivia at any moment.

Catherine nodded. She was clearly and absolutely on the edge, but she was now maintaining her composure and had changed from her pajamas into slacks and a sweater. She wore no makeup; her hair was pulled back. "But you know how to look at facts and make a judgment," she said to Gary.

"And sometimes, that judgment is wrong," Gary said. A member of the staff slipped in and placed a cup of coffee at his elbow. He nodded to them in thanks. "As a judge, you don't ever have *all* the facts. People don't always tell the truth. Sometimes they do, and you have more of the facts than usual, and it's still possible to make the wrong judgment." He leaned back in his chair and placed his hands on his knees. "I can admit that, now that I no longer sit on the bench. People don't like to hear it."

"I understand that, too." Catherine seemed to have made up her mind to trust Gary, at least temporarily.

"All right, then," Gary said. "Did Olivia leave a note, or any indication as to where she might be?"

Catherine handed him a piece of paper. Ellery recognized it as one of the blank pages in the welcome books, torn away neatly along the side.

"*Please don't worry about me*," Gary read. He looked up. "That's all?"

"Yes."

"No signature," Gary said, studying the note. "And this is definitely her handwriting?"

"Yes." Catherine's tone was one of absolute certainty.

"It *is* distinctive." Gary handed the note back. Ellery caught a glimpse of it from where she was sitting in her chair next to him. She was not entirely sure why she had been allowed to stay, unless Rachel had vouched for her to Catherine at some point.

"What is missing, in addition to Olivia?" Gary asked.

"Her phone. Her wallet. Some of her clothes."

"Boots and coat?" Gary asked.

"Yes," Rachel said.

"What kind of coat and boots?"

"A Burberry waterproof coat," Catherine said. "Sorel boots."

"I think she's actually wearing her Salomons," Rachel said. Something passed between the two women, a kind of tension. From the way Gary was watching, Ellery was sure he had seen it, too.

"We can double-check," Gary said. "So it's possible she left on her own. She's not completely underdressed or unprepared. What is her outdoor experience?"

"She's a good hiker," Catherine said, her voice desperate, hopeful. She appealed to Rachel. "You two did that backpacking trip a couple of summers ago with your friends."

"Yeah, but we had a guide," Rachel said. "One of our friends, who's really outdoorsy. I don't think either Olivia or I would have been able to lead something like that or do it on our own."

"That's true." Catherine deflated slightly. "I can't imagine her choosing to hike out of here by herself."

"Perhaps she just went to look at something," Gary said encouragingly.

Catherine's limited supply of patience seemed to have come to an end. She stood. "We should be out looking for her."

"I cannot stress enough that we need people to stay in the main buildings," Brook said. "The rain's stopped, but it's still extremely dangerous out there."

"You let Andy go," Catherine said accusingly.

"Andy has more outdoor experience than most of the other guests, and we paired him with one of our staff," Brook said. Ellery's mind flickered to Grace. Was she qualified to look for a missing person? Or was the wilderness first-responder certification more of a medical thing, like splinting someone who got hurt on a trail?

Either way, Gary wasn't suggesting that Grace go out and look for anyone. "Do you know what else she was wearing?" he asked instead, redirecting the conversation back to Olivia's attire.

"I'm pretty sure she had on her clothes from yesterday," Rachel said. "She'd been leaving her dirty clothes in her suitcase in the closet. I went through them before we came over here, and I didn't see the stuff she was wearing last night." Rachel looked stricken. "Should I have been wearing gloves for that?"

"I don't think that's likely to matter," Gary said. "What was she wearing last night?"

"Leggings," Rachel said. "Fleece lined. They're her favorite because she's always a little cold and this whole place has been chilly since it started raining. A long-sleeved running shirt or something. And then her Ben hoodie was over that."

"Her Ben hoodie?"

"Yeah. We all have them." Rachel stood. "I'll go get one. Then you can see what they look like."

They all turned as someone opened the door to the Main House. Morgan and Maddox entered, followed by a few guests that Ellery hadn't met yet. The other guests beelined straight for the front desk, which another staff member was manning. Morgan and Maddox came through the open doorway into the social room.

"Sorry to interrupt." Maddox hadn't bothered to take off his muddy boots at the door. He stopped short of the rug and stood on the hardwood. He had a bag of something heavy looking—tools, Ellery would guess—slung over his shoulder, and he held Morgan's hand. She was wearing one of Maddox's oversized work shirts, and she looked a bit worn around the edges.

"I spoke too soon," she said aside to Ellery. "I've been throwing up all morning."

"*You* look hardy," Catherine said to Maddox. "Why haven't they tapped you to be out on the search?"

"I'm not a staff member." Maddox's tone was weary.

"Neither is Andy," Catherine said.

"I'm going to take another look at the generator," Maddox said, addressing Brook and Canyon. "Morgan's coming with me. But I'm not hopeful that I'm going to get it working again."

"Thanks for trying, man," Canyon said. "Do you want any of us to come with you?"

"If it's not going to start running again, I think your time would be better spent looking for my daughter," Catherine said. "Perhaps the two of you could go." She looked from Maddox to Canyon.

"We can't ask a guest who isn't related to the wedding party to risk themselves in that way," Brook began, trying to rescue Maddox.

But Maddox didn't need rescuing. "I won't be searching," he said. "I'll be staying with my wife."

At that moment, Rachel returned with the Ben hoodie. As she entered the room, Morgan and Maddox exited, still holding hands. *From a small Midwestern town!* Ellery remembered Morgan saying brightly. Something about it had sounded forced, but watching them now, Ellery felt that the deep bond between the couple was almost visible.

"This is the shirt." Rachel held it up. "Because of what happened, Olivia didn't end up giving them all away."

"Thank you," Gary said. "This is helpful to see. It's a decent-weight sweatshirt, but not exactly survival gear. Still, she wasn't egregiously underdressed, she left a note, and there isn't any indication of a struggle. Those are good signs."

Catherine nodded. She seemed to be taking Gary's measure, and the more he spoke, the more she bought into what he was saying. Ellery hoped she could remember everything they were discussing so that she could tell Ravi and Nina all of it later.

"Unless she went with someone she trusted," Rachel said.

"That could only be you, me, or Andy," Catherine said. Her husband looked up, noticing the omission. Ellery watched as a look passed across his face, as he decided not to say anything. Had Catherine left him out because Olivia *didn't* trust him? Or because he simply didn't register? Ellery couldn't tell. But before she could say anything, Grace burst into the room.

"What's going on?" She strode over to the chair where Gary was sitting and put her hand on his shoulder protectively, turning her gaze on Ellery as if she knew Ellery was responsible for his being there.

"Olivia is missing," Ellery said.

"I'm sorry to hear that," Grace said, momentarily tempered. "But what does that have to do with my dad?"

"He's the only person who has any kind of experience with this type of thing," Ellery said apologetically. "That we know of."

"He's not a police officer," Grace said. "Or a detective."

"That's exactly what I told them," Gary said. "But I'm glad to help how I can."

"This isn't his job." Grace glared around the room at them all. Ellery was reminded of her oldest daughter, Kate, who was gentle and accommodating most of the time, but when you came up against her inner core of steel—if someone made fun of Ethan, or if anyone tried to get her to do something she truly didn't want to do, or think was right—watch out.

"It's all right, Grace," Gary said. "I may as well *try* to be of use. I've only been retired for a few years."

"I mean, we could ask that security guy, Craig, to help," Rachel said, her tone a little snippy. "He'd probably be able to figure it out immediately, right?"

Everyone contemplated that for a few moments.

The door to the Main House opened. Everyone turned. Through the doorway of the back office, they could see Andy, Craig, and a couple of the staff members entering the foyer. Catherine called out, "What did you find? What is it?"

Craig walked toward them, leaving footprints on the polished wooden floor, the richly colored carpet. He stopped, his legs covered in mud up to his knees and his face grim.

"I'm afraid it's nothing good," he said.

36.

Catherine's face crumpled.

"It's not related to Olivia," Andy said, coming up right behind Craig. "It doesn't have anything to do with her."

Craig looked annoyed, as if he'd intentionally set the stage with his dramatic announcement and had hoped to draw the moment out longer. "It's this," he said, gesturing to a staff member who held up a plastic garbage bag. "Show them." The staff member, a young guy with long blond hair, reached into the bag and pulled out a...crown? It was made of driftwood and covered with glass, shells, and stone. It was so beautiful that Ellery caught her breath.

Brook made a sound low in her throat and rushed forward to take the crown. "I didn't even know another one was missing!" She stopped herself short, as if she'd given away too much, but only Ellery seemed to note the phrasing. Perhaps because the other guests weren't aware of the earlier art theft? Maybe they thought "another one" could refer to missing things in general—first Olivia, now the crown? It was more likely they didn't notice what Brook had said at all.

"We don't *know* that it doesn't have anything to do with Olivia." Craig shot a glare at Andy. "Do you think your daughter might have stolen it?"

"He's really bad at this," Rachel muttered.

"Olivia would *never* take a piece of art." Catherine reached for the crown, and, after a moment's hesitation, Brook gave it to her. Catherine turned the crown over in her hands, looking for anything out of place. "It appears to be undamaged. I'll take a further look later, and Brook and I can return it to its proper place." Catherine's spine was straight, her voice firm. "In the meantime," she said, "since this is all you've managed to locate, why don't we come up with a viable plan for finding my daughter?"

37.

"Well, *you've* had an eventful twelve hours," Ravi said.

Once Catherine rallied, Ellery and several others, including Craig, had been summarily excused. Catherine, Rachel, Brook, Andy, Gary, and Grace (who had insisted upon remaining with her father) had reconvened in the staff lounge for privacy to discuss next steps. Ellery had watched them go, Catherine carrying the driftwood crown before her as if she were a queen, Brook trailing behind like a lady-in-waiting. (Ellery wondered if Rachel and the others had cleaned up the lounge after the memorial, or if there were still beer bottles on the table and boxes of baby Ben sweatshirts on the floor.)

Canyon had left as well, muttering about needing to find Maddox.

"I know." Ellery tucked her feet up under her, trying to get warm. She'd come to find Ravi and Nina as soon as she'd left the Main House, and now the three of them were sitting in Nina's room, comparing notes. Ellery had finished filling them in on the events of the morning and what everyone had said at the memorial last night. To keep warm, they'd all kept their coats on and wrapped blankets around their shoulders. The midmorning sun coming in through the windows was weak, but enough to light the room.

"So the search party came back with the driftwood crown," Ravi said. "And no Olivia."

"Right."

"I wonder what plan they'll come up with for finding her," Nina said. "And if Brook and Canyon will be able to execute it. There's a bit of a power vacuum right now without Nat and Carlos."

"I'm a little worried Craig will try to establish martial law," Ravi said. "Now that Nat's gone, he's got a glint in his eye."

"He still answers to Brook," Nina said. "She's the assistant manager. Second-in-command under Nat."

"Will he respect that, though?" Ravi asked.

"I think Canyon will help make sure that he does," Nina said.

"Where do you think Olivia went?" Ravi asked.

"I don't know." Ellery pressed her lips together. "But I don't like this pattern. Since Sunday, we've discovered that someone is dead or gone every morning. Ben, Matt, Olivia."

"Nat and Carlos," Ravi said.

"True," Nina said. "But they did tell people, face-to-face, that they were leaving. And they know this place better than Ben or Matt or Olivia. They have better gear and access to the all-terrain vehicles. They might be all right. It's unlikely they'd be back by now, even if everything were going fine."

"Maybe they've driven off into the sunrise together," Ravi said. "But I didn't get that vibe from them. I do take your point. Ben, Matt, and Olivia seem more connected." He flipped open his welcome book, clicking his pen.

Ellery opened her book, too, and turned to the page marked *Questions:*

Who was the last person to see Ben?
What time did he die?
Why was he still wearing his wedding suit?
Did he ever leave Broken Point?
What exactly *did Ben's text say?*
How did Ben die?
How do I get home?

Some of the questions now had partial answers. Trevor had likely been the last to see Matt, no one was sure who'd been the last person to see Ben (or they weren't admitting to it, anyway), the text had said *I can't do it. I'm sorry.* But some questions remained as unknown as they had two days ago when she'd written them down. She added a few more.

Who was the last person to see Olivia?

Did she choose to leave?

Is the art connected somehow?

"What's the connection?" Ravi asked. Ellery looked up, surprised. That was what she had been about to write next: *What is the link between the three dead/missing people (besides the wedding)?* She wasn't including Nat and Carlos in the dead-or-missing group. Not yet.

"They're all young," Nina offered. "They're all members of the wedding party."

Ravi was writing busily in his notebook. "We need to figure out this murderer's calling card." He lifted his head, tapped the pen to his lips. "Or would that be called the method? The means?"

"The modus operandi," Nina said. "I think."

"Do we know if Matt had been hit in the back of the head before he fell?"

"I didn't hear anyone say anything about that," Ellery said. "Trevor and the groomsmen had to identify him, and they only saw pictures."

"So Trevor specifically said that Matt's head looked fine?"

"Well, no."

Ravi reached over to tap Ellery's notebook, which he had apparently been reading upside down. He let his finger rest on her question *Is the art connected somehow?* "The crown was in the gallery," he said. "I saw it the night we snuck into the cocktail hour. It was in a glass case, in the room on the other side of the main room from where we entered."

"How would someone steal it from the gallery?" Nina mused. "How would they get up there with all this weather? It's not part of the resort's main area."

"In some ways, that makes the theft easier," Ravi said. "Maybe the power was out up there and the alarms and cameras weren't working. The crown would be easier to take. And with the murders and the landslide, everyone was distracted."

"Did they say where they found the crown?" Ravi asked.

"No, but Andy might know," Ellery said. "I'll check with him."

Ravi leafed back in his welcome book until he reached the pages with the art descriptions. "Let's go through and label which art we've found and where it is," Ravi said. "Maybe that will give us a better idea of what other piece is missing."

Ellery and Nina followed suit. "Okay," he said. "*Driftwood Crown*, the piece we *know* was stolen, was in the gallery. So is *Intimation*, the giant oil painting by Clare Han. It was in the main room." He appealed to Ellery. "You saw it, didn't you? It was hard to miss."

"Yes," Ellery said. She glanced at the list. "I don't know where *Untitled* is."

"I saw it," Nina said. "It's on one of the trails, near a small pond."

"Can you show us where?"

Nina pointed, and they all marked the spot on their maps.

"And none of us know where the Warhol sketch is," Ravi said. "Right?"

"Right," Ellery and Nina spoke in unison.

"Okay," Nina said. "*Altar*. We've talked about that one before. It's in the grove. What about *Parts*? It sounds amazing. But I haven't found it."

"Me either," Ravi said.

"I *have* seen this one, on a trail near the grove." Ellery tapped the description for the sculpture where she'd found Olivia crying the night of the wedding.

Love
by Casey Hoyt
1994
wood

While not intended as a direct response to the bright boldness of Robert Indiana's famous *LOVE* sculptures, Hoyt's *Love* is nonetheless a powerful organic counterpoint, putting the human concept of "love" within the context of the natural world. The sculpture's cursive letters soften the angles of the word.

Had she mentioned that she'd seen Olivia there? She knew she'd told them about talking with Olivia earlier in the weekend, but couldn't remember what specifics she'd given.

Neither Ravi nor Nina had seen the *Love* sculpture. She showed them where to mark the location on their maps, and then they all turned to the next description.

> *Carnelian*
> by Cody Carter
> 1995
> limestone, red lacquer

The cracked-open shapes of the stones used for this sculpture evoke geodes, where secondary formations occur inside sedimentary or volcanic rocks. Carter used rich red lacquer in the hollows of the stones to arrest the eye and symbolize the molten core of the earth breaking free.

"*Carnelian*," Ravi said. "I like saying that. It sounds regal. Or carnal. Or both."

"Isn't it a kind of gemstone?" Nina asked.

"I think so," Ellery said. "I feel like one of the characters in *Little Women* had one. Or wanted one. Or something. Maybe they stole one?"

"They'd never steal," Ravi said.

"Jo would," Nina said.

"Amy too," Ellery said.

"Okay, okay." Ravi held up his hands. "I didn't realize some of them were so deviant. I thought they were all sweet."

"Just Beth and Meg," Ellery told him.

"I've seen *Carnelian*," Nina said. "It's easy to notice, right off one of the trails in a small clearing. You don't have to leave the trail to find it. It's huge. Kind of stops you in your tracks."

"Well, there's no way *that* piece of art is the one that got stolen," Ravi said. "In fact, we can probably rule out most of the sculptures, can't we?"

"It seems like it," Nina agreed. "But let's keep going to make sure we've seen them all. Some could be smaller, like the crown."

Fin
by Page Horowitz
2018
glass, steel, granite

In naming *Fin*, Horowitz referenced a quote by painter Ala Bashir ("Darkness is where we begin and where we end"). *Fin* refers not only to the shape of the piece, but also to the French word for "end." The glass and steel formation mounted on granite calls to mind several possible shapes—a dorsal fin, a liquid bonfire, or a spray of water.

"This was the one on our card this morning," Ellery said.

"That's quite a quote," Ravi said. "'Darkness is where we begin and where we end.' Do you believe that?"

"Yes," Nina said. "Literally, it's true. We begin in the dark, and then we go into it alone when we die."

"You don't think there's anything after?" Ravi asked.

"No," Nina said.

They both looked at Ellery.

She thought of Annabel, and her heart ached.

"I think it's true, too," Ellery said quietly. "I don't want it to be. But darkness is also where you were held when you were inside your mother. Where you were safe." *And who knows what the next darkness brings?*

"Well, we know no one could have moved *Fin*," Ravi said. "They make a big deal about how enormous it is. And I've seen it. We all have, right? By the main firepit, off to the side?"

Ellery nodded and so did Nina.

"This next piece might be possible to steal," Nina said after a moment, as they were all reading through the description. "It's small."

Leap
by Cora Beck
1973
pastels

Acquired by our curator after the passing of the artist, this
lively work evokes the sense of joy and play that the wilderness
can inspire in us. Beck shows children jumping from a low cliff
into the ocean, each child captured in a different moment of
motion. Over the years, we have observed many guests smiling
when they come across this delight of a painting.

"I have unfortunately not smiled when I've come across this painting, because I haven't seen it," Ravi said. "Have either of you?"

"I feel like I have," Ellery said. "I can't say where."

"Same, and me either," Nina said.

"Maybe that's because *it was stolen!*" Ravi's face lit up. "I'll mark it
down as a candidate." He read the next description out loud:

Thoughts and Prayers
by Maggie Morgan
1996
steel, granite

This piece was created by the artist as part of a series. Each
bench is crafted in varying shapes of steel and granite. The
names of the works are partial phrases taken from platitudes
commonly used to describe or comfort the bereaved.

They were all quiet. "I heard that one's out at the top of Broken
Point," Nina said. "Under one of those towering fir trees."

"Unless it's been stolen," Ravi said.

"Or slid away," Ellery said.

Media Res
by Lin Marsh
1987
lacquer

This screen, inspired in part by Japanese screens of the 18th and 19th centuries, consists of six panels depicting poppies in various states of their life cycle. Both abundance and decay are trademarks of Marsh's works. Regarding this piece, they said, "Life and death are at the forefront of all we do, but I like— most of the time—giving life the center of the stage."

"We've all seen this one, right?" Ravi asked. "It's in the reception area of the Main House." Nina and Ellery both nodded. "I'm so glad I'm friends with people who notice beautiful things," Ravi said. "What are the odds that Jason et al. would have a clue where the screen was? They probably think the sculptures are cool outdoor furniture."

"Catherine knows what she's doing," Nina said with admiration. "The art itself is interesting, and she's selected pieces from a diverse background. Plus, they were mostly purchased from artists who were living at the time of sale. So she's supporting and drawing attention to people working *now*, not just a lot of old dead white people."

"So it's most likely that the missing piece is either the Warhol sketch, or *Leap*," Ravi said. "Interesting. Not only are they both smaller, but they're the only two artists who aren't living. I think. Unless Marsh is dead." He paused. "So does that mean they're the most valuable?"

"Not necessarily," Nina said. "Still, what I wouldn't give for Google."

"You know how there's a shadow celebrity here?" Ravi said after a moment.

"You keep saying," Nina said. "But don't you think that would have come out by now? And if someone truly famous were here, wouldn't the police have put us higher on the rescue list?"

Ravi was undeterred. "Well, I think the secret famous person might be an artist. Someone so famous we can't believe it." He pointed to the list. "Nina, you can't weigh in because you're somewhat familiar with art. But Ellery and I are not. Ellery, did you recognize any of the names of the artists in here, besides Warhol, who we know is dead?"

"Only Clare Han," Ellery said. "And wait. Casey Hoyt." She flushed. "I should know more."

"Not at all," Ravi said. "Those are the two names that stood out to me, too. And do you see what I see? The commonalities?"

"No," Ellery said, after a moment. "They don't work in the same medium."

"The initials are the same," Ravi said.

"Oh, for heaven's sake," Nina said.

"C. H." Ravi beamed.

"Okay..." Ellery wasn't entirely sure what he was trying to prove.

"They're the same initials as *Catherine Haring*," Ravi said exultantly. "What if she's a secret artist? What if she's not only a curator? What if her work is here? And someone stole it? Or *she* stole it?"

"Why would she steal her own work?" Nina asked. But something was nagging at Ellery. Something about Ravi's suggestion felt—not quite right, but not quite wrong.

"Maybe she needs the money," Ravi said. "Who better to steal a work than the artist?"

"Wouldn't she make something new and sell that?" Ellery asked.

"Maybe she's not as good anymore," Ravi said. "Or the piece had sentimental meaning."

"We are getting very, very lost in the woods here," Nina said.

"Okay," Ravi said. "Whether or not Catherine Haring is a shadow-celebrity-famous-artist, I think we can all agree that *Leap* and the Warhol sketch are the most likely items to be stolen. Right?"

"Right," Ellery said. That made sense to her. The other items were so...unwieldy. How did you steal a statue or dismantle a chandelier? Walk away with a bench or a sculpture?

It seemed even harder than getting away with murder.

38.

The staff set up lunch in the Main House rather than the restaurant, which Ellery imagined was because it was easier to keep warm. Both the social room and Wildrye had fireplaces, but the restaurant had high ceilings and was much larger, and therefore would require more to heat. When Ellery, Nina, and Rachel entered the social room at the same time, they all sighed involuntarily at the warmth.

"*Much* better," Nina said. "My room was getting cold."

Grace was stoking the fire, and Maddox and Andy were piling logs in a rack next to it. The furniture in the social room had been pushed away so that they could all sit in folding chairs set up in rows, as if they were attending a seminar. Beyond the plate-glass windows, the round terrace of the lawn bellied out for the view of the ocean, but the ocean itself wasn't visible. The clouds had not yet lifted enough for that.

"No ice, no glasses," Ravi said glumly, looking at his room-temperature bottle of resort water as they settled into three of the chairs. "We're in the after times now."

"Please, sit down," Brook called out over the group. "We're going to make sure everyone is accounted for before we begin, and it will make it much easier for us to call roll if you're all seated."

"They're calling *roll*," Ravi said. "Seriouser and seriouser."

"Makes sense, with people disappearing all the time," Nina said.

"Did either of you bring your welcome book?" Ravi asked. "We could write down everyone's names. We still don't know all the guests."

"I brought mine," Ellery said.

"Great." Ravi shifted, trying to figure out a way to hold his lunch and water bottle in one hand while retrieving his book from the pocket of his coat. "We can both take notes." His water fell to the floor and rolled under the seat of the person in front of him. He exhaled in frustration and Grace, who had taken a seat next to Gary in the front row, turned around to hand it back.

"Thanks," he said.

They were much more cramped than they'd been in the restaurant. The guests, both the ones Ellery knew and the ones she didn't, appeared worse for wear. They sat in their chairs with hair less combed, shoes muddy, eyes tired and fearful. *They are survivors now,* Ellery thought. She knew the look.

Except for Andy, who was sitting near the front with Olivia's parents, the groomsmen were sitting behind Ellery, Ravi, and Nina.

"Every morning, we find out that someone else has died," Trevor said. "And now Olivia's missing. It can't keep going on like this."

"No," Jason said grimly. "It can't." His voice held an edge of male bravado. *Not on my watch,* Ellery could almost hear him saying. Except it *was* happening on his watch. On *all* their watches. *Where was Olivia?*

"What do you think?" Ravi whispered to Ellery. "Is Jason about to go vigilante on us? Is he going to take matters into his own hands?"

Ellery glanced over her shoulder. Jason looked unkempt and red-eyed. He met her gaze and she thought she recognized, fleetingly, the depths of his despair, the darkness of losing someone you loved. She faced the front of the room again. Brook and Canyon were standing shoulder to shoulder, their backs to the plate-glass windows. They had drawn the blinds and the social room, though large, felt close with so many people in it.

Brook held up her hand. "I need your attention, please," she said. *"Everyone."* When some of the guests didn't seem to hear her, she put her fingers in her mouth and issued a piercing whistle. The room fell silent.

"Thank you," Brook said. "We have quite a lot of information to cover, and we'd like to do it as efficiently as possible."

Craig folded his arms.

"We are taking additional emergency measures in light of our current situation," Brook said. "Please pay close attention and save your questions for the end."

"Right now, we're going to call roll." Canyon held a clipboard in his hands. "Raise your hand when we call your name."

Ellery answered when it was her turn and scribbled furiously in her notebook when it wasn't. She felt people's eyes on her, probably wondering what she was doing. Hopefully Ravi would catch whatever names she missed.

"The buddy system, for lack of a better phrase, is now imperative," Canyon said. "We are also going to consolidate quarters. We're moving guests staying in the cottages into rooms, anyone currently staying on their own into a room with someone else in their party, and consolidating the occupied rooms into certain areas." The guests erupted into a series of small murmurs, but Brook held up her hand and they quieted.

"This is for everyone's safety, and because we're trying to restore power. It'll help us if we have less square footage to heat," Canyon continued. He held up the clipboard. "When we're finished with this meeting, let Brook know who you'd like to stay with. We're basically asking you to double up, and we know that's an inconvenience. But we do not want anyone else to go missing. The staff will help you move your things, if you'd like."

"So we're going to be sharing beds?" someone asked. A few people laughed nervously.

Canyon nodded, not countenancing the laughter. "Right," he said. "Everyone's going to sacrifice some comfort."

"It's not that," another guest said. "It means that one of us is probably going to be literally sleeping with the murderer."

That did give Canyon pause.

Brook stepped in quickly. "If you have concerns about anyone you're planning to room with, let us know," she said. "We'll figure something out."

They're a good team, Ellery thought, *like Nat and Carlos. Like Ravi and Nina, Grace and Gary. Me and Abby.*

"But that means we have to trust *you*," Trevor said. "Maybe the murderer is a member of the staff." He glanced at Jason, as if trying to get him to agree, but Jason's gaze was faraway and distant, his brow furrowed in thought. "Only people from the wedding party are dead or missing."

Brook ignored him, continuing. "We'll keep looking for Olivia. We're discontinuing housekeeping services to free up more staff who are acquainted with the area and who have outdoor experience to help with the search, but you, as the guests, can help us by staying off the grounds and in your rooms or in the Main House as much as possible. We do *not* want anyone else to go missing while we wait for Nat and Carlos—and the police."

"You think they're really going to get through?"

"I do," Brook said, and Ellery wondered if Brook really felt the confidence her voice was projecting. "Dinner will be at six p.m. here tonight. Until then, you're welcome to be in the Main House or in your rooms with the person you've chosen as your buddy. A staff member will be manning the reception desk at all times if you need anything."

"Two staff members." Rachel's voice carried across the room.

"What?" Brook asked.

"The staff should also stay in twos," Rachel said. "For *your* own safety. And so none of *you* murder any of *us*."

One of the groomsmen gave a slight cheer.

"Yes," Brook said. "Will do."

Canyon held up the clipboard a final time. "Please, come and let us know who you'd like to room with. Again, staff will be available to help you move your things if you'd like."

People began talking with one another. Those who were already staying together made their way over to the desk to confirm with Brook—partnerships like Morgan and Maddox, Grace and Gary, Jason and Trevor, the fifty-something couple, and other pairings who knew they trusted each other and were ready to get out of crowded Main House. Morgan gave Ellery, Ravi, and Nina a little wave as she and Maddox lined up at the desk. Canyon ducked through the back door toward the staff lounge.

Ellery had that *alone* feeling again, but this time it felt even more panicky.

Ravi and Nina would go in together, of course. Who could she be with?

She glanced at Rachel. Did they trust one another enough? Or would Rachel and Andy want to room with each other, since they kept getting thrown together and they knew Olivia and Ben so well? But when Ellery located Andy in the room, she saw that he had already been approached by one of the groomsmen and was nodding.

"You can come in with us," Nina said to Ellery. "We could take turns sleeping on the floor. Or whatever. Maybe they have a rollaway bed."

"It's okay," Ellery said. "I'm fine on my own."

"You are *not*," Nina said. "There's a killer here somewhere."

"My, how times have changed," Ravi said. "Now Nina's the one taking things seriously."

"Stop joking and convince her to stay with us," Nina said.

"It's easy to forget that we've only been friends for a few days." Ravi looked at Ellery with understanding. "I wouldn't want to room with us. I get it if you don't."

"It's not that I don't trust you," Ellery said. "It's that I don't know you." She shook her head. "I mean, I do, but not the way you know each other."

"Okay," Nina said, after a pause. "I get that."

"Tell them you'd rather stay on your own," Ravi said. "We'll back you."

"Okay." They were inching closer to the desk. Everyone seemed to have something to say to Brook about the new situation, and she was bearing it stoically.

"We should ask if we can stay in my room instead of yours," Ravi said to Nina. "It's bigger. I swear it's not in my mind."

Ellery looked past Brook to where Canyon had reappeared through the back door. Something was nagging at her. What *was* it?

It took a few seconds for her to register what was off. When she did, she touched Nina's arm, leaning in so that Ravi did, too. "You guys," Ellery said. "I know which piece of art is missing."

39.

"The *screen*." Ravi caught on immediately. "It's gone."

"Maybe they moved it out of the way for the group to gather," Nina said.

"It should be right there," Ravi said, pointing surreptitiously. "Behind the desk. They aren't using that area for seating. They didn't need to move it. And that *is* something you could fold up and move." He opened his welcome book and flipped to the description of the screen.

"When did you last see it?" he asked them.

"I noticed it at check-in," Ellery said. "I remember thinking how beautiful it was."

"Same," Nina said.

"Hat trick," Ravi said. "Because I did, too. But do either of you remember noticing it after that?"

"I bet it was gone when Brook took us to housekeeping yesterday," Ellery said. "I'm almost sure. Because we went that way, behind the desk. I know a lot had happened, but I swear I'd remember stepping around it."

"I would have, too," Ravi said.

"But did either of you note *then* that it was gone?" Nina asked.

"No," Ravi said, after a pause. "I can't say that I did."

Ellery shook her head, too.

They fell silent as Brook gestured for them to come forward to the desk. "Who would you like to room with?" she asked Ellery.

"I don't know anyone here," Ellery said. "I came alone. I'd feel more comfortable if I could stay on my own."

She spoke quietly, not wanting to draw the attention of anyone else, but her tone was firm.

Brook hesitated. "I can't really recommend that." She glanced behind Ellery at Ravi and Nina, who were standing a few feet back. They were the last in line besides Rachel, who was waiting behind them.

"I met Ravi and Nina when I came here," Ellery said, her tone still quiet. "It's been nice to spend time with them, but I don't know them much better than you do."

Brook hesitated. "Okay." She wrote something down on the map of the resort. "You're staying in one of the areas where we're trying to consolidate people anyway, so I'll keep you there."

"Thank you."

"Nice work," Ravi said approvingly, after they were back in the social room.

Rachel walked in from the reception area and came over to them by the fireplace. "Hey."

"You okay?" Nina asked her.

"No," Rachel said. "Ellery, could I talk to you for a minute?"

"Of course," Ellery said, surprised. Did Rachel want to room with her? Would she end up saying yes, if so, despite what she'd said to Brook? There was something about Rachel that made it hard to say no to her.

Rachel drew Ellery over to a spot in the social room lined with bookshelves. A female guest was glancing over the volumes, but when she saw the expression on Rachel's face, she moved away.

"I want to go down to Slipstream," Rachel said, her voice low. "The trailer bar. Would you be up for going with me?"

"Um," Ellery said.

"I know we're supposed to stay here. But it's only half a mile down to the bar. I took some of those hiking poles the resort has. We can use them."

"I'm not sure it's a good idea," Ellery said. *Why ask* me? *And why do* you *want to go down there?*

She didn't ask either question out loud, but Rachel answered the first one anyway.

"You're one of the most outdoorsy people here, besides Andy," Rachel said. "And he's off with the staff helping out with something. You've got the right boots and outside gear. I don't want to go out there alone. And I'm not worried that you're going to kill me."

For a second, Ellery felt oddly affronted. *Why not?* she wanted to say. "Why the trailer bar?" she asked instead.

"Something Olivia said made me wonder," Rachel said. "I want to take a look for myself."

40.

The rain might have ceased for the time being, but the path to the trailer bar was alive and shifting. The water had made rivulets in the earth, small canyons, lakes, puddles. Within only a few steps, they had walked on landscapes upon landscapes.

The trail went down an incline through the trees in the direction of the highway. Unlike the trail out to the point, there weren't sheer cliffs on either side. Rather, it was a gentler slope through the woods. Still, it wasn't easy going as they skidded out repeatedly, the hiking poles helping them keep their footing. Ellery thought of Gary's hiking pole, Stabby, as she shoved hers into the mud to stop herself from completely wiping out on the trail. "It's harder going down than up," Rachel said. "The way back will be easier. Right?"

"Right," Ellery said, concentrating on her footing, and then she was sliding, falling right on her butt.

"Whoa." Rachel reached out to help Ellery get back up. "You all right?"

Physically, she was fine, only muddy. "Yeah. Sorry."

"No worries," Rachel said. "But I've got to take care of you. Your friends are going to kill me if you don't come back in one piece."

Ellery had told Ravi and Nina where she was going. They'd both stared Rachel down, but ultimately promised they wouldn't tell Brook that they'd gone off. "You have two hours," Ravi had said severely to Rachel. "Otherwise, we'll have Brook send out a search party."

"Did you think about asking anyone else from the wedding party?" Ellery wondered now. "Since Andy couldn't go?"

Rachel snorted. "Who would I ask? Catherine? Trevor? Jason?"

So Andy was the only person from the wedding party that Rachel really trusted. *Interesting.*

The clearing that held the bar looked as if it had been staged as a setting for a movie about the end of the world—the subtle, creepy kind that isn't only scorched-earth, but life going on just fine without humanity there to alternately rape and pillage it or try to tidy it up. *Let's fill the ocean with plastic, but heaven forbid we leave these fallen leaves where they are!* The silver, pill-shaped trailer had not been washed away and looked to be in reasonably good shape, but the rest of the clearing was almost unrecognizable.

"Shit," Rachel said. "What a mess."

Having seen what amounted to the *Before* picture on the website, Ellery knew they were definitely looking at *After.* The globe lights strung among the trees had been smashed by tree branches brought down by the rain. A larger redwood had fallen in the middle of the clearing, bisecting several of the picnic tables. The firepit had apparently filled with water and then washed out, the stones holding it together breaking like a dam. The Adirondack chairs were tipped over and partially submerged in mud. The colors of the clearing, greens and grays and russets and rusts, were enriched and deepened by the water.

"Canyon said that he and one of the other staff members came down here and checked to make sure no one was in the trailer or the restrooms," Rachel said, pointing to a small wooden outbuilding tucked into the trees on the opposite side of the clearing from the bar. "But they didn't stay long. They were trying to cover as much ground as they could, looking for Olivia."

Ellery was hoping against hope that she and Rachel would find

Olivia safe and sound. Perhaps she'd gone out on a hike this morning and gotten injured—nothing fatal, but something that would slow her down, a sprained ankle, let's say. Maybe Olivia had taken one look at that slippery, mud-soaked trail up to the resort and decided to take refuge in the silver loaf-shaped trailer. You could seal yourself up safely in there—it looked like a winsomely designed above-ground bunker. And there would be plenty of booze and snacks inside.

Maybe Olivia *was* inside the trailer, waiting for them to find her. Ellery could picture it. Or perhaps Matt hadn't actually been killed, only hurt, and he'd gotten up from wherever they'd put him and made his way over to the trailer to hide out from his would-be murderer. It was far-fetched, but why not? *Why not?* What if everything *wasn't* as bad as it seemed? What if things turned out to be okay?

But Ellery couldn't pretend Ben was anything but dead. She had been there. She had seen him up close. There was no arguing with it.

She and Rachel squished across the clearing. If they hadn't been wearing lace-up boots, the mud would have sucked their footwear right from their feet. As it was, Ellery could feel the cold of the mud slipping over the top of her boot when she squelched down in a particularly deep, waterlogged spot.

"You can't resurrect things," Luke had said to her once, when she had been trying to reconstitute one of Maddie's favorite stuffed animals that had come apart in the wash. "Everything *does* end." The toy was a goner, even though Ellery had washed it in a lingerie bag, on gentle, in cold water. She'd been thinking of how Maddie would feel when she woke up the next morning and found that Molly the elephant wasn't nice and clean the way Ellery had promised she would be, but instead disintegrated and undone.

"There's got to be a way," Ellery had said, her voice the slightest bit choked up, Molly's entrails dripping through her fingers as she tried desperately to put them back into the now-almost translucent stuffed-animal skin from whence they'd come.

"There's nothing you can do," Luke said. "Stop trying. Stop *crying*." She had looked up, surprised, at the harshness in his tone, so rare in their marriage in the early years and still so startling even in the past few.

She'd thought of the words again later, during a conversation several weeks after the one in which he'd told her he wanted the divorce. She'd been teary and pleading, willing to try to do anything he needed. He didn't like his life? They could fix that! They could try a new marriage therapist. They could go on a vacation! Remember, they had that anniversary trip planned? She was willing to move, if that would help. Did he want to look for a new job somewhere else?

"There's nothing you can do," he said.

Stop trying. Stop crying. You can't resurrect things. Everything does end.

Not us, she'd wanted to say, *not this family,* because even though she knew they were all mortal she hadn't thought they'd end *this* way, *this* soon.

She and Rachel checked the restrooms first. They were locked. Rachel pulled some keys from the pocket of her raincoat. They were on a brass loop with a leather tab imprinted with the resort's logo. "Maddox," she said, without explanation, and with an expression that didn't invite questions. Another splinter of unease slid under Ellery's skin. She barely knew anyone here, and that included the bridesmaid who apparently had access to the resort's keys via the electrician the staff had decided to trust. Did Morgan know Maddox was handing out keys? To attractive single women? She'd thought you could hang your hat on Morgan and Maddox being one tight, cohesive unit. She remembered again his hardened face, the way he'd looked straight through her that time outside of the guest rooms.

After a moment's pause, she followed Rachel inside.

Rachel flicked on the lights and the two of them stood still, looking around. Ellery couldn't immediately see anything of note, only a faux-rustic setup with wooden stalls, rubbed bronze fittings, and a long, stainless-steel trough sink flanked by bottles of the same fancy handwash found throughout the resort. There were a few sets of muddy footprints to and from the stalls and the sinks. The stalls were all open and empty.

"Those footprints are probably from when they searched earlier,"

Rachel said. "It wasn't muddy when we were all down here for the rehearsal brunch."

They closed the doors and locked them, Rachel keeping the keys in her hand instead of putting them back into her pocket.

As they drew closer to the trailer, Ellery saw where the bar's sign had fallen to the ground, torn from the nearby tree to which it had been affixed. The word *Slipstream* was carved in relief in redwood. The shape of it followed the outline of the letters, bumping up on *S* and *t* and down for *p*.

"Do you know where they found the crown?" Ellery asked.

"It was in the closest valet stand," Rachel said. "Andy went inside to see if anyone was there, and the crown was sitting on the shelf below the counter. He wrapped it in his sweatshirt and then Craig took over from there." She exhaled. "I really don't think Olivia took it."

Rachel fitted another key to the lock on the Airstream. The door swung open easily, with a slight metallic creak. Rachel stepped inside and moved over so Ellery could enter and stand next to her on the threshold.

It was fairly close quarters inside the bar, even though it was one of the larger trailers, not the tiny, nearly round model that had always delighted Ellery when she'd come across one at campsites or trundling along the road like a cheerful roly-poly bug. A large panel had been cut into the trailer, creating an opening through which people could place orders and receive their drinks. The trailer contained a sink and prep area, a small fridge, and all the accoutrements one usually saw at a well-equipped bar—silver shakers, glass bottles of different sizes filled with liquids and emblazoned with a variety of labels, a pile of ivory napkins, a stack of menus, spigots and taps.

Ellery's eyes traveled fairly quickly over all of this to land on the muddy footprints covering much of the trailer's floor. "Someone's been here, too," Ellery said. "Probably at the same time they searched the restrooms?"

She looked down at her own filthy boots. Were she and Rachel going to go farther inside? It was clear from where they stood now that no one was in the trailer. They could see the full width of it from end to end, and there wasn't anywhere large enough for a person to hide. Olivia wasn't here.

But as Ellery looked closer, something felt different than it had in the outbuilding across the clearing. There were gaps in the bottles on the shelves, like a few missing teeth. A glass had been placed in the sink and another rested precariously on the edge of the counter. Ellery longed to reach out and move it so that it weren't teetering there, but perhaps she shouldn't touch anything.

"Probably," Rachel said slowly.

The prints were dried. Ellery wasn't sure how fast that would have happened. Just since this morning? It was possible, she thought. Maybe Canyon and whoever was with him had come in and looked around and had a drink. She wouldn't blame them.

Ellery picked up one of the menus from a box mounted on the wall next to the doorway. She recognized both the ivory color and the font used in the printed goods throughout the resort. However, unlike the other menus she'd seen, the ones for the bar were laminated. A nod to the likelihood of people spilling drinks on them, perhaps? Or to the general damp of the forest?

Slipstream Draft, one of the items said. *Our house beer, made with hops and local cassis.*

Ellery knew that a slipstream was the airstream behind something that was moving very fast. She had the sense of being in that stream herself, caught in a current created by something much larger and stronger.

"Should we go farther in?" she asked. She wasn't sure she wanted to.

Rachel also seemed hesitant. "I don't want to mess anything up in case it matters later. And I think we can tell she's not here, right?"

Ellery nodded. "Right."

She noticed something crumpled up on the bench inside. It was too large to be a bar towel. And it was striking a familiar note. "Is that—?"

Rachel looked over. *"Oh,"* she said. With a few quick steps, she was across the trailer. Ellery stayed in the doorway. Suddenly she had no desire to be in any kind of enclosed space with *anyone.*

Rachel was back within seconds, holding out the item for Ellery to see.

It was a crumpled sweatshirt, streaked with something…red.

Ben's face looked back at them.

41.

"This can't be good," Rachel said, as she and Ellery stared at the sweat-shirt. "What should we do?"

"We need to tell someone," Ellery said. Dr. Anand flashed into her mind. Although she didn't need a medical expert to tell her what dried blood on a piece of clothing looked like. She'd been a parent for eighteen years.

And, of course, there had been the accident.

Rachel laughed. She stopped abruptly and looked at Ellery. "I'm sorry. I don't know why I did that. What you said isn't funny. Nothing's funny."

"It's shock," Ellery said.

"You're right. We have to tell someone." Rachel reached for something under the counter—a large clean plastic bag from the roll the bartenders must use for trash. "And it's good that two of us know this. About the sweatshirt. Two people should know everything, right? If only one person knows something, then they die, right? Like Ben? Matt?" Her hands were shaking as she bundled the sweatshirt into the bag. "And the information dies with them."

"Do you *know* that that was Olivia's sweatshirt?" Ellery asked. "What size did she wear?"

"Extra small," Rachel said. She looked at the sweatshirt in the bag. "Should I get it out to look at the size? Will that get more fingerprints on it? Mine are already on there." Her hands were still trembling. "We need the *police*."

"Here." Ellery reached for the plastic bag. Rachel hesitated. "I promise I won't touch the shirt." After a moment, Rachel handed the bag to her. Ellery shook it gently until the tag on the inside of the shirt was visible. *XS*.

They looked at each other.

"Did anyone else have an XS?" Ellery asked.

Rachel shook her head, her face pale. "I went through them with Olivia when we got here. She ordered a small for me, a medium for Andy, and then she got extra larges for all the frat guys because she didn't want to deal with asking them for their sizes."

"What about Catherine?" Ellery asked. "And Olivia's stepdad?"

"She didn't get them shirts," Rachel said. "They were for the younger people in the wedding party."

"Got it." Ellery glanced around the trailer. Other than the muddy prints and the glasses that had been used, there didn't appear to be signs of a struggle. Was that good? Or had Olivia been here with someone she trusted? They'd had a drink, and then…? Ellery's stomach turned.

"There's nowhere you could hide a whole person in here," Rachel said. Her voice wavered, and she cleared her throat, as if she were trying to stay calm. "So Olivia's not in here. We should lock it up and get back."

"Should we take the glasses?" Ellery asked. They might have evidence. Fingerprints, DNA?

"I don't really know how to do that without contaminating them."

"I don't, either," Ellery said. "But I don't want them to be tampered with."

"I guess we have to lock the door and hope for the best." Rachel sounded unconvinced. "Because if we put them in the bag with the shirt, won't that rub off any evidence there is from the glasses? And if we put them in their own plastic bags, does that do the same? Maybe we shouldn't have touched the sweatshirt and bagged it up at all." She exhaled in frustration. "I don't know what the hell I'm doing. If only we had cell service. If only I could look up *anything* or we could get a freaking call out."

"I know." Ellery stood next to Rachel as she locked the door, hands still shaking. They took their hiking poles from where they'd propped them up against the outside of the trailer. As they passed the firepit, they both stopped, looking at the remnants of the ashes that hadn't washed away. "Is that cloth?" Ellery asked, pointing to a lighter piece of what looked like charred fabric under the ashes.

"I think so," Rachel said.

Their eyes met. Should they take it with them? Were they ruining everything? Compromising each part of the scene?

"What was it that Olivia said that made you want to come here?" Ellery asked, remembering.

"It was at the brunch." Rachel reached up to push back a piece of hair, leaving a smudge of dirt on her forehead. "She and Ben were super taken with the trailer. She said they should get one someday of their own. I overheard her." Rachel looked at Ellery, her eyes full. It was the first time Ellery had seen Rachel on the verge of tears. "They were so in love. None of this makes sense."

Ellery couldn't say, *I know,* because she hadn't known Ben and she'd barely known Olivia. So she said nothing at all. Just stood there with Rachel, and the trees, and the bloody sweatshirt in the bag and the splintered picnic tables.

"We should go," Rachel said quietly.

"Okay." Ellery felt it, too, like something was off. Before, this was a place where people had laughed and toasted one another with drinks and perhaps danced under the now-shattered string lights. A spot where a wedding brunch had been held and where an almost-bride might have come back to remember what was almost the best day of her life. It now felt watched, too enclosed, too cut off from the rest of the resort. Who might be hiding in the trees around them?

They began to climb.

———

"Damn it," Rachel said. "Most of them are gone." She and Ellery stood in their stockinged feet back in Olivia's room, their muddy boots outside the door. Rachel had used her extra key to let them in and they were now staring into a cardboard box that held only a single Ben-emblazoned shirt.

"What the hell were we thinking?" Rachel said. "Giving out those shirts after everything? Now a whole bunch of people have them and Olivia might have been wearing one when she—" Rachel broke off.

If she's acting and knows something she isn't revealing, Ellery thought, *then she's very, very good.*

"Can I see the shirt again?" Ellery asked. "The one in the box, not the one we found in the trailer." She kept herself from saying, "Not Olivia's."

"Okay." Rachel sounded faintly puzzled, as if she wanted to ask what good that would do. She slid the box across to Ellery.

She picked up the shirt and shook it out. There was Ben, in his penguin costume, his adorable puppy-dog eyes looking up mournfully. The quality of the photo was, of course, compromised by its having been printed on fabric, but there was no mistaking the sweetness of his expression, the way he was looking at the person taking the photo with absolute love and trust. Ellery swallowed hard. She had seen Ben's eyes in death, borne witness to his very last expression.

Ellery realized there was a figure sitting on the doorstep behind Ben. *The shadow self.* She looked more closely, trying to get a sense of the picture without getting *too* close and having it dissolve into colorful fabric fibers. It was a youngish man with a gentle expression.

"That's Ben's dad," Rachel said. "According to Olivia. His mom was taking the picture."

It wasn't clear that the man would have known he was in frame. In fact, he seemed to think he was sitting out of it, on the front steps behind the carved orange jack-o'-lanterns that flanked the stairs. But Ben's mother had captured him in the shot, and in doing so had captured him looking at his son with a quiet joy so real that it crossed years and mediums and being transferred to an article of clothing. There was so much love in all of it—the child in front of and mother behind the camera looking at each other, the father the third point of the triangle in the tender scene, the fact that Olivia had, Ellery was certain, selected the photo not only for the outright, undeniable darlingness of Ben but also for the way the love his parents had for him infused every pixel of the scene without being overt. A picture of the three of them would have been too sad or poignant, had likely been saved for another moment in the wedding celebration. But this—Ben might have laughed at seeing his own childhood face waving him off on his honeymoon, but also would have recognized the photo, the way his parents weren't central but were both present in some way.

Were they going to find Olivia? Would it be in time?

Ellery peeked inside the box, but there was no invoice or receipt.

"Do you remember how many were left?"

Rachel shook her head. "I carried the box back from the staff lounge last night. But I didn't count them. I just dumped them here."

"You, Olivia, and Andy were all wearing them when I came in," Ellery said, trying to remember. "So that's three. And then Trevor took a few. Do you know how many?"

"No," Rachel said.

"Do you still have yours?"

Rachel nodded. "It's in my room. The new one next to yours. I packed up everything and brought it over. I remember seeing it then."

"And you're sure it's still there?" Ellery asked. "No one could have taken it?"

"I should check." Rachel's face had paled. "I mean, no one would come and take something out of my room, right?" She glanced at the pocket of her jacket, where she'd put the borrowed keys from Maddox. Her eyes met Ellery's. "I guess nothing is secure."

"I think that's safe to assume." Ellery was thinking of her own room, the mirror she could have sworn was a painting before. "The art," she said. "I think I know which piece was stolen." She hesitated. Should she tell Rachel? She and Ravi and Nina had kept secrets among themselves so far. But could Ellery really hold out on telling Rachel something that might help her find Olivia? However unconnected it might seem to be?

"Which one?" Rachel asked.

"The screen," Ellery said. "The one with the poppies painted on it, that used to be in the reception area."

She was surprised to see Rachel visibly deflate. "That wasn't stolen," she said. "Catherine has it."

"What?"

"Catherine requested that Olivia be able to use it while she was dressing for her wedding."

Ellery wasn't sure she understood.

"That way, Olivia could get ready in the same room with all of us but have some privacy," Rachel explained. "Catherine was staying in one of the cottages. It was the home base for the wedding preparations, since it's bigger than any of the rooms. That's where Olivia got ready for her wedding day."

"Right," Ellery said. She supposed that asking to use the screen did make sense. She'd seen something like it in movies, maybe. People handing things to the bride behind the screen, the bride emerging to gasps as everyone saw her in her wedding dress.

"Catherine oversaw the transfer of the screen to the cottage, and she paid for the expense of having to move it," Rachel said. "The owner of the resort had to sign off for her to do it, and he did."

"Do they usually let people do that?" It seemed like the art in this place was turning out to be curiously mobile. There was the roving Warhol, the crown that disappeared and reappeared, the screen—and, still, the missing piece of art, whichever one that was.

"I don't think so," Rachel said. "But with Catherine having curated the collection, they were willing to make an exception. Apparently the screen had some kind of special association for her. And Catherine gets what she wants."

"Sometimes it feels like this is Catherine's resort more than anyone else's," Ellery said.

Rachel gave a short laugh. "Brook says it feels like that whenever Catherine stays here."

"How often does she come?"

"I think a couple of times a year, to check on the art."

"Does she drive the staff nuts?"

"I get the sense that they feel it's like having one of the bosses visit,"

Rachel said. "They're on notice, and it stresses them out. They want things to go well. They want to impress her."

Ellery could picture that. "So the screen is still in Catherine's cottage?"

"I think so," Rachel said. "It was due to be removed on Sunday when we left, but then everything happened. And I can't imagine they'd want to move it in the rain."

"Do you think the staff has told Maddox which piece is missing?" Ellery wanted to know more about Rachel's relationship with him—was it simply that he, like Ellery, was empathizing with Rachel's plight? That could be enough reason to lend her the keys the staff had trusted him with. Or was it something more? Was his relationship with Morgan *not* as airtight as it seemed? And how long had he—or through him, Morgan or Rachel—had access to the keys?

"No," Rachel said. As if she were reading Ellery's mind, she said, "He understands why I might need to bend some of the rules to try and find Olivia. More than Brook or Canyon do, anyway. I get it, though. They've got their hands full. This whole thing is a dumpster fire."

"Should we tell him about the shirt?" Ellery asked, as they locked the door to Olivia's room. "Do you trust him?"

"No." Rachel pocketed the key. "I wouldn't say that."

42.

Ellery was going to be late for dinner. If she didn't show up, Ravi and Nina would send out a search party. Her head was still swimming with what she and Rachel had found and what they should do about it. *I think I'm going to tell Brook,* Rachel had said, when they'd gotten back to their rooms. *But can you not tell anyone else? At least for an hour or two?*

Dr. Anand, Ellery thought again, removing her muddy boots just inside her door. She wasn't sure why his name kept coming to her mind. Perhaps because he had been kind to her, or because at least he was an expert in *something.* The rest of them were blundering around, trying to figure out how to get out of here without dying.

Ellery closed her eyes and took a few deep breaths. *Be careful. You need to make it home.* She was about to peel off her socks when there was a knock on the door. Carefully, she looked out through the peephole.

It was Brook.

Ellery glanced around behind her wildly, as if she needed to hide the evidence. But what evidence? The sweatshirt in its plastic bag was with Rachel. And Rachel was likely telling Brook about it soon anyway.

She opened the door. Brook was holding a package. "I'm sorry," they both said at the same time, and then they both smiled, or what passed for it at this stage in the situation.

"Please, go ahead," Brook said, indicating that Ellery should speak first.

"I'm trying not to get the room too messy," Ellery said. "I went out for a little walk, not off the paths or away from the main areas or anything, but it's still really muddy."

What the actual hell are you doing? she could hear Abby asking. *Could you be any more obvious? You're the worst liar! And you're drawing attention to the very thing you don't want her to notice!* Ellery bit her lip to keep from laughing. She missed Abby so much.

But Brook barely gave Ellery's muddy gear a glance. "Don't worry about it. Here. This is for you." She held out the package for Ellery to take.

"Thank you," Ellery said, accepting it.

"Again, my apologies," Brook said. "It came on Saturday, with directions to deliver it to your room Sunday morning before you left, but then with the wedding being canceled, and then your discovering Mr. Taylor, and our being trapped here..." She paused. "It had to be refrigerated, so it wasn't behind the desk, and I forgot..."

Ellery's heart leaped for a moment. Could it be from Luke? What if he'd sent her something to mark their anniversary?

If it had to be refrigerated, could it be flowers? Was he missing her, too?

She wanted to open the box right away, but Brook was lingering as if she had something to say. "I was wondering," Brook said, and then she stopped. She glanced over her shoulder. Her expression when she looked back at Ellery was fearful, as if she didn't want to be overheard.

"Would you like to come in?" Ellery pushed the door open wider.

"Yes, thank you," Brook said. She ducked inside, and Ellery used her muddy sock to nudge her even muddier boots out of the way.

With the door closed behind them, the room dark except for the emergency lantern emitting a low glow, Ellery couldn't see Brook's face as well as she'd like. She had a sharp pang of misgiving—she didn't really *know* the assistant manager; they'd only spent a few days trapped at the same place. Ellery would never have let Canyon into her room, even though she liked him, too. But women could be killers as well as men. She held the parcel out in front of her in a way that she hoped didn't look protective. It wouldn't do anything to stop a knife or a gun, but it was all she could think of without seeming paranoid and asking Brook to leave. Interesting, her mind noted, that she would accept an increase in the risk of death over looking rude.

If anything happened, she'd scream. Rachel would be sure to hear it on the other side of the wall, wouldn't she? It wasn't as if Ellery were trapped in the sauna.

Brook spoke again in a rush. "I know you and Ravi and Nina have been asking about the missing art, and I was following protocol and being discreet about it. But now that the crown was stolen, too—it made me wonder if the murders are connected to the art in some way." Brook took a deep breath. Ellery felt her heartbeat quicken. Was Brook going to tell her which piece of art was gone?

"Have you come up with anything else?" Brook asked. "Any connections, or new information?"

"No," Ellery said. She hoped her discomfort didn't show. Technically, she wasn't lying. She and Ravi and Nina *hadn't* come up with anything new, since it turned out the screen hadn't been stolen. Any discoveries Ellery had made that day had been with Rachel, which wasn't what Brook was asking.

"Okay," Brook said. "We still haven't heard from Nat and Carlos, or the police, and Olivia's family is very concerned. Of course." She exhaled. "I'm sure the police will be here tomorrow. We don't have a safe helicopter landing area nearby like some of the other resorts, or I'm sure they would have tried that option during that window when the weather was clear."

"Did the police know about the art theft, too?" Ellery asked.

"No," Brook said. "We told the owner of the resort, of course, but they didn't want us to call it in yet. And we haven't been able to reach them lately, either."

"Right." Ellery shifted slightly. If Brook wasn't going to tell her which piece of art was missing, and she wasn't going to tell Brook what she'd really learned, then the conversation had come to its natural end. She was impatient to see what was inside the box and who had sent it. "Well, thank you again for bringing this over."

"I think you should be careful," Brook said, her voice quiet, the words catching on the heels of one another.

"Careful of what?" Ellery asked.

"Everything," Brook said. "Everyone." She sounded on edge, near tears. "I can understand why you and your friends want to figure things out. But really, you have to stay safe. Let the police do their work when *they* get here. *Please* follow the rules." She looked pointedly at Ellery's muddy boots, and Ellery knew Brook hadn't missed them after all. She knew Ellery had gone farther afield than she should have. But before Ellery could say anything else, Brook straightened up, her shoulders square, her jaw set. "Anyway! I'm sorry again about the package."

"It's fine," Ellery said. "Really." And then she couldn't help herself. Brook was leaving, and, in spite of the admonition the young woman had just given, Ellery had to push, had to ask at least this one thing. "Can you give me a hint?" she asked. "About the missing art?"

To her surprise, Brook answered. "It's one of the sculptures," she said. And then she was gone.

———

The package had been overnighted at great expense, Ellery saw, and the return address was from a gourmet bakery whose name she felt she might have heard somewhere. *Madrone Bakery.* But she'd never eaten or ordered anything from there. And who would have sent her a cake?

Luke, hope said.

She told hope to shut up. She didn't have time for it right now.

No return address, except that of the bakery. Across the front of the package, Nat or Brook or someone had written *Refrigerate* and *To be delivered Sunday morning* in red Sharpie. Ellery had to use her house key to open the package, the metal slicing through the cardboard in a jagged way. The sound set her teeth on edge. The outer packaging revealed another box stamped with the logo of the Madrone Bakery. When Ellery opened it up, she saw that it was a gorgeous white Bundt cake, snowed under in creamy white coconut frosting. There was a tiny card in a waxed envelope affixed to the cake. She opened it.

Was it supposed to be a…wedding cake?

Ellery and Luke's wedding cake had been of the era, so it was covered in white fondant that looked elegant but tasted terrible. They had each had one bite for the photos and then moved on to the next thing— she couldn't remember quite what, perhaps throwing the bouquet? Her mother had saved the top layer for them to eat on their first anniversary, as apparently was the custom, and Ellery remembered moving the cake from freezer to freezer (they changed apartments three times in their first year of marriage, always looking for a better, cheaper deal). They'd landed at last in the basement apartment of a friends' parents, and they'd taken out the cake and excavated it, hollowing out the decent actual cake part and leaving the white fondant shell behind, like an emptied igloo, a modern work of art. *Scale up that cake and name it* Excavation, *she thought.* You could place it as a sculpture somewhere on these grounds, a perfect example of a torn-out heart.

Congratulations, the card said. It was typewritten. *You made it.*

Ellery swallowed a laugh. *Not yet,* she wished she could say.

Although she supposed she *had,* in the sense that if the cake had been delivered on time Sunday morning, the day of her anniversary, Saturday, would have ended. Ellery would have made it through that particular first—the first anniversary that no longer marked a marriage—and been about to return to her kids. Instead, she'd had no time since discovering the body to think about marking the occasion. She'd been too busy trying to solve a murder—*murders*—and finding a way to get home.

Underneath the first lines, another sentence. *Trust your gut.*

There was no signature.

43.

You're going to get killed for this cake," Ravi said hungrily, as Ellery unboxed the coconut-covered dessert on one of long tables at the back of the social room.

"That's why I'm sharing it," Ellery said. She had asked a staff member who was helping with the food (name tag: *Gavin*) for a knife, but there must be some kind of memo about not giving potential weapons to any resort guests, because Gavin was now cutting the cake into thin slices himself.

Dinner was over. Guests had either headed back to their rooms or were lingering—rummaging through the board games, looking at books on the library shelves, conversing in small groups. The fraternity brothers had commandeered the pool table in the small alcove at the back of the social room. With them at a slight remove, the Main House felt as safe as anywhere in the resort could feel. There was a reasonably sized group, a fire crackling. The staff were folding up the extra chairs and clearing up the last traces of dinner (a crumpled napkin on the floor here, an abandoned brown paper box there).

Gavin had finished setting out the cake on round porcelain dessert plates, and Ravi reached to take one. "I think this is the biggest piece," he said. "Ellery, do you want it?"

"No, thanks." Ellery took a plate with a smaller slice. Ravi offered the largest piece to Nina, who shook her head.

"I won't be having any," Nina said. "Not if Ellery isn't sure who it's from."

"The package hadn't been tampered with," Ellery said. "And Brook agreed I could share the cake after dinner."

"That's good enough for me." Ravi picked up a fork. "Here. I'll eat this piece, and then if I don't die, you can eat some, too."

Ellery thought again of the message that had come along with the cake.

Congratulations. You made it. Trust your gut.

Were the words supposed to be ominous or encouraging?

In any other context, she might have considered them platitudes, so basic as to be almost meaningless. But now they seemed infused with importance, particularly the last line. *Could* she trust her gut? She couldn't trust her heart. All it wanted was her family, and that could make you dangerous.

"My friend Abby might have sent it," Ellery said, as they settled into a few chairs around a small coffee table tucked away in one of the corners of the room, near a window. Other guests were drifting over to the dessert table and taking plates as well. She smiled at Grace and Gary, gave a little wave to Morgan and Maddox. They were hand in hand as usual. Perhaps he really was just helping out a fellow guest by giving Rachel the keys. "My anniversary was Saturday. And this was supposed to be delivered Sunday morning, after I'd made it through."

"That makes sense," Ravi agreed. "And you two are close, right? So maybe she thought a signature wouldn't even be necessary."

"Or maybe it was from—" Ellery paused.

"No," Ravi said. "Don't even think it. It wasn't Luke."

"You're right." She now lived in a world where one of the most important dates of her life was being erased by the person she'd shared it with.

Ellery lowered her voice. "So. Why do you think Brook only warned me about being careful? Why not the two of you?" She'd told Ravi and Nina about her conversation with Brook—the warning, the new information about the missing art—when they'd met to walk over to dinner. She'd also filled them in on what Rachel had told her about the missing screen and their walk to the trailer bar (including the footprints, the two used glasses, and the missing bottles they'd seen in the Slipstream).

She hadn't yet told them about the bloody sweatshirt, however. It had been an hour or two at least, as Rachel had asked. Surely it would be fine to tell them now.

"She had the package to deliver as an excuse," Ravi said. "Plus, she knows Nina and I are staying in the same room. Maybe it was less intimidating to talk to one of us alone. She probably assumed you'd tell us later, anyway."

Of course, Brook and the staff all knew that Ellery was on her own. Even if it had escaped the notice of most of the other guests, or if they assumed she'd figured out some arrangement with Ravi and Nina, since she was often with them, the staff knew the truth.

"Maybe this cake wasn't even meant *for* you," Nina said. "Maybe it *was* a delivery that was forgotten in all the craziness of Saturday evening and Sunday morning, but it was intended for someone else. All of this makes me think it's not safe to eat. It could be poisoned."

They both looked at the cake, and then at Ravi, who put another bite into his mouth.

"This," Ravi said, closing his eyes and chewing, "is incandescent."

"I think it really must have been for me," Ellery said. "I mean, the box was sealed up tight. The label had my name on it."

"Maybe there were two deliveries from the same place," Ravi said. "And they swapped out the boxes and redid the tape perfectly because they wanted you to get *this* cake."

"Do you *want* it to be poisoned?" Ellery asked.

"At this point, I don't even care." Ravi took another bite, closing his eyes again.

"While we're waiting for Ravi to die," Nina said, "I have some thoughts about the art."

"The missing piece?" Ellery asked.

"Yes." Nina pulled out her welcome book. "Earlier, we were saying that the most likely pieces to be missing, based on size and how easy they'd be to steal, were the painting called *Leap* and the Warhol piece. But now we know it's a sculpture." She paused. "If we trust what Brook said."

"Do you think she was trying to throw us off?" Ravi asked.

"No," Ellery said. "I don't. But I could be wrong."

"Okay," Nina said. "For the moment, let's assume we trust Brook, so it's a sculpture that's gone missing. And, in going back over the descriptions in here"—she tapped the welcome book, which she'd opened to the pages featuring the art—"it seems to me that the only sculpture that could have gone missing would be the bench on Broken Point. The piece called *Thoughts and Prayers.* Remember?"

"But that doesn't make sense," Ravi said, his fork halted midair. "Wasn't that made of, like, steel and granite? It would be impossible to move."

"Not as impossible as the other pieces," Nina pointed out.

"And no one's been all the way out to the point to confirm that the bench is still there," Ellery said.

"Why would anyone steal a bench?" Ravi asked. "How are you going to resell *that*?"

"There's always illegal channels for selling art," Nina said. "Private collectors. Sales off the books. People have been doing this for decades. Centuries."

"But a *bench*." Ravi looked profoundly unconvinced.

"It's still a piece of art," Nina said. "And valuable."

Ravi shook his head. "Brook's leading us up the garden path. Or the cliff path, as it may be."

"Matt died out by the point," Ellery said. "That's interesting."

"Right," Nina said. "And people often commission benches as memorials. It might have had particular significance for someone, or they wanted it for that reason."

Ellery reached for Nina's welcome book, and Nina handed it to her. Ellery scanned over the description of the piece. "It doesn't sound like a commission was the case here, but it's still meaningful. It's a work about loss and grief. And it was part of a series. Maybe someone had the other pieces, and wanted it too?"

"Art and meaning and money." Nina's voice was soft. "There's often an uncomfortable relationship between the three."

"Excuse me," someone said. Ellery started. Morgan and Maddox had come up to their table, and Ellery had been so deep in thought that she hadn't even noticed. Nor had Ravi and Nina, judging by the surprised expressions on their faces. Had Morgan or Maddox overheard what they were talking about?

She hoped not.

"Hello there, Morg," Ravi said cheerfully. "Madd. How are you holding up? Have you had some of this?" He gestured to his cake plate.

"Yes, and it was *fabulous*," Morgan said. "I can't believe we got the Aidan Stone cake here. Do you think he sent it?"

"The what?" Ellery asked.

"You recognized it," Ravi said, applauding lightly. "I'm so glad *someone* here did."

"Fill us in, Morgan," Nina said. "Since Ravi apparently wasn't going to." She shot him a glare.

"Well, you know Aidan Stone," Morgan said. "The famous movie star?"

Everyone nodded.

"On special occasions, Aidan Stone sends people this cake," Morgan said. "Like, as a gift. People he works with, colleagues, family, you know. For their birthdays or whatever. Everyone feels like they've made it if they get the cake. They feel bad if they fall off the list. It's got to cost him thousands of dollars every year."

"How do you know this is the same cake?" Nina asked.

"I've seen pictures," Morgan said. "And I saw the box over on that table. Madrone Bakery. Anyone can order from the bakery. It's fancy but not, like, only for celebrities."

"It was actually sent to Ellery," Ravi said.

"Wait," Morgan said. "You *know* Aidan Stone?"

"I do not," Ellery said.

"*Okay*," Morgan said. She winked at Ellery. "Got it."

"I really don't," Ellery said. What surrealness was this?

"Then who is it from?" Morgan asked. "What did the note say?"

"'Congratulations,'" Ellery said.

"That's it?"

"Yeah." She didn't want to tell the rest of it. *You made it. Trust your gut.*

"Incoming," Nina said under her breath. Then she lifted her chin and spoke to someone behind Ellery. "Hi, you two."

"Hello, there," Gary said. "I hate to interrupt, but could we interest you all in a game of Monopoly?" He held out the box.

"Oh, *yes*," Morgan said. "I love that game."

They settled at one of the tables in the social room, pushing aside a few decorative books and candleholders. Rachel and Andy showed up right as they were about to begin, so they made room for them. "I'll be the banker," Andy said.

"Is that what you do in real life?" Ravi asked casually, picking up the fake cash Andy was dealing them.

"No," Andy said. "It's much different from my day job."

"Which is?" Ravi asked.

"Graphic design," Andy said. "Freelance."

"I would have guessed surfer," Ravi said.

"I wish," said Andy. "But I do work as a guide at one of the National Parks in the summer. Eden."

"That sounds like a sweet gig," Ravi said, and Nina burst out laughing. "What?" Ravi asked. "I say 'sweet gig' all the time."

"You never do," Nina said. "And you never go to National Parks."

"That's not true."

"Next summer, just say the word," Andy said. "I'll take you canyoneering."

"You'll take me *what?*"

Andy was the most animated Ellery had seen him since the hike. "Canyoneering," he said. "You'll love it." He gestured to Ellery. "Ellery knows the area, too. She grew up there."

"Is that so?" Ravi asked, raising his eyebrows at Ellery.

"It is," she said.

They rolled the dice to see who got to go first. It was Gary, who pumped his fist. Grace laughed and rolled her eyes.

"What do *you* do, Rachel?" Ravi asked, a couple of rounds later.

"I work for a senator," Rachel said.

"Ugh," Nina said. "Please tell me it's not Blaine Welch. That guy's the worst."

Rachel didn't say a word. She picked up her game piece—the thimble—and moved it two spots. "Reading Railroad," she said. "Anyone own that?"

"You're kidding me," Nina said. "Did I guess right?"

Rachel handed Andy two hundred dollars and he handed her the deed card to the railroad. "Your turn, Gary," she said.

"You work for *him*?" Ravi asked. "The one who looks like a bunny?"

"A bad bunny," Nina agreed.

"But not Bad Bunny," Ravi clarified. "He's no rap artist."

"He is not," Rachel said.

Ravi's face lit up. "A woodchuck! He looks like a woodchuck. Yes, that's it. It's more of a woodchuck vibe."

"That's the one," Rachel said. "I did an internship in his office when I was in college through my university. And then he hired me on. His politics are horrible. He's horrible. I've sold my soul. But the money is so good." She smiled. "The rest of his family is nice, though. His wife, his son. They're great."

"Rachel," Ravi said. "Does his son also look like a woodchuck? Because that's no life for you."

"His son does not," Rachel said. "And his politics are not the same as his dad's. He and his dad fight about that all the time."

"I'm still going to need to see a photo for confirmation that you're not dating a Woodchuck Jr.," Ravi said. "And maybe a voting record to prove that you're not voting for his father."

"I'm not *dating* the son," Rachel said. "All I said was that he isn't anything like his dad."

Before anyone else could say anything, Catherine's husband came crashing through the door.

"Who did this?" he demanded. He looked both livid and frightened. He held up...a face? Dirt dripped from it onto the floor like damp, clotted blood, dark and thick. Ellery blinked, twice. The room swam, spun.

"I don't feel well," Ellery said, and she felt herself sink to the floor.

I AM A HAUNTED house, she thought. I am not art or construct or anything difficult made beautiful. I am only a natural thing, a human being, with all the people I love echoing through my bones, breaking me from the inside out.

WEDNESDAY

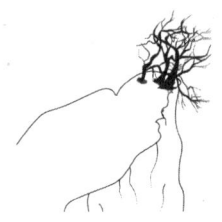

Today at The Resort at Broken Point

"We have forgotten how to be good guests, how to walk lightly on the earth as its other creatures do."

—*Barbara Ward*

Weather: Rain

SUNRISE: 7:16 A.M. .... HIGH: 56° F

SUNSET: 6:27 P.M. .... LOW: 45° F

ABOUT THE ART:
Nocturne
by Holland Corrigan
1996
glass, steel

This exquisite glass-blown chandelier is a tribute to the colors and feelings of night. Made of over 700 free-blown and mold-blown glass pieces, *Nocturne* was assembled by the artist herself on-site.

44.

Where am I?" Ellery asked.

"You're in the infirmary," Ravi said.

"They have an infirmary?" It was a place that Ellery thought only existed in books about boarding schools, or in East Coast summer camps for rich and mosquito-bitten children.

"I don't know if that's what this is actually called," Ravi said. "I'm guessing."

"What happened?" She could remember some things, but not everything. "Did I poison everyone? With the cake?"

"You didn't poison anyone," Ravi said. "Everyone else is fine." He paused. "I mean, everyone continues to lose their shit because we're in a dire situation, but no one else got sick. So it's not the cake."

"From what the others have told me, you seem to have experienced some kind of vertigo," Dr. Anand said. "And dehydration."

"It's very Hollywood starlet of you to succumb to dehydration," Ravi said.

"Does your family have a history of vertigo?" Dr. Anand asked.

Her head still felt slightly dizzy when she nodded. "Yes," she said. "My dad has it. But I've never experienced it until now. Is it a the-room-is-spinning, don't-know-which-way-is-up feeling?"

"Yes," Dr. Anand said. "When you get home, I'd suggest that you have your primary care physician run some tests. But as far as I'm concerned, you can return to your room after noon if you're feeling steady enough."

"How close are we to noon?" Ellery asked.

"Pretty close," Ravi said. "It's eleven now."

"What happened last night?" Ellery asked.

"We brought you here, you were pretty out of it. Dr. Anand gave you an IV to rehydrate you and something to help you sleep. Do you remember any of that?"

She did, now that Ravi said it. She remembered Dr. Anand asking her a few questions, she remembered signing something to agree to treatment, she remembered the grateful feeling of sinking onto the small bed and giving in to the spinning in her head.

"Wait," she said, remembering something else. "Was Andy here?"

Ravi nodded. "He carried you here," he said. "Nina came, too. And Grace and Gary. Rachel. Oh, and Brook. Morgan and Madd checked in on you later."

"You had quite an entourage," Dr. Anand said. "Just like a Hollywood starlet, as your friend observed." He smiled at Ravi, who smiled back.

Ellery took a closer look at Ravi. He appeared even more exhausted than she felt.

"Wait," she said. "Have you been here the whole time? Since last night?" She was embarrassed to find her eyes flooding with tears. These people had known her for only a few days, and they were willing to do more than Luke had been willing to do when she and Ethan had been in the car crash.

"Nina and I have been taking turns," Ravi said in a stage whisper. "We don't trust the doctor. Even though he seems very trustworthy."

"Thank you," said Dr. Anand. "I appreciate that." He stood and went to the door. "I'll be back shortly to check on you."

"Oh," Ellery said after he'd left. She was remembering more and more what had happened. "What was that *face* Catherine's husband brought in?" She paused. "What is his name, anyway?" Was this the murkiness of vertigo, or had she ever known it? "Is it Bill?"

"It might as well be," Ravi said. "It's Rick."

"He looked like he was ready to kill someone," Ellery said.

"Apparently Rick's salient characteristic is that he's very protective of Catherine," Ravi said.

"Well, one of the mysteries is solved, right?" Ellery said. "The missing piece of art?" Now that her head wasn't pinwheeling, it was clear that that was what the metal face must have been.

Ravi nodded. "It's one of the faces from the *Parts* sculpture. Someone buried it in the flowerbed near Catherine's cottage, and the rain washed away the dirt and exposed it, I guess. Which freaked Catherine the hell out."

"Catherine is still in a cottage?" Ellery asked. Hadn't she moved to another room like everyone else? Then she flushed. That was not the most important fact in what Ravi had told her.

"Catherine's gonna be Catherine," Ravi confirmed. "I think they kept her there because it was hard to make her move after her daughter went missing. Plus, then they'd be leaving the screen unattended."

"So someone steals a face from the *Parts* sculpture, buries it by Catherine's cottage, and then it gets found later?" Ellery asked. "That doesn't seem to make a lot of sense. Why steal only one part of a sculpture? And if they wanted to scare Catherine, wouldn't they have just put it on her doorstep? Or at least made it easier to find?"

"I know!" Ravi said. "That's what I've been saying, too. And if they really wanted to hide it and come back for it later, after this whole thing is over, why bury it in a shallow grave so close to the guest quarters?"

"Maybe they stole it after the restrictions came down," Ellery said. "No, wait. We knew there was a missing piece of art *before* the mudslide."

"And it's not like the restrictions have been keeping people from going walkabout," Ravi said dryly.

"What else is happening?" Ellery asked. "Olivia?" But she knew Ravi would have led with that if there had been good news, or bad.

"Nothing yet," Ravi said.

"And the weather?"

"Not raining," Ravi said. "But looking cloudy, and apparently

another storm is on the way. Canyon got a signal when he was out trying to see if we could leave yet, and he checked the weather."

"He got a signal?!?" Ellery struggled up. Her head swam again
briefly, but it was nothing like the night before. She had to contact her
kids.

Ravi held up his hand. "Don't even think about it," he said. "It's
way too dangerous. He and the other staff member he was with rolled
the ATV trying to get back here."

"Oh no," Ellery said. "Are they okay?"

"Yeah, but Brook is freaking out," Ravi said. "Understandably.
The staff is really drilling down on no one leaving. Canyon and the
other guy had to walk all the way back to the resort, and it took them
almost the whole night."

"I'm so glad they're all right," Ellery said. If something had happened to two *more* people…

"They were trying to get to a high point to see the main road, and
to see if they could find out what had happened to Nat and Carlos,"
Ravi said. "And they *were* hoping for a signal. They discovered that
the lower roads are all total soup from the runoff and the mudslides.
Canyon sent a couple of messages asking for help, they checked the
weather and took a screenshot of it. They tried to make a couple of
calls, but they dropped. They're not even totally sure their messages
went through or that the weather was properly updated. But it's all we
have to go on."

Ellery exhaled.

"It's really dangerous out there, and who knows what happened to
Nat and Carlos."

Ellery swung her legs over the edge of the bed.

Ravi put his hand on her arm to stop her from standing up. "That's
the main news," he said. "Admittedly, I should have led with it. But
it's not noon yet, and the last thing we need is you leaving here before
you're ready and falling down and cracking your head open." He
winced. "Bad choice of words."

"That's okay," Ellery said. "There are no good words right now."

"Plus, your being in the infirmary gives me and Nina another place to visit," Ravi said dryly. "Now we can go to our room, the Main House, *and* here."

Ellery sat back.

"Nina and I have been talking," Ravi said, his voice low. "And we both think Catherine is a likely suspect for killing Ben. She didn't like him. The sculpture was found outside her door."

"That's all circumstantial," Ellery said.

"Agreed, but circumstantial is all we've got." Ravi glanced at the door through which Dr. Anand had disappeared. "But there wasn't any extra blood at the pool. We got that much out of Canyon. So if Ben was killed somewhere else, we're not sure Catherine would be strong enough to bring him all the way to the pool."

"She might be," Ellery said. It would be difficult for a woman of Catherine's size, but not impossible. "And she might have had help?" If protecting Catherine was indeed Rick's salient characteristic, surely he would have helped her if needed? "What would her motive be for killing Matt? Because Matt knew that she had killed Ben?"

"Right," Ravi said. "Again, there's a lot of hypothesis happening here. But it does add up."

"What about Olivia?" Ellery said. "Catherine would never hurt Olivia."

"Maybe she really did go off on her own and got lost or hurt out there somewhere."

Ellery nodded. "I agree. If Catherine's the killer, she'd draw the line at Olivia."

"And if Catherine's *not* the killer, maybe Olivia was on the track of whoever *is*," Ravi said. "We don't have any concrete evidence that she's been hurt, do we?"

Ellery remembered the bloody sweatshirt that she and Rachel had discovered. *Rachel*. She needed to talk to her, to make sure that she could tell Ravi and Nina about what they'd found. Should she go ahead and tell him now?

Ravi was looking at her with what seemed to be a watchful, waiting expression. Did he already know? She hated being caught in this in-between place, where loyalty to one person might mean disloyalty to another.

"Wait," Ellery said. Another thought had struck her. "You said before that Catherine might be the shadow celebrity. What if Ben found her out? That could be another motive."

"Could be," Ravi agreed. "But I think I had it wrong. Catherine's not a shadow celebrity. She already *is* fairly famous, at least in the art world. And she's not completely unknown outside of it."

"That's true," Ellery said.

"Besides," Ravi said. "It wasn't her the Aidan Stone cake got delivered to."

Ellery wasn't sure what he meant. She looked at him quizzically.

He raised his eyebrows. His expression was still waiting.

Was he saying *she* was the shadow celebrity? Because that was ridiculous. She hadn't done any of the kinds of things that Ravi had suggested on the first night they met. She wasn't the head of a movie studio, the developer of an app, a cryptocurrency founder.

But a sick feeling had begun in her stomach. A voice around the edges of her mind that she didn't like. *What if he'd seen that awful* People *article? What does he know?*

She tried to laugh. "Ravi," she said. "It's not me."

Ravi held her gaze. "Okay."

Wait—did that mean he thought she was capable of killing someone?

The trust she'd felt moments ago wavered.

"Okay," she said. "You were right. I'm still kind of dizzy. If you don't mind, I think I want to rest alone until noon."

"I don't think that's a great idea," Ravi said.

"You really don't trust Dr. Anand?" Ellery asked. "He's not a killer. His whole job is to take care of people."

Ravi raised his eyebrows. "Doctors kill people all the time."

"If he wanted me dead for some reason, I'd be dead already," Ellery said.

"No, you wouldn't be," Ravi said stubbornly. "Nina and I have made sure of that. We've never left you alone."

"Excuse me," Dr. Anand said, reappearing through the door. They both started. "I was in the other room, and I couldn't help but overhear that my patient would like to rest." He smiled at Ravi, but the message was clear. *Time for you to leave.*

Was Dr. Anand protecting her? Or did he think she was the killer, and he was protecting everyone else?

She looked at Ravi. You never knew who you could trust. You just didn't. The world and the people who loved you, the surest things, could turn on a dime.

"Would you like to leave?" Dr. Anand asked quietly, after Ravi had gone. "I can't keep you safer here than anywhere else, really. But it seemed that you wanted to be on your own, so I asked him to go."

"Yes," Ellery said. "Please. I want to get back to my room."

"Come back if you feel dizzy again, or need another IV," Dr. Anand said.

"Okay." But she wouldn't. She was grateful to him for helping her to get Ravi to leave, and there was a time she would have trusted Dr. Anand. But that had passed.

Ellery saw that he knew this. And she was sorry for that, and for situations that made people not trust one another anymore.

And of course he wouldn't tell her more about Ben's death or how long he might have been gone when she found him. Why would he?

"I recognize you," Dr. Anand said.

She froze.

"You must be mistaken," Ellery said.

"No," he said. "I don't think I am." He smiled gently. "I was in Colorado a few years ago for a work conference. I watch the news every night when I'm traveling. I like to know what's happening where I am."

Ellery felt a swim of dizziness come over her.

"It is admirable to want to fly under the radar," Dr. Anand said. He nodded to her and left the room, closing the door tightly behind him.

They hadn't put her in a hospital gown or anything, thank goodness. Someone had removed her boots. They were tucked underneath a nearby chair, and someone had brought over her coat as well. Ellery stood up and checked the pockets. Everything was still there—her welcome book, her pen, her wallet, her phone, her room key.

Shaking, she pulled on her boots and coat. They did nothing to warm her.

It was almost midday, but she knew that both a storm and the night were on their way.

Things were about to get very, very cold.

45.

Please don't let me run into anyone, Ellery thought as she made her way back to her room. She was in luck—in the distance, she saw a few people gathered around an unlit firepit, bundled up against the coming rain or the chill that seemed to be seeping into all of them. But no one was near her room. She quickened her pace. Her head felt all right. So one person had recognized her, or thought they did. No big deal. She could do this.

As she was fumbling for her key in her pocket, Rachel came out of the room next door.

"Oh, hi," Ellery said. This wasn't the worst person she could see. "Any word yet on Olivia?"

"No." Rachel's tone made Ellery look at her more closely. Something had changed. What was it? Why?

"Are you still staying alone?" Rachel asked.

Ellery hesitated, but what was the point? "Yes," she said. "You?"

"Yeah," Rachel said. "Interesting. I wonder why they didn't make us move in together."

"I guess because we don't know each other very well," Ellery said.

"Right," Rachel said. *Was* her tone cold, or was Ellery imagining it?

"Okay," Ellery said. "Well. Feel free to let me know if you need anything."

"I'll do that," Rachel said. "And if you hear any screaming coming from my room, keep yourself safe. Don't try and save me."

Why had she said that? And what *was* in her voice? The earlier civility and understanding were gone. Something felt off, strange. Had Ellery offended Rachel without meaning to? Was there an undercurrent of mockery in her tone?

"Okay," Ellery said after a beat. Rachel left, her stride purposeful along the walkway.

The daily card had fallen off the doorknob and to the mat again. Ellery leaned down and picked it up.

"Hey," a distant voice called out behind her. "Ellery."

Startled, she dropped the card. Bending down to pick it up, she saw that someone had written on the back.

> *Please meet at the altar at five tonight. Please don't*
> *tell anyone else about this invitation, and please come*
> *alone. —O*

O—for Olivia? Was she alive? Was this her handwriting? Ellery didn't know. She hadn't gotten a good enough look at the earlier note Olivia had left when Catherine had been showing it to Gary.

"Oh, hell no," she could hear Abby saying. "You're not going to an *altar* around the time of day the wedding was supposed to happen because someone summoned you there via a scary hotel card."

Ravi would say the same thing, given the chance.

She missed him already.

"Ellery?" The voice was Andy's. He was almost to her. She shoved the card into her coat pocket and turned to look at him.

Andy was dressed as if for a rock-climbing excursion. Athletic gear, close-fitting clothes, a rope slung over his shoulder.

"I can't do this anymore," Andy said. He seemed as if he were wound so tightly he might burst. She understood the feeling exactly. "I'm getting out of here. Do you want to come?"

46.

Had Ravi really figured out who she was?

Had Rachel?

Who had written that note? *Was* it Olivia?

Ellery's thoughts clambered over one another in her mind as she followed Andy down the path. They were taking the one that also led to the trailer bar, but Andy said another branch veered off before reaching the bar and ran along closer to the resort's main drive. He'd been paying attention to where things were when he'd been out helping look for Olivia.

Andy had waited outside her room while she changed, layering on her warmest clothes and throwing a pair of sneakers into her backpack before slinging it over her shoulder. They'd be better for gripping if she and Andy ended up climbing over anything significant. As she'd left the room, she caught her reflection again in the mirror, and she'd noticed how wide her eyes were. *What are you doing?* she almost asked.

She couldn't trust anyone.

Not even herself.

She didn't trust Andy. But he had things she needed. Rope and expertise and the will to leave Broken Point. He also had a plan. "I'm going to try and get to the closest resort," he said. "The Coldwater Inn. Nat and Carlos said that it was too washed out to get up there, but they weren't on foot. We might as well try. Maybe they have a signal."

It had seemed as sound a plan as waiting for the police to come while one by one the guests died. And it had the added benefit of motion, of moving your body so you didn't lose your mind, which was what Ellery was beginning to worry was happening to her.

She could not stay here another minute like this. If Olivia had left of her own volition, Ellery understood that. She wanted to get back to her kids, and she imagined those close to Ben felt like they were climbing the walls, trapped in the place where he'd died without anywhere to run, scream, cry.

"You met Ben when you were really young, right?" Ellery asked Andy as they picked their way single file along the trail toward the resort road. Leaves, tiny mudslides, and debris were everywhere, and she was glad for the hiking poles they'd taken from the Main House.

"Kindergarten," Andy said. "We were on the same soccer team. We both sucked."

Ellery laughed in spite of herself.

"We liked to go hiking and stuff like that more," Andy said. "Skiing, rock climbing, surfing. You're part of a team, but in a different way. And you only need two of you."

They made their way along the trail in silence for a time, concentrating on the placement of their feet, the land around them. It was not easy going, but it helped that she could follow what Andy did and either go along with it or, if he stepped somewhere that ended up not being ideal, try a different option.

"Ben's dad took us camping a bunch before he died," Andy said. "We came here to Big Sur once. He was super into the outdoors."

"And your dad isn't?"

"Oh, my dad's outdoorsy." Andy's voice was bitter. "In the way that he likes to snowmobile in federal land that's been closed off to prove a point. Or chop down a tree for a photo op. He's also amazing at posing with big game that someone else has helped him shoot."

"He sounds like the opposite of you," Ellery said.

"Thank you," Andy said. "He is." His voice had loosened since they'd begun the hike, but she could still sense the wound-tight tension in it.

They paused for a drink of water. Ellery stayed more than an arm's length away from Andy, giving herself space to run if it were necessary. But *could* she outrun him? She studied his face as he drank, tried to see the kindness in his eyes that she'd noticed before, remembered how she'd told Ravi that Andy was the person she'd trusted immediately. It was still true to some extent—she didn't know that she would have tried to hike out with anyone else—but she was not taking any chances. Nothing was safe.

"My dad was—is—really hard," Andy said. "Ben's dad was great. Like Ben. They got me through a lot of hard times." And then, for the first time since she'd known him, Andy sounded full-on *angry*. "It is total shit that people like Ben and his dad are dead and people like the rest of us are still living."

As soon as the anger had come, it disappeared. Andy passed a hand over his face. "I'm sorry."

"It's okay," Ellery said. "Grief is hard."

She was struck again by the unorthodox nature of Andy and Ben's friendship—how they'd given each other so much space and understanding—but why did that seem so rare? Wasn't that the way friendships should be?

"Why didn't you ask one of the groomsmen to come with you?" Ellery asked, as they started moving again. Was that the highway she saw through the trees?

Andy snorted. "Why would I do that? They're Ben's friends, not mine."

"I don't completely understand his friendships with the groomsmen," Ellery said. "From everything I know about Ben, which isn't much, he doesn't seem like the frat-guy type at all."

"He liked it because it was an instant family," Andy said. "Sure, these guys can be idiots, and Jason is pretty toxic a lot of the time, but they all genuinely looked out for and liked Ben. He was the kind of person that, if you were around him, made you want to be better."

An instant family. Ellery could see how that would be appealing.

Andy came to a sudden halt. She almost ran into his back but stopped in time. She looked past him, to the road and the landscape that had opened up in front of them.

Her breath caught.

It was astonishing. The mountain, the trees, the world—it had all come down.

The highway was entirely covered in places in both directions. The trees had slid down with the earth and were in every possible condition—snapped in half, fallen over, splintered, prone, upright and hanging on to the banks of earth that had come away like huge chunks of snow in an avalanche. Most of the road had disappeared.

Her heart sank. Now that they were confronted with the staggering reality of the disaster, she realized how foolish they'd been for even thinking it might be possible to get out. And this wasn't even the main landslide, the one that had taken out the bridge.

"Holy shit," Andy said.

She remembered how he'd said that earlier, at the view on the hike the day of the wedding.

Now she wondered about the way he'd come out of the woods that day in a place she didn't expect. What had he been doing off the trail? Who *was* he, really? The second-best man. A person who knew the men who had died and the woman who had gone missing.

Andy glanced back at her. "Well?" he asked. "I guess there's nothing to do but keep going. We're going to need two of us to get up to that road that leads to Coldwater. I don't think anyone should try to climb anywhere alone. It's too dangerous."

"You're planning on trying to go *over* this?" she asked, gesturing at the road in front of them.

"Yeah," Andy said. "I don't see another choice. And I can't stay at the resort anymore."

Earlier, she'd thought she understood why. Because there came a point when everything was too much and you had to *move*. But was Andy really trying to get to the other resort? Why had he brought her along? Matt had likely died from knowing too much. Did Ellery know more than she thought she did?

Ellery felt shaky, and it wasn't only the vestiges of the vertigo from the night before. "You're the one who was most likely to have access to Ben's phone. You were the person he trusted most." She swallowed. "Did you send the text? Did Matt figure things out?"

"What are you talking about?" Andy asked. She took a step back. He had that rope and who knew what else in his backpack. He was bigger and stronger and younger than she was. She gripped the hiking poles in her hands. She wasn't entirely defenseless. But she was going to have to be smart.

"The text that was supposed to be from Ben," she said. It had always bothered her. "The one the day of the wedding. Did you send it?"

Andy looked confused. Then his face shifted. To anger? Pain? She couldn't quite tell. "Why would I do that?"

"Because," she said, "you're in love with Olivia."

There was a pause. Somewhere in the woods behind them, a stick snapped. She wanted to whirl around and see what it was, but she kept her gaze locked on Andy.

"It's not Olivia," Andy said. "It's Ben."

He was in love with *Ben*? But then wouldn't he have been more likely to kill Olivia if he was jealous?

Or had he killed Ben to keep him from being with anyone else?

Ellery remembered something. The note, about meeting at the altar. Signed with an *O*. Andy wouldn't have left it and then suggest that they try to hike out. So maybe Andy *wasn't* the killer?

There could be more than one.

Why had Andy asked her to come with him? Was he working with someone? Was something else happening back at the altar? The person he seemed the most likely to work with was Olivia. But she was gone. Wasn't she?

Was the note really from Olivia, or was it a decoy, like she thought Ben's text must be?

Ellery kept her eyes on Andy. "You couldn't lose Ben," she said. Her hands were cold. "So you killed him."

"*No.*" Andy's voice was somehow both a shout and a silence. He took a step closer.

Ellery's heart thudded in her chest.

"You don't understand," Andy said. "Let me explain."

No. She knew how this went. One minute you were perched at the top thinking you were safe, the next minute you were going over the side and there wasn't even time to scream.

She could not linger and ask the questions that people in movies always asked because the audience needed to know, needed to hear the killer say the terrible things out loud so that there wouldn't be even an inkling of doubt. *Did you kill him? And him? Did you kill her, too?*

But there was no audience who needed to know anything. There was just Ellery, standing in a ruined landscape with a man who might be a murderer.

47.

At first, Ellery ran, trying for footfall on the driest parts of the terrain, jumping to avoid mud and slick grass and upturned roots. In her haste, she dropped first one, then the other of her hiking poles and didn't dare stop to pick them up. *Don't catch me,* she thought, *please.* She couldn't hear Andy over her own breathing and the terrain required all her concentration. To fall would be fatal—she might hit her head, she might break something, and Andy would certainly catch her if she lost any of her head start. When she glanced over her shoulder she didn't see him, but that didn't mean he wasn't there.

When she was too exhausted to run anymore, she kept moving, working her way back through the trees toward the resort, the grove. Would she be in time? She wanted to try.

———

No one was at the altar. Her watch told her she was late. But Ellery saw, on the ground, an arrow made of stones set into the earth. They pointed along one of the paths into the trees. Someone was leading her.

The light was low and stormy. It was the gloaming. The rain was coming down in a fine and perfect mist.

She went deeper into the forest. This was the way to the *Love* statue, she realized. But when she reached it, there was another stone arrow, pointing to a thin, barely visible offshoot of the trail that Ellery hadn't noticed when she'd come upon Olivia in the dark.

After a few moments of following the path, the trees opened up in a way that Ellery did not expect. Her eye caught immediately on the glint of metal reflecting back the last of the light. The storm, the night: both were almost here, bearing down inevitably.

It was the sculpture of a crane, its beak pointed to the sky. *Untitled.*

The small pond was so swollen with water that the second part of the sculpture, the nest, couldn't be seen. Without the nest visible, the bird looked to be alone in agony at the edge of a drowned world, its children nowhere to be found.

Ellery and the crane were not alone in the clearing.

Grace. Nina.

Olivia.

Ellery stopped short.

"*Olivia,*" she said. "You're all right." So Olivia *had* left the note?

Olivia laughed. The sound was sharp and desperate and sad. "So to speak." She was dirty, her hair was tangled. Her eyes were shadowed, exhausted.

"Are you the last one?" Nina asked Ellery.

"I don't know." Ellery glanced around.

"No," Olivia said. "Someone else is coming."

Ellery was at once confused and illuminated. Something felt inevitable, as if she'd walked this scene half-awake, half-living, in another slipstream universe. The grove, the altar, these women.

Catherine entered the clearing.

"*Olivia,*" she said. Her face lit up, the way a mother's always does when she sees a child she loves and could have lost. She looked beatific, electric with joy. "Thank God." She moved toward her daughter, arms outstretched.

"*No,*" Olivia said. The word was sharp, bulletproof. Catherine pulled up short. "No. Not yet. There's something we all need to talk about."

"So *you* brought us here?" Nina asked Olivia. "I'm sorry. I'm not sure what's going on?"

"I brought *all* of you here," Olivia said, "because one of you killed Ben."

48.

There are hundreds of beautiful places," Olivia said. "Thousands. Ben always used to say that. *'It's crazy that we terrible humans get to live in a place that's so wonderful.'* But we're all here at this *particular* beautiful place for certain reasons."

She was right, of course. Ellery clenched her fists tightly. She wished she hadn't lost the poles. That she'd brought her flashlight. That she had any kind of weapon at all.

"Why would you think *I* killed Ben?" Grace sounded genuinely baffled. "You don't even know me."

"Because I saw you burying the face," Olivia said. Her voice was ice-cold clear. "Outside our cottage."

"Oh, shit." Grace closed her eyes briefly.

"What?" Nina said. "*You're* the art thief?"

"No," Grace said. "I can explain." She paused. "And why would my burying the face have anything to do with what happened to Ben?"

"Maybe he caught you stealing it," Olivia said. "I overheard you talking to your dad." Olivia took a deep breath, her eyes locked on Grace. Catherine's were on her daughter. "You said, *'Dad, you didn't have to do it. I could buy the whole resort, and just give it to you.'*" She spoke in a surprisingly good imitation of Grace.

"You're right," Grace said. "I did say that. But I didn't say anything about killing anyone, and it's taken out of context."

"The two of you were also the ones to find Matt," Olivia said. "You could have pushed him to his death without any trouble at all."

"My dad didn't kill Ben," Grace said. "And neither of us killed Matt. I promise. But you're right. We did come here for a reason." She exhaled. "My dad came here to honor my mom, and I came here to protect him."

"To protect him, or to protect people *from* him?" Olivia asked.

"Listen." Grace held out her hands. The humidity was curling the escaping tendrils of her hair, and she sounded earnest and direct. "We came here because it's a place that meant a lot to my parents. It would've been their fiftieth anniversary this weekend, and he wanted to scatter her ashes at Broken Point, which is totally illegal, so that's why we were trying to get out to the point the morning Matt died, even though it was stupid and dangerous." Grace's eyes were bright. "What I didn't realize was that my dad also wanted to come here to take a piece of that sculpture. *Parts.* He wanted a specific face from it, the one where the model is smiling slightly."

"Your father," Catherine said. She had had her gaze fixed on Olivia, but now she glanced at Grace. "He's Anonymous."

"Yes," Grace said. "He made that sculpture. And the model for all the different facial expressions and hand gestures was my mom."

"Why did he want a sculpture of her?" Olivia's tone was skeptical. "Couldn't he make another one? He knew what she looked like."

"No," Catherine said. "You can't ever repeat the art." Her voice held a note of understanding.

And you can't ever recapture the expressions, Ellery thought. *Not when they are gone. When they don't look at you anymore.*

"When I confronted him, he told me it was because he was forgetting her. He made *Parts* when they were at their best. He hasn't been able to work since she died, and he was slowing down before then anyway." Grace sighed. "He wanted a piece of her back."

"And the crown?" Nina asked.

"I took it to distract from the face being stolen," Grace said. "I left it somewhere I knew it would be found." She shook her head. "I know it wasn't a great idea. This is all such a mess. If he'd listened to me—if *I* hadn't been so stupid—"

But Olivia didn't want to hear more. She believed Grace's story, Ellery could tell. Enough to move on to the next person, anyway. Olivia looked at Nina.

"Enlighten me," Nina said, almost gently. "Why do you think I killed Ben?"

"Because of the reason *you* came here," Olivia said.

"Which is?"

"Because you're Ben's shit godmother," Olivia said. "The one who dropped the ball. Or, in this case, the orphaned child."

Nina flinched. Only slightly, but Ellery saw it. Was it because the accusation was *true*, in part? Maybe Nina hadn't killed Ben, but what if she *was* his godmother? If so, did Ravi know? *Everyone is hiding something. Everyone has a shadow self.* "I'm afraid I don't understand what you're talking about," Nina said.

"You fit the description," Olivia said. "You're the right age, you're beautiful, you have dark hair. That's everything he remembered about his godmother. She and his mom lost touch when he was small. He was fourteen when his parents died, and he kept hoping she'd show up and rescue him. Spoiler alert: you never did."

This was a different Olivia than the one Ellery had seen before. She was knife-blade angry, honed sharp.

"He told it like a joke, like he was stupid for thinking the whole fairy-godmother-rescues-lonely-teen thing could be possible." Olivia's voice wavered. "But you could tell it hurt. He went to live with his best friend's parents. With Andy. Because he didn't have anyone else."

Ben had lived with Andy's family after his parents died?

Ellery hadn't realized that when Andy and Ben had referred to one another as being "like family" that they meant they had actually lived in the same house for years. She'd known they were best-friends close, but not almost-brothers close. *Andy.* She had left him back there alone.

"At first, I thought you'd showed up to try and do something for Ben since he was getting married," Olivia said. "Better late than never. But now I think you came here to see if you could get some of his money. You must have heard how well he was doing. Maybe you thought you were next of kin in his will. So he had to die before we got married and it all came to me automatically."

"I'm sorry for everything you've gone through." Nina's expression and tone were inscrutable. "But this is quite a stretch. I am not Ben's godmother. And I'm not sure that's even how legacies *work*."

"Olivia," Catherine said. "*Please.* Can we go back to the resort? You need rest. Where have you *been*? Are you sure you're all right?"

"I've been sleeping in the trailer," Olivia said. Her eyes flashed to Ellery's. "It was a lot colder after you took my sweatshirt."

"Your sweatshirt?" Catherine said, looking back and forth between them.

"Rachel and I went looking for Olivia," Ellery said. "We went to the trailer bar and found her sweatshirt. Rachel didn't want to tell anyone. I'm sorry we didn't tell you. And I'm sorry we took the shirt, Olivia. It was bloody. We thought it might have been evidence."

"I knew people might search the bar during the day, so I tried to keep away when I could," Olivia said. "And I fell down and cut up my arm and the shirt got bloody, so I tried to get some of it out in the trailer sink and left it to dry."

"How did you get into the bar?" Ellery asked. "It was locked when we got there."

"Maddox took a key for me," Olivia said.

"*Why?*" Catherine asked. "Where did he get it? Why didn't he tell me where you were?"

"He didn't know where I went," Olivia said.

"But he could have guessed, if he gave you a key! At the very least, he could have told me you were alive!"

"This isn't the point right now," Olivia said. "Ben is the point." And now her gaze turned to Ellery. She felt her knees threaten to buckle. She knew what was coming, what had been coming for her for a long time, and while she was not ready, she was resigned.

"Okay," she said quietly to Olivia. "Why do you think I killed Ben?"

"Because you're the one who found him," Olivia said. "And because I know who you are, and what you did."

"What did she do?" Catherine asked.

Olivia took a deep breath. "She killed someone else."

49.

And there it was.

The words out in the open at last. Someone saying them to her face.

"I didn't," Ellery said.

Everyone was staring at her, shocked.

"She was the hero in a bus accident, where she saved a bunch of her students' lives," Olivia said. "But she also moved one of them who had a back injury, and that student died."

"I didn't move her," Ellery said.

"Even if you did, you would have been safe under the Good Samaritan law," Grace said, her tone gentle, practical. "All fifty states have some version of it. And I can't imagine a jury convicting in a situation like that. You were trying to help."

"Maybe you didn't kill Ben," Olivia said. "Maybe you were just the one to find him. And you did the wrong thing. It's a pattern, right?"

"I promise," Ellery said. Her voice shook, which she hated. "I promise that all I did was get Ben out of the pool and go for help. I promise he was already dead when I found him."

Did Olivia believe her? About the student? About Ben?

Please believe me.

No one spoke. The trees moved in the wind, warning the women that they were running out of time before the storm.

"I've been trying so hard to figure out who could have done it," Olivia said, her voice desperate. "Who all of you *are*. It seemed like it had to be one of you. You've all acted strange or suspicious in some way. And no one who really knew Ben could have done it. It had to be someone who wasn't in the wedding party. Everyone who knew him loved him."

Olivia looked at her mother. "Except you."

Ellery felt that they were at an edge here in the stirring forest, at the swollen pond, with the mother crane and her drowned chicks. She had a sense of something—or someone?—coming for them. Did the other women feel it, too? When she looked at them, their faces in the fading light, she thought they did.

"Mom." Olivia's voice was hushed. "Was it you?"

50.

Olivia," Catherine said. "I'm so sorry." Catherine sounded utterly weary and unbearably sad.

Olivia shuddered. She took a step back.

Someone else was coming. They could hear them through the trees. Whoever it was wasn't taking care to be stealthy, or to go unnoticed— they sounded almost like an animal, twigs snapping, branches moving. Ellery and the other women exchanged glances, edged slightly closer to one another. Who was out there?

"Why?" Olivia was dialed in on her mother, her body braced as if for further impact. Her feet were planted and her shoulders squared. Ellery was reminded of her children when she and Luke had told them about the divorce, the way they had frozen before they shattered.

"It was an accident." Catherine took a step toward Olivia, who held up her hand.

"*No,*" she said. "Stay there. *Don't touch me.* Just tell me what happened."

Catherine halted. "We were arguing, and I pushed him." She swallowed. "He fell backward."

Olivia gestured toward the crane, the pond. "It happened here, didn't it?"

Catherine nodded. "He hit his head on the second part of the sculpture. The baby birds have these sharp, upturned beaks." She took a shuddering breath. "They're all underwater now. You can't even see them. But that night was before the rain."

"*Why?*" Olivia asked. "Why would you push him?"

"Because of what he did to you."

"What did he do to me?" Olivia asked.

"He left you at the altar," Catherine said.

"No," Olivia said. "He didn't."

"Someone's coming," Nina said.

A voice spoke from the trees. "Someone's here."

51.

Jason walked into the clearing. *"Olivia,"* he said. "I'm so glad you're all right."

"What are you doing here?" It was clear from Olivia's voice that he had no place in the gathering. She wanted him gone.

"I've been out looking for *you.*" Jason sounded taken aback. His blond hair was damp with rain and he wore a dark jacket and the kind of expensive outdoor boots Ellery had seen on many of the groomsmen over the past few days. His mouth twisted wryly. "The staff's still telling us not to leave our rooms or go off alone or whatever, but they're just worried about covering their asses. Are you okay?" He looked around at the group. "What's going on?"

"Most of us are leaving," Nina said. "I'll walk back with you, Jason. If you're all right, Olivia?"

Olivia nodded. Her gaze was still locked on Catherine.

But Jason didn't move. "I'm not leaving Olivia out here with a murderer," he said. He pointed at Catherine. "I heard you. You admitted to killing Ben." Ellery could feel the anger rolling off him, and his finger shook before he dropped his hand to his side.

"Jason," Nina said. "Why don't we head back now."

"I'll come with you," Grace said, catching Ellery's eye. An understanding passed between them. Ellery didn't think Olivia was in any danger from Catherine, but someone staying behind with them seemed like a good idea. Jason, however, should go. He had no business here.

"No," Jason said. "I want to stay and hear what her excuse is for killing Ben. For murdering my best friend." Ellery felt her muscles tense. She saw Nina and Grace register the enraged tremor in his voice, too.

Nina stepped closer to Jason. *You don't have to take this on,* Ellery wanted to tell her. *He's not our responsibility.*

"Why?" Olivia asked her mother again. "Why were you angry enough to push him?" Jason did not exist to her. It was Catherine, here, and Ben, gone. And that was all.

"Because he *left you at the altar,*" Catherine said again.

"He didn't," Olivia repeated. "I keep telling you that."

Catherine's voice was soft, as if Olivia were having a break with reality and needed her mother to bring her back to the world. "He *did,*" she said. "We all saw the text."

Ellery remembered what Olivia had said Ben had sent in that message: *I can't do it. I'm sorry.*

"That didn't mean that he was leaving me," Olivia said. "It meant he couldn't go through with the wedding."

"Right," Jason said. "Ben would *never* leave Olivia. He'd die first. Which he did, thanks to you."

Shut up, Ellery wanted to say.

"You were wearing your wedding dress and standing in the grove waiting for him when you got the text," Catherine said. "How is that not leaving you at the altar?" Olivia started to speak, but Catherine barreled on, as if determined to get this out once and for all. "I should never have touched him. I shouldn't have been so angry. Olivia, I'm so sorry. But he *did* leave you there."

"What happened?" Olivia asked. "Tell me. All of it."

Catherine took a deep breath. "After we all left the grove, I went straight to Carlos and quizzed him about the cars belonging to the wedding party. They were all accounted for. And it wouldn't make sense to leave on foot."

"Why were you looking for him?"

"I wanted to give him a piece of my mind," Catherine said. "You wouldn't talk to me. You were with Rachel."

Rachel, Ellery realized, was not in the clearing. Did that mean Olivia still trusted her absolutely?

"I went and told Nat and Brook to open the dinner to everyone at the resort," Catherine said. "Once that was underway, I knocked on Ben's door until he answered it. I told him we had to talk." Catherine swallowed. "And I brought him here."

"So *that's* why you were so generous," Olivia said. "Why you invited everyone at the resort to the dinner." There was something of Catherine in Olivia, in her commanding presence, her absolute focus on accomplishing what she needed to do. "I thought it was out of character that you didn't try to get your money back somehow."

Ellery had seen Olivia at the *Love* statue. What time had that been? Had Ben already been lying dead only a few yards away in the forest? Or had Catherine killed him after that? Or—Ellery's heart thudded—while Olivia was nearby, weeping? No. Olivia would have heard them. Wouldn't she?

"Olivia, he was acting strange," Catherine said. "Like he was on something."

"Mom," Olivia said. "You know he wasn't. You know he never used anything, ever, because of his parents."

"He was on something that night," Catherine said stubbornly. "He seemed out of it. He kept telling me he hadn't left you at the altar, and he wasn't making sense. I think that's partly why he fell."

"*Stop,*" Olivia said. "Stop making excuses. Ben wouldn't have been on anything. He didn't leave me. I know him better than you did. You know nothing."

There was a pause in the grove. Even Jason didn't speak.

"Did you find him?" Catherine asked. "Olivia, when you texted and called him and knocked on his door, did he come and talk to *you*? Or was he drugged up and avoiding you and didn't answer?"

Olivia lifted her chin. "He didn't leave me." She and her mother stared each other down, across the small expanse of the clearing between them, the rained-down grasses, the dimming light.

After a moment, Catherine took a long breath. "He was still wearing his wedding suit when he answered the door," she said. "As if nothing had happened. As if he hadn't left you standing in the middle of the grove alone." She exhaled sharply. "I was so angry with him. I didn't want anyone to come along and interrupt us, so I told him to come with me into the grove and then on down the path to this sculpture." Catherine glanced over at the crane. "I pointed to it and told him that mothers always protect their babies, and what the hell did he think he was doing, not showing up for the wedding? I told him that I'd never thought he was good enough for you."

"Why would you say that to him?"

"He said he knew, and he said nothing was ever good enough for me. He said that you love me, and that Rick loves me, and it's still not enough." Was Catherine crying? Ellery couldn't tell. "He said that the wedding could have gone exactly as planned and it wouldn't have been good enough for me. He said *he* would never have been good enough for me. He said, 'You've made a living and a life out of acquiring things, and that's still not enough for you.'"

"He's right," Olivia said.

"I know," Catherine said. "That's what made me so angry. And why I think he was on something. He'd never spoken to me that way before."

"And that's when you pushed him?"

"Yes," Catherine said.

"I was *at* the *Love* statue," Olivia said. "That night. You're right. I hadn't been able to get him to respond to any of my texts or calls, and he didn't answer when I went to his room. The *Love* sculpture was our favorite piece, so I went there to think. To see if he might be there." Her voice wavered, the slightest bit. "Were you killing him *then*?"

"No," Catherine said. "No. I swear. No one else was out here. I'm sure of it."

"You couldn't know that."

"I did," Catherine said. "We walked right past the *Love* sculpture and you weren't there yet."

"Then *when?*"

"Everyone was still at the dinner," Catherine said. "I thought you were with Rachel. After he fell, I left him behind. I told myself that it was okay, and that if he wasn't, it was his own fault. I couldn't process what happened. I told myself he'd get up and walk back to the resort when he came to. I returned to the party. I'd been drinking, too."

"You came back to the party," Olivia said. "You knew he was hurt, and you left him there."

"Yes," Catherine said. "But I didn't know he was dead. I didn't know that until the next morning."

"So when I came out here, he was already dead. A few feet away." Olivia was crying, now, and her voice was wild and unhinged with grief. "Or he was hurt, and I could have helped him. *What if I could have helped him?*"

Olivia folded, sank to her knees. Ellery couldn't bear it.

"Why?" Olivia asked, for a third time. She was weeping. "Why would you push him? Why were you so angry with him?"

"I already told you," Catherine said, her tone one of absolute misery. "Because he left you at the altar."

"And I already told *you,*" Olivia said, "that he didn't." She exhaled raggedly, the sound one of utter despair and loss. "We were already married."

52.

Catherine stared.

"Holy shit," Jason said.

"We wanted to have our own wedding," Olivia said. "We got married at city hall in San Francisco two months ago. Rachel and Andy were our witnesses. Andy's mom came, too, since she and Ben are close from when he lived with them."

"But then," Catherine said, "all of this—"

"Was for you," Olivia confirmed. "Was for nothing."

"He didn't tell me you were already married." Catherine was trying to wrap her mind and grief around what she had just learned.

Olivia laughed, an incredulous, heartbroken sound, as she got to her feet. "Would that have made a difference? Would you not have pushed him then?"

"*No,*" Catherine said. "I wouldn't have been as angry with him. I would have known he was leaving the wedding, not you."

"No," Olivia said. "It wouldn't have made a difference. I've been telling you all along that Ben wouldn't—didn't—leave me. And you didn't believe me. And, like Ben said, he would never have been enough. Nothing ever is."

"Why didn't *you* tell me?" Catherine said. "About the wedding? Why didn't you want me there?"

"Because you would have been angry we didn't do it your way,"

Olivia said. "Before, that's why I didn't tell you. And then after Ben died? Because I didn't know what had happened. Because I wondered what you'd done." She breathed in, seeming to draw strength from the trees and the forest around her. "Tell me what happened. Don't skip over it. You pushed him. He fell. And then."

"And then," Catherine said. She stopped.

"Did you check his pulse?" Olivia asked.

"No," Catherine said.

"Then *what*?" Olivia asked. "You dragged him to the pool? Why?"

"No," Catherine said. "I left him here. I promise." She had begun to shake. "I don't know how he got to the pool."

"Did you call anyone?" Olivia asked. "Tell anyone?"

Catherine shook her head.

"You left him for dead," Olivia said. Her voice was cold. "How could you? How *could you*?" Then she paused, breathing shakily. "Because you did what you always do. You survive at any cost. If other people bear the hurt, it doesn't matter, because at least you made it through."

"Olivia," Catherine began, but Olivia held up her hand.

"No," she said simply. "No." How was she not breaking? "I know what I need to know."

Catherine fell silent.

"You left him to die," Olivia said. "Alone."

The grove was quiet.

"Everything you did," Olivia said. She took a deep, shuddering breath. "For me, for my whole life. It doesn't matter anymore. Because of this."

Catherine, Ellery saw, could not make a sound. Standing in the clearing near the pond, next to the bird with its beak raised to the sky, shrieking for its drowned nest.

53.

They needed to get back. Nowhere was ever safe, but this was not the place to be anymore, out here where Ben had fallen. It was going to storm again.

Ellery was close enough that if she stretched out her arm, she could touch Olivia. But should she? What did Olivia want? They were all extraneous, except Olivia and her mother and Ben. Ben was gone, but he still mattered here. Now.

Ellery had told Olivia the truth. She hadn't moved a student, she hadn't caused that death. And when she'd moved Ben, he had already been gone. Should she try to move Olivia now, to get her to walk away? Olivia looked like someone who had lost her footing, like she didn't recognize the people in front of her or the world around her. Ellery knew the feeling.

"Let's go back," she said gently to Olivia. "Let's all go to the resort. All right?"

"It was her," Olivia said. "I didn't want it to be her."

"It wasn't only her," Grace said. "Someone else moved the body. Who's to say he didn't drown?" She put her arm around Catherine, tried to get her to come along the path. But the elegant woman had frozen in grief, a physical reaction that Ellery's entire body understood.

We need to go, Ellery wanted to say out loud. *There is danger here.*

Olivia shifted slightly. Did she feel it, too? Ellery hoped she would take a step, start down the path, but instead Olivia looked back at Catherine. "Mom." Her voice shook. "Did you kill Matt, too?"

"I had nothing to do with what happened to Matt," Catherine said, shifting slightly. Ellery saw a flicker of the survivor rekindling. "I didn't even know for sure which of the group *was* Matt, until he died."

"Because you sure as hell didn't bother to learn our names," Jason said.

"Mom," Olivia said, her voice broken.

"You're right." Catherine closed her eyes. She looked like she might fall. "I shouldn't have said it like that."

Thunder rumbled. The storm was upon them.

"Okay." Jason sounded resigned as he flipped the hood back up on his jacket. "I'm going back now. She'll go to jail for Ben at least, whether or not she's telling the truth about Matt. Are you sure you don't want any help getting her to the resort?"

"I'm sure," Olivia said.

Jason turned, and Ellery expected some of the tension in the clearing to dissipate as he left. But there was still that latent energy evident in the line of Jason's shoulders as he disappeared along the trail into the trees, and she felt it, too. Her heart had not settled. Somehow, the danger was still here.

Without a word, Nina started down the path as well.

Grace took Olivia's arm. The bride allowed it. As Olivia walked away, she looked over her shoulder at Catherine but didn't speak. Ellery could tell there was nothing left to give.

She and Catherine were alone. "Are you coming?" Ellery asked, her voice as gentle as she could make it. She was not afraid of Catherine anymore. When she looked at Catherine she saw a woman who had done—inadvertently, perhaps, but still irrevocably—her worst, and who did not yet know if she was going to be able to survive the consequences.

"No," Catherine said.

The crane still shrieked to the sky, which was darkening.

Ellery hesitated. And now they had come to the point in the murder mystery where, if you left the murderer alone, they killed themselves out of guilt. More likely, in real life, this was the point where if you left the murderer alone a myriad of outcomes was possible. Catherine's survival instinct might kick in and she might return to the resort, wait for the police to come and arrest her, hire a lawyer, face a trial. Or she might wander into the forest and slip, fall, slide away, her body found later, in two years, ten years, not at all.

Catherine admitted to killing Ben. She denied killing Matt.

There might be another murderer out there.

They might never know.

Because life was like that. You couldn't ever know everything that might happen, and sometimes you didn't even know what *had* happened when it all took place right there, before your very eyes.

54.

As Ellery jogged along the trail that led past *Love* and back to the grove, she felt a drop of rain on her hand, another on her neck. The light was lowering fast and the forest had turned deeper, more ominous shades of green and gray. A sliver of panic cut through her heart—what if she couldn't catch up, or took a wrong turn? She didn't want to be alone. She was tired of being alone.

Ellery came into Ceremony Grove and pulled up short in relief. She'd caught up. There, standing by the altar, were Nina, Grace, and Olivia.

And Ravi and Rachel.

"What are you doing here?" Nina was asking Ravi. For some reason, she sounded angry.

"We were looking for all of you." He glanced at Ellery. She stayed a few feet back. She wasn't sure how he felt about her sending him away earlier at the infirmary.

"Well, you found us," Nina said. "Let's all get back to the resort." A spatter of rain hit the canopy of trees above them, a fit, a start of the storm to come.

"Are you okay?" Rachel asked Olivia. She put her arm around Olivia and Olivia leaned into her bridesmaid's shoulder wearily, as if it might be the last safe place in the world.

"She did it," Olivia said. "She admitted it."

"Wait," Rachel said. She looked over Olivia's head at Ellery, Grace, Nina. "Is she talking about—"

"Catherine," Grace said. "And Ben. His death."

Another spatter of rain, dappling the altar.

"Have you seen my dad?" Grace asked.

"He was in the social room when we left a few minutes ago, looking right as rain," Ravi said. He twisted his mouth wryly. "Bad choice of words." The rain appeared to have heard its name and answered with another sputter of drops.

"You saw Jason, right?" Nina asked Ravi.

"What?" Ravi asked. "Frat boy Jason? Why would I have seen him?"

"He went ahead of us on the path," Nina said. "He should have come right through here."

"I haven't seen him." Ravi glanced back at Rachel as if to ask her, but she and Olivia had begun walking up the trail to the resort, Rachel's arm still around Olivia. Another motion caught Ellery's eye—a long, dark green ribbon tied to a tree fluttering in the wind, a leftover from the wedding.

"Shit," Nina said. "Where did he go?" She sounded worried, out of sorts. "We can't lose anyone else."

"Maybe he got turned around," Ravi said.

"Catherine is still out there, too," Ellery said. It now seemed unimaginably callous that they—*she*—had left the woman in the clearing. "She wouldn't come."

"I need to get back to my dad." Before anyone could say anything, Grace darted away like a gazelle, sprinting up the path through the woods.

There was a kind of sharpening in the air. It smelled of foliage and earth and ozone and electricity.

"It's too late," Nina said, and Ellery knew she was right. "We should go back. *Now.*"

Crack.

The world shivered.

Light struck through the dim, the smell of burning filled the air.

And something large and ancient began to fall. Somewhere very near, a bolt-struck tree coming down, tearing at the forest as it went.

A scream.

"Catherine," Ellery said. Without thinking, she was off, back down along the path.

55.

The clearing with the *Untitled* sculpture smelled of burning, and even with the rain, the air was full of dust and debris from the treefall. Blinking, Ellery tried to take stock, to see clearly what was happening. It seemed the tree had fallen just past the clearing, thank goodness, and Catherine was there, and so was Jason, who was holding something in his hand, something that was—

"Do you *ever*," Jason said, "mind your own business?"

Ellery heard something behind her. "Shit," a voice said—Ravi's— and then she heard Nina say, *"Oh no,"* and she wished furiously that they had stayed back, that they weren't here now, because the thing that Jason was holding in his hand was a gun, and it had been pointing at Catherine, and now he had it pointed at her, and they were all going to die. That was what happened when someone had a gun and pointed it at people.

"What are you doing?" Nina asked.

"What does it look like I'm doing?" Jason asked.

"It looks," Nina said coolly, "like you were thinking about taking someone's life, Catherine's life, because she killed Ben." Moments ago, when she was asking about Jason, Nina had seemed agitated. Now she was deadly calm, her sights trained on him in a way Ellery couldn't quite decipher.

Jason raised his eyebrows but did not lower the gun.

"Which is an understandable feeling," Nina said. "But not an understandable action. Let's put the gun away and go back to the resort."

Ellery felt the weight of the moment, as if it were again the breath before the lightning. Would it hit here? Who would be standing afterward, if it did? She wanted to look over at Catherine, to see if she were all right, but she kept her eyes on Jason, his face, his hand, the gun.

"It sounds like you're trying to tell me what to do," Jason said.

"No," Nina said. "I'm not."

"There's just one problem," Jason said. "Catherine seems to think that I killed Matt."

He shifted the gun, training it again on the mother of the bride. The killer of the groom. She didn't speak. Her face was drawn tight, but Ellery saw the intelligence in Catherine's eyes, heard the careful weight of her silence. Any one of them could say the wrong thing.

"I'm sure she doesn't think that," Nina said. "None of us do."

Don't argue with her. Ellery willed Catherine to hear her thoughts. *She is trying to get us out of this alive. She's trying to talk him down.*

Ravi, usually so good at smoothing things over, was quiet. Ellery didn't dare take her eyes off Jason and Nina, but she felt Ravi's presence, the way he held very, very still.

"Come on," Nina said. "Let's go back to the resort." Carefully, slowly, palm up, she held out her hand for the gun.

Here we are at the point of the slide, Ellery thought. It was all the rain that had come down recently, and it was also all the dryness of years past and the structure of the land itself, underneath.

"Nothing's done that can't be undone," Nina said, which was both true and untrue. Jason hadn't shot anyone, not yet.

But people were dead.

For some, the earth had already come down and the world would never, ever look or feel the same. The geography of their lives would always have a before and an after, would always have scarring and ruin and new roads.

If they were lucky.

If they didn't die, too.

Grief could make you do terrible things. But not *all* the terrible things, not usually. The important thing was that Jason did not feel trapped.

Jason moved as if to hand Nina the gun. There was a flash of metal as the cuff of his shirt shifted up slightly, and Ellery saw that he was wearing cuff links. Like the ones she had seen on Ben, when she found his body.

Oh.

In that moment it came crashing together.

Did she draw in her breath? What sudden, near-imperceptible motion or sound did she make that made him look at her? Or was it nothing at all? Did something in the air, in his own intuition, give him the realization, too?

Jason looked at her. And when he did, she saw that he knew.

A million little things she'd seen and heard, because she'd come to Broken Point broken and alone, because she'd been watching in ways that everyone else hadn't, came together now.

He lifted the gun and pointed it at Ellery.

He was so close.

He couldn't miss.

56.

Ellery's chest was on fire. Or was she cold? Had lightning hit her? Or had the tree fallen on her? Wait. No. That wasn't it.

There had been a gunshot...

A face loomed over her. Her oldest, her daughter Kate! Was Kate here? Fear bloomed along with the pain. *No.* As much as she wanted to see Kate, this was the last place in the world she wanted Kate to be. And then she felt herself begin to shake. Was it Annabel? Had Annabel come for her?

Was Ellery dying?

Whether she was or not, there was something she had to say to Annabel.

"I'm sorry," she said.

"You'll be okay," a voice was saying. "I've got you."

Everything was suddenly very clear to Ellery.

It was not Kate, or Annabel. It was Grace. Jason had shot Ellery, and Grace was helping her.

"Please," Ravi said. "Do something." He was holding Ellery's hand.

This is good, Ellery remembered. *Grace is a certified wilderness first responder.* Was that how she had snuck up on Jason? Because now Ellery was remembering how right when Jason had gone to shoot, Grace had come out of nowhere from the forest behind him, leaping, grabbing his arm, the gun skewing slightly to the side instead of straight on, then falling to the ground—

Where was Jason now, though? Where was Catherine? And wait, was that Olivia's voice—*no, no, Olivia shouldn't be here*—

Ellery lifted her head.

"Careful," Grace said firmly. "Don't move." Ellery let her head fall back to the ground. This time it was Ellery being told not to move, Ellery the one laid flat with injury; she was not dead, but was she going to die?

"I'm sorry," she said again to Annabel. Was this what it had been like for her?

"It's okay," Grace said. She didn't know Ellery had been talking to Annabel. Annabel, who was not here.

But Ellery *had* seen Olivia. Just now. In the clearing. She had seen Olivia in the clearing holding the gun Jason had dropped, and it was pointed at him. He had his hands up, he was talking now—what was he saying? And where were Nina and Catherine, and had more shots been fired—

"You moved Ben," Olivia said. "You're strong enough to get him to the pool on your own."

"Maybe *you* moved Ben," Jason said. "Maybe you and your mom are killing people together and you staged this whole thing. The rest of us are next. Like I've been saying all along."

Grace was not wearing her jacket anymore. She was going to get cold. She was not wearing her jacket because she had taken it off and was pressing it against Ellery's chest, Ellery realized. She realized this because Grace said, very low, "I'm going to need yours," and then Ravi was handing Grace his coat and taking Grace's blood-soaked one and Ellery felt worried, because now Ravi was going to be cold, too, and was that her blood?

Olivia laughed. "Your *all the white boys are in danger!* idea never caught on, did it? Because it was ridiculous."

"It's not that ridiculous," Jason said. "Your mom admitted to killing Ben. Why aren't you pointing the gun at her?"

"Because you were pointing it at Ellery," Olivia said. "You *shot* Ellery. Are you forgetting that we all saw that?"

"I had a gun pointed at her because I didn't know then who killed Matt," Jason said. "And I wouldn't have shot her if you all hadn't snuck up on me. It was an accident. You're the reason she's over there bleeding out."

Ellery closed her eyes. Was she bleeding out? Was Jason telling the truth? Was Olivia? She didn't know what to believe. She did.

"You're doing great," Grace said, her voice tight. "Keep holding still."

She's so good at this, Ellery thought. *If I get home, I'm going to get a wilderness first-responder certification, too, so I can sneak around in forests and try to save people's lives instead of watching them die.*

When *I get home,* she amended. *When.*

When Grace had said, *I've got you,* things had begun rolling into place again in Ellery's mind. They were all lining up, like when that lottery ball on TV with all the little balls inside it stopped and the right numbers came out in a row. *Was that how it worked?* Ellery's gambling knowledge wasn't strong. But she knew what she knew. Ben. Cuff links. Jason had killed Matt.

Part of her wanted to keep her eyes closed. Wouldn't that be the best way to get back to her kids? Play dead, do nothing, hope for the best?

Or if she played dead, would she die?

"The cuff links," Ellery said. She opened her eyes. *"Have your back."*

"Shh," Ravi said. "It's okay. You're right. We do have your back."

"Someone needs to know this," Ellery said, her voice as firm as she could make it. Grace was still leaning over her, so she addressed Grace. "Tell Olivia. Jason is wearing the same cuff links that Ben had."

"That's very possible," Grace said gently. "A lot of times, all the members of a wedding party wear the same cuff links."

"It *is* weird that he's wearing a shirt with French cuffs out in the wilderness, though," Ravi said consolingly. His voice was still bright with fear, but he was trying to calm her. "You're right about that, Ellery."

Ellery wanted to cry out in frustration. It wasn't Grace or Ravi's fault that they didn't understand. They were distracted by Olivia and Jason and the gun and by taking care of Ellery.

"Someone will be here soon," Grace said. "They'll handle Jason. They'll figure it out."

But Ellery knew what had happened *now*. And some of the people who came to help might really be there to help, but some might not. She knew some things but not everything.

Ellery had to keep it short so they would listen and understand. She knew from the bus accident that it was hard to listen when you were in this kind of situation.

"Maddox has been helping Jason," she said. "He could have a gun, too."

"Shit," Grace said. "Rachel's alone on the trail. She went back for help."

"Maddox might not hurt anyone," Ellery said. "I don't know for sure." She tried to clear her mind. Telling them what she didn't know wouldn't help. She had to tell them what she *did* know, clear and neat, so they believed her.

"Jason moved Ben because he wanted Ben found more quickly," Ellery said. "He'd be found sooner at the pool than he would be out here."

"Why?" Ravi asked gently.

"Because back then, when Jason found Ben's body, he didn't know who had killed him or that the police wouldn't be able to come." Ellery knew the words weren't coming out as clearly as she wanted them to— her head was muddy—but she had to try. "And Jason knew that he had the best motive for killing Ben." It was harder and harder to talk. Could she tell them enough?

"Okay," Ravi said.

"Money is the motive." Ellery was getting cold. What was Olivia saying? What was Jason saying? She could feel the storm swallowing the air in great gulps, getting ready to breathe out on them again in full force. *"Have your back."*

"Shit," Ravi said to Grace. "Are we losing her?"

Ellery knew she wasn't making as much sense as she wanted to. But it was all there, lined up like winning numbers.

She closed her eyes. *Maybe*, she thought, it would be a while before she opened them again.

"Okay," Grace said. "One of us needs to tell Olivia that Jason killed

Matt. I'm not sure how Ellery knows that, but she seems to have figured it out somehow. And I believe her."

"Me too," Ravi said. "I mean, it stands to reason, since he's the one trying to kill people now."

Grace's voice was steady. "We need Olivia to keep the gun on Jason but we can't startle her into shooting him. And we have to keep an eye out for Maddox, or whoever else might be coming, since we're not completely sure who is on our side."

"They won't kill all of us," Ravi said. "They can't explain away *all* of us dying. Right?"

"Right," Grace said, but now her voice had the same waver in it that Ravi's did. They were in the dark in the woods. They were not the ones with weapons.

Ellery felt Ravi stand. "I'm holding up my hands," he called softly. "I'm here where you can both see me. Ellery just told us something that we need to tell you, Olivia. Keep the gun on Jason. He's the one who killed Matt."

Jason laughed. "She doesn't know shit."

"She does," Ravi said. "Have your back."

No, Ellery wanted to say. *Don't say that.*

Ellery could tell from the way the world flickered that Ravi realized he'd made a mistake. You didn't show your hand. You didn't *tell* them the lottery numbers.

She was getting her gambling all mixed up. She couldn't keep her eyes open anymore. "You're such a dork, Mom," she could hear Kate say fondly, and Ethan looked at her with wide eyes as she picked him up from his crib, he was small again, and Maddie was somehow grown up, but Ellery didn't know what that looked like yet so she needed to see.

She opened her eyes.

Ellery lifted her head in time to see Jason rush at Olivia. She felt the pressure Grace was applying to her chest leave as Grace stood—to run? to help?

And then the rain came down.

ELLERY HAD NEVER SEEN anyone die before. Around her were kids crying and Annabel's friend Daisy had curled up into a ball. Her hands were over her ears.

Annabel's eyes flickered open. "My mom."

"She'll be here soon," Ellery lied. Did Annabel believe her?

She looked up. Abby was still on her phone, giving a location. Ellery lied again. "It looks like Ms. Brown just got ahold of her. Okay. What?" She acted as if Abby were talking to her. Annabel, of course, couldn't turn her head to see.

"Okay," Ellery said, turning back to Annabel. "Did you hear that?" She rushed on, not wanting Annabel to try to acknowledge something she couldn't hear, that hadn't been said. "Ms. Brown said your mom is on her way. Your mom said to tell you she loves you. She'll be here soon."

"Okay," Annabel said. "Tell her I love her too."

"I will," Ellery said. She was not crying. She was holding Annabel's eyes with everything she had. "She loves you so much." Ellery said it over and over again, her voice soft and sure of what she was saying. She loves you so much. She loves you so much. She loves you so much.

She would not look away. Maybe it would be enough.

It was not.

57.

"Where there's life, there's hope," Jason said. "Right?"

He did not sound hopeful. He sounded like someone who was going to kill them.

Everything was happening fast and slow. Ellery was still on her back in the clearing. She couldn't see much. But she could tell that Jason had the gun again, and that somehow Olivia was next to her, and she was saying something to Ellery. "You have kids. You did this for me."

Olivia raised her voice. "Jason," she said. "Ellery has kids. You're not going to do this."

"Stand up, Olivia," Jason said. "Now."

Olivia had not run. She was not wired to leave people behind. She had come back for Catherine. She had stayed for Ellery. She had never left Ben. But there was one thing that Ellery could wager everything on. That she could trust her *own* instincts regarding another, stronger instinct that might kick in for Olivia, that might get the bride to leave Ellery and run. It was the instinct that Ellery had, too. It was red in tooth and claw and deep as her own soul.

"You are a mother, too," Ellery said. "Run."

———

What happened next was a storm.

In the same moment,

Olivia ran
Ellery pushed herself up to standing
and someone shouted Jason's name.
It was Nina, from somewhere in the trees. Jason turned.
Maddox came into the clearing. He had a gun, too.
Ellery was dizzy.
Her blood was in a rush. Away from her head, away from her.
Had she stood up
only
to fall back down?

58.

"We reverse-*Lord of the Flies*'d it!" Ravi said. "We were left in the wilderness without the proper authorities, and we didn't all kill each other!"

"Um," Ellery said. "I think our body count might be higher than the one in *Lord of the Flies*."

"That can't be true," Ravi said. "Don't they all die?"

"I don't think so," Ellery said. "But I teach history, not English. I could be wrong."

"But you weren't wrong about Jason!"

"Ravi," Nina said. "Calm down. She just got out of the infirmary."

They were in the social room. There was still no cell service and only the emergency generator was back up and running, but the police had arrived at last with Nat and Carlos who were (mercifully, wonderfully) alive. The officers were using the back office and staff area as their headquarters, and they'd taken both Catherine and Jason into custody. "We'd like you to stay close by for at least the next twenty-four hours," the lead officer had told the guests, which they had reacted to with both stress-induced hilarity (how would they even get out of the resort?) and relief (it seemed to indicate that Broken Point was due for evacuations soon).

"I know!" Ravi said. "The infirmary, twice in two days! First for vertigo and then for a gunshot wound! I can't believe you're out and about."

"Well," Ellery said. She was lying on a chaise lounge in the social room, shielded by the screen that had, at last, been removed from Catherine's cottage. Dr. Anand had wanted her to be close at hand, but now that he'd stitched her up, he'd allowed her out of the infirmary to be with her friends. "I'm not exactly out and about."

"But you're here, with us." Ravi indicated the lounge. "Chaising."

"True," Ellery said.

"And you solved the murder," Ravi said. "By *chaising* down clues." Nina groaned and Ravi had the grace to look embarrassed. "I'm sorry," he said. "I'm wired. I don't think the adrenaline has actually left my body."

"Can you explain it to me?" Nina asked Ellery. "I'm still not sure how you figured everything out."

"Please," said Rachel. "Tell us. And then I can explain it to Olivia."

They all went quiet at the mention of the bride. She was somewhere with her stepfather, discussing what they would do next.

"*Olivia* solved Ben's murder," Ellery said softly. "She figured it out when she was on the grounds. In the trailer bar. She brought us all to the grove, but I think she knew it was Catherine."

"I still don't understand how you knew it was Jason who moved Ben and killed Matt," Nina said. "I mean, we all suspected by the time he was pointing that gun at you, but you *knew*."

"'Have your back,'" Ravi said. He put his hands over his face. "I can't believe I said that out loud. I almost got you killed."

"The cuff links are kind of what locked it into place," Ellery said. "I saw that Jason was still wearing them. And I knew what the letters on them meant, thanks to Trevor. *Have your back*."

"Enlighten us further," Ravi said.

At that moment, Grace slipped behind the screen, Andy following close behind. "Hey," she said. "Is it all right if we hang out here for a minute? The police are interviewing my dad. Brook told me you were back here."

"Of course." Ellery's heart surged at the sight of both of them. "You saved my life," she said to Grace. "Thank you."

Grace shook her head, like it was no big deal.

"And I'm sorry for what happened when we were hiking out," Ellery told Andy. "I thought—"

"It's okay," he said. "I wasn't being totally honest with you. I hadn't told you about Olivia and Ben already being married."

"That's okay." She understood. He hadn't felt like it was his story to tell. He thought Ben was dead and Olivia might be dead, too, or lost. "When did you get back?"

"Not long ago," he said. "I made it to Coldwater. They had radios there, so we called in the latest information to the police. It turned out they were already on their way." He smiled at her. "And you're a hero."

"Again," Ravi said. "Have you heard about the bus accident?"

"No." Ellery felt tears threatening. "I wasn't a hero either time. I was just *there*."

Ravi reached out to hold her hand. "I'm sorry," he said. "But you *were* a hero. Olivia told us about the article she read. You called 9-1-1. You stayed with the kids until the ambulance came. You kept them calm and tried to help."

"But anyone would have done that." Ellery's throat ached, and she couldn't say the rest. *And someone else might have figured out how to keep Annabel from dying. Someone else might have been able to process the whole situation better so that it wouldn't be one of the final straws breaking the back of her marriage. Maybe someone else wouldn't have failed their own kids as well as the ones who were hurt in the accident.*

"Ellery's telling us how she figured out that Jason moved Ben's body and killed Matt," Nina said, briskly changing the subject.

Ellery used her free hand to wipe her eyes. This wasn't about what had happened to Annabel, or to Ellery's marriage. They were living this *now*, and despite what Ravi had said, she hadn't solved anything. All she'd done was guess right, and there were still things she didn't know, spots she wanted and needed the others to fill in. "Do you remember Matt the day after Ben died?" Ellery asked. "He was a wreck. More than anyone else."

"Yeah," Andy said.

"He was the best man, right?" Ravi asked.

"At *this* wedding," Ellery said. "Andy was the best man at the real wedding."

"Oh, right," Ravi said.

Just then Morgan slipped behind the screen. "Oh my gosh," she said, kneeling down next to the chaise, making Ellery feel like she was in a movie from the 1930s, one of those recline-and-die ones. "Maddox told me that Jason freaking shot you."

"He did," Ravi said, standing up. "And he freaking shot Maddox, too, as you are well aware." It was getting crowded in the area behind the screen, and he gestured for Morgan to sit in his place. "How is Maddox doing?"

"He's doing great," Morgan said, perching on the edge of the chair. "The bullet just grazed him in the leg. But Dr. Anand's not letting him out of the infirmary yet. I'm going right back there." She was wearing one of Maddox's shirts again and her large gray eyes were full of life. "Maddox wanted me to come make sure you're all okay. And I want to hear the full story of what on earth happened last night."

"Even we aren't entirely certain," Ravi said.

"Everyone's saying that Olivia's mom killed Ben and that one of the frat guys killed one of the other frat guys," Morgan said. "Is that true?"

"Basically," Ravi said. "We've been going over it all. And Maddox saved the day by showing up when he did. Nina, too. She called out Jason's name to distract him, he turned, he saw Maddox, Maddox shot him in the arm like a marksman from an old Western, when Jason went down he shot back at Maddox, and then Nina took Jason's gun when he hit the ground."

"Good grief," Morgan said.

"And that was only the second installment of shooting," Ravi said. "You missed the first. That was when Ellery got winged."

"In the shoulder," Ellery added helpfully. The wound was a constant low throb, even with the pain medication, reminding her exactly where that part of her body was, the way pain tended to do.

"Everyone was brave as hell except for me," Ravi said. "I may be the one summarizing the story, but I was not actually there for that final scene because I had run off into the woods."

"You *were* brave," Ellery said. "You stayed for a long time. You and Grace saved my life."

"Who figured out that Jason killed Matt?" Morgan asked.

"Ellery." Ravi gestured for Ellery to speak. "She was telling us about it. She was talking about how Matt was an absolute mess after Ben died…"

"And I realized that was because he was getting it from both sides," Ellery said. "Someone he loved—Ben—had died. And someone else that he loved was putting him in an impossible situation regarding Ben's death."

"Jason," Nina said.

"Yes," Ellery said. "Trevor told us that Ben looked out for everyone. He'd take on clients who couldn't afford to pay him. And helped his friends out when he could. They had a whole ongoing thing about it that started years ago, when he first wanted to go out with Olivia." She paused. "'Have Your Back.' They all said or texted that to each other when they needed the others to show up for them. Ben had *HYB* engraved on the cuff links for his groomsmen." She glanced over at Andy. "But not for his real best man."

"Ben knew I didn't wear stuff like that." Andy swallowed. "He gave me something else instead." He stretched out his wrist to show them the watch Ellery had noticed earlier. "He was such a good guy."

Ellery nodded. "That's what everyone always said. And I kept thinking, *No one is that nice. Ben's too good to be true.* But the more I talked to people about him, the more I realized that Ben really *was* that good. And that that's why he died. I *think* that what happened is that Ben asked Jason to handle something with one of his clients. Like, gave him a job. Remember how Trevor said that Ben had paid for Jason's room, that Jason wasn't doing well financially? I think Jason did something shady and was trying to cover it up."

Ellery looked at Morgan. "I'm wondering if you could help us know if that's true or not."

Morgan didn't feign surprise or shock. She didn't say *"Me? Why would I know anything about that?"* Her long blond hair was loose around her shoulders and she wore no makeup. There was both a weariness and an ease about her, a sense of someone who had made it through to the other side of something, and not for the first time.

"Yes," she said. "That's true. Maddox told me."

"How did Maddox know?" Grace asked, surprised. "Do he and Jason know each other from outside of the resort?" Grace tipped her head, her long wild curls knotted in a bun on top. "And where did Maddox get the gun?"

Morgan hesitated.

"You don't have to tell us," Ellery said quietly. "He saved our lives."

"It's okay," Morgan said. She took a deep breath. "You saved our lives too, after all." She fixed her gaze on Grace, on Nina, on each of them in turn. "But you won't tell anyone outside of this group, will you?"

"I'd want to tell Olivia," Rachel said.

"Of course," Morgan said. "That's fine." She scooted back from the edge of her chair, settling in but still upright, attuned. "Maddox had a gun because the staff trusted him early on and gave him keys to just about everything. He had access to Craig's office, even, and Craig had the gun unsecured in a desk drawer."

"What the *hell*," Grace said.

Ravi pinched the bridge of his nose. "Of course he did."

"And Maddox knew about Jason because Jason spilled the beans." She took a deep breath. "They weren't friends. We didn't know Jason before we came here. But Maddox had several conversations with Jason because Jason was blackmailing us."

Nina inhaled sharply. Ravi blinked.

"With what?"

"He figured out who we really are." The scattering of freckles across Morgan's cheekbones and the bridge of her nose were especially evident without makeup. She looked so young. "Our real names aren't Morgan and Maddox. We changed them when we were sixteen." She paused.

"Okay," Ravi said, encouragingly.

"We changed them because we ran away from home," Morgan said. "We were both raised in a religious fundamentalist group. On the Arizona border."

"*Oh,*" Ravi said. "Is it—" He stopped short.

"Yeah, it's the one you're thinking of," Morgan said. "And yeah, it was bad."

The group behind the screen was quiet.

"Maddox and I grew up together," Morgan said. "We were always good friends. We talked about how we were going to leave and get out of there. And we did. When we were sixteen, we actually did it." She blinked, looked at Ellery, as if she still couldn't believe it had happened. "I had an aunt who left the group before I did. We ran away to Utah and she helped us when we got there. We changed our names. We tried to look like everyone else."

"No wonder you're so good at braiding," Ravi said. "Don't you guys *have* to wear braids in those places?"

"Ravi," Nina said. "Stop."

"What?" Ravi held out his hands. "When she braids her hair, it always looks unbelievable."

Morgan was laughing slightly. "Thanks, I guess?" she said. "Anyway. I bleached my hair, and Maddox got the same haircut he saw on all the guys out in the world. We paid attention to what people were wearing and did our best to copy it. We hadn't graduated from high school, so we went to trade schools. Maddox became an electrician; I became a masseuse." Morgan smiled. "It was hard, but we both liked our jobs. We liked our lives. Then the influencer thing happened, kind of by accident. I got hooked on LikeMe."

"It's addictive," Grace said dryly. "Literally. It was designed to be that way."

Morgan nodded. "We were lonely, and the app was so fun! People liked what I was posting. I felt like I had so many friends. And then we started to get sponsorship offers. More money than we were making at our other jobs, and chances to go places we'd never even heard of growing up." She gestured at the resort. "Like here."

"So you're not in touch with most of the people in your family?" Ravi asked gently.

Morgan's voice was tight and sad. "When you leave, they hate you." She reached into her pocket and took out her phone. She didn't turn it on, instead holding it thoughtfully in her hand. "Sometimes I think I did all of it—the LikeMe stuff—because I wondered if *anyone* was missing us. Or cared if we were okay. And I think, on some level, I wanted them to know we'd made it."

"Is that safe?" Ravi asked.

"Nothing is," Morgan said.

No one had any argument for that.

"Wow," Ellery said. "You and Maddox have done this all on your own? Together?"

"Yes," Morgan said. "For the past eight years."

"It's Romeo and Juliet," Ravi said.

"No," Morgan said, her voice steel. "It's not. It's real, not a story. And we didn't die."

"You didn't." *You're both survivors,* Ellery wanted to say. But she knew how that might sound—she had some sense of the guilt it could carry.

"And Jason figured out where you were from?" Ravi asked. "Who you were?"

Morgan nodded. "Ever since my LikeMe account blew up, I've been worried someone was going to out us." She frowned. "And that's what Jason threatened to do. As famous or whatever as we are on social media, he's the only person here who recognized us as Morg&Madd from LikeMe."

"Who admitted to it, anyway," Ravi said.

"And that made him think we were rich," Morgan said. "Really rich." Her brow furrowed. "So I guess he decided to do some digging on us. This was before Sunday, when we still had power and cell phone coverage." She shook her head. "I still don't understand why he would do that. Why you would meet someone and go looking for dirt on them. Be out to get someone you didn't even know."

"Because you're beautiful and well-known and you didn't care about him or pander to him or even notice him and it drove him crazy." Rachel leaned forward and put her hand on Morgan's arm. "Because he always has to have another angle. Because he's the kind of person who always thinks everyone else is hiding something because *he* is always hiding something."

"Well, in this case we were." Morgan sighed.

"Everyone is," Ravi said. "Don't feel bad about that."

"Somehow he found an old Google review from when Maddox was an electrician," Morgan said. "It was from one of the places he worked and the reviewer mentioned that one of the electricians reminded them of someone who came from the town where we used to live. And they said the name of the town in their review. I guess Jason went from there and figured it out. He didn't exactly walk us through the whole thing."

"And then Jason started blackmailing you," Ravi said. "What did he want you to do?"

"At first, he wanted us to help him steal the roving Warhol," Morgan said. "I guess he thought he could sell it on the black market or something. Then the slide happened and he saw how much the staff had started trusting Maddox, so he began asking him for other stuff. To get him keys, to do a couple of other things." She exhaled shakily. "We didn't know he'd killed Ben."

"No one did until last night," Nina said. "Not even me. I feel sick about that."

"Don't," Ellery said. She thought again of that moment outside of the guest rooms. *Maddox stumbling, his face white, realizing Jason might tell the world their deepest secrets.* "None of this is your fault."

"Maddox shouldn't have let Jason get to him." Morgan's voice was tired. "We knew someone would figure out who we were someday. But…" She trailed off.

"The fact that it ended up being a blackmailing murderer really sucks," Ravi said.

"And Maddox did what he could," Rachel said. "He gave Olivia the key to the trailer bar, and he gave me keys when I asked for them. I guess I should apologize for that. I wasn't blackmailing him like Jason, but I *did* notice the staff trusted him. I decided to use that to my advantage and ask him for things, too."

The sun streamed through the windows, further gilding the screen with its toppling, scattered flowers, its vibrant colors. Someone— Brook perhaps?—had set out water and glasses and the light caught them, too. *I am so glad*, Ellery thought, *to be alive.*

"So," Ravi said. "Back to where we started. You confirmed that Jason told Maddox—"

"Right," Morgan said. "Jason told Maddox that Ben had fired him. Jason was mad, saying that Ben wasn't as great as everyone said he was, that he'd fired Jason for a stupid reason."

"So," Ravi said. "Ben had given Jason a job. Jason screwed it up."

Morgan nodded. "Based on what Maddox could deduce from the things Jason said, Jason stole the clients' money."

"And," Ravi said, with enthusiasm, "Ben was *pissed*. He found out all of this right before the wedding. He confronted Jason about it when they both got to the resort."

"Is that part hearsay?" Nina asked.

"Conjecture," Ravi said.

"It's confirmed," Andy said. "By Olivia. She knew Ben was planning on pressing charges against Jason. But she didn't know Ben had talked to Jason about it *here*. She and Ben had agreed he'd do it after the wedding, so they didn't mess things up for Catherine. It's not like Jason was the best man, he was just in the wedding party. And they knew if they asked Jason not to be at the wedding, the other groomsmen would want to know what was up, and it would turn into a whole mess." He shook his head. "You're right. Ben was good. He was too nice."

"But Ben *did* end up confronting Jason when they got here?" Ellery said, making sure she understood.

Andy nodded. "And then what I think happened," he said, "is that Jason panicked. Based on Jason's response, there might have been even more going on than Ben knew. I think Jason decided that everything could *not* come out, and that he should take care of things here, because at least at the resort it could be blamed on an accident or something. At least here, he could construct an alibi, and there would be other people with potential motives."

"Especially if he made sure that Ben didn't make it to the wedding," Ellery said. "More people would have a reason to be mad at him after that. Do you think Jason drugged Ben?" She'd been thinking about how he hadn't answered Olivia, how Catherine had basically had to pound on the door to get him to respond, how she'd said he seemed out of it.

"Yeah," Andy said. "And I think he's the one who sent the *I can't do it, I'm sorry* text from Ben's phone."

"So Jason drugs Ben and then comes to the party, making sure everyone sees him and that he has an alibi," Ravi said. "Is that what you're thinking?"

Ellery nodded. "And then Catherine went and managed to wake him up and Ben went with her. And *she* killed Ben by accident. Which, at first, probably seemed like ridiculously good luck to Jason when he found Ben in the woods."

"Jason must have lost his mind when he went to his room to kill Ben and he was missing," Morgan said.

"How do you think he knew where Ben might be?" Grace asked. "When Ben *wasn't* in his room?"

"Jason knew Ben and Olivia liked the *Love* sculpture," Andy said. "We all knew that because we took some pictures there the day we arrived. And then maybe he just kept looking? And found Ben farther along the path, in the clearing?"

"Or maybe Ben *wasn't* dead yet," Rachel said, softly. "Maybe he was moaning or calling for help."

Ellery closed her eyes against the awfulness of that thought. Everyone was quiet for a moment.

"But why would Jason move the body? Why not let Catherine take the fall?" Grace asked.

"Remember, at that point he didn't know that Catherine was the one who had hurt Ben," Ellery said. "And he wanted Ben to be found soon so that his alibi would still work. That wasn't a guarantee with Ben out in the forest and a storm coming. So he got Matt to help him move the body later, after the party was all over."

"Why would Matt even *do* that?" Grace asked.

"*Have your back*," Ravi said. "He followed the code."

"People will do a lot when they're part of a group," Morgan said quietly. "You don't want to be cut off."

In the pause that followed, they could hear the fire crackling in the

Main House's fireplace. Ellery wanted to tell Morgan, *It's not just you. We've all done things we regret when we were following a crowd or a person.* But maybe it didn't need to be spoken.

"I think he took Matt out in the woods and 'found' the body again," Ellery said. "I think Jason told Matt they couldn't tell people they'd found Ben because then they'd be suspects, but that they needed to bring Ben's body to a place where it would be found. I think he told Matt that they were doing this for the greater good—helping Ben's body get discovered, keeping themselves safe. I don't think Matt thought Jason killed Ben. Jason could have been pretty convincing about that, since he *didn't* actually kill Ben. But then moving the body and messing up the crime scene and realizing later that they might have made it harder to catch the killer started to eat at Matt, as we saw, and Jason decided Matt had to go."

"You seem to know Jason very well," Nina said.

"I don't," Ellery said. "But I teach high school."

The others looked puzzled, but Rachel nodded as if she understood. "The real dicks are always dicks," she said. "They don't usually change."

"So Jason killed Matt," Ellery said. "He threw around the whole serial killer idea. He thought about framing Matt for Ben's death. Matt wouldn't be able to defend himself, obviously, since he was dead. Remember, Jason still didn't know about Catherine. But then yesterday he found one of the notes Olivia had left for us, and came to see what was going on, and it all worked out so well for him. Better than he could have dreamed. Except. He always has to push. He decided that he wanted Catherine dead."

"Why?"

"Because then people would think she killed Matt, too," Ellery said. "Everything would be tied up neatly and he could walk away."

"How did he get the gun through security?" Ravi asked. "They check you at the airport."

"He drove, right?" Ellery said. "From San Francisco. He didn't have to go through anything."

Ravi smacked his forehead with his hand. "Of course. Forgive me. My brain is mush right now."

"How did Jason know he'd need a gun?" Grace asked. "When he packed to come up here, he didn't know that Ben was going to confront him."

"That kind of guy always thinks he needs a gun," Nina said. "They're always living their lives wandering around self-defending or whatever."

Ellery met Nina's gaze. And then she said to Nina the same thing that Nina had said to her, moments ago. "You seem to know Jason very well."

"I don't," Nina said. And then her shoulders sagged. "But I should have."

"You weren't Ben's godmother," Ellery said. "But you *were* Jason's. You hadn't seen each other in years, decades even, but his mother died recently. Had she reached out, asking you to look out for him? Did she know something was wrong?"

"Yes." Nina put her hand to her face. There were shadows under her eyes. "Before she died, she asked me to look Jason up again, keep an eye out for him. She was worried about him. I felt awful that I'd dropped out of their lives. Things had gotten so busy. She'd moved across the country. I knew I had to do what I could."

"And that's why you picked this resort for a vacation, this weekend," Ellery said. "Right? Somehow you found out that he would be here?"

"Yes," Nina said.

"Wait," Ravi said to Ellery. "*I* didn't even know that." He was staring at her in wonder.

They were *all* staring at her. "What?" she asked.

"You're kind of scary," Morgan said. "The things you've figured out. Everything you put together."

"It's because you were here alone," Andy said. "You were the one on the outside, watching. The rest of us were all here with—or for—another person. Or other people." He spoke like someone who was often in the same position. But this time he hadn't been, of course. He'd been here for Ben, and Olivia, and, to some extent, Rachel. There had been a real wedding, and the four of them had known it. He belonged in that circle.

"That's true," Rachel said. "You were having conversations with lots of different people, getting bits and pieces of information that not everyone else had."

"And you were smart enough to put all those pieces together," Ravi said.

"I guess," Ellery said, trying to laugh. "It's nice that my divorce came in handy for something."

"It's not that," Nina said. "Or maybe that heightened it, but you're a noticer. You pay attention to people anyway."

"You figured out that Olivia is expecting," Rachel said.

Morgan gasped and put a hand on her stomach. "Her *too*?!?"

"She *is*?" Andy said. And then, suddenly, he burst into tears. Grace put a tentative arm around him. "That's good. That's so good." He looked across at Rachel. "Isn't it?"

"It is," she said gently. "It's going to be hard, but it's good. We'll be there for her. Right?"

"Yes," Andy said, and then he put his head in his hands and sobbed unabashedly. Grace kept her arm where it was, her face gentle. Rachel brushed tears from her own eyes, fiercely, and Nina patted her knee twice before drawing her hand back, respecting Rachel's space.

"What else do you know about all of us?" Ravi asked.

"That's all I've got," Ellery said. But that wasn't true. She thought she'd figured out a few other things. "And some of it could be wrong." That part *was* true. She might know something, but she was also, always, wrong. *Luke.* She had been so sure of his love. Of the two of them, together. And how wrong had she been about that?

"You came here to start healing," Ravi said. "And instead you ended up solving murders."

"I didn't solve them," Ellery said. "We all did." She looked around at them. Andy and Rachel, both wearing deep grief and hope. Grace, who looked out for her father, who had helped save Ellery's life, her arm around Andy. Morgan, with a brightness about her in spite of everything she'd been through.

And Ravi and Nina. Her friends. The people who had taken her in almost the moment she arrived. Who had made her laugh and feel part of something on one of the most fraught weekends of her life. Their good humor, their kindness, their intelligence and flaws. She had kept secrets from them and they had kept secrets from her. She still had no idea what Ravi's was.

Brook peered around the corner of the screen. "Ellery," she said. "There's someone here for you."

"What?" Ellery asked. Her heart had begun to pound. "Who?"

"How?" Ravi asked.

"They hired someone to ATV them in," Brook said.

"I bet the police are *pissed*," Ravi said. "This makes them look bad." Then he glanced at Ellery's face and said, "Okay, everyone. Let's get out and let whoever it is come in." As they stood up and sidled through the opening in the screen, Ellery's breath kept catching in her chest. *Who would it be?* Who would have come all this way for her?

Someone pulled the screen back, wider. There, standing in the opening, wearing filthy boots and a mud-spattered jacket with actual leaves in her hair, looking absolutely exhausted, was Abby.

"I know," she said into Ellery's ear as she hugged Ellery, tears streaming down her cheeks. "I know who you were hoping I'd be. I'm not. But I'm still someone."

Ellery's throat was too tight to swallow or cry or do anything at all. She let Abby hold her tight.

"I'm sorry I said on the phone that you've been through worse," Abby said. She smelled like shampoo and ocean air and forest. And mud. "I was clearly tempting fate."

A laugh caught in Ellery's throat. Abby was hugging her in her Abby way, patting her back. "Oops," Abby said. "Did I just burp a laugh out of you? Or a cry?"

"Either," Ellery said. "Both."

"Your kids are fine," Abby said. Ellery's eyes flooded with tears. "They sent you this." Abby drew back to hand Ellery an envelope, Ethan's adorable handwriting scrawled across the front. *MOM.* "They each wrote a letter for you."

Ravi peeked around the screen. "Everything fine here?"

"Ravi!" Nina appeared, trying to haul him away. "For heaven's sake."

"You must be Ravi and Nina," Abby said. "I've heard a lot about you."

"*Really?*" Ravi asked, sounding thrilled. "Already?"

"Well, only a couple of texts," Abby admitted. "But I had a feeling."

"We'll let you get back to it, then," Ravi said. "There's so much to say about us. And we're looking forward to hearing about you, too." He withdrew again. Ellery could hear them all talking on the other side of the screen, out of sight but still there. Giving her space but not leaving her behind.

She was holding an envelope her kids had touched. There were people who had her back, and she had theirs. The wholesomeness of what Ben had intended with the phrase was still there. No matter what some people chose to do with the love you gave them, there would be others who would take it in the purest sense, who would give it back to you in ways singular and beautiful as a note written by hand, as a redwood tree, as a piece of art.

59.

At last the texts came through, fast and furious, showing her how well, and by whom, she was loved.

From Abby:

> *I know you're not able to contact me but I'm going to keep trying to send these until one gets through. The news is crazy. They say the Bixby Canyon Bridge is out and that this looks to be even worse than the slide in 2017. I'm so sorry I told you to go! I swear I had no idea this would happen! You can fire me as your best friend. (But don't.)*
>
> *I hope you still got the cake I sent. I wanted you to know someone was thinking about you and that I knew you'd make it. You'll make it through this, too.*
>
> *I talked to Luke and he sounded like Luke. The boys and I baked cookies and took them over. We saw your kids and I promised them this would all turn out okay. They seemed to believe me.*
>
> *I believe me. You're going to be okay.*
>
> *Love you.*

From Kate:

> *Abby called Dad and told him what was going on*
> *with the resort. I'm sorry you're stuck there. I hope you're*
> *okay. I've been following the news constantly. I'm going*
> *to try to keep sending this text until I see it go through.*
> *I love you. Please let me know when you get this. Text as*
> *soon as you can.*

From Ethan:

> *Kate is helping me write this. I miss you. There is a*
> *mudslide and you are stuck. I am here. You will come back.*

Maddie sent texts from Luke's phone. Her messages read like e.e. cummings and postmodern poetry had had a darling haiku-adjacent baby:

> *mom this is maddie please call me*
> *i know you cant call me now*
> *Because of the mudslide and phones not*
> *working*
> *But please call me*
> *As soon as you can*
> *I love you*

I love you, she texted to them, over and over again. *I'm okay.*

The first thing was truer than the second, but she could feel the door opening.

THURSDAY

Today at The Resort at Broken Point

"The wilderness holds answers to questions man has not yet learned to ask."

—Nancy Newhall

Weather: Sunny

SUNRISE: 7:17 A.M. ....HIGH: 67° F

SUNSET: 6:26 P.M. ....LOW: 52° F

ABOUT THE ART:
Media Res
by Lin Marsh
1987
lacquer

This screen, inspired in part by Japanese screens of the 18th and 19th centuries, consists of six panels depicting poppies in various states of their life cycle. Both abundance and decay are trademarks in Marsh's works. Regarding this piece, they said, "Life and death are at the forefront of all we do, but I like— most of the time—giving life the center of the stage."

60.

I like how you're requiring everyone to make pilgrimages to see you," Ravi said. "Receiving visitors again, even if you're not on the chaise."

"Ugh." Ellery was sitting out on the bench at Broken Point. Abby stood a few yards away, taking in the view. Ellery hoped her friend was finding it as heartbreakingly, healingly beautiful as she did.

Ellery's body still ached from the gunshot wound, and she was reminded of the careful way she'd had to move after her c-section with Maddie. But there was something she needed to do, and she'd decided this was the spot. The path to the point had been just dried out enough that she'd been able to walk carefully, with Abby helping her, past the place where Matt had been pushed to where the point overlooked the ocean. To the metal bench on the giant stones, the piece called *Thoughts and Prayers*. "I'm sorry."

"Don't apologize." Ravi's tone was so firm that she looked at him, surprised. "I shouldn't have teased you." He and Nina sat down. It was a tight fit with the three of them, but they managed it. Gary and Grace were several yards farther along the point than Abby was, a few steps back from the ledge. They were scattering ashes to the wind.

"I got this for you." Ravi handed Ellery one of the daily house-keeping cards. She lifted it closer to read it, but Ravi gently pushed her hand back down. "For later," he said. "After we're gone." He and Nina were leaving that morning. Ellery and Abby were staying another day. Dr. Anand had wanted her to wait another twenty-four hours before she traveled. It was pure, distilled torture being away from her kids, but at least she could text and FaceTime them now.

"Morgan and Maddox said to tell you goodbye," Ravi said. "They're leaving today, too. But they'll be back."

"I heard," Ellery said. "Nat hired them?"

Nina nodded. "It was a smart move," she said. "They're both skilled. And the Morg&Madd LikeMe account can do some damage control for the murders. Morgan's sharp."

"She is," Ellery said. "They both are. And if they stay here for a bit, they can have a sort-of extended family for that baby. It wasn't the staff who were dangerous."

"I like that Nat makes exceptions to the no-kid rule for staff," said Nina. "What a place to grow up this would be." The ocean sang beyond the point, the reds and greens of the trees shimmered like the water in the sunlight. And there were all the paths, the secret places, in which children would easily find magic.

"Morgan said that having a place to belong feels good," Ravi said.

"Everyone needs that." Ellery closed her eyes against the glint of the sun on the water, the sharp bittersweet pain in her heart.

"Rachel and Olivia asked us to tell you goodbye, too," Nina said. "They're leaving on the same helicopter we are."

"And Catherine?" Ellery asked, opening her eyes.

"She'll go later today, on the police helicopter," Ravi said.

Ellery understood why Olivia was leaving Catherine behind. This is how it was as a parent. You looked forward, to the children *you* had, first. Not back at the mother, the parents who had done the same with you. It broke your heart and you understood it completely at the same time.

Footsteps, on the path behind them. The wind swelled, as if the ocean were taking a good deep breath.

"Hey," Andy said. "It's crowded out here."

"Ellery doesn't like to make goodbyes easy," Ravi said.

"I thought Grace could use some help getting Gary back to the Main House," Andy said. "He's a good hiker but, you know."

"I do know." Ellery couldn't help but smile as her gaze flickered from Andy out to Grace and back again. "When do you leave?"

"I'm actually flying out with Grace and Gary and a couple of other guests the day after tomorrow," Andy said. "We were okay with being farther down the list."

"That's nice of you," Ravi said, with a twinkle in his eye.

"They're good company." Andy changed the subject, the flush on his face giving away that he knew exactly what Ellery and Ravi were noticing. He addressed Ellery. "You know, I didn't believe you yesterday. When you were telling us all that stuff about everything you'd figured out."

"Oh?" Ellery asked. "What part didn't you believe?"

"When you said that was all you'd got," Andy said. "You figured out some things you didn't say, didn't you."

"Yeah," Ellery said. "I could be wrong, though."

"What did you figure out about me?"

"Well." Ellery hesitated. Then she decided to go ahead with it. "Senator Blaine Welch."

Andy nodded. "That's my dad."

"*What?*" Ravi said, in real shock. Ellery felt slightly pleased that he hadn't figured it out. "The one who looks like a chipmunk?"

"A ferret," said Nina.

"Impossible," said Ravi. "You're too handsome. Too decent."

"It's true," Andy said.

"Is he as bad in real life as he seems on TV?" Nina wanted to know. "Sorry."

"He's worse," Andy said, his mouth a grim line. Then his face softened. "But my mom is great. And Ben's parents were the best, and I had them, too. And Ben." His voice caught. "My mom came to the real wedding at city hall with me and Rachel, and Olivia and Ben. She loved Ben, too. And Olivia has already asked me to be the godfather to the baby. I said yes."

Life going on. Ellery loved it and hated it. She hated it when everyone seemed to forget about Annabel and Pete dying. But she loved that the kids who had been on that bus over two years ago could still go running in the early morning, take an AP test, eat oatmeal in the front seat of their parents' car on the way to school, go to college, hold hands in the dark with a crush, shovel snow with their younger sibling during the first storm of the year, fall in love, have babies, get old.

"Rachel works for my dad," Andy said. "Did you know that?"

"She told us," Ravi said. "We forgave her."

Andy laughed. He looked out to where Gary and Grace were making their way back and jumped up, ready to help them. "All done?" Ellery asked gently, and Gary, to her surprise, shook his head.

"All done here," he said. He still held the urn; Grace held his arm. "I decided to take the ashes to a few other places, too. You don't have to have only one favorite place. Or perhaps—even one great love?" He smiled at Ellery. "I've had mine, and I'm old. But you're so young. There's another one for you. I'm sure of it."

"Oh," she said. She would not cry. She would not tell him he was wrong. She was not ready for that, could not even conceive of it. But she appreciated the sentiment, and the kindness of what he wanted for her.

"Your daughter saved my life," Ellery said.

"She's good at that," Gary said fondly. "She's good at a lot of things. Did you know she—"

"No, Dad," Grace said.

"—invented an *app*?" Gary said the word *app* the way most dads did, with careful enunciation and articulation.

"*Dad.*" Grace shook her head. "You *promised.*"

"What?" her father said. "After everything that's happened, you think my bragging about you is a problem?"

"Wait a second," Ravi said, delighted. "*Grace.* Are you the inventor of LikeMe?"

"*No,*" Grace said vehemently. Then she covered her face with her hands. "Something worse."

"What could be worse than LikeMe?" Abby asked, deadpan.

"I started out with good intentions," Grace said, her hands still over her face.

"That's how roads to hell get paved," Ravi agreed.

"You created a beautiful thing!" Gary protested. "It's not your fault some people have made a mess of it."

"I wanted teens to care about nature," Grace said. She removed her hands from her face. "All of it. Not just sexy megafauna, like, panda bears and whales and—actually—redwood trees. So I had this idea that I thought was genius. I would make an app that kids could use that would help them find the smaller things in the world that also matter, like make them *pay attention* to something meaningful while they're always on their phones, and I made the app so that finding those things was like finding Pokémon."

"Oh my word," Ellery said, realization striking her. "You invented MiniFauna. My son is obsessed with that app."

"It's a freaking global sensation," Ravi said, with admiration.

"Every kid in our high school won't leave that thing alone," Abby said. "They're always trying to find, like, a weird bug in the classroom. It's *worse* than Pokémon Go."

"I *know*," Grace moaned. "There was a whole article in the *New York Times* about it. About how I've ruined nature."

"Grace," her father said severely. "That is not what the article said."

"It's partly what it said." Grace looked genuinely miserable. "The app took on a life of its own. There have been kids—and adults—who have endangered animals and vegetation by looking for them."

"Adults ruin everything," Ravi said.

"There have been *incidents*," Grace said mournfully. "I created a monster."

"You're the shadow celebrity," Ravi said. "All along it was you."

Ellery reached over and patted Grace's knee. Grace was the creator of something that had taken on a life of its own. She was also so much else. It was true that everyone had a shadow, and it was also true that if you were casting one, you had chosen to come out and stand in the light.

"My son *loves* MiniFauna," Ellery said. "Grace. Seriously. It brings him actual joy. And it's connected him with the world."

"Thank you," Grace said. She sighed.

"It will go away," Andy said kindly. "Eventually. Everything does."

Grace looked up at him. She didn't say anything, but her expression lightened the smallest amount.

"I'll help you guys get back to the resort," Andy said.

"That's nice of you." Grace reached to take the urn from her father so that Andy could hold on to his other arm. The breeze lifted her curls, brushed against Andy's.

"Stay in touch," Gary said. "All of you. All right?"

"We will," Ellery promised.

She watched as they walked down the path back toward the resort, back to their newly shifted lives. The sun cast their shadows, and those of the trees, across the uneven ground.

61.

If it hadn't been for the deaths, this would have been a perfect vacation," Abby said, when the others had gone and the two of them were alone at the point. She sat down on the bench with Ellery. "A lot of good people."

"And some murderers," Ellery said.

"Right," Abby said. "You can't forget that. You can't forget who died." Ellery reached over and gripped her friend's hand.

The ocean rose and fell. The sun shone as if it had never rained, but the roads were still out and the very land they were on might still crumble.

"So," Abby said. "How *was* the cake?"

"Amazing," Ellery said. "Why didn't you sign the card?"

"I told them to," Abby said. "The person who took the order and wrote down the note took my name, too. Did they leave it off?"

"They did," Ellery said.

"So you didn't know who sent the cake and you ate it anyway?"

"Yeah," Ellery said. "I shared it, though."

That made Abby laugh. "Smart. So is it delicious? The Aidan Stone cake?"

"It was," Ellery confirmed. "But I didn't know it was the Aidan Stone cake. I didn't know the background."

"How did you not know that?" Abby sounded shocked. "There was a whole article about it in that issue of *People* magazine."

"Which issue?" Ellery wanted to know, but then the moment the words were out of her mouth, she knew. *Their* issue, the awful one, the "Track Team Tragedy" issue. "Wait. You *read* that issue?"

"Yeah," Abby said. "Didn't you?"

"No," Ellery said. "Luke summarized it for me."

"Well, I read the whole thing." Abby's voice caught. "Cover to cover. I think I was trying to put it in perspective, you know. Or context. Or something? Which of course didn't happen, not in *People* magazine. But for some reason the story about the damn cake stuck with me."

"I should have saved you a piece."

"I wanted to, you know, remind you that you had made it through a lot," Abby said.

"Thank you." Ellery reached for her friend's hand.

"Some really bad things happened to you while you were here," Abby said, after a moment. "And some good ones, too. You have space for both."

Ellery's heart ached. "I only want to hold the good stuff."

"You can do that," Abby said. "You absolutely can. But I think that if you do, you'll always know you were half of who you could be." She stopped. Her eyes were thoughtful. "No," she said. "That's not quite right. You'll always know you're being half of who you really are."

Ellery felt the truth of this swimming in her bones.

"Even with everything," Abby said. "Or, maybe, because of it? It seems like you made some good friends on this trip."

It was true. Ellery had fallen into friendship with Ravi and Nina the way you got to do now and again in your life. She'd been lucky enough to have it happen several times. She remembered the first day she met Abby at the school. They'd been at a faculty meeting. Abby had leaned over and said something snarky and hilarious to Ellery when the vice principal was talking and Ellery had almost laughed out loud. She had loved Abby immediately. Like love, friendship could sometimes be a falling, immediate and absolute, and it could last and last.

She looked at the card Ravi had brought her. He had torn it off below the quote:

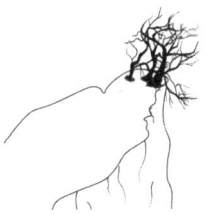

Today at The Resort at Broken Point

"I've loved the stars too fondly to be fearful
of the night."

—Sarah Williams

Underneath the lines, Ravi had written: *You're not finished yet.*

He was right, and so was Williams. At times the stars seemed high and cold, but sometimes they felt warm and low, like you could pluck one down and hold it in your hand for comfort. It depended on the season, and the place you were, and what you were feeling, how you felt when you looked upon them.

"I feel like I've lost the way time works," Ellery told Abby. "Since the divorce."

But it had been before that, too. When Luke had begun drawing away several years before, time had seemed to change. When the accident had happened, it had shifted even more. She felt *unmoored*, as if years were somehow passing in a blur while simultaneously she lived every painful second. There were nights she clawed her way through till morning, when all she did was breathe and tell herself, "Stay here." In her body, in her life. Don't go.

Going on would hurt. It would be bone-breaking, heart-stopping pain.

But so would dying.

"And I feel like I've lost my real life," Ellery said. "The person I married and knew so well. Who knew *me* so well. He's gone."

"That guy is so dead," Abby said gently. "That guy doesn't exist anymore. Luke's not the same man you fell in love with."

"You've told me that before."

"No, I mean, like literally," Abby said. "Every cell in his body is different from when you fell in love with him. Every single one of them has died and been replaced. So he's one hundred percent not the same guy."

"Is that true?" Ellery asked.

"I mean, it has to be," Abby said. "I read something about it somewhere. But remember. I'm a history teacher, not a cell-death scientist."

That made Ellery laugh. It hurt.

"You get to keep the pain, you know," Abby said, looking out at the water. "That's the part people don't get."

"I don't want to keep the pain," Ellery said.

"I don't mean you hold on to the stuff that is killing you," Abby said. "I mean the other part. The good part that isn't easy. I don't know the right word for it."

Below them, a gull cried out.

"The way it hollowed you out," Abby said. "You get to keep that. The way you let yourself love someone and really feel it, and the loss. All the things you learned about yourself and the world: yours forever, if you want."

There was a catch in Ellery's throat. "Being with the people you love is the only thing. You know that, Ab."

"I do," Abby said. "But not everyone does."

The two of them kept their eyes on the view. There were the waves. Here was the wind.

Luke was going, he was going, he was gone.

The Luke who had looked down at her in wonder and joy that first wedding night, his eyes locked on hers, hers on him, every bit of them in love with one another. The man who had held each of his children for the first time. The man who had talked late into the night side by side with her about places they wanted to go, hopes for their children, friends they both loved, days they'd shared or not shared but were telling each other about now, the one who cared about his family, first and foremost—that man was gone.

It was no longer her job—it never had been—to keep him alive.

The trees rose above them. The land held for now.

Abby put her arm around Ellery. Ellery rested her head on Abby's shoulder. They heard the sound of the helicopter, coming back.

"Wait," Abby said, staring down at Ellery's right hand. "Where's your ring?"

"I don't know," Ellery said. "I lost it somewhere in all of this." She couldn't say when. Was it when she'd pulled Ben from the water? In the sauna with Ravi and Nina? When she'd changed into a robe before the massage in the spa? Down in the trailer, when she was looking for Olivia with Rachel, or when she'd been trying to hike out with Andy and find help? Had she simply taken it off and forgotten it somewhere, without realizing either action—the removal, or the leaving-behind?

When she'd realized that the ring was gone, and that she was not going to look for it, she glanced up and caught her eye in the mirror in her room. She'd been startled by her own reflection, her own existence. But the mirror had always been there, and so had she.

This was still the beginning of the loss and the unknowing, but not the very beginning. Ellery had the sense that she would emerge with only her bones.

She would hold on to nothing; she would keep it all.

She could not put her children's lives back together so that they could glide through the world as easily as fish, glimmering silver in the stream, but she could love them, and she could show them the forest and the land, and the water.

Suspended in the air, lapping at the shore, running in rivulets, cutting away cliffs, falling from a great height, gathering in secret springs. The water was everywhere, and so were they.

Look at us, she would say to her children when she saw them again. *I love you.*

We are still here.

ACKNOWLEDGMENTS

I am grateful above all to my children: Calvin, Ian, Truman, and Lainey, for being here for the writing of this book and for our lives together. I love you.

Without the women to whom this book is dedicated, and many other friends who have changed my life over the years, including (but not limited to!) Krista Lee Bulloch, Libby Hughes Parr, and the Celtic/Rangers '08 parents, my life would be much less beautiful (and I wouldn't have laughed nearly as often).

My parents, Robert and Arlene Braithwaite, have taught me about beautiful places since before I could walk, and they still show them to me now. I am also grateful for my siblings, Elaine Braithwaite Vickers, Nic Braithwaite, and Hope Braithwaite, with whom I have had so many adventures.

Jodi Reamer, my agent, has walked every path with me and is the one who sent the cake when I needed it most. Thank you for everything.

I am grateful to Karen Kosztolnyik, my warm, wise, and gracious editor, for acquiring this book and for guiding it along the way. I am delighted and lucky to work with her and with the team at Grand Central Publishing. Many thanks as well to Lauren Bello, Albert Tang, Kamrun Nesa, Andy Dodds, Theresa DeLucci, and Luria Rittenberg.

And to every reader who has ever read any of my work: thank you, with all my heart.

ABOUT THE AUTHOR

Ally Condie is the #1 *New York Times* bestselling author of the Matched Trilogy, and of many other books (including the Edgar Award Finalist *Summerlost*). A former English teacher, she enjoys hiking with her family in the mountains near their home in Utah.

For more information, please visit:

allycondie.com
Instagram: @allycondiebooks
Facebook.com/allycondiebooks